The Target

Catherine Coulter

The Target

WHEELER
PUBLISHING, INC.
ROCKLAND, MA

★ AN AMERICAN COMPANY ★

Published in Large Print by arrangement with G.P. Putnam's Sons,
a member of Penguin Putnam Inc. in the United States and Canada.

Wheeler Large Print Book Series.

Set in 16 pt Plantin.

Library of Congress Cataloging-in-Publication Data

Coulter, Catherine.
  The target / Catherine Coulter.
    p. (large print) cm.(Wheeler large print book series)
  ISBN 1-56895-586-3 (lg. print)
  1. Large type books 2. Kidnapping—Fiction.
3. Mute persons—fiction.
I. Title. II. Series
[PS3553.O843T3 1998b]
813′.54—dc21
                                                    98-29236
                                                         CIP

My thanks to Alex McClure, Esquire, for her intrepid assistance on the workings of the federal justice system.

To Dr. Anton Pogany, who has the instincts, the patience, a light touch. In other words, he's got the right stuff. Let's keep on cooking.

Prologue

He saw the man clearly: tall, with dark clothes, a stark figure against the misty gray sky. He was walking into the big granite building, ugly and flat-looking, with scores of windows that didn't look out over much except if you were up high. Then, suddenly, he was behind the man, just over his shoulder, keeping pace with him, watching him take the elevator to the nineteenth floor. He was nearly beside him as he walked down the long corridor and opened the door to a large office. A smiling receptionist greeted him, laughing at something he said. He watched the man greet two other people, a young man and a young woman, both well dressed, both obviously subordinate to him. He went into a large office with the man, saw a United States flag, a huge desk with its computer on top, the built-in bookshelves behind him, the windows beside him. He punched up the computer. Then, he was right behind the man, he could have reached out and helped him put on the long black robe. He watched him fasten the two clips closed. The man opened a door and walked into a big room, the look on his face somber, becoming cold, all the earlier humor wiped clean. There was a buzz. It stopped abruptly when he came into the room. Then the place went deathly silent.

Suddenly the room began to spin, faces blurred into one another, the very air of the

1

room turned dark and darker still, and then the great main doors burst open and three men slammed into the room. They were carrying guns, assault guns like Russian AK47s. They were shooting, people were screaming, blood was spewing everywhere. He saw the man's face tighten with horror and fury. He saw the man suddenly leap over the railing that had separated him from the rest of that roomful of people, his black robe swirling. His leg was up, he was turning, striking out, his motion so fast it was hard to see it clearly. Someone screamed loudly.

He was right behind the man now, heard him breathe, could feel the controlled rage in him, the vicious tension and determination, and wondered.

Suddenly, the man whirled about again, turning this time to face him. He stared at himself, looked deeply into the eyes of a man who had just killed and would kill again. He felt the spit pool in his mouth, the coiled muscles, and felt his arm fly out, striking a man's throat.

He jerked up, flailing at the single sheet that was wound tightly around him like a mummy's shroud, a yell dying on his lips. He was soaked with sweat, his hair plastered to his head. His heart was pounding so fast and hard he thought he'd explode. Again, he thought, that bloody dream yet again. He didn't think he could stand it.

An hour later, he let himself out of his house, carefully locking the door behind him.

He was on the way to his car when a man jumped out of the bushes and blinded him with a good half dozen photo flashes. It was too much.

He grabbed the photographer, hauled him up by his shirtfront, and yelled right in his face, "You've gone over the line, you little bastard." He grabbed his camera, pulled the film out, and threw him aside. He tossed the camera to the man, who was lying on his back, gaping at him.

"You can't do that!"

"I just did. Get off my property."

The man scrambled to his feet, holding his camera to his chest. "I'll sue you! The public has a right to know!"

He wanted to beat the guy senseless. The urge was so strong he was shaking with it. It was then he knew he had to leave. Otherwise it might not stop before he went nuts and really hurt one of the jerks. Or he simply just went nuts.

1

Rocky Mountains
Spring

He stood at the edge of the mountain that sheered down a good two hundred feet before smoothing out into tree-covered ledges and gentle wildflower-covered slopes and sharp gaping ridges. He breathed in the thin air that was so fresh it burned his lungs, but, truth be told, it burned less today than it had yesterday. Soon, the frigid clean air at nearly six thousand feet would become natural to him. It had been only yesterday that he'd realized he hadn't thought all day about a telephone, a TV, a radio, a fax machine, the sound of other voices coming at him from all sides, about people grabbing at him, shouting questions six inches from his face. And those blinding explosions of white from the ever-present flashbulbs. Now, he figured, at last he was beginning to let go, to forget for stretches of time what had happened.

He looked across the valley at the massive, raw mountains that stretched mile upon mile like unevenly spaced jagged teeth. Mr. Goudge, the owner of the Union 76 gas station down in Dillinger, had told him that many of the locals, lots of them Trekkies, called the whole mess of knuckle-shaped mountains the Ferengi Range. The highest peak rose to twelve thousand feet, bent slightly to the south, and looked like a misshapen phallus. He wasn't about to climb a mountain with so unsubtle a shape. The folks down in Dillinger joked about that peak, saying it was a sight with snow dropping off it in the summer.

He was aware again as he was so often of being utterly alone. At his elevation there were thick forests of conifers, mainly birch, fir, and more ponderosa pine than anyone could begin to count. He'd seen lots of quaking aspen too. No logging companies had ever devoured this land. On the higher-elevation peaks across the valley, there were no trees, no flowers as there were here in his alpine meadow, just snow and ruggedness, so much savage beauty, untouched by humans.

He looked toward the small town of Dillinger at the far end of the valley that stretched from east to west below. It claimed fifteen hundred and three souls. Silver mines had made it a boomtown in the 1880s, nearly bursting the valley open with more than thirty thousand people—miners, prostitutes, store owners, crooks, an occasional sheriff and preacher, and very few families. That was a long time ago. The descendants of those few locals who had stuck it out after the silver mines had closed down now catered to a trickle of summer tourists. There were cattle in the valley, but they were a scruffy lot. He'd seen bighorn sheep and mountain goats coming down the slopes really close to the cattle, pronghorn antelope grazing at the lower elevations, and prowling coyotes.

He'd driven his four-wheel-drive Jeep down there just once since he'd been here to stock up on groceries at Clement's grocery. Had it been Tuesday? Two days ago? He'd bought a package of frozen peas, forgetting that he didn't have a freezer, just a small high-tech refrigerator that was run off a generator sitting just outside the cabin. He'd cooked those frozen peas on his wood-burning stove, then eaten the entire package in one sitting next to the one bright standing lamp that also worked off the generator.

He stretched, caught a glimpse of two hawks flying low, looking for prey, and took his ax back to the stump beside the cabin where he was splitting logs. It didn't take him long to pull off his down jacket, then his flannel shirt, then his undershirt. And still he worked up a sweat. His rhythm sped up. The sun felt hot and good on his skin, seeping in to warm his muscles. He felt strong and healthy. He was in business. He knew he had more logs than he could use for the next week, but he just kept to that hard smooth rhythm, feeling his muscles flex and loosen, grow tight with power, and release.

He stopped a moment to wipe the sweat off his face with a sleeve of his shirt. Even his sweat smelled fresh, as if his innards were clean.

He heard something.

A very faint sound. It had to be an animal. But he'd gotten used to the owls and the sparrow hawks, to the chipmunks and the skunks, and to the wolves. This sound wasn't one of them. He hoped it wasn't another person invading his mountain. His was the only cabin in the high meadow. There were other cabins, but they were lower, at least a half mile away. No one came up here except maybe in the summer to hike. It was mid-April. No hikers yet. He hefted his ax again. He froze in midswing when the sound came again.

It was like the desperate cry of something— a kitten? No, that was crazy. Still, he pulled on his flannel shirt, and the down jacket. He leaned down and picked up his ax. The weight felt good. Had another man come onto his mountain?

He paused, holding perfectly still, letting the silence invade him until he was part of it. He felt the cool afternoon breeze stir the hair on his head. At last it came again, a soft mewling sound that was fainter this time, broken off into two distinct parts, as if suddenly split apart.

As if a creature was nearly dead.

He ran fast over the flat meadow where his cabin stood. He ran into the pine forest that surrounded the high meadow, slowing because of the undergrowth, praying he was going in the right direction, but uncertain even as he ran.

He heard his own hard breathing and stopped. Little sun could cut through the dense trees. Now that it was late afternoon, it was nearly dark here deep in the forest, where there were suddenly no sounds at all. Nothing. He calmed his breathing and listened.

Still nothing. He heard a slithering sound. He whipped around to see a small prairie rattlesnake winding its way under a moss-covered rock. The snake was higher up than it should be.

He waited silent as the trees on all sides of him. He felt a cramp in his right bicep. Slowly he lowered the ax to the ground.

Suddenly he heard it again, off to his left, not too far away, muffled and faint, a sound that was almost like an echo of itself, a memory of what it had been.

He moved slowly now, eyes straight ahead, his stride long. He came to a small clearing. The afternoon sun was still bright overhead. There was rich high grass waving in the breeze. Blue columbine, the Colorado state flower, was blooming wildly, soft and delicate, already welcoming spring. It was a beautiful spot, one he hadn't yet found on his daily treks.

He waited now, his face upturned to the slanting sun, listening. There was a squirrel running up a tree, a distinct sound, one he'd learned very quickly to identify. The squirrel scampered out on a narrow branch, making it wave up and down, its leaves rustling with the weight and movement.

Then there wasn't anything at all, just silence.

He knew the sun wouldn't be shining on him much longer; shadows were already lengthening, swallowing the light. Soon it would be as dark as Susan's hair in the forest. No, he wouldn't think about Susan. Actually it had

8

been a very long time since he'd thought about Susan. It was time to go home, back to his cabin where he'd laid wood for a fire that morning, still waiting for a single match. He'd gotten good at building fires both in the fireplace and in the wood stove. He'd slice up some fresh tomatoes and shred some iceberg lettuce he'd bought two days before at Clement's. He'd heat up some vegetable soup. He stepped back into the thick pine forest.

But what had he heard?

It was darker now than it had been just two minutes before. He had to walk carefully. His sleeve caught on a pine branch. He stopped to untangle himself. He had to lay down the ax.

It was then he saw the flash of light yellow off to his right. For a moment, he just stared at that light yellow. It didn't move and neither did he.

He quickly picked up his ax. He walked toward that light yellow patch, pausing every few seconds, his eyes straining to make out what it was.

It was a lump of something.

He saw from three feet away that it was a child, unmoving, lying on her stomach, her dark brown hair in tangles down her back, hiding her face.

He fell on his knees beside her, afraid for an instant to touch her. Then he lightly put his hand to her shoulder. He shook her lightly. She didn't move. The pulse in her throat was slow but steady. Thank God she was unconscious, not dead. He felt each of her arms, then her legs. Nothing was broken. But she could be injured internally. If she was, there was nothing he could do about it. He carefully turned her over.

There were two long scratches on her cheek, the blood dried and smeared. Again, he placed his finger against the pulse in her neck. Still slow, still steady.

He picked her up as carefully as he could, and grabbed his ax. He curved her in against him to protect her from the low pine branches and underbrush. She was small, probably not older than five or six. He realized then she wasn't wearing a jacket, only the thin yellow T-shirt and dirty yellow jeans. There were white sneakers on her feet, one of the laces unfastened and dangling. No socks, no gloves, no jacket, no cap. What was she doing out here alone? What had happened to her?

He stopped. He could have sworn that he heard the sound of a heavy foot snapping through leaves and small branches. No, he was imagining things. He pulled her closer and quickened his step, the sound of that scrunching step hovering just behind him.

It was heavy dusk by the time he walked through the door of his cabin. He laid the little girl on the sofa and covered her with an afghan, an old red-and-blue-checked wool square that was probably older than he was, and very warm. He lit the lamps throughout the cabin.

He turned to look at the front door. He frowned at it, then walked to the door, locked it, and turned the deadbolt. His hand paused as he lifted the chain. Better to be certain. He secured it. Then he lit the fire in the fireplace. Within ten minutes the single large room was warm.

The child was still unconscious. He lightly patted her cheeks, and sat back, waiting.

His day certainly wasn't ending as it had begun. "Who are you?" he said to the child. Her face was turned away from him. The scratches were bright and ugly in the lamplight.

He fetched a bowl of tepid water that had been sitting on the wood stove all afternoon, a clean pair of white gym socks, and a bar of soap. He washed her face, as carefully as he could with a gym sock pulled over his hand, blotting the blood off the long scratches.

He brought one of his soft white undershirts that was warm and soft after years of laundering, and began to strip her. He had to examine her as best he could. He was shocked, then furious, at what he saw.

She was covered with bruises and welts, some of them crusted with dried blood. Blood was smeared between her legs. Oh, God. He closed his eyes a moment.

He bathed her thoroughly, examining her as well as he could, but he didn't see any signs of wounds or cuts, just abrasions and deep bruises. He turned her onto her stomach. Long thin welts scored her child's flesh, from her shoulders to her ankles, welts that didn't overlap, as if made by a careless enraged hand, but that had been carefully placed, by someone who wanted to mark every inch of the child, to obtain a certain result, a certain effect. She was thin and as white as the clean undershirt he pulled over her head. The undershirt came to her ankles. He smoothed the covers back over her, and spread out her hair about her head on the pillow with his fingers, gentle as he could be, easing out the worst of the tangles. It was just as well that she wasn't awake while he'd taken care of her. He sat back, staring at the silent child.

He realized he was shaking with fury. What monster had done this to a child? He knew, from firsthand experience, that there were many monsters out there, but to come face-to-face with this made him want to puke and kill at the same time.

He willed her to wake up. She didn't move. He considered whether to take her to the hospital now. He had no phone so he couldn't call. He'd even left his cell phone at home. It was late. He didn't know where the hospital was, how far. And he didn't know who had done this to her, who'd abused and beaten her, or where they were. No, tomorrow he'd take her, and he'd stay with her. He wouldn't leave her alone. Tomorrow, he'd drive with her to the sheriff. There had to be a sheriff in Dillinger. Tonight he'd take care of her himself. If she awoke, if she was hurting, then he'd take her to the hospital, no matter what the hour. But not now.

Had she saved herself, escaped somehow, and run into the forest? Had she tripped on a root or a rock and struck her head? Or had the monster who'd hurt her dumped her, leaving her to die in the forest? He leaned over her and gently ran his fingers over her head. He couldn't feel any lumps. The pulse in her throat was still slow and steady.

If she had escaped the man who'd done this to her, that meant he was still out there looking for her. Of course he'd known this in his gut when he'd brought her into the cabin and that was why he'd locked the door. He checked his Browning Savage 99 lever action rifle. It was already chambered with a .243 Win. On the table by the sofa was his Smith & Wesson .357 Magnum revolver. He loved that gun, had since his father had given it to him on his fourteenth birthday and taught him how to use it. It was called the Black Magic because of its black finish on stainless steel. He liked to shoot it, but he'd never used it on a person.

He picked it up. It was fully loaded, as always. He looked toward the door, the revolver in his hand, gauging the distance there.

What man had done this?

He fixed himself a salad and ate it, never taking his eyes off the child. Then he heated the soup. It smelled very good. He waved a spoonful beneath her nose. "Come on now, wouldn't you like to have a taste? Campbell's is good stuff and it's hot, right off an old-fashioned wood stove. It takes a while to heat anything, but it does work. Come on now, sweetheart, wake up."

Her mouth moved. He got a smaller spoon, dipped it into the soup, and lightly pressed it against her bottom lip. To his surprise and relief, her mouth opened. He dribbled in the soup. She swallowed, and he gave her more.

She ate nearly half a bowl. Only then did she open her eyes. She looked confused. Slowly, she turned her face toward him, and stared up at him. He smiled and said, "Hello, don't be afraid. My name's Ramsey. I found you. You're safe now."

She opened her mouth and there came the strange noise he'd heard, a soft mewling that sounded of bone-deep fright and helplessness.

"It's all right. No one will hurt you. You're safe now with me."

Her mouth opened but no sound came out this time. Her arms came out from under the afghan and she flailed at him, the only sound her small mouth made was that awful mewling that made him want to pull this little scrap of humanity against him and protect her.

He quickly set down the spilled soup and grabbed her wrists. Her eyes fluttered closed, but not before he saw the flash of pain. He released her wrists. Both wrists were raw. She'd been tied up. "I'm sorry, sweetheart. I'm really sorry. Don't fight me, please. I won't hurt you."

She huddled into a small ball and turned her

14

back to him, her arms over her head, and didn't move.

He sat there wondering what he should do. She was terrified. Of him. He couldn't blame her.

Why didn't she scream at him? She'd just made those strange sounds. Was she mute?

He said very quietly, hoping she could hear him, "Your wrists and ankles are in bad shape. Can I bandage them for you? They'll feel better."

Had she heard him? She still didn't move. He pulled an old undershirt from beneath the pile of clothes he'd brought and ripped it into strips. He felt every scrap of fear in her as he washed her wrists and ankles really well, smeared on some Neosporin, then wrapped the soft material around them, knotting them off. There, he'd done everything he could. He stood slowly, knowing now he shouldn't make any abrupt moves, and stared down at her. She was still in a tight little ball, her hands, now freed of him, tucked inside the covers.

She'd eaten a good bit of the soup. She wouldn't starve. She was warm. She was clean. He'd smoothed antibiotic cream on the worst of the scratches and cuts. He looked toward the front door, then the front windows. He pulled down the shades and closed the curtains. Now no one could see in. He slid the bolts home on the windows. To get in, someone would have to shatter them. He walked to the back door in the kitchen and flipped the

15

deadbolt. The door didn't have a chain. He pulled one of the kitchen chairs over and shoved it beneath the doorknob. Someone could shove the door open, but the chair feet would screech on the floor and certainly wake him up.

He looked at her one last time. "If you awaken, just call me. My name's Ramsey. I'll be here with you. You're safe now. All right? If you have to use the bathroom, it's just beyond the kitchen, behind you. It's clean. I just washed up in there yesterday."

The covers moved just a little bit. Good, she'd heard him. But she didn't make a sound, not even that gut-wrenching mewling noise.

His bed was on the far side of the single room. He remained fully clothed. He put both the rifle and his Smith & Wesson on the small table by the bed, right next to the reading lamp. He carefully marked the page of the thriller he was reading and set it on the floor.

He left the single lamp lit. If she awoke during the night, he didn't want her to be terrified in the dark.

He didn't sleep for a long time. When he did finally, he dreamed there was a man's face staring in through the window at the little girl. He awoke and walked to the window, stumbling with fear and panic, but there wasn't any face staring in. The curtains were tightly drawn. He couldn't help it, he pulled the curtains open. He looked into the darkness and saw instead the contorted face of someone else, the woman who'd screamed at him that she would kill him.

He awoke at dawn at the sound of that ghastly mewling sound.

2

The child's face was leached of color, he could tell that even in the early-morning light that was mixed with the stark overlay of lamplight. Her eyes were wide open, staring up at him, her fear so palpable he could feel it crawling inside his skin.

"No," he said very slowly, not moving. "It's all right. It's me. Ramsey. I'm here to take care of you. I won't hurt you. Did you have a nightmare?"

She didn't move, just lay there, staring up at him. Then, very slowly, she shook her head. He saw her arms move beneath the covers, saw her small hands come up over the top. The small hands were clenched. The bandages on her thin wrists looked obscene.

"Don't be afraid. Please."

He turned the lamp off. It was getting lighter quickly. Her eyes were light blue, large in her thin face, her pupils dilated. She had a thin straight nose, dark lashes and eyebrows, a rounded chin, and two dimples. She was a pretty little girl, and she'd be beautiful when she smiled and those dimples deepened. "Are you in any pain?"

She shook her head.

He felt profound relief. "Can you tell me your name?"

She just stared at him, all frozen and tense, as if she were just waiting for her chance to run, to escape him.

"Would you like to go to the bathroom?"

He saw it in her eyes and smiled. Her kidneys were working. Everything seemed to be working fine except she couldn't speak. He started to touch her, to help her up, but didn't. He kept his voice low, utterly matter-of-fact. "The bathroom is on the other side of the kitchen. The kitchen's just behind you. Do you need any help?"

Slowly, she shook her head. He waited. She didn't move. Then he realized she didn't want to get up with him watching her.

He smiled and said, "I'm going to make some coffee. I'll see what I have that a little kid would like to eat, all right?"

Since he knew she wasn't going to answer, he just nodded and left her.

He didn't hear anything until the bathroom door shut. He heard the lock click into place.

He shook some Cheerios into one of the bright blue painted bowls and set the skimmed milk beside it. At least it wouldn't clog her arteries. He went to his store of fresh fruit. There were only two peaches left. He'd bought a half dozen, but eaten all the rest. He sliced one on the cereal.

He waited. He'd heard the toilet flush,

then nothing more. Had something happened?

He waited some more. He didn't want to terrify her by knocking on the door. But finally too much time had passed. He lightly tapped his knuckles against the pine bathroom door. "Sweetheart? You all right?"

He heard nothing at all. He frowned at the locked door. Well, he'd been stupid. She probably believed she was safe from him now. She'd probably never come out willingly.

He poured himself a large mug of black coffee and sat down beside the bathroom door, his long legs stretched out nearly reaching the opposite wall. His black boots were scuffed and comfortable as old slippers. He crossed his ankles.

He began to talk. "I'd sure like to know your name. 'Sweetheart' is all right, but it's not the same as a real name. I know you can't talk. That's no problem now that I understand. I could give you a pencil and a piece of paper and you could write your name down for me. That sounds good, doesn't it?"

Not a whisper of sound.

He drank his coffee, rolled his shoulders, then relaxed against the wall, and said, "I'll bet you've got a mom who's really worried about you. I can't help you until you come out and write down your name and where you're from. Then I can call your mother."

He heard that soft mewling again. He took another drink of coffee. "Yeah, I bet your mom is really worried about you. Wait a

19

minute. You're too young to know how to write, aren't you? Maybe you're not. I don't know. I don't have any kids."

Not a sound.

"Well, so much for that. Okay. Come on out now and have some breakfast. I have Cheerios and a sliced peach. All I bought was skimmed milk, but you can't tell any difference by the taste. You just don't want to look at it. It's all runny and thin. The peach is really good, sweet as anything. I ate four of them since I bought them two days ago. You're getting the second to the last one. I'll make you some toast too, if you'd like. I've got some strawberry jam. Come on out. I'll bet you're getting hungry.

"Listen, I'm not going to hurt you. I didn't hurt you yesterday, did I? Or last night? No, and I didn't hurt you this morning. You can trust me. I was a Boy Scout when I was young, a real good one. That person who hurt you, he won't come anywhere near here. If he does, I'll shoot him. Then I'll beat the crap out of him. Well, I didn't mean to say that exactly, but you know, I'm not around kids very often. I've got three nieces and two nephews I see at least once a year and I like them. They're my brothers' kids. I taught the girls how to play football last Christmas. Do you like football?"

No sound.

He remembered his sister-in-law, Elaine, cheering when Ellen had caught a ten-yard pass in the makeshift end zone. "I'll try to be careful with my language. But you can count on this. If that monster comes anywhere close, I'll make him real sorry for hurting you. I promise.

"Please come out. The sunrise is beautiful. Would you like to see it? There are lots of pinks and soft grays and even some oranges. It's going to happen pretty quick now."

The lock clicked open. The door slowly opened. She stood there wearing his undershirt that came to her small feet and was nearly falling off her shoulders.

"Hi," he said easily, not moving a muscle. "You want some cereal now?"

She nodded.

"Can you help me up?" He held out his hand to her.

He saw the fear, the wild panic in her eyes. She looked at his hand as if it were a snake about to bite her. She scooted around him and ran into the kitchen. Okay, it was too soon for her to begin to trust him. "The milk's on the counter," he called out. "Can you reach it?"

He walked very slowly back into the kitchen. She was sitting in the corner, pressed against the wall, the bowl of cereal hugged to her chest. Her face was very nearly into that bowl, her dark brown hair in thick tangles, hiding her face.

He said nothing, just poured himself some more coffee, slid two slices of wheat bread into the long-handled metal toaster, and held it over the wood stove. It only took about two minutes to brown the toast on each side. He sat down in one of the two kitchen chairs, straddling the back. The other one was still shoved beneath the back doorknob.

It came to him quite clearly at that moment that he wasn't about to give her over to strangers. She was his responsibility and he willingly shouldered it. No, he couldn't begin to imagine what they'd do to her in a hospital: doctors, nurses, lab people, all of them poking around, terrifying her, shrinks showing her dolls and asking what the man had done to her, male doctors not understanding, treating her as if she were like any other little girl, when she wasn't. No, none of that, not now. And then the sheriff would get involved. Well, he would speak to the sheriff, but not just yet. Let her ease a bit more. Let her come to trust him, just a little.

"Would you like a slice of toast? I've learned how to work this toast holder really well. I haven't burned any bread now for nearly a week."

The small head shook back and forth.

"Okay, I'll eat both slices. If you change your mind, I've got some really good strawberry jam, made right down there in Dillinger by a Mrs. Harper. She's been here for all of her sixty-four years.

"I've been here for nearly two weeks now. I come from San Francisco. This cabin was built by the grandfather of a friend of mine. He loaned it to me. I've never been here before. It's a beautiful place. Maybe later you can tell me where you come from. I wanted to be alone, to be completely away from everything and everyone, to be isolated, you know what I mean? No, I don't guess you'd have any idea, would you?

"Who said that life is too much with us? Maybe I did and just forgot. So much stuff can happen to you when you're grown-up, but then you're supposed to be able to handle it. But you're just a little kid. Nothing bad should have happened to you. I'll fix things if I can.

"But you know," he continued slowly, eyeing the strips of undershirt on her wrists and ankles, thinking of that small battered body, knowing she'd been raped, "I think we should see a doctor, maybe in a couple of days, then we should see the sheriff. I hope Dillinger has a sheriff."

The mewling sounds began. She laid the empty cereal bowl on the floor beside him and raised her face. She began shaking her head, back and forth, back and forth, the mewling sounds coming from the back of her throat, raw and ugly.

He felt goose bumps rise on his arms. "You don't want to see a doctor?"

She pressed hard against the wall, her legs up, the undershirt wrapped around her like a white tent, her head tucked in, and she was rocking.

"Okay, we won't go anywhere at all. We'll stay right here all safe and snug. I've got lots of food. Did I tell you that I went into Dillinger just two days ago? I got stuff even a kid would like. I've got hot dogs and some of those old-fashioned buns that don't taste like anything, French's mustard, and some baked beans. I cut up onions in the beans, add mustard and some catsup, then put it in a pot on the stove for about twenty minutes. That sounds good, doesn't it?"

She stopped rocking.

Slowly, she turned her face toward him. She pushed back her hair.

"You like hot dogs?"

She nodded.

"Good. I do too. I bought some of those old-fashioned potato chips. The real greasy kind that makes your hands all oily. Do you like potato chips?"

She nodded again. She eased, just a little bit.

The kid liked food. It was a start. "Did you mind the skimmed milk?"

She shook her head.

What now? "Do you mind if I eat my toast? It's getting cold." He didn't wait for her to nod again, just smiled at her and began to butter his toast. When he'd slathered strawberry jam on one slice, he held it out to her. "You want to try this?"

She stared at that piece of toast with a glob of jam about ready to fall over the edge. "Let me put it on a napkin." Thank heaven he'd bought napkins.

He handed it to her. She took three fast bites, hardly chewing, then sighed and ate more slowly. She licked strawberry jam off her lower lip. For the first time she looked happy.

"Has it been a long time since you've eaten?"

She was chewing slowly on a bite of toast. She seemed to think about it. Then she nodded slowly.

"I see I've got to ask you only yes or no questions. Do you feel better this morning?"

Fear washed all the color from her face.

She was looking at her bandaged wrist holding the half slice of toast.

"I'll put some more medicated cream on your wrists and ankles after you finish your toast." He said nothing more, just ate his own toast. What about the rest of her body? He knew he should examine her again but he didn't want to, not with her awake and terrified.

When they'd both finished, he rose and said as he walked away from her into the living area, "Would you like to have a bath? I can heat some water over the stove and pour it into the tub. I've got a couple of really big pans just for that purpose." He knew without looking at her that she was probably shaking her head, pressed against the kitchen wall. "You're a big girl. You can bathe yourself, right?" He turned, smiling toward her.

Slowly, she rose. She nodded.

"I've got some shampoo in the bathroom. Can you wash your own hair? Good. Then I can put more cream on your wrists and ankles. There are a couple of other spots that need some medicated cream too. Now we've got a clothing problem. Tell you what. When you're through, just put the undershirt back on. I'll see what I can scrounge up for you."

He'd gotten so used to silence over the

past two weeks that hearing himself talk on and on felt strange. He felt the echo of his own voice inside himself.

After he'd heated enough hot water and poured it into the tub, he heated more for her to rinse her hair and set the pots beside the tub. While she was in the bathroom, he sat down at the old Olivetti typewriter that had belonged to his mom. It felt comfortable hammering away at those dinosaur keys. He put on his glasses and began reading what he'd written the day before.

He didn't know how long he read. But suddenly he looked up to see her standing there beside his desk, making no noise, just standing there, her hair wet and tangled around her face, her wrists and ankles raw and ugly, her face shiny and clean, wearing his undershirt.

"Hi," he said, taking off his glasses. "I'm sorry I didn't hear you come out. When I work I tend to forget where I am. Why don't you come over and sit on the couch."

He took his own comb, washed it first, then spent the next ten minutes combing the tangles out of her hair. Then he put more medicated cream on her wrists and ankles and bandaged them again. He knew he had to check her over but he couldn't see himself pulling off that undershirt. No, he'd have to be more devious. He rose. "Now, clothes for you."

He wasn't about to put her back into what she was wearing when he'd found her. He could only begin to imagine what sorts of memories those clothes would bring her.

"You're going to be a Ralph Lauren Polo girl. What do you think?" It was a long-sleeved soft wool pullover sweater. At least it would keep her warm. No underwear, no pants, no shoes.

He handed her the sweater. "Why don't you change in the bathroom?"

She left him. This time she came back in five minutes. He was gaining ground. The sweater came to her ankles, the sleeves flopping a foot beyond her hands. He rolled the sleeves up to her elbows. She looked ridiculous and endearing.

What was one to do with a little kid?

"Do you know the capital of Colorado?"

She nodded. He pulled out a map then realized he didn't know if she could read. Well, it didn't matter. She pointed to Denver. It had a red star beside it. So she lived in Colorado.

"That's really good. I don't think my nieces and nephews know the capital of any state, even Pennsylvania, where they live. Do you know where we are?"

Fear, cold, frozen fear.

He said easily, "We're in the Rockies, about a two-hour drive southwest of Denver. There aren't any ski resorts close by, so it's pretty empty. Still, it's a really pretty place. Do you watch *Star Trek?*"

She nodded, some color coming back into her face.

"I'm told the local folks call the mountain peaks opposite us the Ferengi Range."

She opened her mouth and rubbed her fingers over her teeth.

He laughed. "That's it. All the peaks are jagged and crooked and spaced funny. Ferengi teeth."

The sleeves of his shirt were dragging on the floor again. He leaned forward to roll them up. She made that deep mewling sound and ran over to the wall by the fireplace. She curled up just as she had in the kitchen.

He'd scared her. Slowly, he got up and walked to the sofa. He sat down. "I'm sorry I scared you. All I wanted to do was roll up your sleeves. Your arms aren't quite as long as mine yet. I should have told you what I intended. Can I roll up your sleeves? I think there are some safety pins in the kitchen drawer. If I can pin them up, you won't have to worry about them."

She got up and started to walk to him. One step, and she paused. Another step. Another pause, studying him, weighing if she could trust him, wondering if he wouldn't turn on her. Finally she was beside him. She looked up at his face. He smiled and slowly lifted his hand. He rolled up the sleeves. Then he said, "I can try to braid your hair. It won't be great but at least you won't have your hair in your face."

The braid wasn't all that bad. He fastened the end with a rubber band that had come around the bag of peaches.

"The sun's really bright. It's not too cold out. If I bundle you up, would you like to go outside?"

He should have known. She was gone in a flash, into the kitchen. He knew she was against the damned wall. At least she didn't lock herself in the bathroom.

What to do?

Whatever he did with her, he had to do it slowly, really slowly.

Thank God there were some old magazines in the cabin. He said, "Would you like to look at the photos? If you like, we could look at them together and I could read to you what they say about the photos."

Finally, she nodded slowly. "First let me get those safety pins and fasten your arms up."

Then she followed him into the living area. It was tough because she didn't want to get anywhere close to him. The magazine ended up between them on the sofa. At least he got her to wrap the afghan around her.

He looked over at her and said, "Socks."

She blinked and cocked her head to one side.

"I was worried about you walking around in your bare feet. Do you want to try some of my socks? They'll look funny and come up to your neck. Maybe you could practice to be a clown. You could wear my socks and see if I laugh. What do you say?"

The socks were a big hit. She didn't try to be funny, but she did give one tiny smile when she pulled them over her knees.

It took them nearly an hour to get through

a *People* magazine from the previous October. He didn't think he ever wanted to see a picture of Cindy Crawford again. She was on every other page. He looked up after reading about a movie star's painful reunion with her long-lost brother. She was asleep, her cheek on her hands, resting on the arm of the sofa. He smoothed the afghan around her and went back to his typewriter.

He nearly knocked his glasses off he roared up out of his chair so quickly. That horrible low mewling sound was louder this time. She was having a nightmare, twisting inside the afghan, her small face flushed, strained with fear. He had to touch her, no choice.

He shook her shoulder. "Wake up, sweetheart. Come on, wake up."

She opened her eyes. She was crying.

"Oh no." He didn't think, just sat down and pulled her onto his lap. "I'm so sorry, baby. It's all right now." He held her close, gently pressing her head against his chest, pulling the afghan around her to keep her warm. One of his socks was dangling off her left foot. He pulled it back up and tucked her in tighter against him.

"It's all right now. I won't let anyone hurt you. I swear it to you. No one will ever hurt you again."

He realized that she was frozen against him. He'd terrified her but good. But he didn't let her go. If ever she needed another person, it was now, and he was the only one available. He kept whispering to her, telling her over and over that she was safe, that he'd never let anyone hurt her again. He spoke on and on until he finally felt her begin to loosen. Finally, he heard her give a huge sigh, then, miracles of miracles, she was asleep again.

It was early afternoon. He was getting hungry, but it could wait. He wasn't about to disturb her. She was nestled against him, her head nearly in his armpit. He rearranged her just a bit, then picked up his book. She whimpered in her sleep. He pulled her closer. She smelled sweet, that unique child sweet. His eyes feral, he said low toward the window, "You come anywhere close, you bastard, and I'll blow your head off."

3

The morning rain slammed against the cabin windows, driven hard by a gusting westerly wind. Ramsey sat beside her on the sofa, one of the many novels he'd brought with him to the cabin in his hand, reading quietly to her as he'd done for the past three days. She was getting more at ease with him, not jerking away from him anymore if he happened to startle her.

The two of them were sitting on the sofa, a good foot between them, his voice quiet and deep as he read to her. He said, "Mr. Phipps didn't know what he was going to do. He could go back to his wife and deal with her, or he could give up and leave her to all the men who wanted her, all the rich men who would give her what she wanted. But then, he'd never given up in his life." He paused. What was coming, he saw in a quick scan, wouldn't be good for a child. No, thinking about killing his wife wouldn't be cool for her to hear. He should never have begun this one. He cleared his throat.

The words blurred as he said quietly, pretending still to read, "But he realized that he had another choice. His little girl was waiting at home for him. He loved her more than he loved himself, and that was saying something. In fact, he loved his little girl more than he'd loved anything or anyone in his life."

She was sitting very quietly beside him. That foot was still between them. He had no idea whether or not she was listening to him. At least she was warm. She was wearing one of his undershirts, a gray one with a V-neck, a cardigan sweater over it that nearly touched the floor, and the afghan pulled to her chin against the chill of the incessant rain and wind. He was getting better at braiding her hair. If she weren't so very silent, perhaps with a small smile on her face, you could take her for any kid, sitting next to her dad, while he read her a story.

But she wasn't like any kid. Slowly, he looked back down at the book. He said with a feeling that was suddenly crystal clear and true inside him, "He wanted his little girl to know that she would always be safe with him. He would protect her and love her for as long as he lived. She was sweet and gentle and he knew she loved him. But she was scared and he understood that. She'd been through so much, too much for a little girl to have to bear. But she'd come through it. She was the bravest little girl he'd ever known. Yes, she'd survived it, and now she would be with him.

"He thought of the little mountain cabin in the Rockies with its meadow of brightly blooming columbine and Indian paintbrush. He knew she'd like it there. She'd be free and he'd hear her laugh again. It had been a long time since he'd heard her laugh. He walked into the house, saw her standing there by the kitchen door, holding a small stuffed monkey. She smiled at him and held out her arms."

He turned to her and very slowly, very lightly, touched his fingertips to her ear. "Do you have a stuffed animal?"

She didn't look at him, just kept staring straight ahead out the cabin windows, at the gray rain he wondered would ever stop. Then she nodded.

"Is it a monkey?"

She shook her head.

"A dog?"

She turned to him then and tears pooled in her eyes. She nodded.

"It's all right. Hey, he's not stuffed, is he? He's a real dog? I promise, you'll be back soon enough with your dog. What kind is he?"

This time she reached over for the pen and paper he'd set on the table by the sofa the previous evening. This was the first time she'd paid any attention to it. He felt a leap of hope. She drew a dog with lots of spots on it.

"A Dalmatian?"

She nodded, then she smiled, a very small smile, but that's what it was, a smile. She tugged at his sleeve. She actually touched him.

"You want the story to go on?"

She nodded. She moved just a little bit closer to him and snuggled down into the afghan. He said, "Funny thing, she wanted a dog, but she loved her stuffed monkey more than anything. His name was Geek. He had very long arms and a silly brown hairy face. She took him everywhere with her. One day when she and her daddy were walking across their meadow in the mountains, they heard this loud sound. It was a milk delivery truck. 'Why did it come up here on our mountain?' the little girl asked her papa.

" 'He's bringing us our weekly milk supply,' her father said. Sure enough there was milk in the truck, but what the man had really brought was a litter of puppies, all of them pure white. Soon the six puppies were yapping at each other and chasing each other around the meadow, hiding in among the flowers, rolling over on their backs, all in all having a wonderful time.

"But Geek wasn't happy. He sat on the porch, his long arms at his side, watching

34

the puppies steal the little girl's attention. He heard her laugh and saw her play with the puppies, saw them climbing all over her, licking her face, whining when she didn't scratch their tummies quickly enough. His monkey head dropped to his legs. He was very unhappy.

"Then suddenly she came back to where he was sitting on the porch. She picked him up and gave him a big kiss on his hairy face. 'Come and play with the babies, Geek,' she said to him. 'Daddy said they have to go back to their own home soon. The milkman just brought them here so we could play with them.'

"When Geek thought about it later, he realized that he'd liked the puppies, once he'd gotten used to them. They were sort of cute. Now that he thought about it, just maybe he could find a puppy and bring it to the little girl. He went to sleep snuggled up next to her, and he dreamed about a little white puppy that would have black spots appear on it when it was older."

Ramsey made a big production of closing the novel. "There, what do you think of Geek the monkey?"

She picked up the pen and paper. She labored over it a moment, then sat back. He looked down to see a stick figure little girl holding what must be Geek. She was hugging him tightly and she was smiling.

"That's great," he said. Was she sitting right next to him? Hot damn, she was.

It was he who fell asleep, his head flopped

back against the sofa. When he awoke several hours later, she was snuggled against him, her head on his chest, boneless as children are when they are utterly relaxed. He leaned down and kissed the top of her head. She smelled like his shampoo mixed with little kid. He liked it. He eased her off him, covered her well, and went to the kitchen. He made himself some coffee, sat down at the kitchen table, and listened to the rain pelt against the cabin roof.

She'd been with him nearly four days now. There'd been no sign of anybody near the cabin. He'd rather wanted the man who'd abused her to show up. He'd like to have the chance to kill him himself. Where was that bastard? Probably long gone. How much longer should he keep her with him, hidden away from the outside world? At least he didn't have to worry about her health. The second day he'd given her a third of one of his sleeping pills. When she was deeply asleep, he'd examined her again, checked all the bruises and welts, applied more antibiotic cream, then covered her again. She was healing nicely. She'd never stirred, thank God.

He wondered if she really had a Dalmatian. He realized, too, that he'd put himself in the place of her real father. Well, too bad. As long as she was with him, she was his. But what about her parents? Had they been there when she'd been taken? Maybe they were responsible, maybe they'd allowed it to happen? What were they like? No, it didn't matter, at least not yet. But, of course, it did matter.

36

He felt good. This was the first time she'd actually gotten close to him. It had taken his falling asleep for her to get closer, but it was a start, a definite start.

He smiled toward the stove, got up, and opened a can of chicken noodle soup. She liked the soup with toasted cheese sandwiches.

• **That** evening after they'd roasted the last two hot dogs, eaten the rest of the baked beans and he'd managed to make some strawberry Jell-O that wasn't rubbery at the bottom, he said to her, "Why don't I say some girl names. If I happen to hit your name, you can nod three times or pull on my arm, or kick me in my shin. Okay?"

She didn't move. Her expression didn't change. Her lack of enthusiasm didn't bode well.

"Okay, let's give it a shot. How about Jennifer? That's a really pretty name. Is it yours?"

She didn't move.

"How about Lindsey?"

Nothing.

"Morgan?"

She turned her back on him. That made her feelings clear enough. She didn't want to play a name game. But why?

"Draw me a picture of your mommy."

She turned back in an instant. Her fingers fluttered over the blank sheet of paper. She didn't look at him, just stared at that paper. Then she began to draw. It was a stick figure wearing a skirt, sneakers, and a head of curly

37

hair. The figure was holding what looked like a box with a knob in the front of it.

He said then, "That's just excellent. Is her hair dark brown like yours?"

She shook her head.

"Red?"

She smiled hugely and nodded. Then she drew more curly hair around the stick woman's head.

"I guessed red because it's my favorite color. She's got really curly hair? Is it long?"

She shrugged her shoulders.

"Okay, it's medium. Is she holding a box?"

She shook her head. She pointed to people on the cover of a magazine on the coffee table. Then clicked her index finger again and again to her thumb.

"Ah," he said. "That's a camera. She's a photographer?"

She nodded, again pointing to the pictures.

"And she photographs people?"

She nodded happily. Then, suddenly, her face fell. She was thinking about her mother, missing her, wondering where she was, and there was not a thing he could do about it. He said, "Now draw me a picture of your daddy."

She clutched the pen the way one would a dagger. Then she made that horrible mewling sound in her throat.

"It's all right, sweetheart. I'm here. You're safe."

Then, somewhat to his surprise, she began to draw a man stick figure and he was playing a guitar and his mouth was open. Her father was a singer? Then she pressed down so hard the pencil tip broke. So could her father have been the one who'd left her vulnerable? Abused her? No, certainly a father wouldn't do that to his own kid. Yeah, right. With everything he knew about life, everything he'd watched and dealt with, he knew, of course, it was very possible. He wanted to ask her questions about her dad, but seeing her reaction, he let it wait.

She wadded up the paper. She slowly pulled away from him and drew up into a ball, pressed against the back of the sofa.

It would take time, he knew. Time. But how much should he take?

• "I'm not going to leave you here in the Jeep. It's just not safe. You're going to come with me. Here, hold my hand. Can you do that?" He paused just a moment, and lightly touched her cheek with his fingertips. "It's all right, sweetheart, I know you're worried about this, but it'll be all right. No one's going to hurt you. You've got me now and I'm big and strong. I know karate. I'm good at it. Sort of like Chuck Norris. You ever hear of him? He can lay flat more bad guys than Godzilla."

She made some chopping motions with her hands.

"Yeah, that's right. I know you don't want to wear those clothes, but it'll just be for a little while, just until I can buy you some new things. Then you can change immediately and we'll throw these out. Better yet, we'll just leave them here at the store." He'd washed the yellow jeans and the light yellow shirt in the bathtub along with his own T-shirts and underwear. He'd hated having her put the clothes on, but there was no choice. He couldn't very well take her into Mr. Peete's Lucky General Store wearing one of his sweaters or undershirts, and barefoot. He chucked her under the chin. "Now, let's go. This will be an adventure. Don't worry. I'll keep you safe. Think of me as your own Geek the monkey, only much bigger. Can you imagine what Geek would do if someone tried to hurt you? I'm sure you can. Geek and I, we're the good-guy monkeys. You ready?"

She smiled, a very brief smile, but he knew she didn't want to leave the Jeep. But he wasn't about to leave her in here, even with the doors locked. He said, "The faster we get in there the faster we can leave."

Finally, she nodded. He lifted her out of the Jeep and set her onto the rough sidewalk. He locked the Jeep door and held out his hand to her. Slowly, she took his hand.

"Real good," he said and lightly squeezed her hand. "Let's go shop 'til we drop."

The Lucky General Store wasn't a Kmart; it wasn't even close, only about one-twentieth the size. When they walked in the door, she shrank against his leg. He just smiled down at her. "You're doing great. Now, let's get you some jeans first, then some shirts. Yeah, it's this way. You point when you see something you like." He could feel her trembling against his leg. He picked her up. In moments, she eased.

The pants she was wearing were a five tall. And the shirt was a 4–6. There was a smiling woman in the kids' section, heavy and pretty, with really white teeth. Ramsey said with a friendly smile, "We need some clothes for my little girl."

It didn't take long. Mildred looked her over and started selecting clothes. "His little girl," as Mildred called her, even pointed to a lime green T-shirt. They ended up with two pairs of jeans, one red, the other plain blue jeans, and four tops, all in bright colors. Her new sneakers were orange. Her socks were green, red, and blue. The lightweight jacket she liked was orange and green patterned. That was a mixed blessing. On the one hand, she'd stand out like a beacon. On the other hand, seeing her go for the vivid colors was positive. He wasn't about to object.

Mildred smiled really big when she showed off her new clothes. "You look a treat, honey. What's your name?"

Ramsey said easily, "She doesn't talk, but she hears everything. She does look pretty, doesn't she?"

"Orange and green are sure your colors. How old are you, honey?"

She held up six fingers.

"Six years old. Aren't you a bright girl. And so pretty. Your mama is going to be so pleased."

She froze. Ramsey said quickly, picking up

41

a bright blue down jacket that looked as though it would fit her, "It might get really cold still. It's still only the middle of April."

"You're right about that. We'll have at least two more snowstorms before it finally decides to heat up."

He nodded. "Yes, better not take any chances." He helped her on with the jacket. He then stepped back and stroked his chin. "You look great in it. You like it? The arms are a bit on the long side, but you'll grow into it soon enough."

She was smiling. She fingered the jacket sleeves. She nodded.

"Your family up here for the week?"

"Yes," he said. "Beautiful country. We're really enjoying ourselves."

"I've lived here all my life. You can lay a twenty on two more snowstorms. Maybe they'll hit after you're gone. You just never know."

He didn't know what else to say. They'd been here too long. He wanted to get her back to the cabin. He gave Mildred a big smile, then said, "Wave good-bye to Mildred."

She nodded to Mildred instead.

He leaned down, saying quietly so Mildred couldn't hear, "Can I pick you up now?"

To his pleasure, she raised her arms. He tossed a bottle of baby shampoo into the cart on the way to the checkout counter. No one had given them one strange look. Everyone had been open and friendly. No more than ten people had seen them together.

Mr. Peete, the owner, was at the checkout counter. "Goodness, kid, you'll be the best-dressed little girl in the Ferengi Range. Here, have a Tootsie Pop on the house, since your daddy's paid our overhead for the week."

They were out of the store after one hundred and sixty-nine dollars, and thirty-five minutes. He put the packages in the Jeep then said, "Now, I've got a surprise for you. See that bookstore? Let's go." Again, she let him carry her.

This stop took nearly as long before they got back to the Jeep. He unlocked the door and put her inside. Then he straightened and stopped cold. Someone was looking at him.

4

The hair prickled on the back of his neck. He slowly turned but didn't see anyone who seemed out of place or overly interested in them. There, just in the alley beside the Union 76 gas station, was there a movement? He stared hard, not moving, feeling a light breeze ruffle his hair. There was nothing at all.

Still he didn't like it. He'd never before ignored his gut. He quickly climbed into the Jeep. She hadn't noticed anything, thank God. She'd pulled the afghan he'd brought to keep her warm close around her, nearly hiding her face. She looked like she was ready to fall asleep. Was she tired or did she just want to escape her fear in sleep?

He looked toward the sheriff's office just

down Boulder Street. Cops might be looking for her. He knew he couldn't keep her with him indefinitely. She had parents. At least she had a mother she loved, if her smile was any clue. He'd asked her if her mom was as cute as she was and she'd smiled. Her father? He'd find out eventually. But her mother, at least, had to be worried sick about her. But he couldn't do it, not quite yet. What the hell had happened? He'd teased over the questions for the past six days, but hadn't found any answers. He had to do something soon, but watching her small face pinch with fear when he turned her over to strangers wasn't in him yet. The more time she had with him, hopefully, the stronger she'd be. Actually, it was she herself holding him back.

He looked down at the sleeping child. There was some color in her cheeks. The taut gray look she'd had even in sleep since he'd found her was finally gone. She looked like a normal little girl. He smiled at the bright colors she was wearing. He remembered the previous evening when they'd settled down for him to read to her after dinner. He'd brought up seeing the sheriff again.

This time she hadn't just shaken her head. She'd grabbed his hand and clung to him. And then shaken her head. He hated that awful empty fear in her eyes.

"All right," he'd said. "We'll give it a while longer. But your parents, kiddo, they've got to be frantic for you."

She lowered her head and began to cry.

44

He wanted to curse, but he didn't. He hadn't snarled a nice meaningful curse in four days, at least out loud, in her hearing.

She seemed terrified that if anyone knew where she was, parents included, she would be hurt again. And she just might. How had he gotten her the first time? Had her parents been careless with her? Left her alone in a shopping mall? Or had the kidnapper simply walked into the girl's yard and taken her?

Maybe he'd go to the sheriff in a couple of days. Almost as soon as he thought it, he was shaking his head. No, she needed more time to trust, to see that he wouldn't let anything happen to her.

But when she was back with her parents, he wouldn't see her again. He wouldn't be able to protect her. They'd failed to protect her before. It could happen again. But the bottom line was, she wasn't his. He'd saved her, but she wasn't his. He didn't know what to do.

He shook his head at himself and speeded up. The Jeep was a workhorse. He loved it. It was a beautiful day, a bit on the cool side, not more than fifty-five degrees, but the sun was bright overhead. There'd been lots of people on the streets. He remembered the feeling of being watched. Had it been real?

He turned at the sound of a low moan. Another nightmare. He leaned over and touched her face. She moved her cheek against his palm, then stilled. He ruffled her hair and cupped her small chin in his palm. She opened her beautiful light blue eyes and blinked up at him. He saw her fear slowly disappear. Her eyes warmed. In that instant he knew he wasn't going to let anyone else have her until he knew for certain that she'd be safe.

"Yeah, yeah, so I'm a big Jell-O. But you know what? Jell-O isn't bad. Another thing, not only are you the best-dressed kid in the Ferengi Range, you're the cutest."

• **The** next afternoon when he came in from out of doors carrying an armful of logs, she flinched and ducked back behind the sofa.

He stopped immediately. "What's up? What's the matter?"

She tried to smile, but it fell away.

"I surprised you?"

She nodded, relieved that he'd explained it as she'd wanted him to. He smiled. "I'll knock next time. I cut us some more wood for the fireplace and the wood stove. Now, after I get this all set, how about you and I go out into the meadow? I want to show you your surprise. While you were trying on your jeans, I got you something really neat." It was, he knew, the only way he was going to get her outside. Since they were in town, she'd refused even to step out onto the front porch. It was time to get her into the fresh air.

Still, she hung back, her small face pale, her expression wary.

"It's really neat," he said again, not acting all that excited, "your surprise, I mean. You need your blue down jacket. It's a little cold out there."

She looked adorable in her stiff new jeans, her orange sneakers as bright as neon lights, red socks, and a bright orange shirt with lime green apples all over it. He was braiding her hair better each time he tried. She looked fresh and sweet and scared. He hated this fear in her, but it had only been a week since he'd found her. Both of them had made strides.

Had the man gotten her easily because she was mute and couldn't scream for help?

"It's a really great surprise. Hey, would I lie to you? Nah, put on your jacket. You can take it off when you work up a good sweat."

She still hesitated. He just set the fire, rose, and waited, leaning his shoulders against the mantel.

Finally, she nodded and ran to fetch her jacket that was hanging next to his. Of course she couldn't reach it. He got it down for her and helped her into it. It fit her great, except for the too-long sleeves that he rolled up.

"Your surprise is going to have you running around. Soon you'll want to take it off."

He led her out into the middle of the meadow and pointed to a dragon-tail kite. He'd spread it out on the ground in all its glory. She just stood there and stared, then smiled, a huge smile that deepened her dimples. It was the first time he'd seen a smile like that.

"You ever fly a kite before?"

Even without her squealing with pleasure, he knew he'd scored big. She was so excited she could barely keep still. He handed her the

rod, waited until she picked up the red diamond body, and arranged the long glittery
dragon tail out behind. She let out some of the
string.

"You're good at this."

She smiled and let out some more string.

She knew what she was doing. Who had
taught her? Her mother? He yelled, "Okay, let
her rip!"

She began running across the flat meadow,
feeding out the line. He released the kite
when he felt it catch the wind. He shouted,
"You've got liftoff!" She stopped running, drew
back a bit, and turned the rod a bit to the left.
The long multicolored tail whirled about in
a big circle.

"Great, let's see you do some more."

She was a lot better at flying it than he
would have been. The kid was really good. He
watched her move her hand first this way,
then that, then flip her wrist, and the dragon's
tail whipped about and whirled around and
around, turning back in on itself, then stream-
ing out again, long and shining in the wind.
He didn't know how she did it, but she turned
her wrist back, wiggled it a bit, and that shim-
mery tail rippled just like a real dragon's tail.

Whoever had taught her was an expert.

She made no sound at all, but she seemed
to be having the time of her life. He stood back
and watched her. It was the best twelve-dollar
investment he'd ever made.

He ended up sitting on the steps of the
cabin, not letting her out of his sight.

Time and his thoughts slowed, leaving only the child who was flying the dragon kite amid the meadow of bright columbine.

Then, suddenly, there was a shot, startling and clear in the silence. The kite dipped and plowed earthward, landing in a bush. She didn't hesitate for an instant, not even to look around. She started to run back toward him as fast as she could.

He was to her in a moment, grabbed her up on the run, and turned back, carrying her into the cabin. Another shot rang out from behind him just as he slammed the door with his foot. He set her down behind the couch. "Stay here. Don't move."

He shoved his pistol into his belt and picked up his rifle. He crouched next to the window, scanning the far forest, searching for something that was different, something that didn't belong in his world. There came another shot, then another, but he couldn't hear any bullet impacts.

He heard a man shout and another man answer. They were some distance away, maybe fifty yards from the front of the cabin, just at the edge of the forest. There were no other voices. There were two men, then. He said quietly to her, "Stay behind the sofa, sweetheart. It will be all right. Just stay there. Remember what I told you. I'm big and strong. I'm also mean when I have to be. Nobody will get to hurt you."

He looked back out the window. To his surprise, two men stumbled out of the thick fir trees, each carrying a rifle. He had the

49

closer one in his sights when he saw they were laughing, leaning into each other, one of the men dragging his rifle. He cursed viciously. The idiots were drunk. Jesus, there was no hunting allowed anywhere near here and here they were shooting and drinking.

The closer man was very tall and thin, he could tell that even though he was wearing thick dark corduroy pants and a heavy dark brown down jacket. He had a plaid hunter's hat on his head. He was waving toward the cabin, yelling, "Hey! Anybody there? We're sorry, we didn't mean anything." Then he giggled as the other man, short, bowlegged, wearing cowboy boots, said, "Yeah, we thought you was a couple of deer. I told Tommy here that deer didn't fly kites."

Ramsey put down his rifle, but held the pistol at his side as he came through the front door out onto the porch.

He was so angry he was shaking. He wanted to bang their heads together, the morons. He yelled at them, "What do you think you're doing firing guns up here? Didn't you see my little girl?"

They waved at him. The drunken idiots actually waved, as if he'd invited them up for a beer. The tall guy called out, "Hey, buddy, it was an accident. Who are you? We didn't think anybody lived up here. We're sorry, real sorry."

The bowlegged guy didn't say a word, just walked along toward him, looking at his rifle or his snakeskin boots, or both.

"You up here a long time?"

When the tall guy asked him the question, Ramsey looked away from the shorter man for just an instant, just long enough for the man to raise the rifle and aim it at him.

Ramsey didn't think, he fired. He caught the bowlegged guy in his shooting arm just as he felt a numbing cold slam against his left thigh. The tall man had his rifle up in an instant, but Ramsey was faster this time. He got him in the shoulder, a clean hit that knocked him backward, off his feet, to the ground.

Ramsey started toward them, then stumbled. He'd been shot in the leg. He hadn't realized it. He yelled, "What the hell do you want? Who are you?"

They were both wounded, cursing, one of the rifles on the ground. The tall guy on the ground managed to jump up, and the two of them had turned and were stumbling back toward the forest. Ramsey raised his Smith & Wesson and fired. He saw a chunk of tree bark fly into the air. He fired again. He heard one of the men yell. Good, he'd gotten one of them with two bullets. He couldn't see them now. They were gone deep into the forest. He wanted to go after them, but he couldn't. He looked down at his thigh. Blood was seeping through the denim. He realized in that instant that he hurt like hell.

Ramsey quickly turned and ran as fast as he could with his gimp leg to the cabin. One of the men still had his gun. He was still at risk. He was in the open and they were hidden in the trees. He saw an old .22 on the ground where the bowlegged guy had dropped it. It was banged up, not very powerful, thank God, but powerful enough to do the job, accurate as hell from close range.

He made the cabin and looked up in shock to see her standing there on the porch, frozen, staring at him. He grabbed her up, ran inside, slamming the door behind him. He felt a new shock of pain in his left leg. He looked down to see his jeans ripped through the outside of his thigh, the blood oozing through the thick denim to run slowly down his leg. Slowly, he eased her down. She clutched his right leg. She was making those gut-wrenching mewling noises again.

He kept her against his right leg. He didn't want to get any blood on her, that would be all she needed to freak her out all over again. But she'd overcome her fear to come outside to see if he was okay. "I'm all right, sweetheart. The bad men are gone, at least I hope they are. You're really brave, you know that? I'm proud of you. You run really fast and that's good too.

"I didn't lie to you. We kicked butt, didn't we? We beat the bad guys. They're gone." But for how long? What the hell did they want? Who were they? What did they want?

• **He** was seated on the single chair in the living room. She stood over him when he pulled down his jeans to examine his leg. The bullet had gouged a gash through the outside of

52

his thigh, ripping away skin, a bit of muscle. Not deep, maybe two inches long. It wasn't bad. He was very lucky.

He poured vodka over the wound. It burned like hell, but she was standing right there, so scared, her face whiter than high mountain snow, and he wasn't about to yell. He gritted his teeth and kept pouring until he was as certain as he could be that the wound was clean. It probably needed to be stitched, but he couldn't do that, no way, since he couldn't sterilize a needle and thread. The last thing he needed was an infection. He pulled the skin tightly together over the gash, then put some sterilized gauze over it. Then he ripped some adhesive tape off with his teeth, stretched the tape tight to hold the edges of skin together beneath the gauze, and pressed it down. Pain hissed out between his gritted teeth. She made a small mewling sound. He saw her lay her hand on his right knee. "It's all right. It just hurt a little bit, not bad. That was the worst of it, putting that tape over it." He laid down more tape, making it tighter. He rose slowly, turned slightly away from her, and pulled up his jeans. "Now, sweetheart, let's get some aspirin down my gullet." He took four generic aspirin from Clement's and drank a full glass of orange juice. He laughed and wiped his mouth. "Vitamin C is good stuff, maybe even helpful for a gunshot wound."

His leg hurt, but that was the least of his problems.

He knew she was watching him, fear leaving her face as pale as new snow. He locked the front door, shot home the deadbolt, and fastened the chain. Maybe later he'd go get that old .22 rifle. He knew the men weren't coming back. They had no idea he had no ability to contact the outside world. They'd think he'd called in the troops immediately. He doubted they'd hang around. It would be too dangerous for them. Besides, they were both wounded. They'd have to get help. He had bought himself some time.

He looked down at her, standing there, not an inch from him, and he knew he had to deal with this and he had to deal with it now.

"Let's sit down," he said, and held out his hand. There were some flecks of blood on the back of his hand. He hoped she wouldn't see it.

Slowly, she gave him her hand. He sat beside her on the sofa. He carefully moved the bowl of bloody vodka to the far side of the sofa.

"I don't know who those men were," he said, looking at her full face, willing her not to be afraid, not to worry so much. "Did you recognize either of them?"

She cocked her head to one side. She was thinking, he knew that look. He wore one remarkably like it on occasion. Finally, she shook her head, but he could tell she wasn't completely certain. Well, that was good enough for now.

Maybe it hadn't been just one man who'd taken her. Maybe it had been two men. Maybe it was the men who'd just shown up pretending to be drunk to get him out of the cabin, then shooting. Maybe they'd both stayed masked when they'd had her. That meant they hadn't planned to kill her. What was their plan then? Keep her a prisoner and play with her until they were tired of her?

It made the blood pound in his temple. They'd been willing to kill him to get her back? But this time they weren't wearing masks. They wanted her dead now?

That first shot they'd fired hadn't been at him, had it? He couldn't remember. He'd think about it later, go over his memories second by second. Still, it was weird. What was going on? How the devil had they found him?

He'd been a fool. He should have left her in the Jeep in town and told her to keep hidden. Well, he'd done it and there was no undoing it now. It was likely they'd seen him with her in Dillinger the day he'd bought her clothes, the day he'd had her with him, holding her hand to the store, carrying her. He felt the aspirin kick in.

About time.

At the end of it, they'd been shooting to kill. He took her hand in his. "We've got to be really careful now. Okay? I want you to stay close to me." As if she'd stray six inches from him, he thought.

She nodded solemnly.

"We'll get out of this, sweetheart. I promise you that."

Again, she nodded, her little face so serious, so pale and tight that he wanted to cry.

5

The aspirin hadn't worked worth a damn. His thigh was throbbing big time. He couldn't get comfortable and he couldn't get back to sleep. He knew he had a low-grade fever. It was nearly two o'clock in the morning. He got up finally, listened for her breathing, heard it, and knew she was deeply asleep because he was used to the rhythms of her breathing now. He walked as quietly as he could to the kitchen and sat down at the kitchen table, balancing the flashlight so it shone on his leg. He knew he had to get that tape and gauze off to see if the wound was infected. If it was, he would be in the Jeep on his way to the hospital within five minutes. And that would mean the cops since it was a gunshot wound. No hope for it. And he would have to bring her into it, giving her over to the authorities, relinquishing all his protection of her.

He was wearing loose sweats. He pulled down the pants and looked at his swelled thigh. It felt warm to the touch, but that seemed normal to him under the circumstances.

It hurt like hell to pull off the tape and lift the gauze, that had, naturally, stuck to the wound, but he took a long swig of vodka, gritted his teeth, and did it. He stared down at his leg. It was swelled and warm, but there was no redness, no pus, thank God. He poured more vodka over the gash, hissing between his teeth.

He felt her presence, then her small hand on his shoulder. He prayed he didn't look as bad as the wound looked when he said, turning slowly, "Hi, sweetheart. I'm sorry I woke you up. I just had to check my leg. It isn't bad, just swelled a bit, and warm, but nothing scary. I'm just being really careful. Now, let me bandage it up again."

She carefully took a thick pad of gauze, then waited. With both hands, he pushed the flesh tightly together on the exit wound, then nodded to her. She laid the gauze over it. Then she pulled out a length of tape, laid it over the gauze and his flesh, and pulled it taut. Then she flattened it down with her palm. He couldn't have done it better himself.

"Maybe you're going to be a doctor," he said, wanting to howl from the pain. He felt sticky sweat on his face, imagined he was as gray as one of his old nightshirts. He took several quick deep breaths. "Thanks, sweetheart. I'm okay, really. Let me get some more tape over this to make sure it holds." He pressed down four more strips.

She stood back, but kept her hand on his shoulder. Every once in a while, she patted him. He appreciated it.

When it was done, he pulled his sweats back up again. "I'd say tomorrow night my leg's going to be all black and blue. Hopefully the swelling will go down a bit by then. Now, let me take some more aspirin." He took three this time.

"You want to go back to bed now?"

She shook her head.

"Me either. You want me to read you a story?"

She shook her head, then mimicked talking.

"You want me to tell you a story?"

She nodded, then, to his delight, she took his hand. He stretched out on the sofa, with her beside him on top of the blanket that covered him, and pulled two more blankets and the afghan over them. The pistol was right beside him on the floor. He settled her against him, feeling the warmth of her against his side, her cheek against his neck. "Once upon a time there was a little princess named Sonya who knew how to fly kites better than anyone in her father's kingdom. One year, her father decided that he would have a contest. He knew no one could beat her. She had a special kite, you see, a dragon-tailed kite that could fly higher and make more figures than an ice skater. There was just one competitor her father worried about. It was Prince Luther from a neighboring kingdom. But he knew she could beat anyone, even Luther, who was a bully and a loudmouth. Do you know what happened at the contest?"

She was lightly snoring. He leaned down and kissed the top of her head. He realized that he'd forgotten all about his damned thigh. He also realized that to this point, his story was pretty bad, probably because he was so tired, his brain woozy. It was lucky she'd fallen back asleep or he would have bored her into yawns.

• **He** tried to stay off his leg throughout the next day. He stuck to the cabin, sitting by the front window, scanning, forever scanning the meadow and the forest that crept up to the edge. He saw nothing out of the ordinary, and no one.

He was going to lie low today, let himself get stronger, then he'd decide what to do.

He knew she was frightened. He knew it and couldn't do a thing about it. He told her half a dozen stories, and none of them too bad, about the little princess named Sonya who beat the nasty little boy, Luther, in the kite-flying contest, then went on to save her father's life, and cook excellent mushrooms and... well, he wouldn't think ahead to the next story. He found it was better if he just opened his mouth and let the story come out unrehearsed.

She sat on the floor next to his chair by the window, drawing with one of his pencils. The afternoon shadows were lengthening. He looked down to see a stick woman with curly hair holding a kite, a little stick girl standing next to her, holding a kite the same size as she was. A curved-up line was the woman's smile; there was a curved-up line for the little girl as well.

Her mother had taught her to fly a kite. He praised the drawings. Perhaps, just perhaps, he could get her to draw him pictures of the man or men who'd taken her and where they'd taken her, what they'd done to her. But he balked at that. He wasn't a shrink. The last thing he wanted to do was make things worse.

"It's time to make dinner. You hungry, kiddo?"

She nodded enthusiastically and gathered up her pages and the three pencils he'd given her. She laid them carefully on the coffee table, lining up the pages neatly. He realized he did the same thing. Then she held out her hand to him.

He took her hand and made a big deal of her helping him up. His leg hurt like the devil, but that was no surprise. The fever was gone. His wound was still swelled up and warm to the touch. The skin near the wound was turning a little black and blue. He wasn't about to pull off the tape again. Best to leave the leg alone to heal. At least until tomorrow.

They didn't have much left in the larder. Tomorrow he'd either have to go in to Clement's grocery, exposing her yet again, or he'd pack up the Jeep early and they'd get the hell out of here. No matter how he cut it, their location was known. Even if there wasn't danger from the two men he'd wounded, the people who'd sent them now knew where she was. He knew he should drive right to the sheriff's office. He knew it. He also knew he wasn't going to do it, not yet anyway. He remembered those desperate mewling noises she'd made. She might snap. But the bigger issue was: How could he send her back home where she could be kidnapped again?

Now that the danger was clear, he had to get off this mountain. He wanted to call his friend

Dillon Savich at the FBI to ask his advice. Of course Savich would tell him to call the FBI. He might even know about her if she'd been abducted. Ever since the Lindbergh baby's kidnapping back in the early '30s, and the resulting tragedy, kidnapping had been the purview of the FBI. But until he could get to Savich, he knew his bottom line was to keep her safe, and that meant, to him, to keep her with him.

Tomorrow, he thought, tomorrow early, they'd get out of here. He did a checklist in his mind of everything he needed to do in the interim before they could leave.

As he opened a can of vegetable soup, he looked at her tearing pieces of lettuce into a big bowl. She had a look of intense concentration on her small face.

"You want French dressing or Italian?"

She picked up the bottle of French dressing.

"Good choice. That was always my favorite when I was your age." He wasn't going to tell her they were leaving until he was ready to load her into the Jeep.

She cocked her head to one side. He realized he did the same thing in just the same way. Had she picked it up from him in only a week? He shook his head, smiling at her. "Yeah, I was once your age. A long time ago. Don't make fun of me because I'm old."

She gave him an impudent grin that was as kid-normal as kicking a soccer ball.

They ate the soup and salad in front of the fireplace. The evening had turned cold, really

61

cold once the sun went down. It was probably in the low forties.

A coyote howled.

• **Just** after dawn, he unbolted the door, unfastened the chain, and as quietly as he could, he went out into a silent world where he could see his breath. He needed to chop wood for the fireplace and the wood-burning stove. He stood very still, looking everywhere for any sign of something that shouldn't be here. Nothing. He finally laid his Browning Savage down on the ground, really close to his left foot. He looked around again but couldn't see anything out of the ordinary.

He split half a dozen logs before his leg began throbbing so much he had to stop. It would be enough. He'd agreed to leave the cabin the way he'd found it, and that included a goodly amount of split logs. He was cursing softly as he cradled the logs in his arms, pressed his rifle against his side, and carried it all back inside.

The dawn light was gray, the forest line blurred and indistinct. There was no movement, not even an early-morning squirrel dashing between trees. He crossed the cabin threshold to see her jerk bolt upright, mewling deep in her throat, her face ashen.

He quickly set the logs and his rifle down by the fireplace, then went to her. He sat beside her on the sofa. Slowly, because he'd learned never to make any unexpected or quick moves, he gathered her against him. He kissed the top of her head. "It's all right, sweetheart. I had to get some more logs." He wouldn't tell her yet that they were leaving. "You just snuggle down again and I'll get the fire going really strong. Okay?"

He laid her back down, the covers in his hands to pull up to her small chin.

"Don't you touch her, you filthy bastard. Step away from her now!"

He and the child both froze at the sound of the woman's voice. He was the stupidest human alive. He'd left the cabin door unlocked. He looked at his Smith & Wesson on the table beside the sofa.

A shot rang out and his gun went flying off the table, skidding across the wooden floor until it was stopped by one of the Indian rugs.

"Try anything at all and the next bullet will go in your head. I promise you that. Get away from her now."

He backed away from her and stood. He turned to see a woman standing in the open doorway, wearing a black down jacket, black jeans and boots, a black knit cap on her head. Her face was very white, her irises showing huge and black. She was holding a Detonics .45 ACP, a nasty little pistol that could blow a man's brains out if he was within twenty feet, which he was.

She looked strung out and quite ready to kill him, but her voice was calm, quiet, filled with hatred. "Move, you creep. I'm not going to tell you again. I don't want you anywhere near her. If I have to blow your head off, I'll do it. Damn you, get away from her!"

"You don't want to kill me. I'm not the one who took her, I swear it to you."

"You perverted piece of filth, just shut up. I saw you touching her. What would you have done to her if I hadn't shown up? Move!" He stepped two feet away from the sofa. She had the gun trained on his chest.

Her eyes darted to the sofa. "Baby, are you all right?"

It was her mother. But how had she found them?

He said, "You really should believe me about this. I'm not the one who hurt her."

"Shut up! Em, are you okay?"

"I found her a week ago in the forest near this cabin. I didn't kidnap her."

"Shut up! Em? What's wrong, baby? Listen to me, he can't hurt you any more. I'm holding a gun on him. Come here, Em, come to Mama."

She was mewling deep in her throat. She threw back the blankets, looking from him to her mother.

"Get away from him, Em. I want you to come over here to me. I'm going to tie him up and take him to the sheriff. Then neither of us will ever have to be afraid again. I know you understand. Come here now, Em."

The woman raised the gun. She said more to herself than to him, "You're very big. You're not going to let me even get near you, are you? No, the instant I try to tie you up, you're going to attack me. It won't ever be over, not until you're dead. I have no choice, none at all."

"Sure you do. You don't want to shoot me. I didn't kidnap her. I saved her."

"Shut up! No, I won't have you lurking about in the shadows, hanging over our lives ever again. I'll do it. I know I can do it. You're evil. You're a monster. Oh God, you abused her, didn't you? I'd prayed and prayed that the kidnapper hadn't hurt her, but you did, didn't you? You don't deserve to live. Em, come here, now. What's wrong with you? Come here so I can make you safe again." She steadied the gun. It was trained right on his chest.

Suddenly, the child threw herself in front of him, her small hands grabbing at his knees. She yelled, "No, Mama, it's Ramsey! He saved me. Don't hurt him!"

Both of them froze. Both of them looked into each other's eyes.

She spoke before he did. "Now, Em, you know he took you away from me. He's using you, he's—"

"No, I didn't kidnap her. I haven't hurt her. But I will tell you that this is the first time she's spoken since I found her in the forest more than a week ago." Slowly, he came down on his haunches, his thigh screaming from the exertion, but he ignored it.

"You're name's Em? Is that short for Emily?"

"No, Emma," she whispered. She was wearing one of his gray T-shirts, washed so many times it was softer than goat leather. She turned to the woman. "Mama, it's all right. Ramsey saved me. Really." She put her hand on his shoulder. She said again in that small tired voice, "He saved me, Mama. He wouldn't let anybody hurt me again. He gets really mad whenever he even thinks about it."

The woman slowly lowered the pistol, but he could tell she didn't want to. "Who are you?"

He picked up Emma and rose, aware that his leg wanted very much to give out under him. "Forgive me, but I've got to sit down. My leg hurts like the devil."

The Detonics pistol jerked up again. "Don't you move, damn you. Put her down."

6

He ignored her. She wouldn't shoot him now. He was holding her daughter. He carried Emma to the sofa and sat down. Only then did he say to her, "I've got lots to tell you. My name's Ramsey Hunt. You can trust me. Please."

"Give me my daughter. Let her go."

He set Emma on her feet, and she ran to her mother. The woman came down on her knees. He watched her as she crushed Emma to her. Tears streaked down her face. She kissed Emma, all over her face, ran her hands all over her, smoothing her hands over her hair, squeezing her until she squeaked.

Emma finally pulled back. She lifted her hand

to her mother's hair and lightly patted it. "I'm okay, Mama, really. Ramsey saved me. He took care of me. You look like GI Joe. I like those black gloves."

The woman laughed as she pulled off the black leather gloves. "I'm your mama again and not a soldier." He watched Emma lace her fingers through her mother's. He saw the close-clipped nails, several broken off. The back of her hands were red and chafed from the cold.

He felt incredibly relieved. And suddenly very tired. He sat back, stretching his leg out in front of him, watching them. Finally, when she was sitting across from him, Emma in her lap, held tightly against her chest, the woman raised her head and said, "Thank you. I'm sorry I nearly killed you. If I had, it would have been wrong." She sounded only mildly sorry. He didn't mind. He could imagine something of what she'd gone through, what she'd thought.

"Yes, very wrong. I'm glad that Emma isn't mute. But you know, we've gotten along just fine. She draws really well."

"Why didn't you say anything, Em?"

She shook her head, then frowned. She whispered, "Nothing would come out. Nothing until I thought you'd shoot Ramsey. I couldn't let you shoot Ramsey. I didn't know what to do so I just talked. Ramsey wanted me to write my name but I couldn't do that either. He didn't think I could write. I couldn't do anything, Mama, except draw pictures."

"You did well," her mother said and kissed

her not once, but half a dozen times. "Oh, Emma, I love you so much." She settled the child again in her lap.

"I'm glad to see you, Mama. I didn't think I'd ever see you again until Ramsey found me. It was scary, Mama. I was so afraid." Emma threw her arms around her mother's neck. She was crying now, deep low sobs that rent the silence.

"It's all right, baby. We're together again. It's all right. I'll never let you go again, I swear it. Oh Emma, I love you. Oh God, I nearly lost hope."

He turned away, giving them what privacy he could, but he listened to them both crying, Emma's sobs, strangely, deeper than her mother's. He waited until they'd begun to quiet, listened to the sniffs, then tossed her a blanket. She pulled it over both of them. She said blankly, "Emma's wearing a man's undershirt."

"Yes, I forgot to buy her some pajamas. At least she doesn't trip over the undershirt."

Ramsey rose, his leg screaming. "Let me lock the door. We can't take any chances."

She didn't say anything, content to wait, he supposed, since she had her daughter back. He knew she watched him closely as he stared through the window, then fastened the chain and flipped the deadbolt. When he turned, he watched her pull off a close-fitting black knit cap. Red curly hair spouted out, most of it in a braid, the rest a riot around her thin face, a pretty face, one that was changing even as he watched. The tension was leaving her face, bringing color to her cheeks. Her mouth was curving into a smile, her eyes were growing lighter even as he stared at her.

There was so much to say, so much to ask, but what came out of his mouth was, "Would you like some coffee? It will just take a minute to make. We're really basic here."

She nodded. "That would be wonderful. I'm so cold I think it's permanent now."

He walked to the kitchen. He felt Emma's hand on his knee. She'd followed him out, his gray T-shirt nearly dragging on the floor and a pair of white gym socks pooling around her skinny ankles. He watched her walk to the small table and measure the coffee into the waiting pan. Then he poured the water over the coffee and set it on the stove. They'd gotten this routine down as of four days ago.

He looked over to the woman standing in the doorway, staring at them, more dazed than not. He didn't even know her name, but at this moment, it didn't seem to matter. What mattered was creating an air of normality. He said to her, "Emma and I are a good act. We got the coffee thing down first thing. We're just about ready to take it on the road. Hey, Emma, who gets top billing?"

"I don't know what that means, Ramsey."

"Does your name go first on the signs or does mine?"

"I'm the youngest. I should go first."

He laughed and ruffled her hair. He looked over at her mother. She was just standing there. He could tell she was trying to make sense of things, not just coming to understand the relationship between her daughter and this man she didn't know, but she was also trying to come to grips with the fact that Emma was safe, that she actually had her daughter back.

She didn't say anything, just stood watchfully. She looked strung out and very tired. He said, "You'd think that boiled coffee would rot your fillings out, and it just might, come to think of it, but it doesn't taste too bad and it does zing your brain. As I said, we're basic here. We've got a small refrigerator and the lights in the living room, due to a generator. But it's a wood-burning stove and we heat the water for a bath."

Emma said, "We toast bread with a metal thing that has a long handle."

The woman shook her head, still trying, he knew, to understand what was happening here. "I'd drink anything that passed for coffee at this point. I've been sitting out there waiting and waiting for daylight, waiting for you to come outside, but when you did, you had that rifle and I was too far away to do anything with my Detonics."

"I shouldn't have left the cabin door unlocked. It was stupid. If it hadn't been you, it could have been them."

"Well, it wasn't. I didn't see anyone else out there. Who's them? Who are you talking about?"

"Let's hold that for just a little bit," he said, and nodded toward Emma. He poured her a cup of coffee that was still bubbling. "Sit down and try to drink it. If anything it'll keep you buzzing until noon, when you'll probably crash. Emma, I'm going to fix you a bowl of Cheerios. You want peaches or bananas?"

"A banana. I don't really like peaches."

"But you've eaten them without complaint."

She said as she took the cereal box from him and poured Cheerios into her bowl, "I didn't want to hurt your feelings. But I do like bananas better."

He sliced the banana over her cereal while she got the milk out of the small refrigerator. "Look, Mama," she said, pointing. "It doesn't have a freezer. We make everything fresh, just the way we do at home."

"I've never seen one that fancy before. It's neat." She didn't know how the words, such ordinary words, had come out of her mouth. She'd passed from blankness to disbelief. Here she'd expected to come in and fight her daughter's abductor and deal with a hysterical hurt child, and now she was drinking boiled coffee at a kitchen table, looking into a high-tech refrigerator, listening to her daughter chew her Cheerios. She looked at the big man who needed to shave. He'd saved her daughter? He'd protected her with his life? Nothing made sense yet.

Emma was eating Cheerios with a banana on top, nicely sliced by that stranger. She didn't say anything more until Emma was down to her last bite of cereal and he was drinking his second cup of coffee, seated across from her at the table. "I've been tracking her for two weeks. When I showed Emma's picture down in Dillinger, I just couldn't believe it. Several people told me she was Ramsey's little girl. I didn't know what to think. I've been watching since yesterday, but I couldn't get to you without taking a chance of hurting Emma. You never came out of the cabin. Neither of you did."

"Who are you?"

"I'm Molly Santera."

Emma looked up as she swallowed a banana circle. "Mama says it sounds like a made-up band's name—our last name—but it's real. It's my dad's name."

Molly smiled at her daughter and leaned close, just to touch her. "That's true enough. But I'll bet you there are lots of Santeras in the New York phone directory."

"I've never been to New York," Emma said.

"We'll go when you're a bit older, Em. We'll have a great time. We'll stay at the Plaza and walk right over to FAO Schwarz. It's really close."

Santera. The name was vaguely familiar. He remembered Emma's drawing of a man holding a guitar and his jaw dropped. He said slowly, "Santera. You mean Louey Santera? The rock star?"

"One and the same," Molly said, her voice clipped, colder than a late-spring freeze.

Ramsey wanted to know more about Emma's father, ask her why the hell the guy wasn't tracking with her, even though he was a famous rock star. But he could tell that Molly didn't want to say more about him right now. There would be time enough for her to answer all his questions and for him to answer all of hers. Emma had eaten her cereal, all the while smiling at her mother, then smiling at him, like any happy well-adjusted kid.

"I know who you are now."

He cocked his head at her. "Me? How?"

"I recognize you now that I've thought about your name. Are you the famous Ramsey Hunt?"

Again, for Emma's sake, he used a light hand. "Infamous is more accurate."

"In your dreams."

He sputtered in his coffee, raised his head, and stared at her. "Men," she said, her hands wrapped around her coffee mug, "if they have a choice, would rather have the world believe them infamous—you know, rogues and bad boys—not heroes, not known for something worthy or moral they've done or tried to do."

"No," he said. "That's not me."

She sighed, and shrugged, looking away from him. "This is tough to believe. You're a federal judge from San Francisco, but you're here. You found Emma."

"Yes," he said.

"Given what you did in your courtroom, I suppose Emma couldn't have been safer."

He said nothing, just took another sip of the afterburner coffee.

A federal judge who was also famous, a

hero truth be told, despite his reticence, and here both she and Emma were with him. Life had kicked her so much in the teeth for the past two weeks that she supposed she shouldn't be shocked at this latest surprise. She said to her daughter, "Em, you look beautiful. How are you, love?"

Emma kept her head down. Reality had crashed in suddenly and she wasn't ready yet. Molly had sounded too serious, too strident. She felt stupid and so very tired. She could have kissed Ramsey Hunt when he said, his voice still light and calm, his attention seemingly on Emma, "She had to have other stuff to wear than just my T-shirts. I put off leaving the cabin for as long as possible, but she had to have some clothes. And that's how you found us. When Emma and I went shopping in Dillinger."

"As I said, I showed her photo around and the town folks all believed she was your little girl. Truth be told, I didn't expect to learn anything at Dillinger. It was the last stop. I guess then I would have had to let the cops and the FBI deal with things. Naturally, they are dealing with things, in their own way. They didn't solve a thing, didn't turn up a thing. I gave them two days, then hit the road. I heard they called off the manhunt for her after four days."

"Where do you live?"

"In Denver." She picked up a spoon and fiddled with it, her eyes down on the white-and-red-checked tablecloth. "Her father is in

Europe. He's on tour and couldn't leave, but he'll be back soon now." She turned to her daughter and took her small hand. "I speak to him nearly every day, Em. He's very worried about you, really."

Emma stared down into her bowl that had one banana slice floating in a bit of milk. She said, never looking up, "I don't know why he'd come. I haven't seen him for two years."

He realized her daughter had knocked her flat. He said quickly, "I see. You're divorced."

"Yes," Molly said. She'd gotten herself together again. "Emma, it doesn't have anything to do with the divorce. Your daddy loves you. It's just that he's so very busy."

"Yes, Mama."

Time to move along, quickly, Ramsey thought, and said, "So you gave the cops all of two days then you struck out on your own?"

"Yes. There was nothing I could do at home except go quietly nuts."

He wanted to tell her that if the kidnappers called, they'd have wanted to speak to her. Then he realized that any female police officer could do that duty. He didn't say anything. Emma was all ears.

"I've been traveling from Aspen to Vail to Keystone and all the places in-between. Dillinger was my final try."

"You lucked out. As I said, if she hadn't needed clothes, I wouldn't have taken her to Dillinger. I'd been here at the cabin for nearly two weeks before I found Emma."

"Why were you here of all places?"

He shrugged, looking down at his coffee. "It got to be just too much," he said at last. "Just too much. The tabloids just wouldn't let up. The paparazzi were leaping out from behind my bushes to catch me unawares."

"They call you Judge Dredd."

"It's ridiculous, all of it." He started to curse, realized that Emma was staring up at him, and took a deep breath. "I took three months off and got away from everything—people, phones, TVs, everything. Then I found Emma." He leaned over and cupped Emma's chin in his palm. There was color in her cheeks. She looked little-kid beautiful, and healthy. "Why don't you go wash up and put on your jeans and a real bright shirt. Your mom and I will talk and decide what we should do."

She looked worried. "Mama, you won't try to shoot Ramsey again, will you?"

"I never drink a man's coffee then hurt him, honey. It's not done."

"Mama, you made a joke." Emma beamed at her.

"Yes, a good joke," Ramsey said. "Go, Emma."

He sat back in his chair and looked at the woman across from him. "Emma drew several pictures of you. In all of them you were smiling really big." But now she wasn't smiling. She was pale and thin and had the reddest hair he'd ever seen, all curly, just like Emma's drawings. Her eyes were a sort of green-grayish color, a bit tilted at the corners, sort of exotic. She didn't have any freckles, and she didn't look a thing like Emma.

"I've been calling her 'sweetheart.' I like Emma. It suits her."

"It was my grandmother's name."

She sat forward, intent, then suddenly jumped to her feet and began pacing the small kitchen, hyper now from the coffee, alert, and ready for answers. "How did you find Emma?"

"It was exactly eight days ago. I was out chopping logs when I heard this strange sound, you know, a sound I shouldn't have heard here. I tracked it down and found her unconscious in the woods. I spotted her only because she was wearing a bright yellow T-shirt. I brought her back here and took care of her. She didn't speak until she yelled at you."

He saw the question in her eyes and slowly nodded. "Yes, she'd been beaten and sexually assaulted. There wasn't any sodomy that I could tell, but then again, I'm not a doctor. She's much better now, even though last night she had a nightmare." He stopped and shook his head. "It took her a good four days to trust me. She's a great kid."

Tears were running out of her eyes and down her cheeks, dripping off her lips. She sniffled. He handed her a napkin and she blew her nose and wiped her eyes.

"She's only six years old. She was kidnapped by a child molester and it was all my fault. If only—"

"Stop it, just stop it. I've known you for an

hour and I know you didn't leave her unattended, wouldn't do anything to jeopardize her. Now, I don't want to hear any more of that crap." He sighed, knowing deep down that she'd probably never stop blaming herself for the rest of her life. "Believe me, I've never felt so helpless in my life. She's such a sweet little girl. She was terrified of me, a man, and I couldn't blame her at all. When she didn't speak, I became convinced she was mute."

He'd kept talking so she could get a hold on herself, which she finally did. He watched her shoulders square. "Maybe it was the trauma. Maybe she felt safer if she didn't say anything and didn't write down her name for me. Maybe she really couldn't speak until it became a matter of life and death. Would you have shot me?"

"In a heartbeat if you'd so much as moved a finger."

"I'm rather relieved that Emma remembered her voice. You've had a hard time of it. It must have been very difficult to go into all the towns and show her picture."

"No, everyone was very nice, all except for the local cops. Almost to the man, they treated me like a hysterical female, all patronizing and pats on the shoulder and leave it to them, the big macho guys. I nearly punched one guy out in Rutland. When I finally found your cabin, I thought a lot about what I was going to do. I know enough about how law enforcement works to realize that if I only captured the man who'd abducted her, he'd probably be out on bail at some point. Would he come after Emma again? Say the judge denied bail, they kept him in jail, then even convicted him. He'd probably get out sooner or later and then be out again to prey on other children or come after Emma again. I'd have to worry about him for the rest of my life. So would Emma, and that's worse. A child molester, a kidnapper. A monster like that doesn't deserve to live."

She met his eyes squarely. "If that monster had been you, I would have at least wounded you. That way, at least, you couldn't have been out on bail. You would have been in a hospital. There maybe someone would have screwed up your medicine and just maybe you would have croaked."

He drained the last of his coffee, an eyebrow arched. "You don't have much faith in our system."

"No, not a scintilla of faith. The system, even if it weren't screwed up, is so backed up that plea bargains are the only way to keep criminals moving. Why am I saying the obvious to you, a judge who lives this every day?

"You know that this guy, even if he were caught, might plea-bargain down to seven years then get out in three. It's not right, but of course the trial lawyers aren't about to let anybody change anything. They don't care about justice, just about getting their hands on as much money as they can. Then they put all the focus on the poor criminal and how screwed up his childhood was, as if that excuses his brutality. It's just not right. You're part of it. You know it's not right."

He said mildly, "No it's not right. Look, no one wants the bad guys on the streets. Most of us work really hard to keep them in prison." He shrugged. "But sometimes the wrong things just happen."

"Spoken like the person you are."

He shrugged. "I guess none of us can escape what we are for very long."

"You said you came here to hide out."

He looked mildly embarrassed. "Things were out of control. I came here to get myself back together again and to give people time to forget, which they will, soon enough."

"You're a federal judge. You have to know lots of people. You must believe in the system. Why didn't you immediately take Emma to the police? The hospital?"

"I couldn't," he said simply. "I just couldn't. She was terrified. I couldn't bear the thought of strangers all over her." His eyes dropped to his running shoes. "I also worried that she could be taken again if she went home."

She just looked at him for a very long time, then, slowly, she nodded. "If I'd been in your shoes, I wouldn't have given her over to strangers either. I wouldn't have sent her home either, not until I knew she'd be protected. Thank you for keeping her safe. She's the most important person in the whole world. I don't know if I could have gone on if she'd been killed."

He thought she would cry, but instead, she shook herself, and stood up. "And that's why I don't want to go back to Denver."

7

If I were in your shoes, I'd feel the same way." He sat forward, his elbows on the scarred tabletop. "I worried about not notifying the police, not taking her to a hospital, but, bottom line, I just couldn't give her over to the care of strangers. Did you see the sheriff in Dillinger?"

"No, I stopped seeing the local cops as of six towns ago. I just took Emma's photo around and asked and asked. I didn't know what else to do. I had this feeling that the kidnapper had taken her west, not up north toward Fort Collins and Cheyenne. No, I just knew it was here in the Rockies."

"Why?"

"The Denver police had this hot line for anyone who had seen anything. They were flooded with calls, none of them relevant, but there was this one, an old woman who claimed she'd seen a white van heading west. The cops thought she was senile and ignored it, but I went to see her. She lives up the block from me. She has really bad arthritis and so she spends a lot of time just sitting in her chair, looking out the window. If there was anything to see I knew she'd have seen it. I told the cops this, but they blew it off."

"How could she know the van was going west?"

"We live on a hill facing west and facing the Seventy. From her deck, she saw the van turn onto the freeway going west. She swears she saw a little girl in the van."

"No ransom note?"

She shook her head. "No, at least not since yesterday morning. That's the last time I checked in. That's what the FBI agents were counting on. They kept telling me over and over that I had to be patient, just sit there by the phone and be patient. I was to let them tell me what to do since they knew everything and I was stupid. I nearly smacked this one agent. I waited for two days and nothing. Still, the FBI agents just kept shaking their heads saying that I had to wait, wait, wait. I was going crazy. Finally I just headed out at dawn the morning of the third day. I call in every day and let them yell at me.

"I've visited more places than I can remember. Really, this one was the last stop. When I came into Dillinger, I couldn't believe it when everyone just nodded and said she was Ramsey's little girl. If I'd seen you then, without Emma, I would probably have cleaned out my Detonics on you."

"You would have gone to jail."

"Yeah, some justice."

"If you had shot me, sending you to jail would have indeed been justice. For my sake, I hope they wouldn't have plea-bargained you down." Of course that wasn't the point. She didn't say

82

anything to that, but he could practically see the hackles rising. He wanted to ask how Emma had been taken, about Emma's father, and a dozen other things, but now Emma was standing in the doorway, looking bright and clean, a hairbrush in her hand. She walked to him and held out the brush. He heard Molly suck in her breath. He smiled, took the brush, and brought Emma to stand between his knees. He combed out the tangles, then began the braid.

Emma said, "Mama, could you teach Ramsey how to French-braid my hair?"

"Yes, I can. He's doing pretty well with your regular braid, though."

"You should have seen the first braid he did. It was all spiky and crooked, like it was broken in the middle."

When he got to the end of the braid, she handed back a rubber band. "There." He turned her around, his hands on her shoulders. "You look great. Everyone is going to ask you who your hairdresser is. I'm the best."

"That was well done," Molly said in a calm voice, but both of them recognized that it was tough for her, this unquestioned trust and affection Emma had for another human being, one she hadn't even known until a week ago. "Can I show Ramsey how to French-braid it tomorrow for you, Em?"

"Yes, Mama."

Ramsey leaned forward in his chair, taking her hands. "I want you to gather up all your clothes, Em, and stuff everything in a pillowcase. Don't forget anything. It's important. If those men come back, I don't want them to see anything that has to do with any of us in here. The three of us are leaving in fifteen minutes. All right?"

She gave him a long look, then nodded slowly.

He waited until he heard Emma rummaging around in the living room, then said to Molly, "I told you that I was relieved that you weren't the bad guys. We had visitors, two of them."

Emma said from the doorway, a half-filled pillowcase in her hands, "Are you going to look at your leg, Ramsey?"

He'd forgotten. He should, just to make sure there was no infection. He nodded slowly. "I'll get the tape," she called.

"What's going on?"

"Two guys stumbled out of the forest into the meadow yesterday, firing their rifles, pretending to be drunk. I got Emma inside and came back out with my rifle and handgun. I got hit in the leg, but I managed to hit both of them. One of them twice. They ran off. I have one of their rifles. Maybe the police can run a check on it.

"I don't know who they were or why they were here. My feeling is that they were after Emma." Then, Emma was standing there, beside him. He said easily, "Emma, hand me a sterile gauze." He rose and pulled down his sweatpants. He heard Molly suck in her breath. He said as he sat back down again, "Let

84

me get this tape and gauze up. There, that's not too bad. It's supposed to turn black and blue. Okay, Emma, give me the gauze. You know, I think the swelling's down a bit."

"I hope so, Ramsey," Emma said, leaning close. "It doesn't smell bad, so that's good."

Molly said as she watched the two of them work smoothly together, Emma handing him strips of adhesive tape, then helping him pull it tight over the gauze, keeping the flesh together, "How'd you know about that, Em?"

"I know lots of things, Mama. I watched an ancient history show, the one Mr. Spock does, and they talked about how this one phara—"

"Pharaoh?"

"Yeah. He had his leg rot and ooze because someone hit him with a spear, and then he died."

"You mean gangrene?" Molly asked.

"Yes, that's it. I don't see any red, Ramsey."

"No, I don't either."

"Is it still real warm?" She didn't wait for him to answer, just lightly pressed her palm next to the bandage. "Yes, it is. How much longer will it be warm?"

"I don't know. Not much longer. I'm a real quick healer."

"But it is better, isn't it?"

He heard the crawling fear in her voice, and came up with a big grin. He rubbed his knuckles on her cheek. "I'm nearly ready to go skiing, sweetheart. You want to go to Vail?"

"Mama likes to ski at Vail. I'm just learning."

"You can be my mascot. I'll carry you around on my shoulders. When I fall, I'll toss you in a snowbank and you can be a snow angel." Still, she looked profoundly worried. She lightly pressed a hand on either side of the bandage.

"It's okay, Em, I promise. If I wasn't sure, I'd be in the ER quicker than I could get the Jeep started."

A small calm voice said, "He said there wasn't a hospital close to here, just a nice big church."

Molly and Ramsey stared at her, not breathing. The air in the kitchen seemed to dry up.

Ramsey sat forward. He'd wanted desperately to question her about the man who'd kidnapped and abused her, but he hadn't. He had no experience in this kind of thing. There was no way he'd risk freaking her out. He said calmly, his voice utterly matter-of-fact, "Who said that, Emma? What man?"

She began shaking her head back and forth so violently the braid slapped her cheek. She said over and over, "No one, no one, no one."

"It's okay, Em." Molly went down on her knees and pulled her daughter against her. Emma was leaning heavily against his thigh, pulling her mother with her, but he didn't feel any pain from the weight. "I love you. It's okay."

He met Molly's eyes over Emma's head. There was murder in Molly's eyes. He prayed that if they ever caught the guy they'd have time to get information out of him before Molly managed to sneak in and kill him. On the other hand, maybe he'd kill him himself before Molly could.

"Em, you got your stuff ready?"

She pulled back, looking at him. Her face was pale, the cheekbones looking as if they were ready to poke through her skin, she was drawn so tightly. "Yes, Ramsey. I'm nearly ready. I just can't find one of my red socks."

"We're out of here in five minutes, red sock or not. Bring the tape with you. Let's leave the leg alone for another day. Come on, you guys, let's get moving."

• **They** didn't see a soul. Of course anyone could be hiding in the forest, watching them. Ramsey herded them into the Jeep as fast as he could.

"Where's your car?" he asked Molly as he slipped into the driver's seat. In one quick motion he'd inserted the key and turned it. The engine was loud in the early-morning silence.

"It's down about a half a mile, just off the road. It's a rental car, a Chevrolet." She paused just a moment, never stopped looking out the windshield, and said calm as a clam, "Look, Ramsey, you're a federal judge. You're part of the system. I don't believe in the system. I'm not about to call the cops or go back to Denver. Why don't you drop me and Emma off and then you can go about your life?"

"What do you mean by that?" He swung the wheel too far in his surprise and instant anger, and nearly went off the rutted narrow road.

"I mean," she said, still looking out the dirty windshield, and not once at him, "that you don't know us. I'm here now. Emma's my responsibility. I'll take over."

"No."

"I'm not calling in the damned cops."

"Fine. For the time being. But I disagree." He knew there was something else holding her back, something she hadn't told him, not that she'd told him hardly anything at all.

"I don't care. I'm calling the shots here. If you can't accept that, then leave."

"Mama, you don't want Ramsey to stay with us?"

Molly kissed her daughter's ear. "He's an innocent bystander, Em. This isn't his trouble."

"How did you reach that brilliant conclusion?" The Jeep crunched over rocks and lurched to the side. "Some guys tried to take me out at the cabin. Chances are they just wanted to get me out of the way."

"I don't suppose you considered that it could have been you they were after?"

He wanted to strangle the steering wheel. "Emma," he said, "stop listening, as of now. Put your hands against your ears. Yes, that's good. Now, I'm going to speak my mind to your mother."

"I don't want to hear any more. It doesn't matter. You've done your good deed. You've even been hurt protecting Emma. It's enough, more than enough. You're now out of our lives. When we trade cars, I'll be really careful to make certain no one follows us. I've gotten very good at being sneaky. I'm not going back to Denver, so you don't have to worry that Emma will be in any danger again. Oh yeah, I'll call the cops and the FBI and tell them it's over. I'll tell them where you found Emma so maybe they can find the cabin where the kidnapper was holding Emma. Then I'll tell them what a dynamite job they all did."

Emma sat perfectly still on her mother's lap, her hands over her ears. But she was making those horrible mewling sounds in her throat.

Molly looked like she'd been punched in the stomach. She gathered Emma close, rocking her. "Baby, it's all right. Oh, God, I'm sorry, Emma. Please, trust me. I promise I'll take care of you. It was my fault that he got you that first time, but we're not going back there. I'll keep you safe. I won't yell at Ramsey again."

Ramsey stopped the Jeep. He turned in his seat to face them. "Emma," he said matter-of-factly, "take your hands away from your ears. Now listen to me. You won't make those sounds any more, do you hear me? If you have something to say, you'll say it, not scare the devil out of me making those sounds. They terrify me to my toes. They make my leg hurt more. Now, I'm not leaving you and your mom. Your mom can yell at me if it makes her feel better. I might even yell back. But nothing could make me leave you. Do you hear me?"

A loud silence, and then, "You promise you won't leave, Ramsey?"

"I promise. I don't break my promises. Your mom will get used to me just as you did. She won't talk me out of it, no matter what kind of reasons she comes up with. I'll even play by her rules, for the time being. You're going to talk from now on, all right?"

She nodded slowly. "I don't like to hear you yelling."

"No, we don't either. But it'll happen sometimes. You can just tell us both to be quiet. Now, enough said."

Molly didn't say a word. She looked as if she wanted to fold up on herself. She looked near the edge. He felt like taking a strip off her, but he didn't. She might just crumble. Or, she might just shoot him. He lightly patted her shoulder and said in that calm deep voice that served him well in the courtroom, "It will be all right, Molly. You'll see. There's nothing wrong with needing backup, and that's how you can think of me. Now, let's get out of here. Emma, look out the rear window. If you see a car behind us, you tell me."

"Yes, Ramsey."

"I'm counting on you. Keep sharp."

"I will."

"About those men," Molly said. "Do you think it's possible that they could have been after you and not Emma?"

"I don't know."

"You've made enemies. I read you'd gotten threats, particularly from that one woman whose husband died that day in the courtroom."

"That's right, I have, but no one has tried to kill me before."

"That would mean that there were two men with Emma, not just the one who abducted her."

"That's right. Could you please pour me a cup of coffee from the thermos?"

She knew he didn't want to talk about it in front of Emma. But there was so much dammed up inside her. For nearly two weeks, she'd been filling up with anger and hatred and helplessness. She'd wait, she had to. The last thing she wanted was to terrify her daughter even more than she already was. She handed the cup to Ramsey Hunt, a man she'd read about, a man she'd wondered about in odd moments along with the rest of the country. Until two weeks ago when her world was blown apart.

She hugged Emma tightly to her.

"Let me loose, Mama. I've got to keep looking out the back window. The Jeep's dirty, Ramsey. We should stop and get it washed."

"That's a good idea. Who would be looking for a spanking clean Jeep?"

They left Molly's rental car where it sat. Molly took all the papers out of the glove compartment. "I'll call them and tell them where the car is. They may not mind too much if I tell them to charge anything extra on my credit card."

They had the Jeep washed when they stopped

for lunch in Rappahoe, a small town just off the 70. No one was following them as best Ramsey could tell.

"How's your leg?"

"Stiffening up on me," he said, taking a big bite of his hamburger. He closed his eyes as he chewed. When he swallowed, he groaned and said, "Fat. There's nothing better in life."

"I heard my dad say that sex was the best thing in life," Emma said, and chewed on a French fry coated with catsup.

"I think kittens and little girls are about the two best things," Molly said without skipping a beat.

He admired her for that. He himself was aware that his mouth had dropped open.

"Did you bring my kite, Ramsey?"

"Oh yes. This kid's a pro," he added to Molly, who'd taken all of one spoonful of her vegetable soup. "You taught her, didn't you?"

She nodded, picked up her spoon, and began stirring the soup. There was a film of grease over the top. She dropped the spoon and took a slice of white bread. She spread butter and jam on it. At least she was eating that.

"Ramsey, two guys just came in. They're looking over here. One of them has a rifle."

• **Melissa** Shaker watched her father move smoothly and steadily on the rowing machine. She wanted to tell him that he looked really good for a guy his age, that he should hang around in jock T-shirts and shorts. The minute he dressed in one of his expensive Savile Row suits, he looked faintly ridiculous. The bottom line was, he looked like a thug, really. The more expensive the clothes, the more they seemed to reduce him to a stereotype of a Hollywood movie Mafia character. But strip her old man down, and he looked just fine.

She said, "I noticed that you've stopped taking Eleanor around to the clubs."

He grunted, never missing his rhythmic pull, release, pull, release. "Yeah, she's so classy she makes me look like a bodyguard."

She blinked at that. She didn't realize he'd known. Eleanor, classy?

He continued after a moment, his voice smooth and calm, despite his exertion, "The younger, the more beautiful the girl, the more like a gargoyle I look."

Melissa laughed. "You're right, but I wouldn't have said it out loud. I saw you with a really beautiful girl out by the swimming pool the other day. You were wearing a bikini and so was she. You looked better than she did. Just wear shorts, Dad, and you'll look great."

He grunted, slowly easing down on his speed. This was his cooldown. He'd been on the rowing machine for forty minutes. Sweat was dripping off him and his muscles were pumped and glistening. If he hadn't been her father, she would have at least looked him over.

The phone rang. He said without looking up, "Answer it, but don't say anything."

She did. When she handed him the phone, he'd finally come to a halt. He was breathing just a bit on the fast side. He listened, then said, "What's the status?"

He listened. Melissa wished she could pick up the extension. She walked over to the weight rack and picked up two five-pound free weights. She began to do bicep curls.

She turned only when she heard him place the phone back into the cradle. He said, "It shouldn't be long now. We'll get three for the price of one."

"I wish it could be different."

He looked at her closely, doing the slow bicep curls, like pulling through water, just as he'd taught her. "No you don't. You enjoy all this crap. But I promised you. You know I always keep my promises."

She put down the free weights and walked to him. She hugged him close, not caring that he was sweaty. "Thanks, Daddy. I know. I appreciate it."

He lightly pushed her away and toweled himself off. "You're a good girl, Mellie, but sometimes you get strange ideas." He raised his hand. "No, it's okay. It keeps life interesting."

Rule Shaker was whistling when he walked into the huge shower stall in the marble bath off his private gym.

8

Emma, keep your head down and eat your French fries. Molly, don't go for your gun, listen to me. I want you and Emma to go through that doorway that says TELEPHONES & TOILETS. If there's an exit, go on out to the Jeep, otherwise, stay in the bathroom. If you get to the Jeep, lock yourselves in. I'll be out as soon as I pay the bill. Go. Act as naturally as you can. Don't look back."

Molly didn't move. "Em, did you see the two men that came to the cabin?"

"Not really."

"So you wouldn't recognize them?"

"No, Mama, but Ramsey would."

"That's right, I would. Go, Molly. There's no time for any more discussion. If they're the guys I'll be out as soon as I can, probably walking really fast."

"You made a joke, just like Mama does."

"Maybe."

Molly gave him a final long look, grabbed her purse, kept her attention on Emma, and walked with her to the back of the small restaurant, through the doorway. Slowly, Ramsey turned around just as he raised his hand to the waitress. They were standing with their backs to him. One was tall and thin, the other short. He couldn't tell if he was bowlegged or not. He didn't think they were the same guys who'd come to the cabin. How could they be? He'd shot both the bastards. He didn't have his Smith & Wesson. The restaurant was pretty crowded. He prayed the men wouldn't do anything stupid.

The waitress smiled down at him. He said without looking at her, "Is there a back way out of here?"

"Yeah, there's a back door just beside the men's room."

"Good. How much do I owe you?"

She wrote down a couple of more things, frowned as she added, then ripped off the paper and handed it to him, saying, "You guys didn't eat all that much so I took a bit off the bill."

"That's really nice of you. My wife was feeling a bit on the edge. She's pregnant."

"Oh, well, congratulations. It happens to the best of us, getting sick that is."

"Hey, Elsa, how's tricks?"

The guy looked like a cowboy with a gut. He was standing behind the waitress. Ramsey couldn't see his face because Elsa was large, had very big hair, and was standing squarely between them. But it wasn't one of the men at the cabin. He didn't know whether to be relieved or worried over a possible new threat.

"I'm mean and pretty as ever," she said, turning to face the man, blocking Ramsey's view of him. "You're new, aren't you? You move here or something?"

"Yeah. Me and the missus came down from Wyoming. Nice around here."

"Yeah. You want some lunch, then go sit with your friend at that booth." She pointed with the pencil then stuck it behind her ear.

"Hey, mister, what happened to that pretty little girl I was smiling at?"

Ramsey slowly rose. Elsa stepped out of the way, alarm suddenly hitting her brain. Ramsey towered over the man, who was middle-aged, losing the war to fat, and looked as sincere and nice as Ted Bundy had probably looked.

"Hey, buddy, that your kid?"

"Yes, she's my kid. Why do you want to know?"

"No reason. She's just cute, like one of my little granddaughters."

Ramsey handed the waitress a twenty, saying to both of them, "Have a good day. Bye now." He went to the front door, but not before he looked for the other man. He didn't see him. Not seeing him bothered him a lot more. Where was the bastard?

His gut was dancing double time. He looked back again. There was no single guy in the restaurant. Why had the man wanted to know about Emma?

It was then he heard the screech of brakes. He was out the door in an instant to see Molly backing up the Jeep, then slamming on the brakes again to miss a parked pickup truck, by about four inches. He saw a man running toward her. She gunned the engine and the Jeep shot forward. The man shouted and dived into the scrawny bushes that lined the wall of the restaurant.

"Molly!"

He grabbed the passenger door, pulled it open, and jumped in.

She was onto the entrance ramp to the 70 before he even got the door closed.

He looked back to see the man dusting off his pants, staring after them. Then the man he'd been speaking to came out. The two men conferred, heads bent close. He lost sight of them as Molly veered onto the 70, tires screaming.

"Ramsey."

He heard the small voice and looked down. Emma was scrunched on the floor at his feet. "Come here, kiddo. We're just fine. Your mama's a heroine. She saved us. Come here and hug me. I need some attention and a kiss. Yeah, a kiss would make my heart slow down and put my stomach back where it belongs."

Emma crawled up and let him lift her onto his lap. Now wasn't the time to worry about his seat belt. She kissed him on the cheek. "That's better. Thanks." He said calmly to Molly, "Slow down, and go out at this next exit."

"But—oh, yes, you're right. Then we'll see if they follow."

"Slow down. We don't want to attract any attention. When you get off, make a sharp right, and drive behind that Mobil gas station. Emma, hug me tighter. Yeah, that's better."

"If I see them, I'm going to get back on the highway. Maybe we can see their license plate. You'd be able to find out who it belongs to, won't you?"

He nodded. She looked calm and steady, handling the Jeep well enough. Emma was hanging onto him like a leech. It felt good, those skinny little arms of hers choking his neck. The kid had grit.

Molly was off the highway, veering right, then turning sharply right toward the back of the Mobil station, all in the space of about twenty seconds. "Well done," he said. "Now, kiddo," he said to Emma, "I want you to look with me back up to the highway. We want to see if those two men are following us."

"I should have waited to see what car they were driving," Molly said. She hit the steering wheel with her fist. "I just had to keep moving. I didn't think it through."

"It's okay. We'll recognize them. Keep looking." A dark green Corolla went by with two women inside. Then a truck with a single guy and a big German shepherd, his head out the window, his tongue hanging long. There was a space of five heartbeats, then a filthy black truck, its bed empty. In the cab were two men.

"That's them," Ramsey said. "Okay, Molly, ease back onto the highway. Keep a minimum of three cars back."

She was already driving out from behind the Mobil station. There was a small white Honda in front of her. She wanted to honk, to run over it, to yell at the older woman driving, but she managed to keep herself calm and steady, but she was whispering, "Move, move, move."

Ramsey just kept his arms loosely around Emma. "You okay, kiddo?"

"I'm scared, Ramsey."

His arms tightened around her. He kissed the top of her head. "I wish I could give you the power not to be afraid of anything, Emma, but I can't. Fear isn't bad, just as long as it doesn't freeze you up. I know you don't like to think about it, but you didn't freeze up that time. You managed to escape and run into the woods and I found you. You were extraordinarily brave. And so you see that if you just keep thinking, if you don't give up, then you can help yourself. You've got a chance." He knew Molly was listening. "You won't forget that, will you, Em?"

"No," she whispered. "I won't forget. There's the truck, Ramsey. Mom's close now."

"Can you see the license number?"

"It's really dirty, but I can see it."

Then he laughed. "You can see it but you can't tell me the letters or numbers. I'm going to teach you how to read tomorrow, okay, kiddo?"

"I know how to read a little. Mama's taught me. She reads to me all the time. She points her finger at the words while she's reading. You think it'll just take one day?"

"With you, maybe just half a day." He said to Molly, "It looks to me like it's a *B,* then an *L,* then mud's all smeared over the next letter. There's a space, then three-eight-eight-something. That last number's too smeared to make out."

"You'll find a cell phone in my bag. Since you're a federal judge, you're bound to know someone who can tell us who owns the truck. Once you find that out, I promise I'll call the cops in Denver and tell them. You don't have to tell anybody anything. Now, I'll hang back until you find out."

A cell phone. She had a cell phone and hadn't told him until they were holding on by their teeth. He wanted to yell at her, but he didn't. He pulled out the slim phone. He started to call Virginia Trolley in San Francisco, then paused. No, she couldn't do anything. He needed someone objective, someone with an inside track who wouldn't butt in, but would give him all the help he could. He dialed the main number to the FBI in Washington, D.C., and asked for Dillon Savich in the Criminal Apprehension Unit.

In two minutes he was talking to Savich. "Why don't you ever use my e-mail, Ramsey? You know I hate phones. I think when I was a kid a phone cord must have wrapped around my neck and nearly choked me to death."

"Sorry, I don't have my laptop with me. Long story. I need help, Savich."

"Talk to me."

No hesitation, no questions. Ramsey said, "I need to know who belongs to this license plate." He gave Savich the information. "I'm on a cell phone." He gave him the phone number. "Yeah, I'll keep it on. I owe you one, Savich."

A grunt, nothing more. Ramsey smiled into the cell phone. He hung up but left the phone button on.

"Who did you call? The police in San Francisco?"

"No. I called a friend of mine in Washington, D.C."

"A good friend, if he didn't ask you any questions."

"Yes, a good friend. We met about four years ago at a law-enforcement conference in Chicago. At that time I was with the U.S. Attorney's office. Savich is into karate, big time, does an exhibition now and again. He got married about six months ago to another agent named Sherlock. Keep further back, Molly."

"Oh no."

The truck was slowing. The man in the passenger seat was looking back. "They've gone far enough to know we're not there ahead of them. Slow down more, Molly. Yeah, let that Chevy get ahead of you. Good."

He pressed Emma against him. "I don't want them catching sight of you, kiddo. Keep down."

"They're pulling out, Ramsey," Molly said.

He wanted to follow. So did Molly, probably. But they couldn't, not with Emma such an open target.

"It won't matter," Ramsey said. "Once we know who owns the truck, we'll have what we need. We don't have to do everything."

"I don't know about that," she said, her voice

all rough and low. Then she smiled at Emma and said, "Sure thing," and slowed down even more.

"They're hanging on the side, just the way we did." He weighed the options. "Drive like a bat out of hell, Molly. In a couple of exits, we're out of here."

She didn't hesitate for an instant. She floored the gas pedal. The Jeep hit ninety miles an hour quickly. They sped by two exits, Molly weaving in and out like a pro, then she slowed and swung off at the third exit onto a high arcing road that flattened finally, headed due south.

"Good going. Just keep driving, then pull over about a mile toward—what's the name of the town in this direction?"

"Paulson, according to the sign we just passed."

"Yeah, it's about three miles to Paulson. Let's go nearly to the town, then take a side road. We'll just sit there for a while. I'll bet everyone's thirsty. We'll have to buy a bottle of water."

"I have to go to the bathroom," Emma said.

"I do, too," Ramsey said, hugging her. "Hold it just three more minutes, Em."

The cell phone trilled a soft high whine.

"Savich?"

"Yes. Since you didn't have a clean set, we have three possibilities."

"Okay. I've got a pen and paper." Molly watched him pull a pad from the glove compartment and write down names and addresses. She heard him say, "Thanks, Savich. I owe you big time." There was a long pause, then, "I'll tell you everything when I can, but not just yet. Say hello to Sherlock for me."

He shut down the phone.

"It appears that we've lost those guys from the restaurant. I still think we should call the cops, Molly."

"No, not yet. Please, not yet."

He sighed deeply. The last thing he wanted was for her to try to take Emma and go off on her own. He had a strong feeling she'd do just that if he didn't play by her rules. It wasn't just that she didn't trust the police. It was something more, something she hadn't told him. "Well, hell," he said, "let's go to Aspen and stay at the Jerome. I'll take you guys to the Cantina for a good Mexican meal."

Molly pulled off the road a minute later. She took Emma to the cover of some bushes. Molly met his eyes over a tangle of blackberries. He had eyes nearly as black as his hair, thick hair a bit on the long side since he'd been away from civilization for three weeks. He had a strong face, high cheekbones, an olive complexion. She wondered if he didn't have some Italian blood lurking somewhere. He also had the beginnings of a five-o'-clock shadow. Actually, now that she was really looking at him for the first time, she realized he was handsome, not drop-dead handsome like a film star, but handsome in a way that was calm and strong, a handsome that you could trust. She owed him the rest of the truth, but not just yet.

She thought, as she helped Emma with her clothes, that it felt rather strange not to be alone anymore. She'd known him for less than one day. It seemed longer, but the fact was that she didn't really know him at all. She knew his reputation, but not the man. He'd saved Emma. That was really the beginning and the end of it. He'd have her gratitude forever.

She smiled at him.

Ramsey did a double take. He smiled back at her automatically. He'd been wishing that he'd gotten a look at the other man at the restaurant. Were they dealing with two new men entirely? Probably so. There'd been no sign that either of them had been wounded. If they were new on the scene, then there might be a lot more going on here. What was Molly keeping from him?

He handed Molly the cell phone when she and Emma got back to the Jeep. "It's time to call the Denver police. It's time to tell them that Emma's safe. Whatever else you don't want to tell them, then keep it to yourself. But at least do that much."

She pulled a small notebook from her large shoulder bag. She looked up a number, then dialed it in. He handed her the paper with the three names and addresses on it. He moved to the driver's side, watching Emma crowd close to her.

She gave no greeting, just, "I've got my daughter back, Detective Mecklin."

"Is that you, Mrs. Santera? What did you say? Are you all right? Are you injured?"

"No I'm not hurt. I said that I've got my daughter back, Detective." She could practically see those wide blue eyes of his narrowing as he stared at the phone, wondering if she'd lost it or not. She really didn't care. She rather hoped she'd never have to deal with Mecklin again, but here she was on the phone to the jerk. She'd thought he believed it was her fault that Emma was taken. She had hated him for helping to pile that guilt on her. She still did. She'd felt enough guilt on her own.

There was a very long silence, then, "I don't understand how that can be possible."

She laughed, the tension beginning to lighten. She was beginning to enjoy herself. The sexist jerk. "It is, believe me. Would you like me to tell you what's happened?"

"But we just got a ransom note last night. The kidnappers want $500,000."

"Don't let anyone pay it. I've got my daughter right here, Detective. Emma, say hello to the detective."

"Hello, Detective Mecklin. I'm with my mom and Ramsey. He saved me and then my mommy found us. We're okay."

"Ramsey? Who the hell's this Ramsey?"

Molly pulled the phone back up. "That's not important for the moment, Detective Mecklin. Listen to me. I've got three names and addresses that go with these license plate letters and numbers. You need to see which of these fits with Emma's kidnappers. One of them does, count on it."

"I don't understand this, Mrs. Santera. You need to come back to Denver and talk to us. If you really have Emma, you need to bring her in to see us. We've got doctors here for her, a shrink trauma team, everything she'll need. Was that really Emma? Are you all right, Mrs. Santera? Where are you?"

"Will you do anything with the information if I give it to you, Detective Mecklin, or am I wasting my time?"

There was another long pause with very controlled breathing. "Give me the info," he said.

She read out the names and addresses very slowly, occasionally repeating. "I don't recognize any of these names myself, but one of them has to be involved with the kidnappers. Now maybe you've got a chance to catch them. Surely there's a drop site indicated on the note. Well, now you don't have to worry about Emma. You can forget the trauma team. Do your job, Detective. Nail the bad guys. Oh yeah, the guy who kidnapped Emma took her to a cabin not far from Dillinger. I'm sure he's not there anymore but you may find out something."

"Are you in Dillinger, Mrs. Santera?"

"No, Detective, I'm not, so please don't bother siccing any local cops on me."

"This sure puts a mighty different spin on things, Mrs. Santera."

"Sure does," she agreed. "You're sure you've got everything?"

"Yeah, I've got it. But you've got to tell me what's going on. The FBI agents just walked in. They want to talk to you. They don't think—"

She spoke over him, slowly and clearly. "The license is on a dirty black pickup truck. It's fairly new. A Chevy. You've got that?"

"Yes, yes. Hold on. Don't hang up, Mrs. Santera. You need us. Here's Agent Anchor."

"I don't think so, Detective. Give them the information. They'll drool, if they bother to believe it."

"We would have gotten this information in a very short time. Now, I believe you, Mrs. Santera, but... well, you see, this is very irregular." It was Agent Anchor, a man with a great deal of experience with kidnappings. He was also a dictator who believed everyone except himself had a brain the size of a pea. He'd ordered the Denver cops around as if they were his personal chattel.

"No buts, Agent Anchor. Catch the men who took my daughter."

"You have no idea if any of these license plates has anything to do with the kidnappers, do you? Look, I don't understand any of this. Tell me where you are. Do you understand what I'm saying to you, Mrs. Santera? You may be in danger. Tell me where you found Emma. You can't just call in and order us around and—"

"Agent Anchor, go catch the kidnappers. Ah, that pickup truck was last seen just west of Rappahoe on Highway Seventy." Molly smiled as she pushed the *Off* button. "I hated to tell him that because he's not stupid and he'll know that's where we are, too. But I had to, otherwise, how could they catch them? I hope they can locate that cabin quickly, maybe find something helpful."

"No, you're right. You had to tell them. By the time they get themselves together, we'll be tucked safely away in Aspen. They really shouldn't care all that much about us, and where we are, but who knows? At least our perps don't know we got them tagged. They shouldn't be hiding out. Were the Fed agents a big pain?"

"Yes. If I hadn't been so terrified about Emma, I would have felt sorry for the local cops. The Feds treated them like gofers. Detective Mecklin isn't really all that much of a jerk, but he's also not what you'd call very flexible. He's got this big handlebar mustache, dyed really black, you know? It droops around his mouth, makes him look something like a basset hound. He's also very fat. I hope he doesn't have a heart attack." Then she just shook her head. "He didn't want to believe that I had Emma. He even asked me if that was really Emma who'd spoken to him. As for Agent Anchor, he has a God complex."

A lot of the Federal people did, but they were getting better, or at least some of them were, like Dillon Savich. He'd like to meet this Agent Anchor when this was over. He'd like to pin Agent Anchor's ears back. "You did well,

Molly. At least we had to do that much. Let's go to Aspen. Let's forget both of them for now. We'll call Detective Mecklin back tomorrow and see what he's got."

"A ransom note arrived last night. The kidnappers wanted a half a million."

"Their bluff," he said. "It's a good try." He looked quickly at Emma, who looked to be nearly asleep, but he wasn't fooled for an instant. "Just a bluff," he said again. "But it gives the cops a real chance at them now. So there are at least four other guys besides the kidnapper. I wonder how many people are involved in this? And why? It isn't just a kidnapping, Molly."

"I don't like it," Emma said, snuggling close to her mother. "I don't like it at all."

Their eyes met. "Neither do we, Emma. Neither do we," Molly said.

Ramsey pulled back onto the highway. There was no sign of the black pickup, thank the good Lord.

9

After Molly showed him a weighty wad of one-hundred-dollar bills and assured him she had lots more in her bra, Ramsey got them a junior suite at the Jerome, providing them a false name and paying cash. They were shown to a huge single room filled with Victorian furniture, long red or gold fringe on the lamps, and wall-to-wall carpeting woven with big cabbage roses and copious vines. There was violent red wallpaper in the bathroom, which had been updated to a rich pink marble. The old with the new—it was a fascinating combination. There was a sitting area at one end of the big room, with the bed, dresser, and a couple of more chairs at the other. There were tall windows with rich velvet draperies. "I always wanted to stay here," Ramsey said, standing back. "I saw the place way back when I was a kid here on a ski break. It's something, isn't it?"

"Yes," Molly said. "They didn't have two beds? Just this king?"

"We're married, remember? Don't look at it too long, it'll make you bilious. Also, don't worry about it. They're bringing up a cot for me." The spread was a bright blue velvet with red tassels that screamed Victorian Wild West.

Emma said, "What's 'bilious'?"

"Bad liver stuff."

He saw her repeat the word a couple of more times beneath her breath. He smiled as he watched Molly go down on her knees and hug Emma until, suddenly, she squealed. Molly let her loose and the both of them began to laugh. "It's a game we play," Molly said. "If Emma can let me hug her for a whole minute without making a single sound, then she gets an ice cream. Actually, she usually wins. Are you feeling sorry for me, kiddo?"

"I just wanted to see you smile really big, Mama."

"Then you won the smile out of me."

Molly had a single duffel bag, Emma had her stuffed pillow- case, and Ramsey had two suitcases. He'd locked his mom's old Olivetti typewriter and all the pages he'd managed to write during his stay before Emma, and some books and novels in the Jeep. The hotel brought up a cot for him, too short, but he just shook his head at her when she would have protested.

Actually, Ramsey didn't care if he slept on the floor. His leg hurt like hell, he had a headache, and he felt as if he'd hit a brick wall. Molly looked as if she had her nose pressed against that same brick wall. She was standing in the middle of the room, running her hand through her rioting red hair.

He smiled. "You want me to give Emma a bath? No, I take that back. She can bathe herself."

"She's really not very good at it, but she does try." Molly grabbed Emma up and sniffed behind her ear. "Smells sweet. You did a good job. You want me to bathe you this time, Em? Just for a change?"

Emma nodded happily.

Molly turned to Ramsey, who looked ready to fall over. "You just lie down. I'll bring you some aspirin. Do you put an ice pack on the leg?"

"I hadn't thought of that. Why not?"

"Good. Lie down, Ramsey. I'll be right back."

After she'd watched him wash down three

aspirin and she'd laid the ice wrapped in a towel over his bandaged leg, she said, "Do you mind if we don't go to the Cantina?"

"I'll see if they deliver."

They did, for a fifty-buck service charge. It was Aspen, he thought, as he ate a ten-dollar taco.

• **Exhaustion** hit big time after they'd consumed a good half dozen beef tacos, and enough chips and salsa for a football team. Emma had some guacamole smeared on her chin when it was all over and she'd looked wonderful. She was asleep ten minutes later, next to her mother, just after they'd gotten her to brush her teeth.

She beat them to sleep by five minutes.

Molly awoke at midnight at the final stroke from a big grandfather clock in the corner out in the corridor. There was a quarter moon sending a white shaft of light through the open window. It wasn't too cold, just cold enough to make you pull the covers to your chin and let the fresh air hit your face.

It was the first time she'd slept over three hours in more than two weeks. Sixteen days, she thought, suddenly sitting up just to look over to see Emma curled up into a ball, the pillow hugged to her chest, her beautiful hair, free of its braid, tangled about her head. She was safe.

She felt tears sting her eyes, felt them ooze out and slowly trickle over her cheeks. They'd been so very lucky. As it turned out, she hadn't been the important one in the equation, not that she'd ever really believed she actually would be.

Ramsey Hunt. He'd saved her daughter. He would have continued to protect her until he'd gotten her back safely.

The tears came more freely. She sobbed. Oh no, that was humiliating. She stuffed her fist into her mouth.

"Molly? It's okay."

How had he heard her? Emma was still sound asleep. He said quietly, "Cry, it's good for you. I'll bet this is the first time you've had the luxury to just let go. Think you can?"

She kept crying and he kept talking, saying nothing really, just nonsense. Then, "Mama, what's wrong?"

Emma sounded terrified.

Ramsey said quickly, "It's all right, Emma. Roll over and hug your mama. She's just crying because she's so relieved you're safe. She's been on the edge for a really long time. She's been really scared for you."

Molly was hiccuping, crying, and now laughing. Emma had wrapped her arms around her.

"I feel better now. Thanks, Em." She kissed her daughter's neck, and felt as happy as she'd ever felt in her life. In that instant, she remembered another moment, a long time ago, when she'd believed there was no way she could have been happier. It had been a lie.

The three of them went back to sleep, Ramsey's feet hanging off the end of the cot. It was

114

Ramsey who woke near three o'clock in the morning.

Maybe he'd heard something. His brain was still turned inward to a pleasant dream. It was about Susan. She was wearing her uniform and smiling. She saluted him, then poked him in the belly. Once he was fully awake, though, bittersweet memories flooded through him. Then suddenly, it all just faded back into time. He wanted no more dreams about Susan.

He heard it again. Could they be that good?

Very slowly, he stood up. He saw that both Emma and Molly were still asleep. He heard only Molly's deep, even breathing. He was glad for that. He didn't want them frightened.

He stood up, felt his stiff leg lock on him, and grabbed one of the high chair backs. Not unexpected. He held very still and listened.

It was a shuffling sound. It was coming from the corridor, just outside their room door. He picked up his pistol from the small circular table beside the cot. He forced his leg to move, one step at a time, quietly, toward the door, pausing every few steps to listen.

He heard voices. No, it wasn't possible that it could be trouble. There was just no way they could have found out where they were. The hotel registration hadn't demanded an ID. There was no way anyone could know they were here. But they had seen the Jeep. They could have easily traced the license plate, or even spotted it coming into town. He cursed. He was an idiot. Tomorrow, he'd have to turn it in, maybe buy a used car, another Jeep, or any four-wheel-drive vehicle. He heard the voices again, too low for him to make out what they were saying.

He held his Smith & Wesson ready.

It was a man's voice, low and urgent, clear now. "Listen, Doris, you want to sneak back in there, you do it. But your old man could be awake even as we speak. I don't want him to blow my head off. No, don't go in there. If you do, just wait until I get out of here."

He leaned his head against the door, relief pouring through him. It was a wife screwing around on her husband.

It wasn't anybody after Emma.

He heard a woman's voice, with just a touch of hysteria in it. It would be better if she didn't try to sneak back in, he thought, but thank goodness, it wasn't any of his business. He silently checked the lock and the chain.

He laid the Smith & Wesson back on the circular table. When he turned to the cot, he saw Molly sitting up, staring toward him.

He whispered, "It's nothing, just a wife cheating on her husband."

Emma said in a sleepy voice, "It couldn't be him, could it, Ramsey? He didn't see really good. He didn't wear his glasses all of the time. That's how I got away. I made my pillow look like me when he was out smoking a cigarette on the front steps. When he came back, he looked for me, and thought he saw me. I crawled out the front door when he was drinking a glass of whiskey. He really liked whiskey.

He kept saying he didn't like it, that it rotted his soul, but he drank it, lots of it."

"Oh God," Molly said. "Do you know his name, Em?"

But Emma folded, just shut down again, her breathing even and slow. She was sound asleep.

They looked at each other. Molly said, "What am I going to do?"

"I told you, Molly. I'm in for the long haul. Now the question is, what are *we* going to do? Tell you what. We're both still too tired to think straight. I've got some ideas. We'll discuss it tomorrow."

She was shaking her head back and forth, her red hair moving in concert. "I can't go back to Denver. I'm never going back to Denver. I don't understand what's going on here. How many people are involved in this? Who are they? How, why, could Emma's kidnapping be a conspiracy?"

"Conspiracy," he repeated slowly. "Why do you call it a conspiracy?"

She shrugged, one corner of her sleep shirt falling off her shoulder.

"I guess kidnapping could end up being a conspiracy if the parents were in on it, or if it was done for another purpose. But you didn't mean that. Did you?"

"I just said the word. It seemed it might be possible. We already know about up to five different men."

"An elaborate scheme then. But a conspiracy? That smacks of something darker, something beneath the surface. It just might mean it would involve people around you."

She was silent. He watched her pull up the shoulder of her sleep shirt. It said on the front: *BIGFOOT WAS HERE.* Her hair was corkscrewed and wild around her pale face. She looked inutterably weary. And also very pretty, he thought, somewhat amazed that he'd noticed and here it was in the middle of the night. Her skin was very white, unlike his, with his olive skin tone. He wanted to put his hand on her, to compare the color difference between them. He was losing it. "Let's get some sleep. We're out of here tomorrow."

• **He** returned to the Jerome at noon. Molly and Emma were playing Old Maid seated cross-legged opposite each other, the card pile in the middle.

"No, don't get up. We're the proud owners of a 1989 Toyota 4Runner with lots of miles on it. It's a two-door model, on the beat-up side, but who cares? It's got four-wheel drive, nearly all the comforts of the Jeep."

He'd gotten the maximum cash allowed from AMEX and paid the car dealer in cash. He added, "Even if they've tracked down the Jeep, it'll take them a good long time to find it in that long-term parking lot over by the lift." But he knew they weren't safe, not by a long shot.

He said quickly, "It's time we checked out

of here. Fifteen minutes okay with everybody? We shop and then we're heading west."

They'd spoken about it briefly that morning when they'd awakened. "It's just our next
destination," Ramsey had said, "but it gets us
closer to my home and my turf."

Molly had said quietly, afraid that Emma
would awaken, "I know we can't stay here.
Where west do you want to go?"

"Truckee. I know the area very well. Let's
just get ourselves lost for the time being in the
Sierras. I had a friend from college who lived
on Lake Tahoe."

Molly didn't say anything more until she got
him in the bathroom with the door shut,
Emma in the bedroom packing her pillowcase.

He said, "Anyone with a brain could trace
the money withdrawal from AMEX that I
used to pay for the Toyota, and I think we've
got professionals here. So our best bet is to get
ourselves lost for the time being. The Sierras
are beautiful and out of the way. Any problem with that?"

"I've never been to Lake Tahoe," she said,
fiddling with a towel that was wadded up.
She was methodically folding it, arranging
it back on the rack.

"It's a little town, quaint, all rigged out
for the skiers in the winter and the hikers in
the summer. Emma'll like it. It'll be safe."

She looked up at him. "How's your leg?"

"Better this morning. You and Emma were
both standing over me when I took up the tape

and gauze. The skin's staying together, a good sign. The flesh is pink. Very little swelling. It just aches."

"You wouldn't lie to me?"

"Yes, but not about this."

"All right. Let's go." She turned away, her hand on the bathroom doorknob, and said over her shoulder, "You don't have to do this, you really don't. I have money. Not just the cash I showed you. I have lots of money, family money and money from my divorce from Louey. I could get Emma to safety."

"Don't, Molly. I couldn't leave Emma in danger."

She sighed as she twisted a corkscrew curl around her index finger. "I know."

She opened the bathroom door and walked out, calling, "Em, love, are you ready? Do you know what? I'm going to buy you a duffel bag, just like mine."

"Can it be a Mingus Raiders duffel? Yours looks like a soldier's."

"Okay, Mingus Raiders it is." She said over her shoulder to Ramsey, "The Mingus cartoon good guys also include Mingus cartoon good girls. They're hot stuff."

• **They** drove all that day and night, spelling each other, and reached Truckee the next evening at just after six o'clock. They spent that night at a Best Western Motel.

The next morning Ramsey went to a local realtor's office and looked over the rental houses available. They didn't want a condo, too many people around, they told the woman. They were a family on vacation. They'd saved their money for this and didn't want to use credit cards.

If the woman didn't believe this, she didn't argue, just showed them properties. Emma fell in love with the third one, a small two-bedroom house that sat off by itself, backed against a forest and fronting a small creek. Tree-covered mountains rose all around it. Lake Tahoe was only about four miles distant. It was safe. Everyone was pleased.

They paid five hundred for the week, including the security deposit. They stocked up for a week at Food Giant.

When they returned to Nathan's Creek, it was well into the afternoon. Emma was asleep in Molly's arms. Ramsey took her and carried her up to the larger of the two bedrooms.

When he met Molly downstairs in the kitchen, she handed him a glass of iced mineral water.

"Come in the living room," he said. "It's time."

"All right," she said. "You're right. It is time. We've got to do some talking and some planning."

He waited until she sat down in a big recliner that was well worn, a real guy's chair, then said, "Now, no more stalling. Who are you, Molly? What are you still keeping from me?"

"I know it's impossible that Emma's kidnapping has anything to do with what you don't know."

"Molly, I'm going to throw this water glass at you."

"I was Margaret Lord before I married."

He just stared at her, then breathed out hard. His leg started hurting.

"Shit," he said. "Your daddy is Mason Lord?"

• **Joe** Elders loved those few precious minutes just before the sun arched up over the low-lying barren hills just a mile or so from his farm. He stood there, breathing in the fifty-degree air, filling his lungs, letting the silence and soft air fill him.

The sun struck his eyes with brilliant light and he smiled into it, closing them. He heard Millie moo. She was soon joined by half a dozen of her cousins. It was time to begin his day, and that meant milking his girls. He whistled as he walked to the cow barn, brand new, just completed a month before, with all the new technology they told him would at least put him in the same ballpark as the big dairy outfits. And he'd had the money to pay for it all. He'd been smart, really smart. They hadn't taken advantage of him, no they hadn't. After his deal, he hadn't had to borrow anything. He paused, sniffing the air.

He could swear it was the sweet clinging scent of marijuana. He kicked one of the goat's favorite old chewing gloves out of his path. He cursed. It was pot he smelled. Nancy was smoking and carrying on again, and after she promised him and her mother that she would straighten up. Pot, of all things. She was six-teen years old, popular at school. He hoped she wasn't that popular. No, she was too young to really have the hots for any of the boys he'd seen around. But pot, hell and damna-tion.

He opened the barn door. He was greeted with a chorus of moos, most of them wel-coming, a couple pissed, he could tell. They didn't like all the new equipment that relieved them of their milk.

Shirley was the one who hated the machines the most. Since she was one of his old girls, he'd decided just the week before to milk her himself. She enjoyed that, turning her head to look at him while he pulled on her teats.

He got all the other cows set up. It still took him a while. Well, he'd get better and faster at it soon. Then he took his old stool down to where Shirley was standing, still and fat with milk, watching him come closer.

"Good morning, old girl," he called out, giv-ing her a wink like the one he'd given her every dawn for the past seven years.

He began to whistle as he set the stool down beside her. "Now, let's make you a couple of pounds lighter."

He heard a soft whooshing sound. It was close, real close. He wrenched around on the stool. There was a man standing over him. He was black, his eyes hard and wide, his head bald. Joe never even had a chance to ask the man who he was.

He felt a huge hand on his shoulder, and saw

a big hammer part the air. He felt the blow throughout his body, but it wasn't exactly painful, just a numbing jarring that made his eyes blink once in surprise. The large hand released his shoulder.

Joe Elders fell beside Shirley's stool, his eyes staring up at her milk-swelled teats.

10

I just heard Emma moving around upstairs. We've only got a few minutes before she comes down. We'll get back to your daddy a bit later. Now our immediate problems: We've got to assume they're professionals. And that means we've also got to assume they have a backup organization to be on us in a flash if we use credit cards. If we're careful, your three thousand and my two thousand should last us just fine until this mess is cleaned up."

Molly figured she'd been frugal for a total of thirteen months in her life. She'd gone from one wealthy home to taking care of herself, and she'd done it, not that it had lasted long. Then she'd gone to another one. From a rich father to a rich husband. But for the past two years, she'd been on her own again. She loved it. She grinned. Actually, it was the first time she'd smiled in a very long time. "I'm going to go scrub a toilet."

"Mama, you're joking."

Emma had arrived, full of energy. Molly hauled her up in a big hug, kissed her small ear, and said, "No, sweetie, this time I'm not. Well, maybe. I'm thinking that if I can take Ramsey in poker, then he can scrub the john. What do you think?"

Emma looked very serious, her head cocked to one side. "I think you could beat him in Old Maid. I beat you last time we played poker."

"Thanks for the support, kiddo. All right, I'll think about it. Maybe I can play him to a draw."

"That's chess, Mama."

"Yes, but maybe I can figure out how to apply it to poker. Hey, you want some hot dogs for supper?"

"Oh yes. Ramsey makes the best. We stuck them on coat hangers and held them over the fire in the fireplace."

Ramsey was sitting in that big recliner, his hands folded over his stomach, a pillow under his leg. "You'll have to go a long way to beat my hot dogs, Molly."

"I know how to make the *secret relish*, handed down from my mother's family in Italy. The relish will make her jump off your bandwagon quick enough."

"We'll see about that. I've got secret other things, like good cheap yellow mustard." He said to Emma, "How come you know about draws and chess?"

"My boyfriend taught me."

"You've got a boyfriend, Emma?"

"His name's Jake. He's my nerd boyfriend."

Ramsey rolled his eyes. "You also got a jock boyfriend?"

"Oh no, Ramsey, they're gross."

"Hey now, I was once a jock and I wasn't gross. Well, maybe I was for a while, when I was real young."

"Young as me?"

He stared down into that small intent upturned face. "No, Em, I was never as young as you."

She giggled, actually giggled. It warmed him to his toes. Molly looked up, smiling. Emma said, "I'm just glad you're not as young as me right now." She lightly touched her palm to the wound in his thigh. "It's not warm anymore."

"Nope, all of me is at room temperature again."

She patted him, then skipped off to the small kitchen to help her mother.

It was an easy evening, with no talk at all about the sword of Damocles that was hanging over their heads, no talk just yet about Molly's criminal father. They played word games, then Ramsey gave Emma a reading lesson using the sets of letters and numbers he'd bought at the bookstore in Dillinger.

The kid was smart and fast. She was writing his name in full sentences, along with her name and her mother's by nine o'clock. "You put the best teacher in the world with the smartest kid in the world, and just look what you've got." He leaned down to stare at the last word Emma had printed: *john.*

Both of them tucked her up in the small single twin bed.

"You want a night-light on, Em?"

"No, Mama. Are you going to sleep with me again?"

"Yes," Molly said easily. "If Ramsey wakes up and gets lonesome, he can talk to us through the wall."

Emma was smiling even as her eyes closed. They stood looking down at her, this child who had changed both their lives.

"She wrote my name," Ramsey said. "It was legible. She wrote it in a whole sentence. Amazing."

"She's got her mother's brains." Molly grinned up at him. "*My Ramsey is smart.* Yep, that has a real ring to it. Can you believe she spelled *john?*"

"And she did it well. It made her laugh, Molly. Where'd she get the hair?"

"Her father." Her voice was clipped. She didn't say anything else. Why hadn't he come back here after Emma had been kidnapped? He'd teased himself with that question at least half a dozen times now. He simply couldn't imagine any father not being frantic about his child. That the parents were divorced made no difference. He said, "Let's go downstairs. Now that Emma's in bed, I want you to tell me everything about Daddy."

"I should call Detective Mecklin and Agent Anchor first. I forgot."

"No, you didn't, but it doesn't matter.

Let's do it. Who knows, maybe they've got something."

"Don't bet your gym socks on it."

She asked for Detective Mecklin and got put on hold. She stared down at the phone, then suddenly banged down the receiver. "They were trying to trace the call," she said. "I know it. The bastards."

"You're probably right. Let's call in the morning. They didn't have enough time. Don't worry."

"I guess you'd know all about that."

"Enough. It's not as if we really have to hide from the cops, Molly."

"I don't want to let them near Emma. Don't you see? They might take her away and give her over to a battery of doctors, strangers, all of them. She's doing so well. I can't take that risk. You didn't want to do it either. Just leave it alone."

"All right. Tell you what. Let me call Dillon Savich, my friend in Washington, D.C. See if he knows what's going on."

"Who is this friend, exactly?"

"He's a computer expert who happens to be an FBI agent. Trust me on this, he's not like Agent Anchor. Actually, he and his partner— who's now his wife, Sherlock—were the ones who broke The Toaster case in Chicago. Do you remember that?"

"That was the young guy who'd killed those families?"

"Yeah. Russell Bent."

"They won't ever let him out, will they?"

"Trust the system on this one, Molly. Russell will be in a psychiatric hospital until he dies."

"Yeah, but I also remember the killer in Boston who escaped when the judge ordered that he be let out of restraints while he was being evaluated by the psychiatrists. The String Killer, wasn't that the moniker the press gave him?"

"Yes, that's what happened."

She gave him a long look. "Some system."

"You know, Molly, our legal system works well most of the time. Since people run it, sure there are screwups now and again. You need to be a bit more objective."

Molly sighed, then rose and walked to the French windows that looked out over a small sloping lawn to Nathan's Creek, full and rushing from melting mountain snow. The half-moon made the snow glisten. "This is a beautiful place. Aren't you going to call Dillon Savich?"

"Yep. You got me sidetracked. I want to tell him what's going on. I want to tell him who you are. He won't do anything unless I ask him to. All right?"

Molly nodded.

He used the house phone and punched the speaker button. The phone was picked up on the third ring in Washington, D.C. Ramsey identified himself.

A very alert Savich said, "You know it's one

A.M. here? Never mind. Where are you? You've got the speaker on. Are you finally ready to tell me what's going on?"

"You know about that kidnapping case in Denver? Emma Santera?"

"Yes. Wait, don't tell me. You're somehow involved in that?"

Ramsey gave him an unedited version of what had happened until they'd arrived in California. "We're all right, hopefully, safely hidden. Mrs. Santera doesn't want anyone to know exactly where we are."

"Including the FBI? Including the cops? This is all very strange, Ramsey."

"Yeah, I know. Bear with me. Can you tell me what's happening there? Has an Agent Anchor said anything that's filtered back?"

Savich laughed. "Has Bud said anything? He's been yelling his head off, claiming he's going to bring in Mrs. Santera for hampering his investigation. It's going to be hard to keep my mouth shut, Ramsey, but I will until you give me the 'go' signal. Can you begin to imagine what folks here would say if they knew you were a part of this and you were getting inside information from me?"

"What about the owner of the truck? We gave the Denver PD and Agent Anchor the three names and license numbers you gave me."

"The truck was reported stolen last month from a dairy farmer in Loveland, Colorado. The wife reported it. Then the husband said it hadn't been stolen, he'd sold it, and hadn't told his wife. Who knows? Did he sell it to the kidnappers? That plays for me."

"Yeah, it does for me too." Ramsey sighed.

"You might consider coming in now. Any more attempts to get the kid?"

"Not since we've come to our new location."

"Come in, Ramsey. It sounds dicey. I agree that this isn't just a simple kidnapping. You got any ideas?"

"Maybe. Look, Savich, let me keep us hidden a while longer. I'll check in on Friday unless something happens sooner. Listen, thanks. I owe you."

"You can bet on it."

"Is that Sherlock I hear? Give her a kiss for me."

"Not on your life. You're too much like the kind of man she likes, all hard and tough. Given your macho demonstration a while back in your courtroom, I'd be hard-pressed to keep her away from you, especially if she's having a bad day and not thinking clearly. No, all kisses are from me. Take care of yourself, Ramsey, and call if there's anything I can do."

"Thanks, Savich." Ramsey slowly hung up the phone. "You heard everything?"

She nodded.

"Now, no more procrastinating. It's time. On to Daddy."

She started shaking her head.

"Listen, Molly, your father is Mason Lord. It's time we thought about him. I don't think it's possible he could be involved directly in any of this, but it's very possible that from what

131

we've seen, just maybe some of your father's enemies had Emma kidnapped to use as leverage against your father."

She didn't turn, just ran her fingers over the thick fabric of the light tan drapes. "I think he would have warned me if someone he was dealing with might consider such a thing."

"Yes, he probably would have, if he'd had warning. Do you agree that perhaps some of his enemies are involved up to their gum lines to get leverage on him, to milk him? You wondered about all the guys who seemed to be involved in this, so far. Well, that could be our answer."

She still didn't turn around. Slowly, she pulled the drapes shut over the French windows and just stood there, head down, saying nothing.

He noticed that she was barefoot. Her toes were painted a pale pink and were chipping. "When did you last speak to your father?"

"Last week."

"And you told him what was going on?"

She nodded.

"Tell me something, Molly. When was the last time you saw your father?"

"That's none of your business. It has nothing to do with this. Stop pushing me on this."

"I just want us to stay alive. You're making that difficult by holding out on me. When, Molly? I deserve to know." He rubbed his leg.

"All right, but it doesn't make any difference. The last time I saw him was three years ago."

He slammed the recliner forward and stood, staring at her. "Three years ago? What's been going on?"

She turned then to face him, but she didn't move from her stand by the windows. "The last time I saw him was when Emma had just turned three years old. He flew to Denver for her birthday. But that wasn't the real reason he came. He was angry at my husband. He came to Denver to see him."

"And did he see your husband?"

"Yes, he saw him. Louey ended up with two broken ribs, a fractured kidney, and bruises everywhere except on his face, that lasted until the next Christmas."

"What had Louey done?"

"I don't want to talk about it. It has nothing to do with this."

"You have no clue what does or what doesn't have to do with anything at all."

"Listen, as I told you, Louey is my ex-husband. We've been divorced for two years. I didn't lie to Emma about her father being worried about her. Louey did call once when he heard that she was missing, which was a big surprise to me. He called me before I even considered contacting him. As Emma already told you, he hasn't bothered to see her since he left.

"It was right after one of his concerts in Berlin. I remember clearly that he asked about

Emma, said he'd heard from somebody in Denver that she'd been snatched, and wondered if I had her back yet. When I said no, he acted all sorry and depressed for about a minute. Then he sort of laughed and said that my daddy would pay the moon to get her back, and not to worry. He told me how the tour was going. He said this *fräulein* reporter—yeah, that's what he called her—from the *Berliner Zeitung* compared him to Bruce Springsteen. He told me the Europeans had better taste than the Americans—in other words they like him better—said he just might spend most of the year in Europe. He talked about his conquests in Europe, in great detail. I don't think you need to know any of that. He never mentioned Emma after the first time.

"The policewoman listening with me just stared at me. She worshiped Louey, prayed he'd call so she could just hear his sexy voice. Or rather, she worshiped him until she heard what that sexy voice said. She patted my shoulder when I hung up.

"I started crying and she kept patting. She thought I was sorry about Louey leaving me, sorry that he was bragging about all these women."

"I remember now," he said after a moment. "There was press about the divorce, but never any details, no hints of infidelity or drugs or anything at all. Just a quiet announcement of irreconcilable differences, something like that. It was out of the public eye very quickly."

"My father is powerful. In this instance it was a good thing. No one had much to say about anything. There were a couple of days of speculation in the tabloids, but even they dropped it. I was very grateful to my father." She looked down at her fingernails. There was mustard from the hot dogs on her index finger. She licked it off.

"Molly?"

"Louey, her biological father, didn't ever want her. After we split up, I think he was relieved to be out of the daddy business. A child didn't go with the sexy footloose image he had of himself. Funny thing is, she's probably just as talented musically as he is. Maybe more so."

"How did Louey know Emma had been kidnapped? You said he called you before you called him."

"I wondered later about that. One of his friends in Denver probably called him. Louey undoubtedly thought that if it hit the press, he should act the concerned papa so he wouldn't be seen in a bad light. Who knows?"

"I wonder which friend in Denver bothered to call him."

"He didn't say and I was too upset to ask. But you know, Louey's friends with a lot of folks in the media, from TV to newspapers. It was probably one of his newspaper buddies."

"Is there a special buddy?"

"Yes, his name is James Hicks and he's with the *Denver Post*. Why?"

"No reason. I just like to gather information. Now, are you going to call your papa and tell him Emma's safe?"

"Yes, I should. He's been very worried. I called him right away when Emma was kidnapped. I knew he'd have some of his people on it right away, and he did. A man and two women came by six hours after I'd called. It drove the local cops nuts. Lots of suspicion. I ignored the cops' bitching about outsiders. I told them everything I could, why not? They wanted to help; my father was paying them to find Emma. I don't know what his people actually did. I saw them several more times. We discussed leads, possibilities. If they found out anything, I don't know about it."

"Did you tell them you were taking off to find Emma yourself?"

"No, I didn't. I'll call him right now. At least he won't try to trace the call." She paused a moment, then said, turning to face him, "I wonder if my father suspected Emma's kidnapping had anything to do with him? I bet he has. I know one thing: If he found out who did this, he wouldn't hesitate to sanction a kill."

11

Sanction a kill. She'd said it so easily, so naturally.

How many times had she heard it said when she was a kid?

"All right, I'm going to call. Hey, wait a minute. What if those men were there to rescue Emma and they thought you were the kidnapper? Of course they'd try to get rid of you. Of course they'd follow you. Oh goodness, there's no end to the possibilities. I've got a headache, Ramsey."

"That goes really well with my leg ache. That theory could fly until you showed up. You think they haven't at least seen a photo of you? You think that there's any way they wouldn't know you're the boss's daughter? Call, Molly. I want to hear what he has to say. Use your cell phone. Come over here so I can hear."

She sat down on the arm of the recliner and began dialing. Area code 312. Chicago and outlying residential areas, like Oak Park. Sure, that was where Mason Lord lived, only the best. He saw her hand tighten around the phone.

Why hadn't she seen her father for three years?

The phone rang twice, then a man answered, his voice deep and mellifluous.

"Miles? It's me, Molly."

"Yes, Molly. You've got news about Emma?"

"She's fine, Miles. She's back with me.

Thank you for asking. I want to give Dad the news."

"Just a moment. Goodness, this is a relief. Mr. Lord's been on a real tear."

"You heard that?" she asked Ramsey. Ramsey was three inches from the receiver.

"Yeah, I heard."

There was a good twenty more seconds of silence, then, "Molly? Emma's safe?"

"Hello, Dad. Yes, I've got her with me. I found her. She's fine."

"I don't understand. I haven't heard a word from my people. Do the Denver police know you've got Emma back?"

"Yes, they know. They don't like the fact that I got her back without them."

"Tell me."

She took a deep breath. "You know I went looking when the cops and the FBI didn't get anywhere. I would have thought your people would know. Well, I found her. A guy had saved her and I came upon both of them. She's safe. We're going to stay out of sight for a while."

"There's no reason to, Molly. Come home. You can bet I'll protect the both of you."

"No, not yet. There are a lot more people involved than just a single kidnapper. I don't want to take any chances. I'm going to keep Emma hidden as long as those people are still out there and looking for her." Her knuckles were white she was clutching the phone so tightly. "It's not a simple kidnapping, Dad."

"But they got a ransom note."

"Yes, but that ransom note arrived after I already had Emma back. It was a lie. Do you understand any of this?"

"No, but I'll speak to Buzz about it. We've already discussed the possibility of some enemy of mine being involved. But the important thing is you've got Emma back. I'm tremendously relieved." He sighed. She could picture him running his fingers lightly through his hair, never enough to mess it up. "We've got nothing as of yet. But I don't like the feel of this at all. How many people have you seen?"

"Probably four different men, but we've managed to get away from them. We're safely tucked away now."

"All right. I'll speak to Buzz Carmen immediately. He's still in Denver. How exactly did you find out about these other men?"

"I knew they were following so I pulled off at an exit. When they went by, I got the license. I checked with a friend who found out for me that the truck was reportedly stolen from a farmer in Loveland, Colorado. The wife reported it; then the husband said he'd sold it. It sounds like maybe he did sell it—to the kidnappers. I phoned in the license plate to the Denver PD and the FBI. I'd appreciate your checking as well, Dad, then I'd know it got done right." She gave him the license and the name of the farmer.

"I've got it. I don't suppose you'll tell me who gave you this information?"

"I can't."

He sighed. "Very well. Come home, Molly."

"I'll call tomorrow. Emma's just fine. Don't worry. Those men won't find us."

"About this man who found Emma. Who is he? How can you be sure you can trust him?"

"If we can't trust him, Dad, then it's all over. Believe me, he's the most trustworthy man in the world. Tomorrow, Dad." She pushed the *Off* button and laid the phone on the table.

"At least you don't call him Godfather."

She smiled at him. It was a charming smile, warm and full. She had a wide mouth and very white teeth. His father was a dentist. Ramsey always noticed a person's teeth. His old man would really like what he saw.

Ramsey liked that smile, too. It was almost as if she was ready to stop being afraid. She said, "Mason Lord is very good-looking. He's black Irish: fair skinned, hair like ink, straight and thick, just a dabbling of gray at his temples. His eyes are such a startling blue, women just stare at him. He doesn't appreciate having a grown daughter, much less a grandchild, but he copes. My mother was the one who told me I should call him by his first name, but I couldn't get the hang of it. Neither could he. I remember thinking Mason jar every time I used his first name. When I told him that, he threw up his hands, laughed, and said to forget it. He's been Dad for a very long time, actually since I was eight years old and moved away with my mother."

"I've never thought of Mason Lord as having human qualities, like a sense of humor. You don't look a thing like him."

"No, I'm the picture of my grandmother. She was an actress in the fifties. Never got very far with it because she wasn't beautiful or very photogenic. Boy, but could she act. It turned out not to be enough."

"You're far from plain, Molly."

She just smiled at him, that same gorgeous smile. "You should see my mother. Now she's what you'd call a looker. She's fifty-five now and still a head-turning beauty. Both she and Father were appalled, I think, when I turned out the way I did."

She honestly believed what she was saying. It amazed him. Didn't she look in a mirror once in a while? "Where's your mother? What's her name?"

"Her name is Alicia and she lives near Livorno, Italy. That's where her family is. She and Dad divorced when I was just a kid. I lived with her in Italy nine months out of the year and the other three months with Dad. I came back to the United States to go to college at Vassar. I've only seen her once a year for the past seven or eight years."

"Does she know about Emma's kidnapping?"

"I don't think so, not unless she read about it in an Italian newspaper, and I strongly doubt the story made it there. I saw no reason to worry her."

"Your father hasn't remarried."

"Oh yes he has, nearly three years ago. Her name's Eve and she's two years younger than I."

"You said that Emma's musical. Does she play the piano or something yet?"

"Don't want to know about Eve, huh? I don't blame you. She'd take one gander at you and lick her chops, but not while my dad was looking. One of my mother's old friends called me and filled my ears with tales of Eve Lord. My mother's friend is a Sunday school teacher, so I guess she's trustworthy. Although maybe she wanted Dad for herself. Who knows? Emma plays the piano."

"I'll buy her one of those two-octave portable pianos tomorrow. I'd like to hear her play."

"Thank you, Ramsey."

"Why haven't you seen your father for three years?"

He swore he could see her stiffen from across the room. He said, "Was it because he'd hurt your husband?"

"You're good at your job."

"Yeah, I am, but this hasn't a thing to do with my job. I'm not being nosy, Molly, just trying to figure out what's going on here. Help me."

"That was part of it."

"That's a lie. I can hear it in your voice."

"All right. Louey said he'd take Emma away from me if I ever saw my father again. He called him a son of a bitch, as I remember."

"Why?"

"Louey hated my father because he found out about him."

"Found out what?"

She sighed deeply. "Louey beat me."

He started to jump out of the chair, grabbed his leg, and sank back down. "That scrawny little fucker beat you? As in he hit you?"

"Yes. Don't think I'm some sort of victim here. I told him if he ever touched me again I'd kill him. To be honest, I don't know if he believed me, but I believed me and I'm sure he must have picked up on that."

"If he had a brain he picked up on it really fast."

"This was three years ago. What happened was that one of my friends found out and called my father. Mason came to Denver and personally beat the daylights out of Louey.

"He told Louey that if he ever touched me again, he'd kill him. So Louey knew that he was in deep trouble, but he hated being help-less, so he told me not to see my father again."

"Would you have killed him if he'd hit you again?"

"Probably not, but I would have left in a flash. That first time, he was drunk, he'd gotten a bad review on his newly released CD, *Danger Floats Deep*, and was really angry. That same day I got a notice from a magazine that they wanted to buy some of my photos. He was jeal-ous, which is ridiculous, if you just think about the relative proportion of things. But it didn't matter. Louey took his anger out on me."

"I don't remember hearing a thing about Louey Santera being hurt."

"No, there was no coverage on it. My dad had a doctor come over and check him out. I kicked Louey out the next year."

"Ah," he said. "What took you so long?"

She sighed, realizing how easy it was to talk to him. "I wanted to try to make a go of it for Emma's sake. Not a smart idea. Actually, when he did officially leave, it was just a formality since he'd moved out of the house and in with one of his girlfriends." Then she laughed. "My father made sure that Louey gave me more money in the settlement than Louey even had at the time. He was royally pissed, but there was nothing he could do about it. He tried the threat again, about Emma, but I wasn't buying it. I told him I'd kill him if he tried to take Emma, and this time, he believed me."

"Why didn't you see your father again? After you and your husband split up?"

"There are two truths. The one I tell people if they ask is that Eve doesn't want to be seen with a stepdaughter who is older than she is. And a step-granddaughter? Please."

"And the other truth? The real truth?"

She began rubbing her arms. "To most people, if they've even heard of my father, they just think he's a very rich successful businessman. He's in Silicon Valley, into communications, he owns lumber mills in the Northwest, he has a chain of restaurants in the South, lots of other enterprises. He's never been convicted of or indicted for anything. His accountants are top-notch, so he'll never go down on a tax-evasion charge. People like you know that he's a lot more than that. He's a kingpin in extortion, gambling, prostitution, just about everything except drugs. He hates drugs.

"My mother was very wise. After the divorce, she took me far away from him, all the way to Italy. I wasn't raised with his influence. I remember how she'd cry every time she had to put me on an airplane to come to the United States, to him, for those summer months every year. I don't want Emma near him. My mother kept me away from him and I intend to do the same for Emma."

"*Sanction a kill*. That's what you said."

"You're right. It came right out. It's insidious, that kind of influence. Can you believe I ever want Emma to even know those words go together? A child growing up with a man like my father—I'd fear for that child and I'd be afraid of the adult that child would become. Now, that's enough. No more for you, Mr. Hunt. I think we should get some sleep. You don't know Emma. She'll be awake and raring to go at six o'clock in the morning."

"I know. She waited until seven after I got shot in the leg. I'd wake up with this soft little hand on my forearm, just lightly stroking up and down." He was silent a moment. "She's a great kid, Molly."

"I know," she said. "I know."

"We'll keep her safe."

145

"I know we will," she said.

It was deep in the middle of the night when a loud piercing scream brought Molly straight up in bed.

She grabbed her daughter and shook her. "Em, wake up, honey. Come on, wake up!"

She shook her again. Ramsey stood in the doorway, his heart pounding, his Smith & Wesson in his hand. He watched Molly sit up and pull Emma onto her lap. "Come on, love, wake up. It's all right. I'm here with you. Ramsey's here too. Wake up, Emma."

Emma suddenly arched then twisted around, throwing her arms around her mother. She was shuddering and sobbing. Ramsey quickly sat down beside them and held them both tightly. After a few moments, he eased his hold and leaned back. He pushed back Emma's tangled hair from her ear. "It's okay, really, Emma, it's okay. We're here. No bad guys, just us."

She slowly stopped sobbing. She hiccuped. He looked at Molly over Emma's head. Her eyes were shadowed, then he saw her mouth was tight, saw the pain deep within her, visible now to him, and he knew what that pain felt like because he felt it as well. Emma said in a flat singsong voice, "I dreamed about him, Mama. He tied my hands and feet to the ˜d. He used twine. He said he didn't need because I was just a little girl. He said I ˜fect and that he needed me more than ˜ded him. Only me. He took that ˜ wrapped me like a package." She fell silent. Ramsey and Molly waited, stiff, enraged, but she said nothing more.

They held Emma between them for a very long time. Finally, Molly said quietly, "She's asleep. Thank you, Ramsey. I'll hold her real close the rest of the night."

It was a very long time before Molly fell asleep again. When she awoke, she felt Emma's wet kiss on her cheek. Emma took her arm and pulled it and she naturally turned over to curl around her daughter's back.

When Ramsey awoke early in the morning, he thought about Emma's nightmare, her flat dead words. Twine. He'd tied her with twine, as he would a package. He hadn't needed rope. She was just a little girl.

Not that it mattered. If Ramsey could get his hands on that man, he would probably kill him. Would he send the man through the system, confident that he'd be punished as he should be? He didn't know. He just didn't know. And he should know. He walked to the other bedroom, stood quietly in the open doorway, watching Emma and Molly sleep.

"Ramsey?"

A little whisper of a voice.

"Good morning, Emma. Did you sleep well?"

"Oh yes. Mama's all snuggled in behind me. This is nice, but I have to go to the bathroom."

He heard Molly giggle.

He saw Molly kissing Emma's neck, telling

her they'd both go and then they'd get her a bowl of cereal, with bananas, none of those disgusting peaches.

He went back to bed and pulled the covers to his chin. Louey Santera had beaten her. He didn't blame Mason Lord one bit for taking the bastard down. He'd have taken him down himself. He wondered, as he got up to go to the bathroom himself, if Molly had loved her husband before that.

12

Emma was jumping out of her skin she was so excited. She started playing the two-octave piano as soon as she saw it, Ramsey standing just behind her, so surprised he couldn't speak.

She was playing a Mozart Sonata that had been the title song to an old film called *Elvira Madigan*.

All the salespeople in the toy store were beginning to gather around along with children and their parents. No one was saying anything, just watching Emma play on that little excuse for a piano and listening to the incredible music she was making.

He looked over at Molly. He could see that she was humming to herself along with Emma's playing. She looked as if it was nothing out of the ordinary.

He bought the piano. The saleswoman said, "It's a pity she can't have a regular piano. She's quite talented. How long has she been playing?"

Molly answered. "Since she was just three. We're vacationing here and forgot to bring her portable piano. We'll make do nicely with this one."

"Amazing," the saleswoman said. "Just amazing. You've got a lovely, talented little girl."

Ramsey nodded. "Yes, she is amazing."

He felt Emma's hand slip into his. He hugged her against his leg, which was feeling nearly back to normal again. He was down to about four aspirin a day. He wondered if Emma remembered her nightmare. He wanted to ask her about it but thought better of it. No, they needed to talk to a professional. He realized he could call and get a reference.

He said low to Molly when he opened the car door, "Do you think Emma's doing okay?"

"I don't know. I haven't asked her. After last night, I'm more afraid than before."

"I could probably find out the name of a local shrink, one who deals only with children. What do you think?"

She chewed on that so hard he could practically see her thinking. Finally, she shook her head. "We don't dare take a chance. I think that for the time being we should just keep her close and let her know she's safe."

But she knew Emma wasn't safe from those terrifying dreams. Molly forced a frown because she wanted to cry.

He nodded, still uncertain. He looked into the backseat of the Toyota. Emma was holding the big box with her piano inside really close. Her eyes were closed. What was she thinking? Or was she just playing music in her mind? He prayed it was music there and nothing else, at least for the time being.

He noticed the Honda Civic a half mile from the shopping center. There weren't many cars on 89, the only road to Lake Tahoe from Truckee. It was another seven miles, give or take a mile, to Alpine Meadows Road, their turnoff. He didn't say anything, just kept checking every couple of minutes in the rearview mirror.

Finally, when he was certain they were being followed, he said quietly, "Molly, look back and see if you can get the license plate number on the Civic two cars behind us. It's fairly new and gray. Be as discreet as you can. We don't want them to notice us looking."

She didn't even change expression, but he saw the panic in her eyes, followed by a hard coldness, the look she'd given him when she'd burst into the cabin that first morning.

She looked back at Emma. She was staring out the window, her piano box still hugged to her chest. She didn't appear to have overheard them.

They were nearly to their turnoff when she could finally make out the license. "It's F A R B three-three-three. That's too easy. Are you sure they're following us? It's a ridiculous plate."

"No. But I'm not about to take any chances. You got your gun?"

"Oh yes. What do you want to do?"

"Let's turn and see what they do. It's two guys, right?"

"As best I can make out. They're being really careful to hang back. I can't tell yet if it's the same two guys. My cell phone is at home getting recharged."

"That's all right. We'll call in the number as soon as we get home." *If* we go home hung silently in the air between them.

Emma said, "Ramsey, I can make out an *A* and an *R* in the license. I remember those letters really well. They're in our names. I need another reading lesson."

He looked at Molly, who just said, "That's great, Em. I got the *A* and the *R,* too. *F* and *B* are tougher letters. We'll make up words this evening so you can learn them."

"We shouldn't have gone out for my piano. That's how they got us. It's all my fault." Her small face was pale.

Ramsey said clearly, "Nothing is our fault. Don't say that again or I'll have to keep you away from hot dogs for a week. Don't be afraid, Emma. We'll take care of you."

"Listen to me, Emma," Molly said, turning in the front seat to face her daughter. "If anyone tries to get you again, I'll shoot them, even if it's the president. Do you understand?"

"Yes, Mama."

"Make sure your seat belt's tight."

"Yes, Ramsey."

They turned right onto Alpine Meadows

151

Road. The River Ranch Motel was sprawled out on the left-hand corner, a landmark for some time, a ski shop of nearly equal age on the right. It looked closed down. There was still some spring skiing, but not enough to lure more than half a dozen cars into the parking lot of the River Ranch Motel. He prayed the car wouldn't turn right after them.

The day was bright and would warm to about sixty degrees. Ramsey said, "Hey, Emma, you want to go hiking with me this afternoon? We might get lucky and see some neat wildlife—foxes, deer, lots of birds, rabbits."

The clothes he'd bought her were perfect. He was trying to distract her, but it wasn't working. "You game, Molly?"

"Maybe. We'll see. Are you hungry, Emma?"

"I don't know, Mama. I'm still trying to see the men in that car. Do you think they're the same men who were in Colorado, at that restaurant?"

"I don't know," Molly said. "They're not close enough to tell yet."

Ramsey looked behind him. The car had turned, dammit. There wasn't another car between them now. They were hanging back about forty yards. "Okay, they're after us. I'm going all the way down to the ski resort. There's a big turnaround. Then we'll head to Tahoe City. It's only a couple of more miles east. I'm not about to let them get anywhere near our house."

He saw that Molly had taken her Detonics out and was holding it loosely by her leg.

He'd put his Smith & Wesson underneath the front seat, loaded and ready to go. There were only about fifty cars at the ski resort and a couple of dozen four-wheel-drive vehicles parked up close to the ticket windows. The snow already looked slushy. The people who were here were either really serious skiers, or didn't know better. He slowly drove by the front of the resort, making the large lazy circle back onto Alpine Meadows Road, heading back toward the main road again.

The Honda Civic paused at the row of ticket windows, but didn't stop. He knew they wouldn't stop. He wondered if they knew they'd been spotted.

He gunned the Toyota as soon as they got back onto the road. When they got to the intersection with Highway 89, he took a right toward Tahoe City. No one had said a word.

He was thinking about how the hell he could lose the Honda behind them in very small touristy Tahoe City with its endless restaurants, ski rental shops, and souvenir kiosks. There was a shopping center. It was good sized. There were walkways all around the indoor center. He didn't know where most of them led, but he was fairly certain he could get them lost there.

It was on the right, he remembered, as you drove into town. He'd have to get rid of the Toyota. Pity, but no choice now. He didn't see them behind him for the moment. He turned into the huge parking lot and eased the Toyota right up front.

"Out. Quickly!"

He grabbed Emma's piano and they were through the shopping center doors in five seconds. "Go directly out the back, Molly. There's a walkway out there. Take the nearest one to the back door. I'll be with you in just a second."

There were just a handful of people in the shopping enclosure. He saw Molly weave her way through, moving as quickly as they could.

He didn't need to wait long before the Honda pulled around. They saw the Toyota and stopped. It was all he needed to know. He was out the back door in ten seconds, several unhappy people behind him.

He took the nearest walkway and started running. He caught them behind a small Louisiana-type restaurant.

"Molly, you and Emma go into this restaurant and stay in the bathroom. In five minutes, I'll pull up out front. Be there. Five minutes, by your watch."

He ran back toward the shopping center. He didn't see them. He walked quickly around the north side, into the parking lot. There was the Honda, double-parked right out front. It was empty.

He smiled.

Four and a half minutes later, he was in front of the restaurant, and Molly was opening the passenger side.

"Excellent. Emma, you all set back there?"

"Yes, Ramsey. My piano's okay, too." She

was hugging that box so tightly her knuckles were white.

It was hard to smile, but he managed it. "Hold on, kiddo. We're outta here."

"Will they follow?"

He looked over at Molly as he pulled back onto 89. "No, they're going to be a while. I took the distributor cap. They probably have a cell phone and will make some calls. Since they know where we are, we can't take the chance of going back to the house."

They were on Highway 80 ten minutes later, heading west.

"We never got to hike, Ramsey."

"We will, Emma, we will."

• **They** drove over the Golden Gate Bridge three hours and thirty-five minutes later. The day was sharp and clear, a picture-postcard day. The fog was just beginning to curl through the arches of the bridge.

"Are you sure this is a good idea, Ramsey?"

"I don't know, but I'm tired of running. My base is here, Molly. It's time we got help. We discussed this before. You didn't disagree."

"But the men who are after us, surely they'll find out who you are very soon. When they find out, they'll be on us like a shot."

He cursed under his breath. "You're right. I'll just bet they already know what I like to eat for breakfast. Okay. Let's just stop at my house so I can change, pack, and make arrangements. We'll fly to your father this afternoon. Sorry, Molly, but I just can't see any other choice unless you want to go to the cops right here in San Francisco."

"No." Molly cursed under her breath. "There's just no good alternative, is there? Let's go to Chicago, then. I'd still rather have her with me than being questioned by police psychologists, hordes of cops, not to mention the FBI. If Special Agent Anchor is representative, then the FBI is scary."

"He's not representative. All right, let's go to Chicago. When the time is right to bring in the cops, we can call them from there."

"I probably should have gone to him sooner. My old man's got more ability to protect Emma than the cops and the FBI. He may be a big criminal, but he'll do his best to keep Emma safe."

"All right, then. Let's use your father, if he'll let us. We'll let him keep Emma safe."

She closed her eyes a moment, then nodded to herself, coming to a decision. Then she smiled as she said to Emma, "Look over there, Em. It's Alcatraz Island. It was a prison for really bad guys until sometime in the 1950s."

"It's pretty. I wouldn't mind being a prisoner there."

"I read they fed the prisoners about six thousand calories a day, to make them fat, so they'd be less likely to try to escape and swim to shore. I think it was a whole lot of hot dogs and beans. They didn't let them exercise much."

Emma's eyes brightened.

156

He grinned at her in the rearview mirror. "They didn't cook them on hangers in a fireplace, Emma. They were boiled."

"Yuck."

Ramsey turned onto Scenic Drive in a beautiful old section of the city called Sea Cliff. "We're the closest houses to the bay. My house is number twenty-seven, right there on the end."

"I knew federal judges must be paid pretty well, but not that well. This place must have cost a bundle, Ramsey."

"It's worth quite a lot, but I didn't buy it. It was bequeathed to me by my grandparents along with a nice inheritance. I'm not as rich as you, but I won't starve. The views are incredible. We'll come back, Emma, and barbecue. We can sit in the backyard and watch the fog roll in. It floats through the Golden Gate Bridge like soft white fingers. I've always loved the fog. I've even got a piano for you, an old baby grand that my grandfather played. He was a great old man."

Ramsey's nose twitched the instant he unlocked the front door and stepped into the tiled foyer. It smelled like rotten food, but that didn't make any sense. He stepped into the living room and quickly stepped back.

The room had been trashed. His high-tech stereo equipment was ripped open and stomped on. CDs were strewn all over the hardwood floor. All the furniture had been slashed. He walked numbly into the kitchen. The stench was pretty bad.

The refrigerator door stood open. Someone had flung food all over the floor, not that there'd been very much. Dishes were smashed, in shards everywhere. Drawers were pulled out, silverware all over the floor. A violent hand had simply swept everything out of the cabinets.

"Don't come in here, Emma," he said.

"Oh no," was all Molly said from the doorway, holding Emma back.

It took him only minutes to see that whoever had done this hadn't forgotten a single room.

He walked into his study, a magnificent dark oak–paneled room that looked toward the Marin Headlands. His antique rolltop desk had been gouged, the drawers pulled out and smashed, all his papers in shredded heaps everywhere. Books lay in broken piles on the Tabriz carpet. His favorite leather chair had been ripped open with a knife. His grandfather's baby grand piano had its legs sawed off. It lay drunkenly on its side, most of the keys stomped in. Someone had even cut the piano wires.

Devastation everywhere.

What had they been looking for? Something to tie him to Molly and Emma?

"I'm sorry, Ramsey," she said at his elbow. "I'm really very sorry. We brought this to you."

He realized then what she'd said, the full impact of it. He turned slowly, took her upper arms in his big hands, and said, "I was feel-

158

ing equal parts enraged and sorry for myself. But now, after what you just said, I realize that this place, no matter how nice, is still just a place. When we get the person responsible for this, I look forward to kicking his butt, but Emma means more to me than a pile of stupid possessions. There's no contest. Do you understand me, Molly?"

She nodded. "I just don't understand why someone would do this. They could have just searched, if they wanted to find some sort of connection between us. They didn't have to destroy everything."

"I don't understand either, but we're going to find out."

"I hope so." She leaned down and picked up an atlas, its pages ripped, the spine broken. She tried to smooth the pages. She looked numb.

He gently took the book from her. "Help me pack, then we're out of here. I'll make some phone calls from a pay phone." But there weren't any undamaged clothes left. Even his leather luggage, a Christmas present from his folks, was mutilated.

Ramsey made four calls from a public phone on the corner of California and Gough. The first was to a cleaning service, the second was to Dillon Savich, the third was to an airline, and the fourth was to Virginia Trolley of the San Francisco Police Department. He made one stop: his bank.

"Let's go," he said, grinning at Emma as he came out of the bank. "This is going to be exciting, kiddo. At least now I'm as rich as your mama." He handed her a twenty-dollar bill. "Keep this, Emma. Tuck it away somewhere safe."

Molly gave him a quizzical look but didn't say anything, just watched her daughter very carefully fold the twenty-dollar bill and slip it inside her piano.

"I think I've had enough exciting things happen, Ramsey," Emma said and hugged her piano to her chest.

Molly said, "Maybe we can buy her some more clothes at the airport."

Ramsey frowned. "I'm thinking. I don't remember any kids' clothes there. T-shirts, but that's about it. We don't have time to stop. We'll get her a new T-shirt at the airport, and work on her wardrobe in Chicago. Ours, too, for that matter."

13

There wasn't a sound, just the slow movement of a finger, a gentle silent stroke, and an instant later, the whoosh of rending paper. The man's chest exploded outward, the sharp, jagged edges fanning out from a huge hole, smelling of char.

Gunther nodded to himself, turning away. He said under his breath, "Not bad."

"What do you mean, 'Not bad'?" she said, staring at the target as she walked closer. "How about perfect?" She watched Gunther blow on the muzzle of his Spanish Star Ten, one of the very few European 10mm auto calibre pistols, Gunther had told her in an unusual show of pride. Of all his acquaintances he had the only one, he'd said, which was just as well since he'd also be the only one to shoot it right. She watched him blow on the muzzle again. Naturally there was no smoke to blow away. She imagined he did it because it was symbolic, a move reminiscent of the gun-slingers in the Old West.

He gave her an irritated look but didn't say anything.

"Don't you like to be perfect, Gunther?" She came closer, running her fingers down his forearm, over his hand, to stroke the barrel of the gun.

He stayed silent. She was doing this just to make him crazy, he knew that, but it was tough not to respond in some way, just a small push, just a tiny shove away from him. But he wasn't stupid. He couldn't lay a finger on her, no matter what the provocation. No, he wouldn't even acknowledge that she was playing a game with him.

He had a feeling that Mr. Lord enjoyed these games of hers, even encouraged her. Maybe he was standing in the shadows at the back of the gallery, watching, chewing on an unlit cigarillo, a habit he'd developed since he'd stopped smoking the year before. Gunther slowly pulled away, cradling his gun in his big hands. He liked the feel of the cold smooth steel against his warm palm.

She shook her head, laughing at him. "The way you hold that gun of yours. What is it with you, Gunther? You think that gun is a woman?"

"No," he said very precisely, "I think this gun is a tool to get my job done." He nodded to her, politely, as always, and turned away from her. He said over his shoulder, pausing just a moment in the gallery doorway, "Mr. Lord appreciates my tool."

She stared at him an instant, then doubled over, hooting with laughter. "I sure hope not," she said. "I sure hope you're wrong about that."

His jaw locked. He felt embarrassment flood him, from inside out, as if his guts had turned red before his face. He hated the feeling. A soft voice said, "Yes, Gunther, I do appreciate your tool. Why don't you go clean your gun. You've used it a great deal today and with excellent effect."

"Yes, sir."

Mason Lord watched his man leave the gun gallery before turning to his wife. His look was indulgent, his voice amused as he said, "You torment poor Gunther."

"Yes, but he's really too easy, Mason. Did you bring my Lady Colt?"

He nodded. "I wish you'd let me teach you how to shoot a real gun, not this ridiculous toy."

Her voice hardened. It was disconcerting in that she looked like an angel, from that smooth thick pale blond hair of hers to the soft blue eyes, the fragile blue of a summer sky. "If I'm close enough, it'll get the job done. I don't want a tool like poor Gunther's. It's not elegant."

He had to agree with that. The recoil from the Spanish Star Ten would also knock her on her butt. He handed her the Lady Colt, stood back, and watched her put six bullets straight through the chest of the target.

She turned, her eyes sparkling, removed her earmuffs, and said in a wicked voice, "And I didn't even have to fondle it."

"No," he said, drawing her to him, "I'm the only thing you fondle."

But though he spoke the words, he wasn't responding to her the way he usually did. Usually she would have been on her back by now. She stepped back, laying her Lady Colt on the counter. "I wonder what your daughter is doing?"

He shook his head. "I called Buzz Carmen in Denver just a little while ago. He said the cops are still acting like idiots, mad at her for saving her own daughter, trying to track her down and this man with her. Buzz and three others have fanned out now, looking for her. Molly's an amateur. Buzz and his people aren't. They'll find her. He admitted he hadn't known she'd left Denver. He said they'd kept their distance because the cops had hassled them."

"No one's found her except whoever did this. Maybe the bad guys got them, Mason. You have to consider that."

"Molly's smart. She may be an amateur, but she's smart."

"I thought she was like your wife."

He stared at her, then laughed. "Like Alicia? Molly thinks of herself as the ugly duckling compared to my former wife. No, Molly might look like a railroad tie, but she's smart." He frowned a bit. "I suppose she's like me in that. I wish she'd just admit she needs me and get over here. She knows I can protect her and Emma."

"I'll bet this guy who's with them is calling the shots. Don't you think?"

"I don't even have an idea yet who he is." He took her arm. "Let's have one of Miles's margaritas."

It was during that first delicious margarita that Miles said from the doorway, "Sir, Molly's here. Emma too, and a man I don't know."

"It took her long enough to come," Mason Lord said, rising slowly. He set his glass on the marble tabletop as Miles went back out. Then he heard a child's voice, soft, high, not frightened, but wary?

"This is a very big house, Mr. Miles."

"Yes, Emma, it is."

"It's even bigger than the one we had with Daddy. This ceiling just goes up and up."

Then the three of them were standing in the open doorway, Miles behind them, his look questioning. "It's all right, Miles. I'll call if I need you."

Then his daughter turned, her hand on Miles's arm. "Can Emma have a glass of water, Miles?"

Miles looked down at the little girl, who was standing very close to her mother, her hand now held by the big man on her other side. "How about some lemonade instead?"

"Oh yes, Mr. Miles, that would be wonderful."

The three of them turned back to face Mason Lord. Three years since he'd seen Molly or her daughter. The little girl was the picture of Alicia, but her dark brown hair was her father's, that low-life runty little scum sucker who'd always reminded him of Mick Jagger when he'd been younger. She was six now, tall and skinny, her skin that pearly white that only children seemed to have. She'd be at least as beautiful as Alicia when she grew up.

He'd wanted Molly to come here. He'd told her to come here. Yet now that she was here, her child with her, and that man, whoever the hell he was, he didn't know how to respond. What was he to say to her? Three years. It had been a long time and she'd been the one who wanted to keep a goodly distance between them. But now things were different. Things had changed, irrevocably.

"Hello, Molly."

"Hello, Dad. You're looking well." She looked beyond at Eve, who was sitting elegant as a Parisian model on a soft yellow brocade love seat. She was wearing tight black jeans and a white blouse tied in a knot over her smooth midriff. "Hello, Eve. I presume you're Eve? I believe we spoke once on the telephone a long time ago."

"Oh, yes, I remember. How delightful to

finally meet you in the flesh. And you are Molly, I presume?"

"Yes. Dad, Eve, this is Ramsey Hunt. He's the one who saved Emma. Then I came along. There are maybe five men after us, and they're very good at tracking us. We don't know why they're after us, but we wanted you to know this right away."

The man cleared his throat and said, "We decided to come here, Mr. Lord, because they know who I am now. We just couldn't keep Emma safe. The people hunting us are good, too good. We trust you to keep Emma safe better than the authorities can."

Mason Lord walked to the man and extended his hand. "This is an honor. It's a pleasure to meet you, Judge Hunt."

Ramsey shook the man's hand. "Thank you. We're here because we believe you're our best shot at keeping Emma safe."

"I didn't imagine for a moment that you were here to visit me, Judge Hunt. Yes, yes, I know who you are. You're a famous man. It's quite a surprise that you're the one who found Emma."

Molly could only stare at them, all civilized on the outside, but she could see each sizing up the other, weighing, assessing. She gathered Emma closer to her. She hadn't wanted to be here, hadn't wanted her daughter exposed to her father, but it was the safest place for Emma.

Mason Lord wouldn't allow anyone to get close to his granddaughter, even though he hadn't seen her since she'd been a toddler. No, Emma carried his blood. He would protect her with every weapon in his arsenal.

Her father finally said, his voice smooth and deep, "You saved Molly and her daughter. I thank you. You brought her home when she refused. You will all be safe here. No one, cops or anyone else, will get near Emma."

"Thank you," Ramsey said. He squeezed Emma's hand, then said to the crook he was trusting with all their lives, "Actually, sir, Emma had saved herself. She'd escaped from the man and run into the forest. I found her there and took her to my cabin. Some days later, Molly found both of us." Ramsey looked down a moment at Emma, who was staring at a huge rhinoceros head, complete with a shining tusk, above the mantel, her mouth open. She was tugging on his hand. He gave hers a squeeze, looked at the rhino, and said, "I wonder what kind of polish they used on the tusk. What do you think, Emma?"

She squeezed his hand tighter. "Soap and water," she said. "Mama always says that soap and water's the best."

Mason said, "I'll call Buzz in Colorado. He will come back here."

"That might be a good idea. I would imagine that the men after us have already tracked us to the airport. We had to show photo ID. Someone will remember, no doubt about that, even though Molly bought her ticket singly and I bought Emma's ticket with mine. Yes, the men will be here very soon."

"You took a cab from O'Hare?"

"Yes, to downtown, Michigan Avenue. Emma needed some clothes, as did Molly and I. None of us were very presentable. Then we took another cab to the Jefferson Police Station, wandered in and spoke to the desk sergeant about nothing in particular, then we got a third cab out here. But they'll find us. I'm convinced of that. They probably already know we're here with you. As I said, they're good, and, as Molly and I have agreed, there's got to be an organization behind them."

Mason Lord nodded, then said, "That was smart of you to go to a police station. It will give them pause. Please, all of you, sit down. As to any organization behind all this, we'll speak of it later. Ah, here's Miles with some lemonade."

"I brought enough for all of you, sir."

"Thank you, Miles," Molly said.

"And I brought some chocolate cake I baked this morning." He looked at Emma as he poured her a glass. "You like chocolate cake?"

"Oh yes, Mr. Miles. It's the best."

Ramsey laughed. "Be careful or she'll eat the whole cake. She hasn't had many goodies for a while."

Miles smiled as he ruffled Emma's hair, even as Mason Lord frowned. He watched his daughter wipe the child's hands on one of the little wet towels Miles had brought. How had Miles known to do that? He was like one of those hovering smiley-faced airline attendants. He was silent until everyone had drunk the lemonade and eaten some of Miles's chocolate cake. He hadn't known of any cake. He loved chocolate cake but Miles hadn't offered him any, either for lunch or right now. He'd had a low-cal, low-fat flan for dessert the previous night. It hadn't even tasted very good. He looked at his beautiful wife. She wasn't looking at the cake. She was looking at Molly. Her face was perfectly still. No expression at all. What was she thinking?

Ramsey Hunt was big, tall, and very well built, but that made sense, of course, given what he'd done in his own courtroom. He was a man who obviously worked out, who took good care of himself, a man who looked as if he could deal with anything that happened to cross his path. Mason supposed he was good-looking enough, his features regular, his coloring olive, his eyes a green color that argued against Italian blood. But who knew in America? All of them were mongrels, himself included. At least he had more good Irish blood than anything else. As for his beautiful Eve, she was Swedish, every beautiful blond inch of her. She'd told him stories about her father falling in love with a German countess, but he hadn't married her. Too many control-freak genes, he'd said. No, Eve was pure Scandinavian. He'd chosen well this time.

He looked again, hard, at the man sitting opposite him. Judge Ramsey Hunt of the

Ninth Federal District Court—who would have imagined that he'd be the one to find Emma?

What were the odds of this man's finding Molly's daughter and saving her? He cleared his throat and said, "Judge Hunt, you said you found Emma in the forest. Did she willingly come with you to your cabin?"

"She was unconscious." He saw that Emma had stopped eating. Those ears of hers were on full alert. He said easily, "I can tell you all about it after we've got Emma settled in, all right?"

Mason Lord said, "Very well. Miles, give them three rooms."

"Emma and I will stay together, Dad."

"Very well, two bedrooms."

Ramsey turned to Molly, and said low, "Your father wants to grill me. Take Emma upstairs, all right?"

She didn't want to go; he knew it. "Please, Molly, go. I'll set your father straight."

"No," she said. "Emma is my daughter. You won't send me off to the kitchen to make tea."

He understood. He said to Mason Lord, "Let's make it a bit later, sir. Molly and I will settle in. If Emma is content to stay with Miles, then we'll come see you as soon as we can."

Mason Lord turned to his daughter. "What's wrong with you? Take your child upstairs. I want to speak to him. You had little enough to do with any of this. I want to thank him for saving you, for bringing you here. You haven't got the sense of a goat. Now, take your child upstairs. Judge Hunt and I need to talk things over."

Molly rose. She was shaking. Odd, she thought, how he could push the buttons so easily, so quickly. Only this time, she wasn't going to fold her tent and slink away. She fought the urge to lower her head, her eyes at her feet, like a whipped dog. She jerked her head up. She'd been through too much ever to let anyone take control of her again. But she had to keep calm, not let him see how she had to fight the hold he still had on her, the pull she was still fighting.

"I see," she said slowly, cutting him off, for he would have continued, she knew. She touched Emma's shoulder. "Emma, love, are you full? Yes, then let me wipe your mouth. Now, we're leaving this place. As it turns out, we just came for a short visit. Come along, Emma." She smiled at Ramsey. "You coming?"

"In a flash," he said. He nodded to Miles. "Thank you for the cake and lemonade. It was delicious."

"You don't talk to me like that, Molly."

"I didn't talk to you in any way at all. Goodbye, Dad. A pleasure to finally meet you in person, Eve. You're a knockout stepmom."

"Just stop it. What do you think you're doing? Where do you think you're going?"

He'd used that cold harsh voice with her countless times when she was growing up.

She turned, saying easily, "We're out of here, Dad. It's obvious that only one of us is welcome and that isn't your daughter or your granddaughter."

"Damn you, I just want to find out what's happened, what his plans are."

"Anything that's happened, any plans made, we've made them together. I'm sorry, Dad, but just because you're men doesn't mean you rule my world."

"Yeah, well, if a man hadn't been around, Louey would still be beating the crap out of you."

Molly knew Emma had heard that. "Be quiet," she said as calmly as she could manage. "Just be quiet."

Mason watched the little girl turn, obviously puzzled, and stare at him. He saw she didn't understand, but she would soon. He saw she was gripping both their hands. Had Molly already taken Ramsey Hunt as a lover? Despite her daughter's presence?

He said to Judge Ramsey Hunt, "Damn you, come back here. There's no way you're leaving my house now and taking them with you. Besides, given who you are, your chances of getting away unrecognized are about zip."

Suddenly, Eve uncurled from her chair and rose. She smiled at all of them indiscriminately and said in a charming hostess voice, "How about some more lemonade? It will make everyone feel better."

• **It** had been a long day, too long a day without Ingrid. Louey Santera rubbed the back of his neck, feeling the painful knots. The performance had hurled him to the heights, the crowd's applause still rang in his ears, as always, but now that it was over, he'd fallen into the pits. He needed Ingrid's clever hands on him.

But he'd given Ingrid the day off. She was with her parents in Frankfurt. Maybe one of his groupie girls could rub him down. He walked to the door and pulled it open.

"Alenon! Get in here!"

A skinny young guy with acne and stringy blond hair stuck his head around the corner. "Yes, boss?" Even the kid's voice was stringy, with little substance.

"Get me one of the girls, one who just might know how to unknot my neck and shoulders."

Alenon was back in under five minutes towing a small black-haired girl who couldn't have been more than sixteen. She looked like a baby. Was she one of the groupies who trailed after him like a pack of puppies? He didn't recognize her.

"This is Karolina, sir. She says her mother's a masseuse. She says she knows what to do."

Louey looked into the girl's eyes. She might be sixteen in years, but not in experience. He nodded. "Hello, Karolina. Can you help me?"

She said in excellent English, "It is my pleasure to help you, Mr. Santera. Is your daughter all right? I read in the newspaper that she was kidnapped."

What the hell was this? "What newspaper?"

"The *Berliner Zeitung.* There was an article about you. At the bottom, there was a sentence about your daughter being kidnapped. The reporter wrote it happened somewhere out in America's Wild West. I'm very sorry."

How had the reporter known? Hell, when she wasn't listening to him speak or writing down what he said or wrapping her legs around him, there hadn't been any time for her to find out anything. He'd just muttered something about Emma, not even a complete sentence. She must have called Denver. He turned to Karolina. "You speak English better than that reporter did."

"My mother is American."

"Oh," Louey said, rubbing his neck. He watched as Karolina efficiently covered the massage table with its soft flannel sheet. She stood back. Louey smiled. Slowly, he undressed for her. She didn't say a word. When he started to pull down his jockey shorts, she stepped forward, holding a towel out wide in front of him.

When she was rubbing his feet, she said, "I'm in Al-Anon. It's for children whose parents are alcoholics. Why do you use it as a name for Rudy?"

Rudy. That was the kid's name? He shrugged, a small movement because he was lying flat on his stomach. "Because it amuses me."

"I see," Karolina said as she moved up the table. He felt her hands dig into his shoulders. He closed his eyes.

It was the best massage of his life. When he woke up two hours later, Karolina was gone.

Alenon was standing there, watching him. For how long? Had he snored? Drooled? "What do you want?"

"I have a message from Mr. Lord for you."

"Oh no," Louey said and sat up, pulling the sheet to his waist. "When did the old man call? What did he want?"

"It was actually a man who said he was calling for Mr. Lord. He said he didn't need to speak to you. He said that your daughter is safe again, with Mr. Lord, at his house. That was all."

Rudy Brinker watched one of the most talented men in the world lower his head in his hands. He looked sad, broken. But his voice, when he spoke, was vicious. Rudy listened to him curse for a good thirty seconds. Then he quietly let himself out of Mr. Santera's room. He went down the hall to Mr. Murdock's room and knocked twice.

The ugliest man Rudy had ever seen answered the knock.

14

Mason Lord swirled the rich golden brandy in the Waterford snifter, watching it lightly veil the sides of the glass. It was magnificent brandy, coating his tongue and his throat as well when he swallowed. He allowed himself one snifter at night, an hour after dinner.

Eve was sitting on the sofa, watching television. He thought it was an idiotic show like *Wheel of Fortune,* only worse. Although he'd felt contempt for her taste even before he'd married her, he hadn't felt anything but lust for her body, and in his way of thinking, contempt couldn't begin to catch up with lust.

She looked up. It must be a commercial. "What are you going to do with them, Mason?"

He took the last drink of his brandy, carefully set the snifter down on a marble-topped side table, then said slowly, "I wanted them to come here. You heard me tell Molly when she called that she was to come here."

"Yes, so she listened to you."

"But she didn't want to. It was the man. It was Ramsey Hunt." He looked at the gold Rolex on his wrist. "He said he would come down to speak to me. Miles told him he wasn't to bring Molly."

"When did he say that?"

"Miles told him what he had to do if he wanted my protection. He'll do as I ask. He knows he needs me." He streaked his long fingers through his hair. Eve stared at him. She'd never seen him do that. "What's wrong?"

"She needs to be controlled. The way she spoke to me. I nearly struck her, Eve."

"But you didn't. When she threatened to leave, you backed off and told her what she wanted to hear—that you wanted to know what she had to say as well as this Ramsey Hunt." Eve paused a moment. The show was coming back on. Then she said, "You flattered her and she fell for it. You did control her, Mason."

"No," he said, "really, she didn't fall for anything. She's scared for her daughter. She'd make a deal with the devil to keep her daughter safe, even if the devil is me." But he knew if he hadn't backed off, she'd have been out of there, and that man would have gone with her. She had to be sleeping with him, to have him so pussy whipped. He looked at his wife. She'd turned back to her game show. He walked to the door of the immense living room and quietly opened the beautiful French doors that gave onto a walled-in, quite lovely English garden. The air was soft, redolent with the intermingling scents of hyacinths, roses, and star jasmine. The jasmine he'd selected himself for the garden. There were no sounds to break the quiet. Very few people knew that half a dozen men were stationed in and around the house. As soon as Molly, Emma, and Ramsey Hunt had arrived, he'd added more guards. He turned to see Miles coming from across the hall, toward him.

"Emma liked the spaghetti I made for her," he said. "The pasta was shaped like Jurassic Park dinosaurs."

Mason Lord could only stare at a man who'd been loyal only to him, at his beck and call only, for twenty-two years. He'd begun here when Molly was a little girl, but he'd never paid her much attention. Why Emma? Sure she was pretty, she was the very picture of Alicia, but so what? He'd never paid any attention to Alicia either.

He saw Ramsey Hunt coming down the wide staircase to his right. He was dressed well in black slacks and a white shirt. No tie, but that was all right. They'd been on the run. He called to him, "Did you deal with Molly?"

"Yes."

"You told her how she was to behave in my house?"

Ramsey wanted to laugh at the heavy-handed tactics. He just smiled. "She knows exactly what to do. Now, I hear from Miles that you want to speak to me."

"Yes, but just you, not Molly. She doesn't understand either business or strategy."

"Last I knew, Molly was in her bedroom, giving Emma another reading lesson. The kid's really bright."

"I read *Moby Dick* when I was five years old."

"I understand that Molly was reading very early on as well. That's remarkable."

Mason Lord had forgotten that. He nodded. "Come to my study. It's quiet there." He shut the double oak doors, cutting off the repulsive sound of that game show in the living room and all those shouting low-class slugs.

Ramsey said without preamble, "I understand that when you heard that Louey Santera had beaten Molly you were out there like a flash. That was well done."

Mason Lord stared at the big man standing in front of his desk, at ease, his face open, his expression even admiring.

He wouldn't have even gone to Denver if it hadn't been for what Louey had done. "I wasn't about to let that little creep hurt one of mine."

And that was the bottom line for Mason Lord, Ramsey thought, relieved and pleased. "And naturally you'd feel the same about Emma. She's also one of yours. Who do you think is behind this?"

"It's a kidnapping. Louey is rich—well, not as rich as he was before my daughter divorced him, but he's doing very well. His European tours net him literally millions, the wretched little shit."

"No, it's not just a kidnapping. I told you there were a lot more men after us. How many more people would you need to mount a tracking operation like that? Say at least two more, all of them professionals. Not a kidnapping, sir. Something else. I'd stake a lot on that." Ramsey paused a moment, then said, "I'm sorry to have to tell you, but you don't know yet that Emma was taken to a cabin in the woods, high in the Rockies, and sexually abused and beaten. It's another thing we have to think about. Emma needs to see a doctor and a child psychiatrist. She has nightmares. Neither Molly nor I have spoken about this because we're afraid of making things worse."

The blood drained from Mason Lord's face. For a moment Ramsey thought he'd be sick—that, or explode. He did neither. Gradually the color returned. His breathing was slow now, calm.

He looked directly at Ramsey. "The bastards have just signed their death warrants."

"I shouldn't, but I feel the same way."

"You're supposed to uphold justice and the precious laws that protect scum like that."

"Yes," Ramsey said. "I'm supposed to uphold the rights of all sorts of scum."

Mason Lord looked at him sharply, but Ramsey's expression didn't change. "As much as I don't want to even consider it, you're probably right that there's got to be either a connection to me or to Louey. I will think about that. Actually, I'd already spoken to Buzz Carmen about my enemies being behind this. We'll see."

"I want to leave Molly and Emma here with you. At least here I know they'll be safe."

"Just what will you do that I can't?"

"Your people didn't do much of anything in Colorado. No, my resources are more far-reaching."

"Just who are your resources other than a whole bunch of cops and lawyers in San Francisco?"

Ramsey shook his head. "You wouldn't approve, so I'll just keep that information under my collar."

Mason Lord felt red creeping up his neck. He rose slowly, his palms flat on the beautiful mahogany desktop, but he didn't have time to say anything. The door opened and his daughter walked in. She was smiling. She said to her father, "Have I missed much? I'm sorry for being late, but Emma wasn't ready to go to sleep. You know, it's true—a mother's work is never done. Now, tell me what you're thinking and I'll tell you what I think."

Ramsey winked at Mason Lord. "Might as well, sir. She's got a really good brain. It'd be stupid not to use it. You should have seen her drive the getaway car."

Mason Lord heard the mindless music from the game show. He shouldn't have, not in his soundproofed study. Had she turned the volume up? He looked at his daughter's face. "Go back to see to your daughter."

"Your granddaughter is peachy. She's with Miles. Let's talk."

"Go watch the game show with Eve."

"I don't know Eve. I don't like game shows. Actually, on my list of priorities at this moment, neither of those is very high."

He wanted to tell her to butt out, that this was his home and he was the boss here. Then he looked at her eyes, filled with pain and defiance and determination.

"Well, hell," he said.

Ramsey Hunt smiled and nodded at him. He still had to tell Molly that he was leaving her and Emma here. He'd been avoiding it. He wondered if she'd take him apart. But he had to do something.

Molly smiled at him, patting his arm. "Don't

even think it," she said. "I overheard you speaking to Dad. No, Ramsey, no way am I letting you go out there on your own."

Ramsey looked at Mason Lord. "Well, hell," he said.

• **Dillon** Savich said to Agent Sherlock, who happened to be his wife of six months, two weeks, and three days, "This whole thing just doesn't make any sense. I've tried lots of different approaches with MAX but he can't seem to get a reasonable handle on it."

MAX was Dillon's laptop and partner, so he called him. Dillon's reputation in the Bureau was that he could make the laptop dance, and he did, that was true enough. Sherlock patted MAX's case. "You've got lots of supposition, but just a few facts. Unfortunately MAX likes solid facts, not wussy guesses from the ether."

"That true, MAX?" Savich punched a key on his laptop. A deep mellow voice said, "Right, boss."

Sherlock laughed. "I still can't get used to that voice. You're a sicko, Dillon. You're going to have to change the voice when MAX has a sex change again to MAXINE."

"You want to audition?"

"Do I strike you as a Maxine type?"

He stared up at her face and just shook his head. "No, but don't worry, I'll think of something when the inevitable sex change happens. You should see Jimmy Maitland's face when I ask

MAX a prearranged question. The first time he nearly fainted. Now he sits forward, just like a kid waiting for a Spiderman cartoon to come on." As a matter of fact, she had seen his boss's face when MAX had come out with "Actually, Savich, I don't think I wish to deal with this confusion anymore." Maitland had run out of his office, shouting for everyone in the vicinity to come in and hear this.

She poked him lightly on the shoulder and said, "We've got to get more information. Ramsey called you this morning from San Francisco to check in. Has he called since then?"

"No. But at least we know where he is."

"Just imagine Ramsey Hunt—a federal judge—at Mason Lord's house in Oak Park. It boggles the mind."

"Just to imagine that Molly's his daughter. Now that's got to be a real shock to Ramsey's system, having to go to Mason Lord. At least the little girl should be safe now. I hear that place is a fortress." He sighed. "Unfortunately, with Mason Lord's resources, I don't blame Ramsey a bit for not wanting to try his protection. I did try to talk him into calling the FBI, but he refused, said this was the safest way to go for the moment, and he's probably right. He also wants the little girl protected from the cops asking her questions, psychologists all over her. At least until we find out who's behind all this." Savich sighed again. "You want to see some photos we just got from a military satellite?"

She smiled at him. "Do you know something of interest, sir?"

"A bit." He punched buttons on MAX, waited a moment, and then the two of them watched photos of Mason Lord's huge house come onto the screen. Dillon hit another button and the photo changed to another view, this one from east of the vast grounds. "These shots just came in. I counted six different men stationed around the grounds. Now on to the boss man himself." He hit a key and Mason Lord's lean, very handsome face appeared on the screen. "He ain't bad, is he?"

"No. Who's that? His daughter?"

"Nope, that's his new wife. She's younger than the daughter."

Sherlock made a rude noise. They looked at more photos. Finally, he hit a key and said, "This is Molly Santera and Emma, her daughter."

Sherlock was silent for several moments. Then she said, "We've got to do more, Dillon."

Special Agent Dillon Savich, chief of the Criminal Apprehension Unit at the FBI, tilted back his chair, looked up, and said, "What do you suggest, Sherlock?"

"For starters I'd go see that farmer in Loveland, Colorado. You know, the one who said he'd sold the truck that later turned up being driven by the guys chasing Ramsey."

He felt a tingling down his spine. He sat forward, his eyes never leaving her face. "You think this guy knows who they are."

"Yes, it makes sense. I think we should go

there, talk to him, have a really serious talk. Besides, at the moment, there aren't any other leads."

"Agreed. I'm with you on this one—that farmer knows. One of the guys from the field office in Denver can take a ride up there and talk to the farmer."

She was shaking her head. "No, Agent Anchor is already involved. I'll bet he's also already verified to his own satisfaction that the farmer didn't have a clue that he'd sold his truck to the kidnappers. In other words, his mind is already made up and I doubt he'd change it unless something smashed him in the nose. The word about Agent Anchor is that he's got an attitude problem. He brown-noses up the chain of command at the Bureau and tromps on local law enforcement. Nope, it's got to be one of us who goes. We're not on the FBI's side. We're on the kid's side."

"And that makes a difference?"

"Maybe this time it does," she said thoughtfully, lightly stroking her fingers over two thick black strips that were MAX's speakers. She remembered hearing Dillon hoot when MAX had made his first statement, which was, if she remembered correctly, "Hooray for the Redskins."

She said, "If it were a simple kidnapping, that would be different. But this is big, Dillon, and no one has a clue who's behind it and what they want. Well, maybe Mason Lord does. You know, that's got to be one of the reasons Ramsey's there."

"All right. I'll phone the field office and let Agent Anchor know we're coming." Savich swiveled his chair back, pulled out his directory, and punched out some numbers on his telephone. The phone rang busy. "Damned thing. I think e-mail should be mandatory for everybody in every department and in every field office in the FBI, maybe even everybody in the world."

She shook her head at him, picked up the phone, and punched in the same numbers. When it was answered, she asked to speak to Agent Anchor. She said to Dillon, "Phones hate you. It's time to face up to it. Just let me do the dialing from now on. Oh yes, hello, Agent Anchor. Agent Sherlock here from the CAU in Washington. I'm fine, you? Good. I wanted to ask you about the Santera kidnapping. Un-huh. Now, about that farmer you interviewed who claimed he'd sold his truck after his wife had reported it stolen?" In an instant she was staring at the phone as if it had bitten her. "You're kidding me."

She waited some more, nodded, then said, "When? How? Any leads?"

She asked more questions, then listened for a couple of more minutes. Slowly, she hung up.

"What happened?" Savich's voice was tense, low.

"You won't believe this," she said. "The farmer's dead. He was found three days ago just after dawn by his teenage daughter. His head had been bashed in with a hammer.

Whoever did it just dropped the hammer by the body. No clues, no leads as of yet. Of course no fingerprints. As for other forensic evidence, we've got to wait to see. Agent Anchor said he'd call us when he found out anything more. He said they just found out about it from the local cops.

"The locals said that no one saw anything or anyone. His wife said he always went to the barn just before dawn to milk the cows."

"And someone was waiting for him."

She stared out the window. "He had three other kids besides the teenage daughter who found him."

"Of course it has to be tied to the kidnapping, or whatever the hell it is."

"Agent Anchor thinks so, at least he now thinks there might be a connection. What do we do now, Dillon?"

Savich pressed one of MAX's buttons and said in a throaty FBI interview voice that imitated MAX's, "We're going to kick butt, Sherlock."

15

I'll say it again. No way are you going out there on your own. We're in this together."

He grinned down at her. "Before we get into it, let me compliment you first. You did really well with your dad. You hung in there, didn't lose your temper, and finally he caved. He's pretty smart himself. What I'm thinking now is that I should go to Denver, get personally involved, work with both the local cops and the FBI. As for you and Emma, you'll both stay here." He saw the fear draining the brilliance from her eyes. "I can handle myself, Molly. I won't get killed. I promise."

The emptying fear left her eyes and anger moved right in. She took three deep breaths.

"Good. You're getting good at control. When my mom gets really mad at my dad, she throws something at him. My father can still move faster than any human I've ever seen."

"I'm trying hard not to kick you in the shin. Listen to me, Ramsey. I know you mean well, but there's no way I'm going to let you go out there alone and put yourself on the line." She smiled at him. "It's all for one and one for all. We're the Three Musketeers. Call me D'Artagnon."

"He was the fourth musketeer."

"His is the only name I know."

"I remember Aramis was one of them. Tell me, Molly, which one is Emma? Do we give her a sword or a gun, in this case, and let her fight right alongside us?"

She walked away from him, rubbing her hands over her arms. Then she hugged herself. "You and I have done a good job of protecting Emma. Besides, I can't begin to imagine what she'd do if you just up and left. Don't you understand? Emma needs us, both of us."

He cursed under his breath and ran his fingers through his dark hair. "Okay. So you're right. I agree. And I really don't want to leave Emma in any case. Now here's what we'll do first thing. You're going to call Louey in Germany and get him back here. It's very possible he's involved. How? I don't know, but it's possible. We need to talk to everyone."

"I can try," she said and walked to the phone. Three minutes later, the speaker on, they were listening to the phone ring at the Bristol Hotel Kempinski in Berlin.

Ramsey asked, "It's what? Six A.M. there?"

"Something like that." She asked for Louey Santera's room.

The phone rang three times, then, "Mr. Santera's suite. Rudy here. May I help you? It's just past dawn here, by the way."

"Good morning to you, too, Rudy. This is Mrs. Santera. I don't know if Louey happened to mention it, but his daughter was kidnapped. Please put him on the phone."

There was a miserable silence.

"Now, Rudy."

"Yes, ma'am."

After a three-minute wait, Louey Santera said, "Molly, that you? What the hell's going on? Is Emma all right? I heard she was safe."

"Yeah, she's just fine. However, all is not what it seems, Louey. You've got to come home right now. Today."

"I can't. I have a concert tonight. Three more before I come back to the U.S."

"Look, Louey, this is important. It's about your daughter's life. Doesn't that mean anything to you?"

"Dammit, Molly, I could probably come back by the end of the week, but not before then. I—"

"Today, Louey," said Mason Lord, his voice soft and very gentle.

"Who's that?"

"Hello, Louey," Mason Lord said. "This is your ex-father-in-law. How are you feeling this morning? It is morning, isn't it?"

"Yes, damn you, it's morning. So Molly went home to Daddy, did she?"

"I suggest you get yourself back here, Louey. You can make the Lufthansa flight from Frankfurt to Chicago."

"I can't, I—"

"Today, Louey. There are many things we need to talk about. Perhaps you have some explaining to do."

They heard a woman's voice in the background. "Who is that, Louey? Why are you breathing so hard?"

Molly laughed. "Bring her along, Louey. No one wants you to get lonesome." She hung up.

Ramsey looked ready to burst into laughter. He said, "If it were between a grand jury and your father, I'd bet any day on your dad getting him home."

"Oh yes," she said, and yawned. "He's good at scaring people's socks off."

"I like your hair," he said, surprising both of them.

She blinked at him. "My hair? What did you say? You like my hair?"

"Yes," he said. "I do. It's substantial, your hair. I like all those curls. It's good hair."

"Well, I like your hair too."

He began to laugh. She joined him. The door opened and Mason Lord looked in. "What is going on here? Why are you two laughing?"

Molly just shook her head. "Will we be picking Louey up at O'Hare?"

Mason Lord looked back and forth between them. "I think Judge Hunt should pick Louey up. That would catch the little bastard off guard."

Ramsey merely nodded. "I'd be delighted. I've got lots to say to Mr. Santera. I'll use my old prosecutorial style."

"My daughter," Mason Lord said precisely, "doesn't have nice hair. She looks like a grown-up Little Orphan Annie. She has her grandmother's hair."

He'd had it. Ramsey walked up to Mason Lord. He got right in his face. "Why don't you tell Molly how happy you are to see her after three years? Why don't you tell her that she's got brains and grit and you're about the luckiest guy alive to have her for your daughter?"

Mason Lord turned on his heel and left the bedroom. Ramsey knew he'd gone too far. Mason Lord was enraged, nearly over the edge. But when he turned in the doorway, it wasn't Ramsey he went after. He said, his voice low and vicious, "Don't bother wasting your time sleeping with her. Louey said she was a cold lump in bed. No fun at all. Of course I had to have him disciplined when it got back to me what he'd said, but there it is anyway."

Molly didn't fold at all from the hurt of his words. Instead, she said, her voice filled with amusement, "Well, Louey's the expert, isn't he? Bottom line, Dad, I'm really glad I didn't get some disease from him."

She saw her father pause a moment, and then he was gone from her view.

Ramsey said, "The two of you are quite the duo. Look, Molly, you're an adult. I know it must hurt when he goes after you, but kiss it off. It's not important. There are lots more important things to think about and the most important is standing right there."

"Mama, why is Grandfather angry?"

Emma was standing in the doorway, her hair long and tousled, her nightgown with its pink bows, nearly to the floor. She was clutching her piano against her chest. It was nearly as big as she was.

Ramsey said, "She needs a doll."

"Your grandfather wasn't what you'd call really angry, Em. It's late and he's older, you know? Older people get cross quickly when they get tired."

"Boy, what a whopper."

"Be quiet. Em, Ramsey is just trying to make a joke. I'm going to give him lessons. Now, come back to bed. I'll tuck you in."

"I'll come with you." Ramsey walked to Emma and picked her up in his arms. "This piano weighs a ton, Emma. I think I'll have to remove an octave."

Emma reared back in his arms and looked at him closely. "That was funny, Ramsey. Not as funny as Mama, but funny. Has she given you a lesson?"

"Thank you, Emma. She hasn't yet given me any lessons at all. Actually, I came out with that one all on my own." He took the piano, handing it to Molly. Emma sprawled against him, her head on his shoulder. She sucked her fingers.

There was a queen bed in the bedroom. It was Molly's old room, he realized. There wasn't a ruffle to be had. What there was were bookshelves all up and down one wall, filled with paperbacks and hardcovers, piled indiscriminately. On the other wall were photos, dozens and dozens of photos. Many were framed, most were arranged lovingly and carefully on cork boards.

"Mama takes pictures," Emma said to Ramsey when he laid her on her back. "She took all these when she was young."

"I see," he said, and leaned down and kissed Emma's forehead. He stroked her hair back from her face. "You go to sleep now, Emma. I don't want you worrying about anything, all right?"

"You won't leave, will you, Ramsey?"

He'd already made that decision, with Molly's help, but still, what if something happened? Something he couldn't foresee made him leave?

She whispered, "You don't know if you should tell me the truth. It's all right. Everybody lies. Except Mama. She never lies."

"Is that so?"

"Yes," Emma said. "Mama, will you come to bed soon?"

"Yes, love, in just a little while. Ramsey and I have bunches of things to discuss."

She turned off Emma's light, but left the door ajar. Just a slice of light shone into the room from the three Tiffany lamps standing at intervals in the wide corridor.

Ramsey said, "I won't leave you, Emma, unless I have to, and then I'll tell you first."

Emma didn't say anything.

"We can hear her if she has a nightmare," Molly said quietly as she followed Ramsey back to his room.

"Now," he said once they were in his bedroom, "tell me what you think we should do."

"Beat up Louey Santera again."

"After we beat him up."

She sighed. "I don't know, Ramsey. So much has happened."

"One of the first things is to take Emma to a doctor and to a child shrink."

"Yes," she said. "I've been thinking about that. I don't want to take her to her regular pediatrician. He's a man. I want to take her to a woman."

"That's probably smart."

"I'll make calls tomorrow, get some names. Where do you think those men are, Ramsey?"

"If they're here, they're cursing a blue streak. There's just no way in here. Miles told me he has six men patrolling the grounds around the clock. I think this place is more secure than the White House."

"I heard Mason tell Gunther to bring in another three men to patrol. He's not taking any chances."

"He loves you and Emma."

"Yeah, right. It's all a matter of possession. He just doesn't want anyone messing with something he sees as his."

"Whatever it is, it's still a start. We'll see. Tomorrow—" He rubbed his hands together. "Tomorrow I'll get to meet dear Louey face-to-face."

"It won't be one of the high points of your day. Trust me."

"As Emma would say, you made a joke."

"Sometimes truth's funnier than fiction."

• **Louey** Santera was furious and it showed. His mouth was tight, his lips a skinny pursed line. Then he saw a reporter and the fury was masked immediately by a charming smile and a little-boy shrug. "Hi," he said to the reporter, turned, and gave a smile to the accompanying photographer, then saw Molly and gave a wave.

The reporter, a longtime friend of Ramsey's, said cheerfully, "I hear you flew back, breaking concert dates, when you heard your little girl was kidnapped."

"I couldn't leave immediately," Louey said,

nose sharp, on the alert instantly. "I naturally came back as soon as I could."

"Is it true your little girl is safe and at her grandfather's house? Her grandfather is Mason Lord, isn't that right?"

"Yeah, he is her grandfather, and yeah I heard she was at his house. It's over now, thank God. Did you hear? My concerts went great, too."

"I've heard you've had your problems with Mr. Lord. Is that right, Mr. Santera?"

A man came from behind Louey Santera to plant himself directly in front of the reporter. He was a young guy, stringy, with acne scars. "Mr. Santera just flew in from Germany. He wants to be reunited with his little girl. He's tired. He's said all he's going to say. Good-day."

The reporter said, "Come on, Mr. Santera, what's going on here? Your little girl was kidnapped over two weeks ago. You're coming back a little late, aren't you?"

"No comment."

The young guy with Louey actually shoved the reporter. The photographer flashed a photo.

Louey Santera was white-faced. Ramsey smiled as he stepped up to him. "Mr. Santera? I'm here to greet you. I'm Ramsey Hunt, currently residing with Mr. Mason Lord. Do come this way, out of all this crowd of people. Ah, yes, here's Molly."

"Get out of his face," the young guy said,

and gave Ramsey a shove. The guy might look scrawny and too young, but Ramsey spotted the moves immediately, the watchful eyes, the stance.

"That isn't polite," Ramsey said, and in a move that was subtle and smooth, he gently clasped the young man's hand and twisted his thumb back. The guy gasped with pain. He didn't move.

"Now, back off," Ramsey said very quietly. "I'm not a reporter." He applied a bit more pressure on the thumb. "All right?"

"Leave be, Alenon," Louey Santera said.

The young guy nodded. There was cold hatred in his dark eyes. It seemed to be awfully easy to make enemies these days. Ramsey released his thumb. "Now, let's get out of here. Molly, say hello to your ex-husband."

"Hi, Louey. How's tricks? Hey, I don't see your girlfriend. She doesn't have a passport?"

"How did you find Emma?"

She batted her eyelashes at him and put her hand on her hip. "I used my considerable sex appeal, naturally."

Ramsey stared at her. Louey Santera barked out a vicious laugh. "Hey, that's a joke," he said. "You're always telling jokes, never serious. You didn't find Emma at all, did you? It's just all hype."

"Why do you think that? I don't have enough brainpower? Not enough guts?"

"Come off it, Molly. You know you didn't have a thing to do with getting Emma back.

You wouldn't know where to find square one if it hit you in the nose. What really happened?"

She leaned close. "I found her but I was too afraid so I slept with the kidnappers. They were so excited, so happy, that they gave her back to me."

"Stop that and tell me the truth."

"Okay, Louey, the game's over." She leaned over to whisper in his ear. "Listen, you selfish jerk, I found my daughter, all by myself. You want to know what had happened? The man who took her sexually abused her and beat her. What do you think of that, Louey?"

"That can't be true. I didn't hear anything like that. No, you're lying, trying to make me look bad."

"No one could make you look worse than you already look. You call from Europe and start bragging about your success there and all the women you're screwing. You're a toad, Louey, you don't give a damn about Emma."

"Then why am I here?"

"Because my father scares you all the way down to your crooked little toes. If he told you to be celibate for a week, I just bet you'd do it."

"He's a murderer, Molly, shouts to the world that he's a big legitimate businessman, but he's nothing but a big-time crook, and you know it. You're no better. You took me for everything in the divorce, you're nothing but a—"

Ramsey broke in. "All right, enough of the

emotional sentimental reunion. It's time to get out of here before more reporters show up." He turned to the acne-faced young guy who was Louey Santera's bodyguard. "You get Mr. Santera's luggage. You can drop it off at Mason Lord's place in Oak Park. Then you can go to a motel or something. Don't think you're included on Mr. Lord's houseguest list."

Louey looked over at the reporter who'd been so rude. He recognized him. His name was something like Marzilac. He was from the *Chicago Sun-Times*. Hell. He was just standing there, speaking low to his photographer. What were they talking about? Maybe they were talking about whether to print any of this. Just his luck. Now he had to face Mason Lord. His kidney hurt just thinking about it.

"Let's go," Ramsey said.

"Do as he says, Alenon," Louey said. "Just call the house and tell me where you're staying."

16

An hour and a half later, Louey Santera faced his ex-father-in-law across the huge mahogany desk in Mason Lord's study.

"This cretin—" He motioned toward Ramsey, who was standing by the door. "He accosted me. He nearly broke my bodyguard's thumb. In fact, I'll just bet you he got a reporter to come there and ask me stupid questions. It cost me a bundle to leave Germany. I was busy, everything was going great with the crowds. Besides, there's nothing I can do for you. I've thought about it, and I don't know of anyone who could have done this."

Mason Lord didn't rise. He sat there, tall and straight in his chair, weaving his black Mont Blanc pen, heavy with gold trim, expertly between his long fingers. He let Louey talk and talk. Finally, when he'd heard more than enough, he said, smoothly, "You're looking thin, Louey. Your eyes look too bright, the pupils too large. I hope you're well."

"Touring is hard work, real long hours. Sometimes I have to take sleeping pills to calm me down. Listen, I didn't want to come here. What can you possibly want from me?"

"I do hope you're not doing cocaine again. I really hate drugs, you know that. I told you that when you were married to Molly. If the coke doesn't kill you, then it's usually something else. Like the guys selling it to you getting pissed off. I've never seen simple sleeping pills dilate your pupils."

"I'm not doing drugs."

"Did you meet Ramsey Hunt?" Mason Lord waved a hand toward Ramsey, who was still standing by the door, arms crossed over his chest.

"I told you, he was the bastard who—"

"It's Judge Ramsey Hunt. Perhaps you've heard of him?"

"No. Who is he? Some gigolo your young wife wanted?"

"Ah, Louey, you do like to push the envelope, don't you? I suggest you think a bit before you open your mouth. If you ever mention my wife again, I'll have Gunther cut off the end of your tongue. Your singing wouldn't benefit from that. Now, since you appear to be ignorant as well as unwise, I'll tell you that Ramsey Hunt is the San Francisco Federal District Court judge whose picture was on the covers of both *Newsweek* and *Time* magazines a while back. He's a real hero, they say. Don't you remember? The big drug murder case in San Francisco? What Judge Hunt did all by himself when they tried to break the defendants out of the courtroom?" Louey looked blank. Mason Lord sighed. "Ah, Louey, I do pray that Emma didn't inherit your brains, your inability to recognize the importance of anything that doesn't pertain directly to you. It would be a pity."

Ramsey said, "Ignorance isn't the same as stupidity."

"In Louey's case, it seems to be."

"She's got his talent, Dad," Molly said, coming into the room to stand beside Ramsey. "In fact, she's got all the talent that he could ever claim. And his talent is good even if his brain isn't."

"Impossible," Louey Santera said, whirling around to see Molly standing beside that damned judge. The guy was too young to be a judge. She'd come in very quietly. How long had she been standing there? "Emma? She's a little kid, only what, five years old?"

"Six, Louey. Your daughter is six years old."

"Yeah, well, what talent?"

"She can play the piano for you. She's incredible."

"Enough!"

Everyone looked at Mason Lord. He relaxed slowly, saying nothing more, knowing that he had all their attention again.

Louey said, "Why did you want me to come back? You got Emma. What else is there?"

"It appears there's a conspiracy afoot. Not just one kidnapper, Louey. Judge Hunt believes there are a goodly number of men involved since it appears to be a very professional operation, and they're all after Emma. Indeed, the men tracked Molly and Ramsey all across Colorado into California. Do you know anything about this, Louey?"

"That's ridiculous! What would I know about that? Emma's my daughter, for God's sake. I don't know anything about any conspiracy."

"Well, there's a problem," Mason Lord continued, his voice suddenly soft, oily with sincerity. It reminded him of Bill Matthias's voice, a lawyer in San Francisco unoriginally called Slick Willie. "I'm not behind any conspiracy, Louey, and there, quite simply, isn't anybody else. There's another little point that's really very disturbing. The man who had Emma. He abused her sexually and beat her."

Louey lunged to his feet, his face white. "No! That's impossible. Molly said that, but I didn't believe her. There must be a mistake... not Emma, no one would dare touch Emma like that."

Mason Lord sat slightly forward. "Didn't you bother to make sure that the man you hired to hold Emma in that cabin in the Rockies wasn't a child molester?"

Louey collapsed back into the chair. "Listen, I didn't hire anybody! I don't know anything about any of it. Dammit, she's my daughter. I wouldn't have my own daughter kidnapped."

"Oh?" It was Molly's voice coming from behind him, cold and hard. "You'd do anything for money, Louey. Anything. I'll just bet you owe some big shot lots of money and you left the country because you couldn't pay. Is that it?"

He turned on her, so furious the pulse pounded wildly in his thin neck. "You have the gall to talk high and mighty about money. You took me for every dime I had. You didn't deserve anything at all. All you managed to do was get pregnant. Dammit, I didn't have Emma kidnapped!"

Mason Lord slowly rose. He pressed his palms against the desktop. He said in that same soft, oily voice, "I think Molly's right. You're in big debt to somebody and this was your way of paying them off. Tell us the names of the men, Louey. Tell us who helped you pull this off. Tell us why they're still after Emma."

"I don't know about any men! I don't know anything! Molly's dead wrong."

"Gunther, please come here."

Gunther, huge and menacing, his big hands relaxed at his sides, said, "Yes, Mr. Lord?"

"Gunther, please take Mr. Santera to one of our guest rooms. He's weary from his long journey. He flew in from Germany today, you know. Yes, he's tired and needs to rest. Take him upstairs and put him to bed. Stay with him, Gunther. Remind him that life is sometimes very difficult. Remind him that I forgave him once, but patience is a precious commodity. Remind him that I'm not always such a patient man. Oh yes, he doesn't need to speak to that creature who is supposedly his bodyguard. Keep Mr. Santera quiet and apart. He needs to rest."

"I didn't have Emma kidnapped!"

"I'll see you after you've had a nice rest, Louey," Mason Lord said. He rose and watched as Gunther wrapped one huge hand around Louey Santera's upper arm and pulled him toward the study doors.

Louey jerked around at the door. "If it's Molly who's claiming I did that, she's crazy. She hates me. Maybe this judge character is her lover and they wanted the money. Yeah, maybe Molly did it."

Gunther quietly closed the study doors, and there was silence.

Ramsey whistled. He said, "I sometimes forget the awesome power people like you wield. Every day I deal with people claiming that they're as innocent as their dear grannies, but you know they're lying through their teeth, you know that most of them are thugs, cons, just plain scum, and many times much worse.

"And the thing is, of course, that in our justice system you can't just beat the crap out of them even though you know they're so guilty they're bulging with it. No, we play by rules that seem absurd in their gentleness, in their lack of focus and force. We use compromise and negotiation, not metaphorical thumb screws." Ramsey shrugged. "On the other hand, your performance hasn't yet resulted in anything, except to terrify one skinny little man. Molly would probably disagree with me on how often we get to it, but the truth is always there, somewhere. Don't beat the crap out of him yet, sir. Your threats are just as potent. I'd like a chance to talk to him myself. From what I could see, Molly should probably keep her distance. She's quite good with that pistol of hers."

Mason Lord said easily, "Of course I know my threats are potent, Ramsey. They wouldn't be potent, however, if occasionally I didn't back them up, and the knowledge of that got around. Talk to Louey, see what you can dig out of the little bastard."

Ramsey nodded, then said to Molly, "I'm thirsty. Would you like to drink a glass of lemonade with me and Emma?"

"Yes. Then I've got phone calls to make."

• **Dr.** Eleanor Loo, a tall Chinese-American woman in her mid-thirties, was wearing a leg cast. She rose clumsily when they came into her office. Molly had gotten her name from Emma's new pediatrician. Her fingers were crossed when, after introductions were made, Dr. Loo turned to Emma. She just smiled at her, then said, "Let me sit down, Emma. My leg makes me a bit awkward and the cast is heavy. At least it doesn't hurt much anymore. I broke it skiing. It was a beautiful fall, right off a twelve-foot cliff. Everyone said I looked so graceful sailing off that cliff. I don't suppose you ski?"

"My mama does. I'm learning." Emma didn't move, just stood there between Ramsey and Molly.

"You've had three lessons, kiddo," Molly said. "You're going to be very good. Maybe you'll be lucky and not go sailing off a cliff, but it happens. Remember when I strained the ligaments in my right knee?"

"Yes, Mama. You had to have physical therapy."

"Me too," said Dr. Loo. "I'll ski again, but not for another year. I miss it. Now, Emma, why don't you come over here and sit by me?"

Emma didn't move. She tightened her hold on Ramsey's hand.

Ramsey said easily, "Tell you what, Dr. Loo, why don't I just let Emma sit on my lap for a while. Is that all right?"

"Sure thing. I understand that you're a very smart girl, Emma. Your mama told me that you escaped from this bad man all by yourself, that you thought it all through and figured out what to do."

Emma was frozen. Ramsey couldn't even hear her breathe. But he forced himself to keep quiet, to wait. He supposed he'd expected the shrink to go easier, to ease into Emma's experience, not just dive in, face first.

Dr. Loo said, "How did you figure out how to escape?"

Emma licked her lips. It was the first movement she'd made. Ramsey wanted so much to pull her against him and cover her with his arms, protect her, but he knew there was no protection when the wound was raw and deep, all on the inside. He looked at Molly. Her face was white and set. She was trying to look relaxed, but she wasn't succeeding. Her hands were fists on the chair arms.

Emma said in a small reflective voice, "I thought and thought."

Ramsey felt as if he'd been punched in the gut. Emma's voice was a whisper of sound. He was surprised any of them even heard her words.

Dr. Loo waited for more, but Emma didn't say any more. Dr. Loo said then, "You thought well. How long did you think about it?"

"All that day. But I didn't know how I could get the string off my hands, and then he forgot. He just forgot and went outside to smoke."

"Then what did you do?"

Emma was pressed so tightly against his chest that Ramsey wondered if he shouldn't intervene. He was on the point of opening his mouth when Emma said in that same whispery soft little voice, "I jumped off the bed. It was real dirty. I was going to go right out the window, but then I knew that he'd know right away. So I stuffed the pillow under the covers. Then I went out the window. It was above the sink. I was afraid I'd fall off, but I didn't."

"You were barefoot?"

Emma thought. "No, I knew I had to run, so I put on my sneakers. I put them on after I jumped to the ground."

"Did that fall hurt you?"

Emma nodded. "Yes, but I didn't make a sound. He'd hear me and catch me."

"Did he drink very much?"

"I counted four empty bottles. I didn't have anything to do, so I counted them. They were really big."

"How long did it take him to drink those four bottles?"

"Five days."

"That's how many days it was until you escaped?"

"Yes," Emma said, her voice not quite so choked now.

"Were there certain times of the day or night that he drank out of those bottles?"

It was loud, that mewling sound that ripped Ramsey's guts. She was trembling, wheezing for breath, making those awful sounds. "No, no, sweetheart," Ramsey said, pressing his cheek to hers, holding her tightly, rocking her, keeping her close and closer still. "It's all right.

You're safe now, with me and your mama. If Dr. Loo had been there I bet she would have kicked that miserable man in his butt."

"That's right, Em. She would have kicked him with her cast. That would really hurt."

The mewling sounds stopped.

"Emma?" It was Dr. Loo. Emma didn't say anything, just pressed closer to Ramsey's chest. "I would have kicked him really hard. Count on it."

Emma jerked. Then, slowly, she raised her head. She looked at her mother, at Ramsey, then at Dr. Loo. "Mama wanted to shoot him," she said at last. "She might have shot Ramsey if I hadn't said something."

"You did well, kiddo," Molly said. "You did really well."

"Can you answer another question for me, Emma?"

The little girl looked at her clearly now. "I don't want to but I know that my mama wants me to, and Ramsey."

"Yes, but only if it doesn't make you sick afraid. Okay?"

"Okay."

"Was this man who kept you at the cabin for five days the same man who took you?"

"Yes."

"How did he get you?"

"Mama was taking pictures in the park in front of our house. I was with Scooter—he's the neighbor's dog. Mama said I could get one just like him. I was throwing his stick. It took me a long time to teach him to bring me back the stick because Mama said that Dalmatians weren't genius dogs, just dumb dogs and really cute. I threw the stick and when Scooter didn't come back I went to him. There was a man petting him. I heard Mama call my name and I called back and said I was getting Scooter. Then the man smiled at me and he hit me on the head. I tried to call my mama but I couldn't."

Ramsey thought: It was that easy. It took just an instant, just that one instant when the adult believed everything was all right. And then it was too late.

He glanced over at Molly. She looked stricken, guilt ridden. He'd have to shake her out of it. It hadn't been her fault, but he knew just how deeply self-blame could burrow in and corrode.

Then Emma just turned her face in against Ramsey's chest. It was as if she'd frozen, stiff and cold. He held her, kissing her hair.

Molly rose slowly at a nod from Dr. Loo. "Thank you, Dr. Loo."

"It was nice to meet you, Mrs. Santera, Mr. Hunt. I like you, Emma. You've got guts. You've got a good mind. You're going to do just fine. Now, I want us to talk some more when you're feeling less overwhelmed with bad memories. All right?"

Emma slowly turned to face the doctor. She said finally, "I don't know, Dr. Loo. Maybe we can talk next week?"

Ramsey noticed that Molly was flushed with relief.

Emma slipped off his lap and went to her mother. She took her hand and held it hard. She dragged Molly out of the office.

"Mr. Hunt, just a moment, please."

He turned and smiled. "You did that very well. I was wondering about your approach, but it worked."

"Emma's a smart child. You've always got to take a chance, though, on your initial reading. I don't know your part in all of this, but Emma certainly trusts you. So, whatever you and her mother have done, it's been good. It's up to me to get it all out of her so she can look at it, dismantle it, study it, then come to terms with it. Are the police in any way involved?"

He shook his head. "Not right now. Neither Molly nor I wanted to give her over to strangers. This is just for Emma. She's had some doozy nightmares."

"No wonder. I understand you had her examined?"

"Yes, the pediatrician put her under, at our request, then examined her. She'd been sexually abused, she'd been beaten, as we thought, but she's healed nicely, at least on the outside. Oh, yes, one other thing. A couple of times, coming out of a nightmare, Emma said things about this man. She talked about him tying her up with twine because she was just a little girl. She mentioned that he told her he needed her more than God needed him."

"Now that's a real lead. Give the FBI this information, Mr. Hunt, if you haven't already."

"I will."

Dr. Loo nodded. "Just you and Mrs. Santera keep doing what you're doing. I'll see you on Tuesday?"

"Yes, that's fine." It was only four days away. "There was something else."

She reached out to pick up a scratching stick. He watched her ease it down into the cast. She smiled. "Ah, that feels good. You never realize how important scratching is until it's a pain to be able to do it. Now, your something else—you think I'm going too fast. I am. But you see, you want to get all the poison out of her as quickly as possible before it has a chance to fester. Talking about all the hideousness is like the psychological equivalent of using a stomach pump. Don't worry, I'll pull back if I think it's too much at a time."

She stuck out her hand. "Tell her mother she's doing a great job. Tell her mother, too, that if she continues to blame herself for what happened then she won't be much good to Emma in the long run. All right, Judge Hunt? Don't look so surprised. You're a famous man."

"I'll tell Molly what you said." He turned, then said over his shoulder, "Dr. Loo, what I am really is a very frightened man."

17

Molly came out of the kitchen to see Emma standing beside a hallway table, one of Miles's chocolate-chip cookies in her hand, staring up at her father. Louey looked profoundly discomfited.

"I remember you," Emma said slowly, and took a bite of cookie. "You're my papa. Mama said you were coming to see me."

"Yeah, well, here I am all right. You've really grown, kid."

"You haven't seen me for a long time," Emma said, staring at a man she dimly recognized. He looked tired and nervous. "Mama says I grow taller than a Dr. Pepper can every month. That's my favorite drink."

"You look pretty tall to me. Look, Emma, I've got to go. I've got to see some people, do some things, you know?"

"Yes, Papa," she said slowly, her eyes never leaving his face. "I know."

Molly caught up to Louey in the upstairs hallway just after she'd tucked Emma into bed an hour later. He was just coming out of his bedroom. Gunther stood some twenty feet away, his arms crossed over his chest, chewing on a toothpick.

"You saw Emma for all of two minutes, Louey. The first time you've seen her, I might add, in two years. I was thinking that you could have her play her new piano for you. You'll be impressed, I promise."

Louey Santera looked more harassed than scared at the moment, and he knew he had good reason to be scared. "Look, Molly, I saw her. What was I supposed to do, for God's sake? She's just fine. Oh, all right. The next time I see her, I'll ask her to play that ridiculous piano."

"All right, how about this after she's played for you—how about telling her you love her? You are her father, and she needs you, although that's a concept that never really took root in your brain."

"You wanted her, I didn't. You were a lot more fun before you had a kid, Molly. Remember those photos you took of me that *Rolling Stone* featured? Now those could have made you, but what did you do? You just laughed and said they were okay, not all that great. The editor at *Rolling Stone* said you were terrific, but you wouldn't hear about doing any more work for them."

"Louey, you're not remembering quite right. I was pregnant with Emma at the time and puking my toenails up on a very regular basis. I've been getting back into it since Emma's older."

"No one has ever photographed me as well as you did."

So that was it. As usual, Louey was thinking about himself. She wanted to roll her eyes and smack him. She did neither, just smiled at him. She really didn't hate him most of the time, actually; she really didn't even think of him except rarely, and even on those rare occasions she felt only mild dislike simply because she understood the bone-deep fears that always festered beneath the surface in him. They occasionally even overwhelmed his remarkable conceit and ego. Because she was sometimes so weak-headed, she forgot about the damage he could wreak. It was fear that was driving him now and so she said without rancor, "You're an excellent subject, Louey. You know how to mate with the camera. Don't be impatient. There are lots of terrific photographers out there, but that's neither here nor there." She stopped, then just shook her head. "Never mind. Sometimes I'm a fool. Now, tell me what you know about Emma's kidnapping, if you want me to help you before Mason gets nasty. And he will, Louey, he'll get nastier than anything you can begin to imagine, nastier than he was to you in Denver three years ago."

"You weren't in Denver when he showed up three years ago, so just how would you know what your dear daddy does?"

"I remember one summer when I was here. I was twelve years old and I woke up late, probably about midnight, and walked downstairs to the kitchen. I saw a light under his study door and I could hear men's voices. I pushed the door open and looked inside." She shuddered from the force of the memory, but she said only, "Tell him, Louey. Don't be cute. When he sets a goal, his focus never falters. His patience is formidable, but when it's gone, it's well and truly gone. Tell him. Or tell me. How were you involved in this? Tell me the names of the men you owe money to."

Ramsey pulled back around the corner. He'd just come up the stairs to go to bed. It was late. There stood Molly and Louey Santera facing off like two gunslingers in the hallway outside his bedroom door. He'd heard her last few words. He knew she didn't really think that Louey had had anything to do directly with Emma's kidnapping. But he was involved indirectly. She was covering all the bases, which was really smart. He wondered if Louey was buying it.

Louey cast a furtive look at Gunther, who hadn't moved a muscle, then leaned against the door, crossing his arms over his chest. "I sure made a big mistake marrying you, didn't I? You were Little Miss Sweet Innocence with a big crook for a father. But I found that out too late."

"What do you mean?"

"You want some truth? I'll give you some truth." He stared down at her, his mouth twisting. "I wanted to fuck you, Molly, not marry you. But your daddy found out about us. He left me no choice."

"That's not true, Louey, you know it's not. He didn't even know I was dating you until I told him we were going to get married. Stop looking at me like I'm an idiot. I tell you, he didn't know a thing until I told him. I remember the surprise on his face. I'm not making it up. He *was* surprised."

He laughed, a nasty laugh that nearly froze Molly where she stood.

"It's not true," she said again. She was crumbling inside. Was nothing as it had seemed in her life? "You're making this up, after all these years, just to hurt me."

"Sure, Molly Dolly, sure I am. It turns out

your old man had us followed—you didn't know that, did you? Of course you didn't. Yeah, and he had me followed to protect his little girl from the scummy coke-snorting rock star. He probably knew to the minute when you lost your virginity to me. And I got a visit from him the very next day. That was the day I really understood who your daddy actually is."

"You're not lying? My father made you propose marriage to me?"

"You don't think it was because I could have possibly wanted a wife, do you? Come on, Molly, even you're not that stupid. I always liked fresh-faced eager girls. You looked at me like I was a god. I wasn't about to deny myself. So I had to be patient and play a few games with you so that you'd fall on your back for me. I wanted to take your virginity. I've always preferred virgins. And so I did, but then there was Daddy standing at my front door just after you left that morning." Louey shrugged. "I remember one of his goons—a guy who got his head shot off a while back—he had huge hands. He grabbed my neck between his hands and lifted me off the ground. Then your daddy told me how things would be. He told me I'd better be real sincere when I proposed to his daughter. He told me if I wasn't faithful to his daughter, he'd make my face so ugly nobody would want to see it. I believed him."

"You were very sincere," she said, and wondered how she could even form the words, much less get them out of her mouth. "I remember that evening very well. But you slept with lots of women."

Louey shrugged. "Yeah, well, what was I supposed to do when I was married to you? Finally, I called your daddy and confessed that I was having sex on the side. I told him you just weren't interested. What was I to do?"

Louey laughed, actually laughed. "Your daddy finally gave me his permission. He told me to be discreet."

Humiliation and rage mingled and flowed over. She drew back her arm and struck him as hard as she could with her fist in his belly. The air whooshed out of him. He gasped, clutching his stomach, bent over.

"You bastard," she said low. "You complete and utter bastard. You'd do anything, wouldn't you? It's true that you're the only man I've ever slept with so I have no comparisons, but let me tell you, Louey, it wasn't ever any fun at all. From what I hear from other women, you were a pig at sex, and I bought it because I didn't know any better.

"You have nothing in you but greed and ego. And you've got street smarts, enough anyway to keep you alive, enough to realize that Mason would have annihilated you if you hadn't done what he told you to do. Did you have Emma kidnapped? You need money. You always need money. You knew Mason would be the one to pay for her release, but you didn't care where it came from." She paused, panting, then smacked her palm against her forehead. "How could I be so stupid? You didn't want my dad involved. You wanted me alone to pay the ransom. You viewed it as getting your money back.

"I really didn't think you'd done it, but I've changed my mind. You don't owe big bucks to anyone, do you? No, you're the one who had her kidnapped. You wanted your money back."

She hit him again in his stomach. "And you got a child molester to take her. *You did that to your own daughter!* What kind of a man are you?"

She punched him yet again. He was still bent over, gasping for air. "No," he managed to get out. "I didn't. Don't hit me again, Molly, I mean it. Remember how I hit you three years ago? I'll do it again."

"You just try it, you worm, just try it." She started to say something else, then just shook her head and walked away.

Ramsey didn't move for some time. People did the most incredible things to each other. He, Judge Ramsey Hunt, without hesitation, walked quickly down the corridor to where Louey Santera was still standing, alternately looking at Gunther and at his own toes.

"Hey, Louey. How's tricks?"

Louey managed to raise his head. "What do you want, you prick?"

Ramsey smiled at him and said in the mildest of voices, "Molly creamed you good. I knew she was strong, but that was quite a demo. You must have really pissed her off."

"She's really tough when her father's nearby or one of his goons. Can you imagine what Gunther would have done if I'd so much as breathed too hard on her? She knew. I had to stand here and let her hit me."

Ramsey kept that smile on his mouth. He lifted Louey Santera up by his shirtfront, straightened him, and sent his fist into his jaw. Louey yowled, staggering back. Ramsey let him go and he hit the wall.

"You're a real piece of work, you know that, Louey? There, that should give you something else to think about. I can't wait to see the back of you. And Molly's right, you know. Mason's just about ready to snap. I have a feeling that when he does, you'll be dead meat."

"You're a bloody judge, a bloody federal judge, and just listen to you. Some officer of the court you are. I'll get you for assault and battery. I'll get you impeached and disbarred, you bastard. I'll get you."

"Hey, you want to try to get me now? I'd sure welcome that, Louey. Anytime you want to play some more, you just come see me." He shook his head. "It looks right now like you hired a child molester to kidnap your own daughter. You probably didn't know that, but it just shows what a real winner you are. You're going to do big time for this, Louey, if you're involved, and that, only if you're lucky. Who knows, maybe I'll see you in my courtroom."

"You're in San Francisco, idiot."

"Yeah, but I've got lots of judge friends."

Ramsey walked away whistling. He said over his shoulder, "Sleep well, Louey. Tomorrow will be here soon enough."

He went to his bedroom. He didn't bother turning on the lights. He knew his way around now. He walked to the bed, lay down, and stared up at the black ceiling. Was Louey involved? It seemed fantastic to him. But on the other hand, the man didn't seem to have a moral bone in his skinny body.

"You heard everything he said, didn't you?"

He jerked to a sitting position. "Molly? Why are you here, in the dark?"

"Waiting for you. I saw you lift him off the ground and hit him in the jaw."

"Between the two of us pounding him, just maybe he might dredge up a bit of humanity, although I doubt he can. Why did you ever think you loved him?"

"I was nineteen years old and stupid."

"And he was the big rock star."

"Yes, and I was super-impressed. A friend of mine who knew him introduced us. You heard him. The only reason he asked me to go out with him was because I was Little Miss Sweet Innocence. I didn't go to bed with him that first night, and that was probably why he asked me out again. I didn't go to bed with him at all until one night I smoked marijuana, drank too much— Oh God, that sounds pathetic. Anyway, I just floated off with him to his bed." She shuddered with the memory of it.

"Just leave it be, Ramsey. At least he gave

me Emma. I would have danced with the devil if the result was Emma."

"Of course you would have," he said, and rose from the bed. He could see her now, standing by the open window. There was a quarter moon, sending just a sliver of white light into the bedroom.

She turned to face him. "You did hear everything he said, didn't you?"

"Yes. It felt good to hit him, Molly. He's a miserable human being."

"Do you really think he had something to do with Emma's kidnapping?"

"Maybe. If he did, you hit it right on the head. He wanted his money back. But you know, I keep coming back to the same questions. Why all the professionals? Who was tracking us? Remember, the ransom note arrived after we'd gotten Emma back. I got the distinct impression that if they'd found us, we'd all be dead. Why? That wouldn't give them any ransom."

"I know."

They heard a scream, a high piercing cry that had them out of his bedroom in an instant and down the hall into Emma's and Molly's bedroom.

Ramsey stood back while Molly gathered Emma to her and rocked her. "It's all right, baby, really, it's all right. That's right, just breathe deeply now for Mama. You're okay. I'm here. Ramsey's here too."

He sat down on the other side of the bed and rubbed Emma's back, saying nothing.

"Was it that awful man, Em?"

Emma nodded against her mother's shoulder. "I woke up when there was this noise. I looked over. He was at the window. He was staring in at me. He was grinning. He had bad teeth, just like before."

Ramsey went immediately to the window and stared out. He didn't see anything. He unlocked the window and raised it. They were on the second floor. There was a ledge outside, wide enough for a man to stand on. He looked and looked but there was no movement in the bushes or trees, no shifts in the shadows, no sounds. He didn't see a single one of Mason Lord's guards.

He turned to Emma as she said in a small broken voice, "He won't go away. He's always there, waiting for me. I knew he'd come back for me, and he did. He followed us all the way from California. He's here now."

Molly looked up at him. He shook his head.

"You sure you saw him at the window, Em?"

"Yes. He was grinning at me. I was so scared."

Molly pulled her tightly against her again. "I know, sweetheart. But you're all right. Both Ramsey and I are here with you."

Ramsey said, "He won't come back again, Emma. And he won't be there for much longer, I promise. Now, I'm going downstairs and we're going to look for this character."

He was at the door when Emma called out his name. He turned to her. "Yes, Emma?"

"Thank you for believing me."

He just smiled. "If he's still out there, we'll get him."

She didn't look as if she believed him. Actually, he didn't either since he believed she had indeed dreamed him up out of a nightmare, but he and the guards would all look anyway. He couldn't imagine that anyone could sneak onto the estate without one of the guards seeing him. But it couldn't hurt to look around, to talk to the guards, to make sure they were on their toes.

Emma was sucking her fingers, hiccuping. Molly said, "I'm going to come to bed now, Emma, we can play spoons. We can snuggle real close."

"Can Ramsey come, too?"

He didn't even hesitate. "Sure, Emma. Tell you what, you get settled with your mom and I'll be in soon. I'll hug you both until you fall asleep. I'm going to go look for that guy."

She sucked harder on her fingers, then pulled them out of her mouth and whispered, "Please be careful, Ramsey. He's a bad man. He even smokes."

"I'll be back soon, Emma. I'll be careful as a judge."

The sucking slowed. She sniffed and swallowed. "That was kind of funny, Ramsey."

• **Miles** knocked lightly on the bedroom door, then quietly opened it. Emma was lying pressed against Molly. Ramsey was sleeping in a chair next to the bed, an afghan pulled up to his chin.

It was late, after eight o'clock in the morning. He paused, not knowing what to do.

"Is that you, Miles?"

"Yes, Ramsey. Should I come back?"

"No, it's time for us all to get up." He sat up in the chair and stretched. "I'm a damned pretzel," he said, and rubbed his neck. He started to get up, then Emma's hand shot out from under the covers and grabbed his hand. Molly awoke. She tried to sit up and not disturb Emma at the same time.

"I'm awake, Mama. I've got Ramsey."

"I see that you do. Miles?"

"Yes, Molly." He suddenly broke off and turned. "Oh, good morning, sir. As you can see, Ramsey and Molly were protecting Emma."

"This is ridiculous," Mason Lord said. "What the hell are you doing in here, Ramsey?"

Ramsey said quietly, Emma's hand still held in his, "If the two of you will please leave, Molly and I will get ourselves together. In case you're wondering why I'm in here, Emma had a nightmare. I stay close. It makes her feel safe again. Let me go now, Em. That's right." He leaned down and kissed her, then lightly patted her cheek.

Mason Lord turned away. They heard him say, his voice hard and cold and very smooth, "Good morning, Louey. I trust you have a whole lot to say to me this morning."

"So she's sleeping with him, huh?"

"You have a very plebeian mind, Louey. I suggest you go downstairs, have some bacon and toast, then prepare to tell me all about the recent happenings in your miserable life."

"I tell you, I didn't kidnap Emma. She's my daughter, too. Why do you call her Molly's daughter? Listen, you've got to believe me, I—"

Miles, thankfully, closed the door.

• **Ramsey** called Dr. Loo, telling her about Emma's nightmare that had seemed so real to her. Dr. Loo would see them right away.

Mason Lord stopped Ramsey on the way to the breakfast room and drew him aside. "I had Gunther bring the Mercedes around for you. You can drive it to the doctor's. I also heard about the search last night."

"We didn't find any evidence of an intruder, and no one really expected to. Emma dreamed about the man, then half woke up and saw him in the window. Adults could do that. It shouldn't be too much of a stretch to imagine a six-year-old seeing the bad man at the window. That's why we're seeing Dr. Loo right away while it's still fresh in Emma's mind." Ramsey frowned, looking just past Mason Lord's shoulder.

"What is it?"

"It's very likely that Emma could describe the kidnapper. I'd thought about it before, but I decided she didn't need that kind of stress. It was too soon. Maybe she could do it now. We could get a police artist out here."

"No police. They poke where they shouldn't. I'll get an artist and have him make arrangements to see you at Dr. Loo's."

Ramsey nodded and walked into the breakfast room. Only Emma and Molly were there. It was a charming room done in the Colonial style, with bowed windows looking over the back lawn with its glittering blue swimming pool. He sat down at the cherry-wood table with its hand-embroidered tablecloth, covered dishes set for them.

"I like Dr. Loo," Emma said as she started on her bowl of the special oatmeal Miles had made for her. "Do you really believe I saw him?"

"It's possible you didn't really see him, sweetheart. I hope we can find out what you really saw. Do you mind?"

"No." She sighed deeply. Ramsey hadn't ever thought a child could sigh like that.

Molly stood up and walked behind Emma. "Let me French-braid your hair, Em. It looks a bit ratty."

While Emma ate her cereal, Ramsey drank coffee, watching Molly do the French braid, her hands sure, her motions smooth. He'd have to learn how to do that. He remembered the pathetic braids he'd managed after he'd found Emma.

"Will you teach me that?" he said to Molly, who was twisting a rubber band around the bottom of the braid. She wrapped a pretty yellow puffy bow around that.

"Sure, no problem. Emma, do you mind Ramsey practicing on you?"

"No, Mama. Ramsey can learn anything."

"Such faith," Molly said and kissed her daughter's ear. "If you're finished, sweetheart, it's nearly time to go. I'll call Miles to get the car."

"Gunther already brought it around earlier, according to your father."

They went out of the house five minutes later to see the car parked on the far side of the wide circular drive.

Suddenly, Louey Santera bolted from behind a thick row of bushes, rushed to the car, and jerked open the driver's-side door of the Mercedes.

"He's trying to escape," Ramsey said, shaking his head. "The idiot."

He yelled, "Come back here, Louey. You can't get out of here, and you know that. The drive is gated. There are two guys there, with guns. Stop, you moron. For God's sake, Mason isn't going to pull your fingernails out. All you've got to do is tell him the truth and nobody's going to hurt you."

Louey gave them the finger. He twisted the key in the ignition.

It was his last act.

18

The car exploded in a ball of flame. Tongues of fire and metal swept upward and outward from the car, shooting into the air, hurtling toward them. Molly grabbed Emma and threw her to the ground, falling over her. Ramsey flung himself on top of them both, gathering them in with his arms, covering them as best he could. He felt the fierce heat of the flames, heard the whoosh of the fire and chunks of metal striking the sidewalk and gravel. Suddenly he felt as if a boulder had slammed into the middle of his back. It was hard and heavy and hot. The pain was intense. Whatever had hit him was still on his back, burning through his sports jacket and shirt. "Hold still, Molly." He quickly rolled off them onto his back. A smoking fragment of upholstery fell to the ground beside him. The pain immediately lessened. He'd stopped the burning.

He looked back at Molly and saw a sharp piece of metal that looked like a spear jutting out of her arm, right above the elbow. "Oh Jesus, Molly, hold still. Emma, you okay?"

"Yes, Ramsey."

"Good. Don't either of you move yet. It's still too dangerous." He ripped off the sleeve of his shirt, took a deep breath, and without saying a word to Molly, he jerked the metal spear out of her arm. "Good," he said. "Don't move, I'm going to wrap it up."

Molly hadn't made a sound. He didn't know how she'd managed it, but she did. The next minutes ground slowly by. Emma was fidgeting. He said things, silly meaningless things, to quiet her. Finally, the car was burning down, consuming itself, the flames collapsed into plumes of black smoke, which then fell, blanketing everything. The smell of burning rubber was nauseating. The Mercedes was a burning corpse. And what was left of Louey was inside it.

Emma twisted onto her back when Ramsey finally moved and looked up at him and her mother, who was holding her arm. "What happened? Why did our car blow up?"

"It's all right, Emma." He couldn't answer her, not yet. He helped Molly to her feet. "You hanging in there?"

"Yes, don't worry about me. I'm lucky I was wearing a long-sleeved dress. Not much protection, but some." Her sleeve was seared off, the blood from the wound soaking his makeshift bandage and snaking down her forearm.

"Both of us need a doctor."

She was staring at him. "Are you all right, Ramsey? I know you're hurt. How bad is it?"

"I'm all right. Come on, Molly."

She looked away toward the burning car. She turned perfectly white. "Oh God, Louey!" She ran toward the burning wreck, holding her hurt arm. "Louey!"

Ramsey grabbed her around her waist, pulling her back. "No, Molly. He's dead." He blinked. It hit him that Emma's father had just been blown up in front of her. He and Molly were both in shock, not thinking clearly or quickly, but now here was Emma, staring at the car. He came down on his knees in front of her and gathered her against him. "It will be all right, Emma, I promise. I'm real sorry, sweetheart. Someone put a bomb in the car. It exploded when he turned it on."

He heard people's voices behind him, coming from the house, but he didn't turn to see who was there.

There was nothing left of the car. Nothing left either of Louey Santera. Then he saw that the Mercedes hood ornament was still recognizable. He turned then to see everyone standing on the front steps gaping at the twisted, blackened car. There were still small spurts of flame eating into the metal, bursting up now and then into glittering showers.

Emma's piano was smashed. Still she held it against her chest. She looked at her mother, then back at him. "I don't understand."

"He's dead, Emma," Molly said.

"Oh," she said finally. She looked at the gutted car, at the licking flames. "I don't see him, Ramsey."

"No," he said. He wasn't about to tell her that her father could be picked up in a wastebasket.

Then everyone seemed to be talking at once, patting, soothing, Mason Lord even holding Molly close to his side for a moment. Gunther had his gun out. Miles was trying to edge close to Emma. Guards had swarmed to the burning wreck, their guns at the ready. All of them were young men, fit and strong, each carrying an automatic weapon. Even they stopped to stare at the devastation.

Eve Lord said slowly, her eyes on Emma, "You three were supposed to be in that car, not Louey Santera."

"It was that bad man," Emma said. "He came

back to get me, but he killed Daddy instead."

She looked at her smashed piano, and gently laid it on the grass. "Look at all the broken keys." She came down on her knees beside it and gently pressed the middle C. A sharp tinny sound pinged out. Her face went very still. She picked up the piano again, clutched it to her chest, and walked back into the house. Molly caught her in a moment, and pulled her up into her arms.

"I'll call the police," Ramsey said to Mason Lord.

"There will be no police on my property."

"Oh, yes, there will."

• **Molly** didn't make a sound as Mason Lord's own personal physician, Dr. Theodore Otterly, sewed up her arm. Ramsey felt the ripples of pain, the tensing of her muscles, but she didn't complain. He'd put two chairs together, sitting on the back one to support Molly in front of him. Dr. Otterly asked him to help support her, so Ramsey put his arm around her, under her chin, his hand cupping her shoulder. She leaned her chin on his arm. Emma was holding her hand. Her wounded arm was resting on the kitchen table. All of Dr. Otterly's medical stuff was spread out on the table. Molly flinched, then drew a deep fast breath.

Suddenly Emma made a small mewling sound. Ramsey said easily, "I know, Em. This is tough, but your mom's hanging in there. If you want to say something, say it."

"Are you all right, Mama?"

Her voice was small and thin, her fear stark. Molly didn't know where she got a smile, but she managed to manufacture one. "Hey, Em, this is nothing. I'm mean and tough, just like Ramsey. I can take these little hits. I'm a macha. Don't you worry, kiddo, I'm just fine."

He felt her shudder again and tightened his arm around her. She leaned back, letting him support her weight. Dr. Otterly had helped him off with his jacket, probed at his shirt a moment, then said he'd deal with Molly first. He was vastly relieved. He didn't want an injury that would shut him down for even a short time. Events had gotten out of control, and he couldn't afford to be out of control as well. But damn, his back hurt.

He was aware that Mason Lord was standing back by the kitchen door, his arms folded across his chest. He hadn't said a word, just stood there. Miles was seated beside Emma, holding her other hand. He knew the police had arrived. He'd heard sirens and voices, running feet.

"Ramsey, your back is all black. I mean your shirt is all black. I hope you're not black underneath."

"Dr. Otterly just grunted when he saw it, told me not to whine, that he wanted to see to your mom first. He knows I'm okay, Emma," he said, glad he couldn't see exactly what that crashing piece of upholstery had done to him.

Dr. Otterly set the last stitch in Molly's arm. He wet a thick cotton ball with alcohol and dabbed it against the stitches, getting off the last of the blood. He straightened. "That's good, Mrs. Santera. All over now. Just a couple of shots. Let me get you bandaged up and then we'll see to Judge Hunt."

Molly ended up with a sling. "To keep those stitches from pulling even a little bit," Dr. Otterly said.

When it was Ramsey's turn, he felt Emma take his hand. "I'm here, Ramsey. It's okay."

"Thanks, sweetheart. I need you to be here."

The pain was bad, but he managed to keep himself still. It felt as if a year had passed, a very painful one, before Dr. Otterly got his shirt off and his back cleaned. He said, "It's not as bad as I thought it would be. Your jacket saved your bacon. You've got a small second-degree burn on your back which means it'll blister and take a little bit longer to heal. You've also got some bruising. I'm going to apply some antibiotic ointment and put a bandage over the area. Leave it be for a day or two. You'll be just fine, Judge Hurt.

"If either of you has any problems, just give me a call. Oh yes, here are some more pain pills like the ones I've already given you. Mrs. Santera, you'll need them for the next three days or so."

Dr. Otterly smiled down at Emma. "Now, young lady, I've got a treat for you."

Emma didn't believe that for an instant. She

took a step back. He laughed. "No, no, I promise nothing horrible. I just want you to drink some orange juice." He nodded to Miles. In a couple of minutes Miles handed her a half glass of orange juice. "Now, Emma, you need to drink it down."

She clearly didn't want to.

Ramsey said, "How can you make sure that your mama and I take care of ourselves if you're not in top-flight form?"

He saw she wasn't sure what that meant, but it was enough. She drank down the juice. Dr. Otterly patted her head, nodding to Molly.

"Em, will you see me upstairs? I'm a little bit shaky. No, I'm all right, but I've got to say that my arm isn't very happy with me. I'm also kind of worried about Ramsey. Yes, I need to lie down for a little while. Will you come with me?"

After Molly and Emma left the kitchen, Mason Lord said, "Will my daughter be all right?"

"I didn't lie to her, sir. The metal didn't slice that deeply, so I didn't have to repair the muscle. I gave her a tetanus shot and an antibiotic.

"Don't get me wrong. Although Judge Hunt's back wound isn't as severe as I feared it would be, your daughter's wound is bad enough. I'd say they were both very lucky with all the burning car fragments hurtling around."

"And Molly's daughter? What did you give her in that orange juice?"

Dr. Otterly had to think a moment, then nodded. He said, "Oh, you mean your granddaughter. Emma's okay. I slipped a bit of a sedative in the orange juice. She'll start feeling sleepy in just a little while."

He turned back to Ramsey. "Both you and Mrs. Santera need to rest. It's the best thing for both of you. No heroics. As I just said, take the pills. Rest." He eyed Ramsey's back, frowned, and pressed down another strip of tape over the bandage. "There, that should hold it. I hope you've got a good psychologist for the little girl?"

"Yes, we do. We were on our way to see her when all this happened. One other thing, Dr. Otterly. I got a gunshot in my left thigh some two weeks ago. Do you think you could take a look at it?"

"Here I thought that a judge's life was pretty staid. Drop your pants, Judge Hunt, and let me take a look."

When Dr. Otterly was done prodding and probing, he said, "You're just fine. Whatever you did, it worked. The flesh has grown together nicely, not even much of a scar. Have you got full strength back yet in the leg?"

"Not all of it."

"Another week or so and you'll be running again. I wish you luck, Judge Hunt. Call me if there's any sort of problem." He nodded to Mason Lord.

Ramsey thanked him again and held himself still while Miles helped him on with a clean shirt. It didn't hurt.

Thank God Emma had escaped being hurt. Only she hadn't escaped, not really. It was another blow, a really big one.

Ramsey walked slowly with Mason Lord to the living room where Eve was answering questions for the police until they got there. Ramsey was relieved that Mason Lord hadn't put up much of a fight about their coming, had even agreed to speak to them. Not even he could try to kiss them off through his lawyers after a homicide. Neither Ramsey nor Molly had seen the police yet. He wasn't surprised that Molly had gone straight upstairs with Emma to try to keep her from the police. He just wished he could have gone with her, too.

Three plainclothes officers sat on the edges of their chairs, looking uncomfortable, as if they had hemorrhoids, amid the stiff opulence and, naturally, in the company of Mason Lord's gorgeous young wife. All three of them rose when Ramsey and Mason Lord walked into the living room.

Mason Lord introduced himself, nodded coolly to each of the three men, then sat down beside his wife. He looked down at his fingernails and began to swing his leg.

Immediately, one of the men turned to Ramsey. "Judge Hunt? I'm Riley O'Connor. It's a pleasure and an honor to meet you, sir." Detective O'Connor was at least fifteen years older than Ramsey, skinny as a one-sided board, and bald. His dark eyes glittered with intelligence and humor. "We're very pleased that you're all right." The two men shook hands. Detective O'Connor introduced the other two officers, Sergeant Burnside and Detective Martinez.

Mason Lord cleared his throat. "Do you have all the information you need, officers?"

Detective O'Connor arched a very black eyebrow. "No, sir, we've actually just gotten started. We've got a murder on our hands, a particularly violent murder. Mrs. Lord hasn't really had time to tell us much. And you just got here. However, I'd like to speak to Judge Hunt first. Then perhaps you'd be free, sir?"

Mason Lord gave Detective O'Connor an infinitesimal regal nod, rose, and walked to the sideboard to pour himself a brandy.

"Fine," Ramsey said. "Let's go to Mr. Lord's study. Is that all right, sir?"

Mason Lord didn't look happy. But he had no choice. He nodded. The other two detectives rose to go back out to the burned-out Mercedes, to join the forensics team combing the remains. Ramsey overheard one of them say, "I heard there isn't much left of him, after the blast and fire."

Detective Martinez said to Sergeant Burnside, "The three of them were lucky beyond belief. This is a weird one, Tommy, really weird. That guy, Gunther, didn't tell us a thing. I've got this feeling that we're not going to find out anything at all from anyone who works here."

"Yeah, and I wonder what Judge Hunt is doing here, with a guy like Mason Lord? Talk about a straight arrow."

Ramsey couldn't make out any more words. A straight arrow, was he? He rather liked that.

Beside him, Riley O'Connor laughed. "This is really something for us, Judge Hunt. I'm really sorry, but it's all going to come out now, everything about the kid's kidnapping, you guys being followed all over the West, and now this. Yeah, both fact and supposition. But I guess you know firsthand what the media spotlight can do. You can be a devil or a saint, depending on the reporters' likes and dislikes, and how nice you've been to them. As for the photographers, I'll bet you've wanted to slug some of them."

"Oh yes," Ramsey said, remembering the paparazzo outside hiding in his bushes, the final straw that had sent him to the Rockies where he'd found Emma and discovered that he really hadn't had any problems worth a damn. "On the other hand, this does need to come out. I want the press to have a field day. I'll personally cheer them on."

"Why?" Detective O'Connor cocked his head, his eyes trained on Ramsey's face.

"One reason: to protect Emma. Maybe the people who are after her will back off once everyone knows there's some sort of conspiracy afoot and that the press is going to plunk themselves in the middle of it."

"Conspiracy?"

Ramsey just smiled at him. "Just a moment, Detective."

They went into the study and Ramsey closed

the door. His back was beginning to ache. He must have winced because Detective Riley O'Connor said, "I heard it was a nasty hit you took in the back."

"Yeah, a slice of burning car upholstery. It's not so bad as the cut Mrs. Santera took on the arm. It landed flat on me, didn't slice the skin. She's with her daughter." Even as he was saying the words, there was a knock on the door. It opened. Molly appeared, pale, her arm in the sling, her hair a wild nimbus around her thin face. Her eyes were large, calm, and very green, not even a speck of gray. He noticed, for the first time, that she had a faint line of freckles across the bridge of her nose. He liked them.

He realized she was near the edge. He took a step toward her, then stopped. "Molly, what are you doing here? Is Emma all right?"

She raised her hand and lightly touched her fingers to his mouth. "It's all right. Emma's just fine. She's asleep or I wouldn't have left her. Miles is keeping watch over her. I wanted to meet the police, tell them everything I know. There's no reason for them to have to repeat everything separately with me. Besides, I imagine that you and I will be the only forthcoming witnesses in this household. When we tell the detective the whole story, maybe I'll remember something you forget and vice versa." She walked forward, her hand out. "I'm Molly Santera."

Detective O'Connor looked at a loss. "The dead man—Louey Santera, the rock star—he was your husband?"

"Ex-husband. Louey and I had been divorced for two years."

"Molly, would you like a brandy?"

She started to shake her head, then paused. "You know, that might just work some magic."

Ramsey poured all three of them a small amount of brandy and handed it around. Detective O'Connor smiled at him, gave a mournful look at the brandy, and set the glass down on an end table. "Thank you," he said. "Perhaps later."

"This will take some time, Detective."

O'Connor took a small tape recorder out of his coat pocket. "May I record our conversation? That'll be best." They listened to him identify himself, them, the date, the place. Then he said clearly, "What I was saying about the media, Judge Hunt, is that with Mr. Santera's death, there'll be almost as many TV vans here as there were in L.A. covering the O.J. trial. When all the stuff about your daughter's kidnapping gets out, the good Lord only knows what will happen."

"It can't be helped," Ramsey said. "Now, I think we should all start with you, Molly. Detective O'Connor needs the whole story. Whoever blew up Louey Santera meant to kill the three of us."

"Yes," she said, her voice just a whisper of sound. She drank some more brandy, and set the nearly empty snifter on a side table. She cleared her throat. "It started with Emma's kidnapping. Goodness, Ramsey, that was only about three and a half weeks ago."

"Emma was taken from your house, Mrs. Santera?"

"No, from the small park just behind our house. I was photographing there." She stopped, just stopped cold. Her hands were clasped in her lap, her knuckles white.

Ramsey said, his voice sharp, "It wasn't your fault, Molly. Just tell Detective O'Connor exactly what happened."

Just then the door opened again.

Special Agent Dillon Savich and Special Agent Lacey Sherlock Savich, both of the FBI, walked into the room.

Savich said, "Hi, Ramsey. I'm real happy to see you in one piece. Things have really turned ugly. We heard about the explosion on the ride in. You remember Sherlock, don't you? Everyone remembers Sherlock."

Dillon Savich looked over at Riley O'Connor, smiled, and stuck out his hand. "We're with the FBI. Don't worry. We're not here to bigfoot you. We're friends of Judge Hunt's. We just want to help."

• **Dr.** Loo looked at Emma's new piano, fresh out of its box. She plunked a couple of keys. She smiled. "Do you know how to play 'Twinkle Twinkle Little Star'?"

"Yes, Dr. Loo. But it's been a long time."

Ramsey grinned at Emma. "Why don't you give her the theme and some variations, Emma?"

Emma gave him a small smile before she looked down at her new piano. The finish

242

was so glossy she could see her face in it. She swallowed hard. She laid one finger gently over F. She didn't press the key down. Slowly, she turned to Dr. Loo. "I'm sorry, but I can't play right now. It doesn't feel right. My old piano just died."

Ramsey thought he'd cry. Oh, shit. He beat Molly to it. He picked Emma up, leaving the piano on the small table, and gathered her to his chest. "You're right, sweetheart. You need to mourn your old piano for a while. Dr. Loo can hear you play on your next visit."

Dr. Loo, who'd heard from Molly exactly what had happened, didn't mention the violent death of Emma's father. Rather, she said, "Mason Lord sent an artist over, Emma. We would like you to describe that man who kidnapped you, that same man you saw look in your bedroom window at your grandfather's house. Can you do that?"

Emma looked worried, then, slowly, she nodded. "I can try, Dr. Loo."

An elderly bald man was shown into Dr. Loo's office by the receptionist. His name was Raymond Block and he'd been a police artist for twenty-seven years. "Don't worry," he said to all of them. "I've worked with children all my career." Then he sat down beside Emma and opened his drawing pad.

"Are you ready, Emma? No, wait a moment, Mr. Block. I need to scratch inside my cast."

Dr. Loo didn't leave them until it was done. It took Mr. Block forty-five minutes of drawing, erasing, widening, elongating, more drawing, more erasing. Finally, Emma said, "That's him."

Mr. Block turned the drawing so that Dr. Loo, Ramsey, and Molly could see it.

"Oh, dear," Molly said, staring at the excellent drawing. "Are you sure that's the man you saw at the window, Emma? The man who kidnapped you?"

"Yes, he was the man who stole me. And then he came back and he smiled at me through the window."

Ramsey just shook his head back and forth, quelling a weird desire to laugh and cry at the same time. "Well, this fellow isn't any pool man who works down the street from your house in Denver, Molly. No, I think he resembles someone who lives in a much more prestigious place."

It was an excellent rendering of President Clinton, only he had very bad teeth.

19

Two hours later, Ramsey and Molly sat opposite Dillon Savich and Sherlock in the small breakfast room off the kitchen. Miles had served coffee and some special nut bread he said he'd baked just that morning. He said Emma had told him she liked nut bread, but only with walnuts. Miles and Gunther stood in the shadows back by the outside door.

"Yeah," said Ramsey. "It was an excellent likeness of President Clinton."

Sherlock, who was drinking some of Miles's rich Jamaican coffee, choked.

Savich slapped her on the back. "Get a hold, Sherlock. It may not have been a coincidence. It may have been a mask. But he wore a mask the whole time? That would get real uncomfortable."

"Yes," Molly said, handing Sherlock a glass of water, "but it also means that they—whoever they are—wanted Emma alive, and they continued the disguise so she wouldn't be able to identify that man later."

"It still doesn't make sense," Ramsey said, picking a big chunk of walnut out of the bread. "Then why the attempts on our lives? Believe me, Savich, someone wanted Emma, alive? Dead? I'm not sure which."

Sherlock took another sip of her coffee, then shuddered. She said, "This coffee is delicious but I think it's trying to kill me."

"You shouldn't drink it in any case. You're pregnant. It's not good for you."

"Thanks for announcing it," Sherlock said, grabbed her stomach, and flew through the door Miles quickly opened for her. "Just down the hall on the left," he shouted.

Savich shook his head. "I forgot. You won't believe this, but usually she's just fine. But when I mention the word *pregnant* in front of her, she has to heave."

Ramsey started to say something, then shook his head, smiling. "I'm not going to go there, Savich." He stuck out his hand. "Congratulations."

"Me too," Molly said.

"She'll be just fine when she gets back, and I'll try harder to watch my mouth. Poor Sherlock. She hates it when she loses control."

"She married you," Ramsey said. "She can't hate losing control all that much."

Savich laughed. "Point that out to her and see what she has to say."

Molly said, "You're both FBI agents, you're married, and she's pregnant. You have a transgender laptop and you took a week off to come and help us. Why?"

Suddenly serious, Savich leaned forward, resting his chin on his clasped hands, his elbows on the table. "I've known Ramsey for a while now. We were both in law enforcement, Ramsey with the U.S. Attorney's office in San Francisco, and I with the FBI. We found we had a lot in common.

"We've kept in touch. I admire him, Mrs. Santera. I don't like what's happening. As for Sherlock, she's been a special agent less than a year now, but she's tough and bright, and although she's pregnant, she wouldn't have dreamed of not coming. Uh, if you could not mention the word *pregnant* in front of her, both of us would appreciate it."

"So it's anyone who says the word *pregnant?*"

Savich grinned at Ramsey. "As in she blames any messenger or just the guy who got her in this condition?"

"That's it."

"I don't know. I thought it was just me.

Maybe you could drop the word by accident and we'll run a small scientific experiment."

"I wouldn't do that to another woman," Molly said. "Thank you both for coming."

"No problem. This is a royal mess. Sherlock doesn't like what's happening to you guys, either. So, this guy was either wearing a Clinton mask or he was a master at makeup and disguises. But it'd have to be a really good mask for Emma not to have realized it was a mask. I vote for a guy who's really good at disguises."

"Yes, that sounds more reasonable," Molly said. "Emma even put bad teeth in Clinton's mouth. Emma's bright."

Ramsey said, "I'm not her mother, but she's right. Emma's three dozen points sharper than Molly's razor."

"I told you not to use it."

"I was lucky not to cut my throat." He turned to Savich. "Did you mean it? You're not here to take over the case from the locals?"

"Nope. Sherlock and I are off for a week. But I've got MAXINE—"

"MAX experienced another sex change just three days ago," Sherlock said from the doorway, a wet washcloth in her hand. She daubed at her forehead, but she was smiling. "It's happened twice since I've known Dillon."

"I might have thought it meant MAX didn't know how to relate to her," Savich said. "That he was trying to make an accommodation since he knew she was here to stay. But the fact is he's gone back and forth now for about four years."

Ramsey said simply, "Molly and I both appreciate your help."

"We know that, Ramsey." He smiled up at his wife. "You okay, Sherlock?"

She nodded. "Just a brief brush with the devil." She turned to Molly. "That's what Dillon calls it every time I'm sick. Now, we'll put every scrap of information we can get our hands on into MAXINE and see what she comes up with." She saw that Molly didn't understand. "Dillon is the chief of the Criminal Apprehension Unit or CAU at the FBI. We don't do profiling, but we work with the profilers and with local law enforcement to catch serial killers. We use a number of programs that Dillon's developed. We plug in all the information we can get our hands on, including everything from the local police, the forensic reports, the autopsy reports, witness statements, you name it. MAXINE isn't better at figuring things out than real people, but he or she, depending on the month, is faster and looks at the data in many different ways. In just the first year, we solved six cases along with the local cops. We think we can apply that experience to help us catch this monster."

Savich said, "Ramsey, I'll speak to Agent Anchor and get all the reports on the cabin where Emma was kept. There's bound to be some physical evidence left. I'll get MAXINE to work on child molesters who have an M.O. of using disguises."

Ramsey said, "Emma said he smoked, had

bad teeth, and drank. Once when she was coming out of a nightmare, she remembered he'd said that he needed her more than God needed him."

Molly said, "He also used twine to tie her up." She swallowed and looked down. "He used twine because she was just a little girl."

"That's a start," Savich said.

Sherlock patted Molly's shoulder as she said, "Dillon and I took a week's vacation. We're at your command."

"I already told them," Savich said, pulling her down onto his lap. "They haven't applauded just yet, but when they see what we can do, they'll do handsprings. I'll also speak to the police in Denver. We can add stuff from forensics from the explosion. Sherlock can help us by translating what you know into data for MAXINE."

"Then we push a button and MAXINE becomes the brightest Cuisinart on the planet," Sherlock said. "While Dillon talks to the cops, why don't we make a list of all the things you guys can remember.

"Where," Sherlock began, "do you think Louey Santera planned to go if he did manage to get the Mercedes off the estate?"

"Nowhere," Molly said. "He hadn't thought that far ahead. He was scared and he lost it. He did that sometimes."

"This time it was fatal," Ramsey said. "Poor bastard."

"Not a poor bastard if he was the one who

staged Emma's kidnapping," Molly said, her voice hard. "How will we prove it if he was behind it?"

"Follow the money," Savich said. "I'll get a warrant to search through all Santera's financial records. There's always something there, always."

"You don't need a warrant. I'll get the records." Mason Lord stood in the kitchen doorway, Gunther standing right behind his right shoulder.

"I'd just as soon you didn't do anything, Mr. Lord," Savich said. "It's our job. Let us do it on the up and up. Admittedly it takes a bit longer. On the other hand, it's legal. There are advantages to being really legal in this situation."

Mason said, "I know Louey's accountant. I will speak personally with him. Warren will plead to tell me everything he knows, to show me every record he's ever entered. Warren has always been useful and informative."

"You know," Sherlock said slowly, eyeing Mason Lord, wondering how he could be so utterly different from her own father yet look so remarkably like him. Both men had power, but they were on opposite sides of the law. "Just maybe since Mr. Lord and Mr. Santera's accountant are such good acquaintances, it wouldn't be a bad thing. What do you think, Judge Hunt? Does that sound kosher enough to you? Would evidence from such a source give the defense a shot at an appeal?"

"Not that I can see. Hey, why not? We're

on Mason Lord's turf. Let him glean information for the case." He grinned at Lord. "I would discourage breaking and entering, though."

In that instant Molly realized her father had been standing there stiff as a poker. Now she saw him ease up, saw those aristocratic hands unclench, the long lean fingers uncurl. The cops were admitting him. They wanted to involve him. He didn't smile, no, he'd never go that far, but there was something in his expression that held at least some degree more warmth than usual.

• **Warren** O'Dell was completely bald—probably through shaving—and looked like a longshoreman, exactly the opposite from what you'd expect of an accountant. He did wear wire-rimmed glasses, though. He had something of the look of Michael Jordan.

When he spoke, you saw he had yellow teeth from too much smoking. He had calluses on the pads of his fingers and his palms. He spared one glance for Ramsey, his full attention on Mason Lord. Then he did a double take. "I know you," he said, staring hard.

Ramsey smiled and said, "I'm Ramsey Hunt."

"You're that federal judge in California who jumped over the railing and chopped up a group of terrorists in your courtroom."

"That's the way things worked out. It was just a little group."

Mason Lord cleared his throat, and suddenly

Warren O'Dell turned pale. "Uh, sir," he said, nodding his head and making a sweeping gesture with his hand toward an expensive white leather sofa. "Please, sit down. I was devastated at the news of Louey's death. I was going to call you."

"Were you now, Warren?" Mason Lord said. "Why?"

It was obvious that Warren O'Dell was scared spitless. He was standing in the middle of his beautifully furnished office on the nineteenth floor of the McCord Building on Michigan Avenue looking as if he wanted to jump out a window.

"Yes, sir," he said finally. "I would have called you as soon as it happened, but it was such a shock, you know. I couldn't pull myself together until just this morning. Louey's dead, blown up by a car bomb. I can't believe it. It doesn't seem possible. I heard you allowed the cops to investigate?"

Ramsey felt a small ripple of surprise in his gut. Did O'Dell consider Mason Lord to be some sort of god with total immunity?

"It was murder, Warren. I'm a law-abiding citizen," Mason said, his voice austere, as if he'd been the one to insist on the cops coming in. He looked toward Ramsey. "Judge Hunt is the man who saved Molly's daughter."

"Oh, yes, now I see. I couldn't imagine why he was here, with you, seeing me. It's the shock of Louey's death. It's shaken me badly. I gave my girl the day off I was so upset."

"I see you have some boxes shoved behind

your desk, Warren. I don't suppose you were planning to destroy some documents? Perhaps in preparation for a nice long vacation?"

"Oh no, sir. I was just cleaning house. Nothing more."

"I'll see that you get any assistance you require," Mason said.

"No, sir, I'm just fine, really."

Mason Lord barely raised his voice. "Gunther."

The huge man was there in the doorway, looking dead on at Warren O'Dell. As if O'Dell were a bug, Ramsey thought.

"Yes, Mr. Lord?"

"We need to assist Mr. O'Dell. See those boxes shoved behind that impressive mahogany desk of his? We'll take those and have a look at them. Ramsey, maybe you would be so kind as to look through Mr. O'Dell's file cabinets."

"I have some questions first," Ramsey said.

"Please, Mr. Lord, there's really nothing—"

Mason Lord raised his hand. O'Dell was instantly silent. "Judge Hunt wants to ask you some questions, Warren. You will answer them completely and honestly."

Warren O'Dell's bald head glistened with perspiration. He watched Gunther carrying out the boxes. He licked his lips. "Yes, sir."

Ramsey felt exceedingly strange. Here he was with a powerful criminal boss who had a potential witness nearly pissing in his pants, and he, Ramsey, a federal judge, was a co-conspirator in what was probably extortion,

253

at least duress. Who cared? "Mr. O'Dell, tell me about Mr. Santera's finances."

Warren O'Dell swallowed. He looked again toward Gunther, who was coming back into the office, his gun in its shoulder holster clearly visible because his coat was open.

"Louey was broke," he said at last. "Dead broke. He was doing this tour to try to pay off his debts. There's nothing now that he broke his contract, not even loose change."

"Louey was broke?" Ramsey repeated. "Did he owe a lot of money?"

"Louey wasn't ever big on denying himself. Then he got butt-deep in debt. There's this small consortium in Las Vegas. I think they arranged for Louey to lose heavily at the craps table, which he did. He was a lousy gambler, but he wouldn't admit it. He thought he was the greatest in just about everything. No, in everything. He was into them for nearly a million dollars. They kept him gambling and he couldn't begin to pay them off. They just kept adding on interest. They made threats. On him, on your daughter, sir, and on your granddaughter."

"Names, please, O'Dell," Ramsey said. "Give me names and then give me records."

Mason Lord rose and walked to the small bar, a chrome-and-glass affair on wheels with three gold leaf–framed glass levels. He picked up the brandy decanter and poured an inch into a snifter. He never turned, just stood there, looking out the wide windows, sipping on the brandy. He said quietly, "I know who it is."

"Who, sir?" Ramsey asked.

"Rule Shaker. Am I right, Warren?"

"Mr. Rule Shaker's the main player, yes sir. Louey had turned him down on a long engagement to play in Las Vegas. Mr. Shaker insisted, Louey kept saying no, even after he was in for all that money. That's when he decided to go on tour in Europe. He thought he could make back all the money. He's very popular in Europe, much more so than here in the U.S. He would have been able to repay Mr. Shaker if he'd stayed on his tour."

Ramsey said quietly, "You must have heard that Emma and Molly were the targets of that bomb, not Louey."

"Yeah, I heard. That's why I was heading out of town, until things settled down, just as Mr. Lord said. Mr. Shaker told Louey that no one he knew was safe. He was the one behind the car blowing up, there's no doubt in my mind about that. But he didn't want to kill Louey. He was after Louey's kid. He wanted to use the kid to show Louey he was serious."

"You think then Mr. Shaker also ordered Emma taken?"

Warren O'Dell said, "Louey was sure it was him. Didn't surprise me either. Louey called me from Germany. He didn't know what to do. I didn't either."

"Yes," Mason Lord said. "Rule Shaker had Emma kidnapped. Rule's killed Louey by mistake. I wonder why?"

Mason had spoken very quietly, but Ramsey had heard him. He said to Warren O'Dell,

255

"How much money did Louey make before he died?"

"About three hundred thousand. There would have been taxes, of course, and some extra overhead we hadn't figured in, but he was getting there. If he'd been able to finish his tour, he might have been able to pay back every cent."

"Where's the money?"

"I don't know."

"You're his accountant," Mason Lord said, his voice soft and clear as he turned from the huge glass window. "His accountant. Louey was particularly feckless, couldn't even seem to understand the most basic concept of how the dollar worked. I'm sure you must have been the one who guided him after he and my daughter divorced. I know that she handled all the finances during their marriage, but after? No, Warren, it was you. Now, tell Judge Hunt where the money went."

"I'm not lying, sir. I swear to you, I don't know. Louey wouldn't tell me. I've got the records, sir. Withdrawals from the bank, nearly all of it. He just took it out, didn't say a thing to me."

"When did he withdraw the money, Mr. O'Dell?" Ramsey asked.

"Just before he went to Germany. He was broke, but he still managed to talk the backers out of a huge advance, nearly two hundred thousand, if I remember correctly. Another hundred thousand was coming later, after he was in Germany performing, and that's gone too.

Louey took all of it. He didn't tell me a thing, I swear it."

Gunther stood by the door, silent.

"You have all of Mr. O'Dell's papers?"

"Yes, sir."

"Then we'll be off. Judge Hunt, do you have more questions for Warren?"

"Yes. Where were you early this morning?"

Warren O'Dell looked as if he was going to faint. He cleared his throat. He swallowed and made himself cough. He said at last, "I was home in bed."

"Was anyone with you?"

"Yes, my girlfriend, Glennis."

"Give me her phone number."

In another four minutes, Ramsey was on the phone speaking to Glennis Clark, a waitress at the Downtown Diner over on O Street. He spoke quietly for several minutes. Finally, he hung up. "Unless you have excellent ESP, Mr. O'Dell, and a very strong connection to Ms. Clark, it appears you're telling the truth."

Ramsey nodded and walked with Mason Lord to the door of the opulent office. He turned and said, "Who are you hiding from, Mr. O'Dell?"

"Mr. Shaker. He already called me. He's very angry, claims I'm responsible for Louey being in that car. Now that Louey's dead, he won't get his money back."

"A million bucks is a spit in the ocean for the likes of Mr. Shaker. Why is he really so angry?"

"Because he can't have Louey," Warren

O'Dell said finally. "He really wanted Louey. When he realized that Louey would earn back the money and he couldn't use the debt as leverage, then he kidnapped the kid. Jesus, he'd kill me if he knew I'd told anybody."

"He wanted Louey to perform in his casino?"

"That, too."

20

It was after nine o'clock that evening. Everyone had finally moved from the dining room into the huge living room for coffee and some of Miles's low-fat apricot tarts. Emma had begged to stay up so she could help Miles load the dishwasher. After she'd left in Miles's wake for the kitchen, Ramsey told everyone about their encounter with Warren O'Dell. When he said, "And then Mr. O'Dell said Rule Shaker really wanted Louey," Molly stared at him, disbelieving. "He's gay? This Mr. Rule Shaker wanted Louey Santera for a lover? Is that what he meant?"

"Yeah," said Sherlock. "What's all this about?"

Ramsey just smiled. Both Sherlock and Molly had understood it just as he had. Their incredulity was as great as his had been.

Savich sat back in his chair and said, "I'll bet there's an unexpected punch line here. Come on, Ramsey, spit it out."

Ramsey smiled wider, nodding to Mason Lord as he said, "As it turns out, it was Mr.

Shaker's daughter who wanted Louey. Her name is Melissa and apparently she's the apple of her daddy's eye. Anything she wants, Daddy gets for her. It was Louey she wanted, and so Mr. Shaker went after him."

"And ended up killing him." Molly was tired to her bones, worried sick about Emma, and now some gangster's daughter had wanted Louey? She continued, "So her daddy rigged a craps game so Louey would lose big time? And when that didn't work, you're saying this Mr. Shaker had Emma kidnapped to make Louey fall into line? Then he sent men after the three of us? Finally he tried to blow Emma and me up and killed Louey by mistake?" Molly jumped up from her chair, nearly knocking it over. She began pacing up and down, her eyes fastened on the toes of her black Bally loafers. "No, that's as nuts as this Shaker guy being gay. What kind of monster is he? That's sick."

Mason Lord narrowed his eyes on his daughter, "Get a hold of yourself, Molly. Louey could have had his own daughter kidnapped so he could get his hands on my money and pay back Rule Shaker. It would further seem that finally Rule Shaker tried to kill Emma so that Louey would be frightened enough to do as he wanted him to do. It was business."

"Mason's right," Eve said. She gracefully set down her coffee cup. "If there's something you want badly enough, then you must be prepared to do whatever is necessary to gain it."

"Despite the costs?" Molly asked.

"Costs are part of doing business," Mason Lord said.

"No," Ramsey said. "Louey didn't have a thing to do with any of it. Don't you see? There wasn't enough time to get another team in there working for a different master. Emma was kidnapped; I found her; then the two men came to the mountain cabin and tried to shoot us. Then two others probably followed us all the way here. No one knew where Emma was except the people who took her. All these acts seem connected, they're all part of the same piece of cloth."

Mason Lord was chewing on an unlit cigarillo. He said slowly, "Well, it's a lot simpler to think that Louey wasn't involved at all."

"I've got a headache," Molly said, going toward the door. "It's late and I don't think I can help us anymore. I'm going to go to bed."

"I'll come with you," Ramsey said. "Sherlock? Savich?"

"I want to speak to MAXINE about all this just a bit longer," Dillon said from where he was sitting near the fireplace in a massive leather chair, his laptop on a small table in front of him. "She's been chewing over some information while we were talking."

Sherlock said, "When she's finished chewing, then, doubtless, MAXINE will want to speak to me. When she's a female, she communicates better with another female. We'll be up soon."

Mason Lord held out his hand to Eve. "Shall we go up, my dear?"

"Certainly, Mason," Eve said, smoothing the silk of her dress over her hip. Every man's eyes followed that move.

Mason Lord turned at the doorway, slight bewilderment in his voice, "I have a judge and two FBI agents staying in my house. This isn't what I'm used to."

He left without another word. Ramsey would have laughed, but he felt too much tension. He rubbed his neck. Emma would have remarked that her granddaddy had made a joke. Mason Lord knew this Rule Shaker, or at least he knew of him. What did he really think of all this? He as well as all his staff had been politely unhelpful to the police. What would Mason Lord do?

Savich stood and said to Ramsey, "You want to go work out? That is, if your back's up to it?"

Sherlock said to Ramsey, "Working out is great for his stress. I usually work out with him. I used to let him throw me around, under the pretext of teaching me karate. He tromped me regularly until he found out that I was in this interesting condition, then he refused even to let me watch him. You two go; it'll be good for both of you. I'm beat. Molly, I'll head on upstairs with you."

Molly gave Ramsey a worried look, but he just smiled, nodding at her. "I'll be up later," he said. "Tell Emma I'll be in to kiss her good night." He knew she was thinking about Emma, whose father had been blown up, and it had to be dealt with.

"Let's do it," Ramsey said. They didn't have to leave the compound or even Mason Lord's house. Gunther took them to the downstairs of the west wing to a state-of-the-art gym, actually more like a sports facility.

Ramsey said when they came out of the locker room, "Look at this. You think we're in the wrong line of work, Savich?"

Savich fastened on a weight belt. "Nah, it doesn't matter. Hey, the equipment might be the best, the mats might be the thickest, the bottled water might be from France, but the end result is still sweat. Let me help you tape your back up really well before we get the kinks out. I can even make you waterproof."

After Savich taped him, they both stretched for five minutes, then, as if of one mind, they began circling each other, poised and focused. Ramsey made the first move, a high clean kick with his right foot. Savich stepped three inches to the left, grabbed the ankle with his right hand, and pushed. Ramsey went flying to the floor, only to roll to the side and be back in position in an instant. He felt a twinge in his back, and Savich noticed.

"You're a bit faster than Sherlock, but not much, Ramsey. I don't think your back's ready for this. Why don't we just spot each other on the equipment?"

After thirty minutes, they ended up on their

backs on the mat, their arms flung out, sweating and feeling better. After twenty laps in the swimming pool, they felt even better.

"Not bad," Ramsey said as he hauled himself out of the pool onto the cool pale blue tile apron. "I'd forgotten how busting my butt relieves the tension. My back doesn't feel so bad either."

"It's always worked for me."

Ramsey gave Savich a hand out of the pool. They sat in silence, soaking in the sweet still air in the huge enclosed pool room. "This place is something," Savich said. "So much foliage, it looks like a rain forest."

"As long as it doesn't have any boa constrictors under those palm fronds."

"Look," Savich said quietly, nodding only slightly upward. "It's a TV camera. Well, what did I expect—our host to give us a welcome kiss and let us roam at will? I'll bet there are microphones as well."

"Who cares? I'll have to ask Miles to show me the equipment," Ramsey said. "It looks like high-grade stuff from here."

"Think he has any female security people?"

"No," Ramsey said, "not Mason Lord. He's not what you'd call a major employer of women. I've seen him look at his wife. There's actually lust in his eyes and a sort of immense satisfaction that she's his and no one else's. I'm a bit surprised that he bothered to marry her, except that maybe he wants to get himself a son." Ramsey shook his head. "Mason Lord probably had to marry her just to get into her pants. Eve's very smart."

Savich said, "Safe bet, huh?"

"As for Molly, well, she seems to deal with him pretty well. When we showed up here, I could practically taste her fear of him, the pressure to be the helpless little girl grateful for her daddy's help, but at the first insult from him, she dug in her heels."

"You backed her up, I assume?"

"Yeah, even though I didn't know the players then. I didn't realize then what a big deal it was for him to back down. I do now. And he did back down, Savich."

"You'd have to be blind not to notice what he thinks of her. That's got to have been tough on her. Jesus, I hope he doesn't show his stripes too obviously in front of Sherlock. She'd take a strip off him."

"I bet she would. Good choice, Savich. I like her. She's tough and she's smart and she seems to think you're pretty hot."

"Ramsey, what do you really think is going on here?"

Ramsey slowly rose. He was nearly dry. His back was beginning to hurt. He'd probably pay for the exercise, but right now, he was still glad he'd done it. He picked up a big dark gold towel and wrapped it around his shoulders. It was very soft, money soft. He shook his head, lifted an end of the towel, and wiped his face. "What's going on here?" he repeated, still drying his left ear. "I don't know, Savich, any more than you do. I'm too close. I care too much for the players. I do know one thing: To put a bomb in that Mercedes means that someone here on the premises had to have done it. No one could have gotten in here and planted that bomb without being seen. But nobody's coming right out and saying it. I wonder what Mason Lord is going to do."

"How much do you know about Molly Santera?"

Ramsey cocked a dark eyebrow not at the question itself, but the seriousness of Savich's voice. He said slowly, "I know she's fiercely protective of Emma. I know she's brave and tough, just like Sherlock. I know she can focus on one main thing and disregard everything else. She's also got great hair. Red like Sherlock's, but not at all the same shade. It's more like a sunset I once saw when I was on the west coast of Ireland."

Savich didn't say anything to that. He looked away, wishing things could be different, but, of course, they weren't. He said finally, "Did you know that one summer when she was about twelve years old she supposedly let her younger brother drown?"

Ramsey dropped the towel. He stared at Savich. He was shaking his head. "No," he said, "oh no. I can't believe that, Savich. That's not at all like her."

"I'm sorry. Sherlock discovered it in fifteen-year-old records. I'm sorry if you think she was spying on something that wasn't her business, but Sherlock is a professional to her fingertips. She looks at everything."

"I have no problem with Sherlock checking out my birthmark if she thinks it's relevant to this case, but I'm telling you that this thing with Molly's brother, it had to be an accident. Molly could never just watch her own flesh and blood die. No way. And that includes that son-of-a-bitch father of hers."

Savich shrugged. "There was an investigation, of course, but the results were inconclusive. The general belief at the time was that she hated her younger brother because Daddy made it clear he was the favorite, the heir, the only one worth anything. You told me yourself that Mason Lord doesn't have much use for his daughter. Maybe you're right, maybe that's one reason he married Eve. He wants another boy child.

"Mason Lord and his first wife, Alicia, were divorced when Molly was around eight years old and her brother was six," Savich continued. "She went with the mother back to her mother's home in Italy and the boy stayed with the father. Molly was visiting here one summer when this happened. When she was eighteen, she went to Vassar. She left after a year and moved in here with her father.

"You can't just dismiss it out of hand, Ramsey. Molly Santera has a past. She may have been innocent, but you know there was a question about it. We can't afford just to ignore it."

Ramsey said, "Are you suggesting that she'd have anything to do with Emma's kidnapping?"

"No, I don't believe that. But how about Louey's murder. What if Louey was the target after all?"

Ramsey said, "Listen, she divorced his worthless ass. There was no reason to kill him. Besides, she couldn't have known that he would try to escape. It was a spontaneous thing; Louey just lost it and ran."

Savich rose to stand facing Ramsey. "What if she convinced him that her father was going to kill him? What if she told him he'd best clear out and he could take the Mercedes, that Gunther had just brought it up? Isn't that possible? Just think about it, Ramsey. None of us have known any of these people for very long. Don't sweep it under the rug because you happen to admire the lady, just because you think her hair's cool."

Ramsey felt his heart pounding against his chest. It made his back ache even more. He didn't believe it. He was a good judge of character. He'd seen Molly in crunch situations. She hadn't faltered, hadn't broken, hadn't flipped out. He said aloud, "She would have no clue how to fashion a bomb. That means she would have had to hire someone in a very short length of time. Not likely."

"She's Mason Lord's daughter, but maybe you're right about her. You really seem to know this woman very well, even though it's only been for a short time." He sighed, and rubbed the back of his neck. "What better person to bring someone onto the estate in secret? And how do you know she wouldn't know how to rig a bomb?"

Ramsey just stared at him. He shook his head. Then he turned and walked away. His back was throbbing.

21

The night was dark with thick clouds hanging low, the air heavy with coming rain and sweet with the scent of the late-spring flowers. Ramsey shifted to his side, pulling the covers with him. He'd flung the pillow on the floor some hours earlier.

He flipped onto his back again, his left arm over his head. Then, suddenly, he was thrust into a dark room where there were blurred images, voices that overlapped one another, growing louder and louder. Suddenly the room was clear, the images sharp. He was in his courtroom, jumping over the guardrail, his black robes flying, his legs straight out, his foot kicking the semiautomatic out of a man's arms, sending it spinning across the oak floor. He heard the snap of the man's humerus, heard his howl of rage, saw the wild pain in his eyes. Then he saw terror and panic, saw him leap toward the gun even as he held his broken arm.

He was on him again, with a back-fist punch to his ribs that sent him sprawling to the floor. The din of screaming people filled his mind. A second man whirled around to face him, the semiautomatic raised, ready, and he'd rolled, coming up to twist his hips as he parried, seizing the man's wrist so he wasn't in the line of fire. With his free hand he went after the man's throat, crushing his windpipe, watching him gag, hearing his gun slam against the spectator railing. The screams were high and loud. They went on and on, filling the courtroom, filling his mind, seeping into his brain. He saw the third man now, whirling around in a slow, very precise movement, saw the point when failure registered in his brain, saw him raise his gun and fire randomly, striking the shoulder of one of the defense team, a young man in a pristine white shirt that was instantly shredded and soaked red. The force of the bullet flung him back against three women who were cowered down in the first row of spectators. The man turned back to him, his eyes filled with panic and death. Ramsey felt the heat of a bullet as it passed an inch from his temple, and rolled, picking up the semiautomatic, aiming it even as he lay on his side, and pulled the trigger. He saw the man flung hard against the wall, his blood splattering against the wainscotting. The screams wouldn't stop, just grew louder and louder.

Ramsey jerked up in bed, breathing hard, sweat sheening his forehead, and covered his face with his hands. So much blood, as if it had rained blood.

"It's all right, Ramsey."

It was Emma. She was sitting beside him, her small fingers lightly stroking his forearm. "It's all right. It was a nightmare, a bad one, like mine sometimes. Don't worry. I won't leave you, not until you're okay again."

"Emma," he said, surprised that he could even get the word out of his mouth. He swung his legs off the side of the bed, pulled the little girl onto his legs, and drew her close.

"I heard you," she said against his shoulder. "I was scared for you."

"Thank you for coming. It was a bad one. It happened three months ago. I haven't dreamed about it for several weeks now."

"I'm sorry it came back. What was it, Ramsey?"

"I had to kill someone, Emma."

She drew back and gazed up at him. His eyes were used to the darkness and he could see her clearly. She looked at him with calm and utter certainty. "You must have had to, that's all. Did they deserve it?"

He stared down into that child's face with her eyes that had felt far too much pain and seen horrible evil. He owed her the truth.

"Yes," he said slowly, never looking away from her. "They deserved it. They broke into my courtroom. They had guns. They wanted to free the drug dealers the jury had just found guilty. They started shooting jurors. So I stopped the carnage."

"What's carnage?"

"Emma? What are you doing here, love?"

She turned toward the door. "Mama, Ramsey had a nightmare. I heard him and knew he needed me. He dreamed about car-nage."

Molly blinked at that.

"Hello, Molly," Ramsey said. "I'm okay now. Emma's made me see things a bit differently."

"Can we help you get to sleep, Ramsey?"

"I smell like sweat, Emma. You don't want to stay close to a sweaty guy."

"You're drying off, Ramsey. It's not too bad." Emma yawned, her head falling forward to Ramsey's chest. He looked toward Molly, who was standing in the doorway, wearing a white sleep shirt that had across the front in blue lettering, *F-Stops Are My Specialty*.

Molly shrugged. "Why not? Emma and I can stay on top of the covers. Here's another blanket I can cover us with. I'm surprised I didn't hear you. I just realized Emma was gone a moment ago."

As Molly climbed in next to Ramsey, pulling Emma next to her, she said, "Next time it'll be my turn to have a nightmare."

"Are you all right, Ramsey?"

"I'm much better now, Em, that you're here."

"Tell me about the nightmare, Ramsey," Emma said, leaning up over her mother. "Mama says it helps when you say everything out loud," and he did. It was easier this time.

Molly said, "How did they get into the courthouse with guns?"

"A guard was bribed. He's in jail." He felt himself begin to ease. He had no more words.

The shadows were reclaiming the blood and the death.

"Yes, I remember now. That was in the articles I read. Well, it's over now. Does your back hurt?"

"No. It wasn't much of a burn, Molly."

"Good," Molly said. Emma was breathing deeply in sleep. Molly lightly touched her hand to his shoulder. "I'm very glad you weren't hurt."

He tightened like a spring. He cleared his throat and said, "I'm sorry I'm sweaty."

"There are three blankets between you and us. You haven't sweated them through."

He heard Emma's rhythmic breathing. She'd crashed. He hated himself, but he couldn't stop the words. "Tell me about your little brother, Molly."

He felt her stiffen, then felt the whisper of her sigh in the silence. "He was such a sweet little boy. He was just ten years old that summer. He was a good swimmer, which was why I was on the dock, not really paying all that much attention. I was probably thinking about some thirteen-year-old boy, I was just about at that age. Then he was yelling and going under. I swam to him as fast as I could but he never woke up.

"It was a reporter who first wrote that it might not have been an accident. My father was a ruthless criminal. Why would his daughter be any different? I was devastated. Teddy was dead and I was some sort of evil seed."

"If there's one thing I'm sure about, Molly, it's the quality of your seed."

She laughed, sadness and relief in her voice, then she leaned over and kissed his shoulder.

He was content when he fell asleep.

• **"The** police have already interviewed Rule Shaker, with his lawyer present, of course," Savich said to a full audience the following morning just after they'd finished breakfast and trooped into the living room. "Detective O'Connor called me just a while ago. He said that Rule Shaker is giving them all the same kind of cooperation the president gives to Congress. That approach stretches things out forever and ends up leading anybody anywhere.

"Rule Shaker just sat there behind his big chrome-and-glass desk, smoking his Cuban cigars, and swearing he just wanted Louey Santera to come play in his casino. He freely admitted that Louey lost a good deal of money at the craps table, so what? What reasonable man, what reasonable businessman, he asked, would kill a man who owed him money?

"When the cops pointed out that Louey might not have been the target, Mr. Shaker very politely informed them that any operation he ever undertook was done right. A screwup would have been impossible with him running it. Then he offered both O'Connor and the Las Vegas detective a cigar."

Everyone just stared morosely at Savich.

Mason Lord said, "That sounds like Shaker. He's an arrogant little bastard."

"Sorry, guys," Savich said, "ain't nothing easy in this life, even when it involves bastards."

Miles cleared his throat at the door. "Detective O'Connor is here."

O'Connor looked very tired; he had bags under his eyes that hadn't been there just two days before. He tried to smile, but didn't make it. "Hello. I got by the reporters and photographers intact. Your men are dealing well with them, Mr. Lord, no violence, but they're firm. There aren't more than a dozen out there today. Ah, I see that Agent Savich is giving you all a rundown of what I didn't accomplish in Las Vegas." He turned to Savich. "Do you have anything for us?"

"MAXINE just might, Detective O'Connor," Savich said, grinning. "Actually, we've had her plugged in all night. We're just waiting for her to cough something up."

Mason Lord cleared his throat. "My dear, would you like to ask Miles to bring in coffee?"

"Of course, Mason," Eve Lord said and rose gracefully from the elegant wing chair she'd been sitting in. She hadn't said a word until that moment, hadn't really called any attention at all to herself. But when she stood, all the men's eyes began to swing toward her. She was wearing tight white jeans, a top tied beneath her breasts, her pale blond hair long and loose, smooth as a silk swatch down her back. Every male eye in the room watched Eve Lord walk to the door, open it, and leave the living room. There was nearly a collective sigh of lust.

Ramsey smiled as he said, "Detective O'Connor, we didn't mean to interrupt you."

"Well, I can tell you that we spoke to Mr. Santera's accountant, Warren O'Dell, last evening, after you'd seen him. He was telling the truth, as far as we can tell. Louey Santera did personally remove three hundred thousand dollars from his account. We won't know what he did with it.

"About the bomb," Detective O'Connor continued. "It was hooked directly to the ignition switch. The parts are common, but we're checking for leads. It was professional, no doubt about that. Mr. Lord, we'd like to speak to your staff again, at some length, beginning with Gunther. You said, Mr. Lord, that he was the man who brought the Mercedes up from the garage."

"Yes, that's right. He brought it around at about five o'clock in the morning. I was awake and so was he. He had the time, so he washed the car. Gunther does that. When he finished, he just brought it around. He doesn't know anything more or he would have told me. This is my estate, and I know everything that goes on here."

"Evidently not," Molly said, ignoring the look her father gave her.

O'Connor said, "Someone could have rigged the bomb in the car, but not turned it on until they were sure who would be in the car. Unless, of course, Gunther told anyone who he was bringing the car around for. You must realize, Mr. Lord, that someone on the estate must have been involved."

There, it was said out in the open.

Mason Lord said in his mildest voice, "That is one opinion, Detective O'Connor. Now, there is, of course, the man who works here to take care of my cars. I have a fleet of six. He also lives on the premises. But I know you've already spoken to him. It's possible that Gunther would have said something to him, I suppose. I'll send him to see you, Detective."

"I would appreciate some cooperation from your people, Mr. Lord."

Mason Lord just looked at him, one eyebrow arched. Then he rose and left the living room, saying nothing more.

"Judge Hunt, can you think of anything else?"

Ramsey said slowly, "I remember vividly when the car blew up. For an instant you just don't register that it's really happening. Your brain doesn't want to accept it as real. It's like this special effect in a movie. Then it hits. It becomes real and terrifying.

"As to whether there was anyone else, no, I saw only Louey rush out of the bushes and yank the car door open. I remember he was wearing a blue shirt, short sleeves, no jacket. He looked frantic."

O'Connor said to Ramsey, "Of course we've searched those bushes. We'll look again. Anything else?"

Ramsey shook his head. "I asked Mason

about Rule Shaker, but he refused to say anything much about him."

"I wouldn't expect him to, Ramsey," Molly said. He suddenly remembered those two kisses on his shoulder blade in the night. He wished now it had been his mouth. He'd told Savich what Molly had told him about her little brother, Teddy. And Savich had looked off into the distance, thinking his own private thoughts, and finally nodded.

"Yeah, whichever way you want to translate that," Detective O'Connor said. "The point is, though, that Mr. Shaker wouldn't ever let a trail, particularly a murder trail, lead anywhere near him. If he was responsible for Louey Santera's death, we don't have what I'd call a very good chance of connecting him personally to it.

"We've got court orders to take a narrow look at his financial records, to see if there's anything to indicate that he had dealings with Louey Santera, and if he did, what they were. The cops in Las Vegas told us he goes out of his way to keep his nose clean. Even the IRS is happy with him at the moment."

Detective O'Connor rose. "I'm really sorry, Mrs. Santera, but we're no closer to finding out who took your little girl and abused her. It really bums me out."

Molly nodded as she rose to face him. "If we're right about what happened, the danger's over simply because Louey's dead. I don't want to live with that, but I guess I'll have to learn how to. Emma's safe now, thank God. But I want that monster who abused her, raped her, and beat her. I want him. I want him to burn for what he did."

"I promise, Mrs. Santera," Detective O'Connor said, taking her hand, "we're just getting started with this." Molly thought there wasn't much hope in his voice.

After Detective O'Connor left, Molly looked around and said, "I've got to get things together for a small memorial service for Louey. I owe it to Emma. He was her father." She and Sherlock left the living room, speaking quietly to each other.

"It's just down to us two," Ramsey said. "I'm depressed."

Savich said, "Miles never brought any coffee." He leaned his head back against the sofa. "How's your back, Ramsey?"

"What? Oh, it's fine. I only took two aspirin yesterday."

"I didn't want to tell Molly, but we really don't have much," Savich said. "MAXINE agreed with Detective O'Connor, indicates there's a high probability that Rule Shaker in Las Vegas is behind all of it. But MAXINE needs facts, and we're short on them."

"You were here, and I appreciate it. Let's go scare up some coffee."

"You know, I was thinking that Sherlock and I might as well fly to Paris," Savich said. "We've still got five days." He laughed. "Doubtless Mr. Lord will be relieved to see us law-enforcement types out of his digs."

"I still wish we could catch the guy who abused Emma."

"I'm sure O'Connor isn't lying to make Molly feel better. No one likes that kind of scum on the loose. We'll all keep working, but for now, well, we can hope that it's over."

22

Ramsey and Molly were standing in his bedroom, he by the window, she at the door. It was early morning, and the house was still quiet. His suitcase was open on the bed, some of his clothes packed. He looked up to see her standing there.

"You're leaving, then?"

Ramsey shrugged, looking over at the suitcase on the bed. "Yes, I think so. I couldn't sleep, decided I might as well start to pack." He paused. "Did you know I was trying to write a novel? It seems like a million years ago."

"No, I had no idea."

"That's why I was there at that isolated cabin in the Rockies. I took a leave of absence for five months. I had to get away from all the media hype, all the reporters. One guy even stuck his head in my bathroom window one morning when I was shaving. I nearly sliced my own throat. That's when I decided to leave town for a while. I decided to write the novel I'd thought about for the past year."

"What's it about?"

"A courtroom novel, about a judge in the federal court system. It's a subject I should know well enough, a subject I'd like to say a few things about."

"I see. So you want to go back to Colorado? To write?"

"Yes, I suppose so." He fiddled with a loose thread on his pale blue sweater, remembering her kisses on his shoulder. He looked at her. "Actually, I was wondering when you would be going back to Colorado."

"I hadn't really thought about it, not yet. All this is still sinking in. I'm willing to accept intellectually that this awful man, Rule Shaker, from Las Vegas, is behind everything that's happened, but there's still that monster who abused Emma. I won't ever forget that. I've got lots of money. I think I'll spend some of it trying to find him myself."

She looked defensive, as if she expected him to argue with her. He said, "I'd do the same thing. In fact, I'm going to be putting the word out as soon as I get home. Pedophiles have networks; they seem to either know one another or of one another. I've got several friends who spend a lot of time on the Internet. I'll see where that leads." He drew a deep breath. "Savich will keep the fire lit by alerting all the FBI field offices. He's not happy about this either."

She looked down at the soft nap of the carpet beneath her feet. "Well, I guess I should thank you, Ramsey. Emma will miss you."

He looked up at her, at the dark shadows in

her eyes, and that dancing line of freckles across the bridge of her nose. He said, "I told Savich that your hair isn't at all the same color as Sherlock's, although most people would just say you've both got red hair. I told Savich your hair was the color of a sunset I saw once in Ireland."

The nap lost her attention. She blinked up at him. "A sunset in Ireland? When were you in Ireland?"

"Two years ago. I was staying in Ballyvaughan. Nearly every day I went to the Cliffs of Moher. You really can't describe how awesome they are, because you just say something like they're rugged cliffs with waves crashing and billowing up against the rocks, that they dip and then push right to the very edge of the sea, but that really doesn't tell you." He shrugged again. "You see what I mean? You haven't got a clue really how it actually makes you feel just to be there, to look over the water into the distance where there's no sign of anything."

"I'm beginning to," she said.

He ran his fingers through his hair, standing it straight on end. "Dammit, you're nice, Molly."

"Tell me about this sunset."

He looked mildly embarrassed. She grinned at his hair, though he was now smoothing it back down. He hadn't shaved yet. He looked tough and hard and she saw him in that moment with Emma on his lap, holding her against his chest, his big hands stroking her

281

back, her face against his shoulder. He was wearing slacks and a T-shirt, his feet bare. She had intruded. He was going to leave.

It didn't matter. It couldn't matter. He had his own life. Hers and Emma's had intersected his briefly and violently. It was time.

He was going to leave.

It wasn't what she wanted, but she wasn't going to try to change it. He said quietly, "I'll never forget this one evening I was at the Cliffs of Moher. The air was crisp and dry and the sky perfectly clear. No Irish rain that day. I sat there and watched that red ball of sun slowly sink into the Atlantic. You almost expected the water to hiss and boil when the sun sank into it. People around me were talking and laughing and joking around, until that precise moment. Then there was a hush and everyone was silent and still. Just staring at that red ball sinking under the horizon." He shook his head, bemused at the memory. "I'll never forget that sight as long as I live." He paused a moment, then looked at her. "I remember the next day it rained so hard it was like payback time for that incredible sunset. You know, Molly, I was just thinking that maybe you'd like it as well, both you and Emma. Not the rain, although that's beautiful too, no, the sunsets."

"Emma and I? Go to Ireland?"

"Yes. With me. I don't want to leave you."

The morning light was dim and gray. Her expression wasn't clear to him, as she kept her head down. After a very long moment, she raised her head and looked across the room at him. She said, smiling, "Yes, I'd like that. I'll bet Emma would too."

He felt a shock of pleasure. The strength of it surprised him. He smiled back at her. "Savich and Sherlock are going to Paris. They're leaving from O'Hare this morning."

"They're very good people."

"Do you think we could go to Ireland soon? We could all just get away for a while. I think it would be good for Emma."

"I don't have our passports. They're at the house in Denver."

"Mine's in San Francisco. We could pick them up and meet in New York. Or back here in Chicago. Or best yet, I could go with you and Emma to Denver and then all of us could go on to San Francisco. How about that?"

She started laughing, her hands splayed in front of her. "I didn't know you a month ago."

"No, you didn't. On the other hand, we've probably been through more in the past weeks than most people have in a decade, or at all, for that matter."

"You really think my hair is the color of that sunset?"

He gave her a slow smile. "Yeah, that's what I think."

"Is your back really all right?"

"Yes. Your arm?"

"It still throbs sometimes, but it's not too bad. These stitches aren't the kind they have to take out. They'll resorb by themselves,

Dr. Otterly said. I couldn't believe you went to the gym with Savich, though. You could have hurt yourself more."

"My back has barely blistered. Besides, I was careful. Savich taped me up pretty well so I wouldn't stress anything, and so I could swim." Then he grinned at her. "Yeah, I was stupid."

She laughed at him, shaking her head. "I didn't say that."

He just smiled at her. "I'm worried about Emma. Is she asleep?"

"I hope so. She wakes up a lot. Three times this last night. Still the same dreams. And she dreams about the car exploding."

"I suppose we need to ask Dr. Loo about taking Emma to Ireland this soon."

"We can ask her this morning how Emma's doing, if she thinks a trip would be good for her. I can't think of anything better."

He was surprised how giddy he felt that she was going to go to Ireland with him. It was as if a knot he felt in his belly were loosening. It had just come out of his mouth, unplanned. He really hadn't thought about it at all.

Well, maybe without knowing it. He hadn't really wanted to be separated from either Molly or Emma.

"What time is her appointment?"

"Ten o'clock this morning."

"Let's see what she says before we make definite plans, then."

Molly straightened the sash on her robe, a glamorous peach silk thing that she'd obviously borrowed from Eve Lord, her stepmama. He wondered what she'd look like without it. She gave him another smile. "Ireland, huh? Did you go there alone before?"

"No," he said. "I didn't."

"No," she said, "I don't suppose you'd do anything alone unless you wanted to."

"What's that supposed to mean?"

"Even with a burn on your back, Ramsey, a lot of women would find you an appealing kind of guy."

"Thank you. Go back to bed, Molly. It's too early to be up and about yet."

"What about you?"

"Yeah, now that we've made some plans, I think I'll sack out for another hour myself. I'm not nervous and uptight anymore. It's a miracle."

She nodded, then her smile fell away. "Oh yes. I've made the arrangements for a small memorial service for Louey this afternoon, here on the estate. I even found a Presbyterian minister to come and give a service."

"It's good," he said. "It's good for Emma."

"I hope so."

• **"Emma,** are you ready to play 'Twinkle Twinkle Little Star' for me?"

"Yes, Dr. Loo, I think so. But I haven't played a piano seriously for a long time."

"It's okay. I don't mind."

Emma straightened her new piano on the low coffee table. Dr. Loo sat in a chair, Ramsey and Molly on a love seat opposite her.

"Don't forget the variations, Emma," Ramsey said.

This time Emma didn't hesitate. She took a deep breath, one that sounded appallingly adult, and played with one hand the simple notes of the song, beginning with F. Once she'd played through the tune, she added the left hand. It sounded classical, like Mozart. The next time through, she changed it to a jazz sound, then to a definite John Lennon feel.

Dr. Loo blinked. She looked shell-shocked. When Emma finished, she leaned forward, took Emma's small hands between hers, and looked her in the eye. "Thank you, Emma. You've given me great pleasure. I hope someday to hear you perform at Carnegie Hall."

"What's Carnegie Hall?"

"It's where great artists from all over the world come to perform. It's in New York City. I heard Liam McCallum play the violin there. It was an incredible experience. You could be there too, Emma."

"Yes," Molly said, "I think she might."

"My papa never played at Carnegie Hall," Emma whispered, not looking up from her keyboard. "But he was a great artist, Mama said so."

"Yes, he was," Molly said. She looked as if she was going to burst into tears. Ramsey sat forward. "I have one of your dad's CDs, Emma. Even though he didn't make it to Carnegie Hall, everyone in the world can hear him. All his music will live on."

"That's what Mama said."

"And when was the last time your mama was wrong?" Ramsey said, lightly stroking his fingers over her French braid, one that he'd done himself. It wasn't bad, hardly crooked at all, and the plaiting looked pretty smooth.

Emma raised her face then. She thought really hard. "It's been a long time," she said finally. "Maybe two months ago."

Ramsey laughed.

"Now," Dr. Loo said. "It's time we talked about you going to Ireland with your mama and Ramsey."

Emma said, "I don't know what Ireland is, Dr. Loo."

"It's a beautiful wild country that's across the ocean. It's a place to enjoy, Emma, a place where you can look at things and maybe see them in a different light. It's a place where you can stop being afraid, where you can play your piano, where you can run in the mornings with Ramsey and play Frisbee with your mama, and have picnics. It's very beautiful, Emma. You can sit on the rocks and dangle your toes into the water. It's so cold you yip in surprise. You'll be with two people who love you and want you to be safe and happy. What do you think?"

Emma drew back between Ramsey's knees. "Will that bad man be there?"

Ramsey rubbed his hands lightly up and down her thin arms. "No, he won't. We'll never let him get close to you again. I promise, Emma."

Emma turned to face him. "He's close,

Ramsey. He's real close now. He killed my daddy. He wants me now."

"No, Emma, he doesn't. He's very afraid, and he's running and hiding now because he knows the police are after him. I'd like him to be caught. Then he'd be in jail for the rest of his life. Everyone is trying really hard to catch him.

"I do know one thing for sure, Emma. We won't ever let him come near you again. Do you believe me?"

Emma looked up at him for a very long time. Molly was aware that she was holding her breath. Emma continued to be silent, but she finally released her breath, letting it out slowly and quietly. She looked at Dr. Loo, who just smiled and shook her head slightly.

Dr. Loo took a quick look at her watch and stood. She pulled Molly aside. "It will take time. Don't push her. I can already see that both you and Judge Hunt are dealing with this very well. I think Ireland is a fine idea. However, I think Emma and I should meet tomorrow. When had you expected to leave?"

"It doesn't matter," Molly said, her eyes on her daughter. "Emma's what's important. We'll leave when you think it's right and not before."

"She's doing well, Mrs. Santera. She really is. But this sort of thing—it will be with her forever. You must face that and find a way to deal with it. Her feelings about it will change as she grows up. Most of it will fade into blurry vague memories, and that's good, but it won't ever disappear. But now, she's just a little girl. She doesn't have a clue about the concept of rape. She knows this bad man hurt her badly, and that it wasn't right, but there are no grown-up connotations. What you're dealing with right now are feelings of fear and remembered helplessness.

"Eventually, she'll have to understand that what happened to her can't be changed, that it was real, and that the trick is for her to learn to deal with it so that it doesn't ruin the rest of her life. It's not going to be easy for either of you. You'll put out a fire then another one will crop up in some other context.

"She's lucky that you're her mother. I know that Judge Hunt has known Emma for a very short time, but they trust each other, their affection seems to be deep and abiding."

"It will be difficult when Judge Hunt returns to his home," Molly said.

Dr. Loo let a couple of seconds go by, then said in that comfortable, matter-of-fact voice, "Well, these things have a way of working out. Tomorrow I'll meet with Emma alone. I want to speak to her about the abuse, try to make her see that the man wasn't normal, that it wasn't in any way her fault, that this didn't happen to her because she was bad."

"But how could she possibly feel that way?"

"Children, Mrs. Santera, children can bring almost everything back onto themselves. Also, we have no idea what the man said to her, how he manipulated her, how he terrorized her, or how he hurt her. It's always the adults who screw up royally. I have to deal with Emma now from the inside of her head. I'm telling you not to worry, but of course you will, both of you."

"You won't want either Judge Hunt or me here?"

"I think it would be better between the two of us. You would find it very upsetting. I can see Judge Hunt becoming quite enraged. No, just Emma and me."

"If you think that's best, Dr. Loo. You will call me, won't you?"

"Of course." Dr. Loo turned back to Emma with a smile. She leaned over and patted her shoulder. "I'll see you tomorrow, Emma. In the meantime I want you to get a lot of rest and try to smile at least three times a day at your mama."

"How about me?"

"And at least six times for Ramsey. I've found that guys need more smiles than girls do. Remember that."

• **Ramsey** smiled down at Emma. It was early afternoon, two hours before Louey Santera's memorial service. He'd brought her upstairs for a nap, just tucked her in. "I like your jazz variation, Emma. Did you know that Mr. Savich plays the guitar and sings? Yep, country and western. He performs in a club. It isn't Carnegie Hall, but it's a neat place, he told me. He also has a friend who plays the saxophone. He and Sherlock want us to visit them."

"I wish they didn't have to leave. Sherlock

290

told me that she hoped she was going to have a little girl just like me. She said that Mr. Savich felt the same way. She said they both thought I was really neat. I told her that that wasn't a good idea. I'm not very good anymore."

Ramsey looked down at the child he'd give his life for. He'd just kissed her forehead, just complimented her on her music, and now this. He gently pushed her hair back from her face. Before he could think of what to say, Emma continued, "Sherlock's face turned red. She was really mad, but she said she wasn't mad at me."

"You, my perfect Emma, not good? Where'd you get a weird idea like that?"

She looked away, into a past that still had a hammerlock on her, a past that hemorrhaged into the present. "That man said I would save him. I didn't know what he was talking about."

Ramsey wanted to kill. He forced down a deep breath, slowed it, tried to calm himself. This was something for Dr. Loo, but she wasn't here, he was, and the rage he felt couldn't help her. "Listen to me, Em. This man who kidnapped you, he's sick in the head, really sick. What he thinks, what he does, it has nothing to do with you—Emma Santera. He would have hurt any little girl he could find. You weren't Emma to him. Do you understand?"

"No," she said finally. "I don't understand. It's scary, Ramsey."

He leaned down, his forehead touching

hers. He kissed the tip of her nose. "Listen up, Emma. We're on a roll here. The three of us together, we'll take on the scariest thing you can dream up. You're a very good little girl, Emma. In fact, you're so good that the thought of not having you with me makes a big dent in my heart. That's how good you are."

She gave him a big smile. One small hand stroked his cheek. "You won't leave, Ramsey, will you? You won't go back to your house?"

He took both of her hands between his and kissed her fingers. They tasted like the gingerbread that Miles had baked for her at lunchtime. He didn't really know what the future would bring, but he knew he couldn't tell that to her. Her life had been smashed, her father murdered, and he said now, without hesitation at all, "I won't leave you, ever, Emma."

"Good," she said, and yawned.

"Emma?"

"Yes, Ramsey?"

"Will you be a brat for me just once? Maybe when you get up from your nap? Or this evening? I know, you could whine about having to drink your milk or finish your dinner or having to go to bed? Throw a kid fit?"

She smiled at him. "Sure."

"You want to take a nap now?"

"Okay." She closed her eyes, then opened one and squinted up at him. "But maybe I won't go to bed tonight."

"Fair enough." Actually, he just wanted to get her through her father's memorial service. He hoped they could continue to keep out all the reporters, the local TV stations, and the paparazzi. The guards had ably assisted one reporter back up over the compound wall and out onto the road. He prayed that Emma wouldn't pay any attention to the impertinent questions that flew at him and Molly whenever they went outside the gates.

23

Melissa Shaker was crying so hard she nearly tripped down the steps leading into the garage. It had been two days now but she still couldn't believe it, didn't want to believe it. That damned ex-wife of his had held a dip-shit little memorial service, no actual funeral because there'd been nothing to cremate or bury.

Louey was gone, just simply gone, and nobody cared. Except her. She tripped again, grabbing the handrail to steady herself as she stepped into the underground garage. A car horn honked loudly. She felt its hot exhaust as it whooshed past her, the driver yelling at her to pay attention.

She wiped her eyes. There was nothing to do. Just nothing. Her father had sworn he hadn't killed Louey, but she'd looked into his eyes and seen guilt. She would never forgive him, ever.

"Miss Shaker."

She didn't want Greg anywhere near her. She wanted to be alone. She wanted to drive out into the desert and let the sun burn into her. She kept walking toward her car.

"Miss Shaker! Please, wait up. You know your father's orders, particularly now."

She waited for him simply because she didn't want to get Greg fired when all he was trying to do was his job.

She stopped by her BMW roadster, painted James Bond blue. It was exactly like the one he'd driven in a movie, except hers was more powerful. She loved that little car.

"Thank you," Greg said as he trotted up to her. "Listen, Miss Shaker, I'm really sorry."

"Thank you," she said, and got into the car. Greg came around the other side.

"Don't try to lose me, Miss Shaker. It's important that I stick close to you, particularly during the next week."

"They gave him a measly memorial service," she said, and turned the key.

The car exploded into flames.

• **It** came on the local Las Vegas news brought in via satellite at twelve-twenty in the afternoon.

> *Melissa Shaker, twenty-three, daughter of Rule Shaker, Las Vegas casino owner, was killed at ten A.M. this morning when she and a friend were in an explosion involving Ms. Shaker's car that was parked in the underground parking lot beneath the Sirocco Casino.*
>
> *Arson experts say a bomb was involved.*

*Police haven't yet said if there are any sus-
pects. Details at five o'clock.*

Ramsey dropped his fork, sending the thin
slice of ham slithering off onto his plate. He'd
heard the TV playing from the kitchen, wondered why it was even on, wondered why it was
turned up loud enough to hear in the dining
room, wondered why it was on satellite to
get a local Las Vegas station, and now this. And
now all his questions were answered.

Obviously someone had known it would
make the local Las Vegas noon news. Obviously someone had been waiting for this.

There was an instant of shocked silence, then
everyone was talking. He heard Eve gasp,
heard her say something, but he couldn't
make out her words. There was a crash of a
pan that Miles must have dropped in the
kitchen. At the head of the table, Mason Lord
continued to eat his casaba melon, not missing a beat. There was a slight flush on his
cheeks, but he said nothing, did nothing out
of the ordinary at all.

Molly had been saying something to Emma.
She stopped in mid-sentence. She looked
over at her father and said quietly, "An eye for
an eye, Dad?"

Mason Lord chewed on the bite of melon,
gracefully laid down his fork, and looked at
his daughter. "I suggest you refrain from
such talk, Molly, particularly in front of your
daughter."

Emma, attuned to the change in the most

important person in her world, pulled on her mother's sleeve. "Mama? What happened?"

Ramsey watched Molly pull herself together for Emma's sake. She banked the horror in her eyes and smoothed her expression into nothing more than a soft smile for her daughter. She turned to Emma, hugged her close for a moment, and said, "I taste something strange in Miles's quiche. What do you think?"

Emma gave her that weary adult look. "The quiche has bacon in it, Mama, and fresh spinach. I watched Mr. Miles make it. He even let me add the eggs. The quiche is just fine."

Molly looked as if she'd just been smashed on the head with a cannonball. She was having a tough time getting it together. "I'm sorry, Emma. You're right, of course. I don't know, love, I guess I just don't feel well."

Molly looked over at Eve Lord, who sat to her right at the foot of the table, her face tight, as white as the tablecloth. She was staring at her husband. Then, suddenly, Eve turned to Emma, and her face was again as smooth as a madonna's. "I gave the quiche recipe to Miles. My mother was an excellent cook. I'm sorry your mother doesn't like it."

"I think it's time we had coffee," Mason said. "Miles?"

Ramsey said, controlling his voice, "I would like to speak with you, Mason. Shall we take our coffee to the living room?"

"It's a beautiful day," Eve Lord said, staring again at her husband. "Mason said that we would go out on the yacht, Ramsey. Perhaps you can speak with him later?"

They heard the phone ring. Miles appeared around the door of the dining room. "Judge Hunt, it's Agent Savich. He, uh, wants to speak with you."

Ramsey tossed his napkin on his plate and walked quickly to the kitchen where Miles stood patiently, holding the phone.

"Sherlock and I are at O'Hare. We just heard about the murders in Las Vegas. I can't believe this, Ramsey. The man has balls, I'll say that for him. You want us to come back?"

Ramsey wanted them back in the worst way, but there was nothing they could do, nothing anyone could do, really. How selfish did he want to be? "No, Savich. Take Sherlock off somewhere and make her happy. Just let me know where you're staying in Paris so I can call if there's occasion to sound the cavalry trumpet."

"It's a little *pension* on the Left Bank," Savich said. "Sherlock wants to show it to me. We'll let you know the number. Did Mason say anything? Have you seen him?"

"Oh yes. We all just heard it on the news at the dining table. It didn't even touch him that there were a federal judge and FBI agents in his house when he gave the orders."

"Here's what I think. Just get out of there, Ramsey. Take Molly and Emma, and check out of the Bates Motel. You don't need this. It's vengeance. Don't get involved. There's nothing you can do in any case."

"I can't believe you're saying that."

"I'm saying it as Molly and Emma's friend. You don't want them in the middle of something that could shape up into a nice little personal war. There's been tit for tat. Don't stay to see if it goes another round. Just get out."

Ramsey said slowly, "You're right, of course." He rubbed his hand over his forehead. "I feel that I should question Mason, handcuff Gunther. No, you're right. It's Molly's and Emma's safety that's most important. I'll call you in a couple of days, let you know what's going on."

They spoke a bit longer, and then Ramsey laid the phone slowly back into its cradle. It was an old-fashioned black rotary, one that Miles had picked out specifically for his kitchen, he'd told Ramsey when he was whipping up pancakes for breakfast one morning.

Ramsey turned slowly to see Miles standing at the island, chopping celery. A chopped red apple stood in a bright pile to one side. Green grapes, sliced in half, formed another pile. Miles said in a very precise voice, "I'm making Waldorf salad."

"Did you know this was going to happen, Miles?"

"You know I can't say anything, Ramsey. Leave, sir, that's my best advice to you. Take Molly and Emma and leave. Since this man Shaker was behind everything, you're safe now that Louey's dead. Just leave."

"Unless Shaker plans his own vengeance now. Unless he plans to escalate. If he does, we're in really deep."

Miles shook his head, chopped some more celery in sure quick strokes, and said, "It doesn't work that way. It's over. One player knocked down, one opposing player knocked down. Everything's even again. Those are the rules. Nobody breaks the rules."

The horror of it bubbled out of him. Ramsey slammed his fist down on the counter. "That's sick and you know it."

Miles just shrugged. "No one will miss Louey Santera. No one will miss this Rule Shaker's daughter. Leave it alone, Ramsey. Get Molly and Emma out of here."

Ramsey, his jaw locked hard from disbelief and tension, left the kitchen. He looked only at Molly when he reached the dining room. "Come upstairs with me, will you?"

"Yes, certainly."

Then he realized that Emma was sitting there, quiche on her fork, staring at them. Ramsey calmed himself. "Em, would you do me a favor?"

She wanted to ask him questions, he could see that, but he shook his head at her. "Would you come upstairs with your mom and me?"

Five minutes later, after they'd settled Emma with a book on animal husbandry for children in her bedroom, all of them knowing it was a ploy, especially Emma, Molly and Ramsey were standing alone in his bedroom.

He said without preamble, "I see no reason to stay. Do you?"

"No, no reason at all," Molly said, pulling a silver ring off her pinkie finger, then pushing it back on. "He's a monster, Ramsey. My father just blew up a twenty-three-year-old woman."

"That's the league he plays in, Molly. The media should be back here anytime, if they haven't already pulled up to the front gates. Let's fly to Denver today, to your house. You and Emma can pack stuff for Ireland, then we'll go to San Francisco. Okay?"

Molly said more to herself than to him, "Ireland would be beautiful, I've seen pictures." Then he saw a sparkle in her eyes. "I could begin work again. I could take my cameras."

He realized it would be a new beginning for Molly. And for himself as well. "Yes, bring all you need. Will you take a photo of Emma for me?"

"You don't think the media will follow us, do you?"

"I doubt that we're interesting enough."

"You know that's not true."

"All right, so we'll have to be smarter than they are. Leaving before they can shove mikes at us is the first step. Oh yeah, what about Emma's Dalmatian?"

"Dalmatian? Emma doesn't have a dog."

"She drew me a picture of her dog."

"Oh, that must have been Scooter. He's a neighbor's Dalmatian. She loves that dog a whole lot."

• **"You're** leaving," Mason Lord said, no particular regret or surprise in his voice. "Miles said you'd ordered a taxi." He smiled. "I can understand why you wouldn't want

300

to take one of my cars or have one of my people drive you."

It was a joke Ramsey hoped Emma hadn't understood. He'd dealt with men like Mason Lord in his professional life. They were men to whom a designated death was just another move on a chessboard. "Yes," Ramsey said, "we're leaving. Molly is ready to return to Denver." He wasn't about to tell Mason Lord where they were really going.

"Eve wanted to go out on Lake Michigan. We didn't go. I knew you'd leave if I left."

"You stayed and we're still leaving. It doesn't matter, Mason. Thank you for your hospitality."

Eve Lord came up behind her husband and said that Detective O'Connor had arrived.

Ramsey cursed under his breath. He should have foreseen this, but he hadn't. He'd been focused on getting the Hell Out of Dodge. He turned to Molly. "You and Emma stick close for a moment. I want to speak to Detective O'Connor." Ramsey got to him before he'd stepped into the living room.

"I was just leaving. Mrs. Santera and Emma are going with me."

Detective O'Connor looked as if he'd slept in somebody else's face. The skin didn't fit, it was loose over his jowls. There were bags under his eyes. "I don't blame you, Ramsey. Before you head out, do you know anything about this?"

"I heard it on the TV. We were all at lunch. I remember wondering why a local Las Vegas station was on the TV in the kitchen, why it was so loud. Then, of course, it was clear. You know as well as I do that Mason Lord arranged for the explosion. I've been told that now things are even again and there won't be any more violence."

Detective O'Connor whistled between his teeth. "I feel like a fly buzzing around with no place to land. I don't suppose Mason Lord admitted to you that he'd done it?"

"No, he didn't say a word. But you know, he had a glimmer of satisfaction in his eyes that he couldn't quite hide. Sure he ordered it. This place is like an alternate universe."

"The cops down in Las Vegas say they ain't got dip. Everything was neat and tidy, except for the two bodies left over."

"You'll be checking to see if any of Lord's men took a quick trip down to Las Vegas?"

"Yeah, but it won't matter if they did. Lots of folks go to Las Vegas. Besides, the chances of Mr. Lord bringing the murders this close to home are slim to none. These guys don't operate like that. It's like dogs and their own backyards. But I got to talk to everyone, go through all the motions, just the way homicide did with me down in Las Vegas. Maybe some of the Las Vegas detectives will come up here, who knows?"

"I still have trouble with what Miles told me about the even-up rules. If it were me, I'd want to up the ante myself, not walk away, not just wipe my hands and say, well, that's how it is. My daughter's dead, but hey."

"Probably Shaker knew when he had that bomb planted that he was putting his daughter's life on the line. It does make him sound like he's not the greatest dad, doesn't it? These guys aren't like you or me, Ramsey. There's something missing somewhere in how they're put together. But they don't get where they are by being stupid. He probably thought Mason would try for him, only he didn't."

"Let's say he didn't expect Mason to go that far. Let's say he doesn't consider things even. What happens then?"

"Listen, go home, Ramsey. I'd say for you it's over. Rule Shaker isn't about to make another mistake. He can't afford to; he's got too much to protect.

"Send the little girl and her mother home. The Denver cops will take care of them.

"It's over now. You can leave the rest of it to us. We'll let you know if we find out anything that would fill a cereal box."

24

At six-thirty in the evening a taxi pulled up to Molly's house on Shrayder Drive. It was a small, lovely house with white window frames and window boxes painted a soft blue. Flowers bloomed wildly over the fence, in bordered flower beds, and in half a dozen flower boxes attached to the porch railing.

The house faced the park where Emma had been kidnapped while Molly was taking pictures. All the front yards were filled with trees and bushes, but no other house had such beautiful flowers.

Emma was a silent ghost. She was holding her piano against her chest, looking straight ahead. She was so very still, as if the quieter she became, the less likely the chance that anything bad would happen to her. He could tell her again that she need not be frightened, but that wasn't true, not really, and both of them knew it. The man was still out there. Probably he was far away, in hiding, but to Emma, he was lurking close, just as he had been, waiting to take her again. It broke his heart.

He looked out over the park, with its small dips and rises, its clusters of flowers and bushes, and banks of elm and pine trees. He wondered where the man had waited for Emma to get close enough to take her.

He saw that Molly was gazing toward a knot of trees at the west corner of the park. So that was where it happened. Her face was tense, drawn, and thin. Even her glorious red hair seemed flat and lank, pulled back and fastened with a pale green clip that matched the color of her silk blouse. He'd bet that if she'd had a piano like Emma's, she'd be carrying it too.

"Emma, we're home." Molly spoke very softly, not wanting to frighten her, just gain her attention slowly and gently. "Remember, we're just going to pack our things and then we're going with Ramsey to San Francisco."

"And then Ramsey is coming with us to Ireland?" Emma said, pressed against her mother's side, not an inch between them. Molly wondered what had gone on between Dr. Loo and Emma. It had been just that morning that Emma had seen her for the final time. She must remember to call her.

"Yes, he is," Molly said. "He wants to go back and he really, really wants us to go with him. He begged, Emma. I'm a nice person, I had to say yes."

"Did you really beg, Ramsey?" Emma asked, shooting a look at him.

"I can beg with the best of them, Emma," Ramsey said, going down on his haunches in front of her. "I decided I didn't want to let you out of my sight. I decided not seeing you would make me very unhappy. Do you mind my staying with you at your house until tomorrow?"

"You can stay with us, Ramsey. I think it's a good idea." She marched through the open gate toward the front door, her piano hugged against her. She said over her shoulder, "Dr. Loo showed me Ireland in her atlas. She said it was so green you had to brush your teeth at least twice a day or they'd turn green too."

"Emma, was that a joke?"

To his delight, Emma gave him a wicked little smile over her shoulder.

He said quietly, "The park, over there?"

"Yes. I used to love this house. We lived with

Louey in one of those estate areas in the western part of Denver. After the divorce, I sold the house and found this one. The thing is, I don't love it anymore. I can tell that Emma's terrified. To be honest, I am too."

"Let's give it time," he said and knew it was a worthless thing to have said. "Actually, we only have to give it the next few minutes, just time enough for you and Emma to pack. We don't even have to spend the night if you don't want to."

"No, we won't," she said.

"Also, there's no reason you can't sell the place, Molly. There's no reason at all why you couldn't, say, move to San Francisco."

The words came out of his mouth, and his eyes fastened on a rosebush just beyond Molly's left shoulder. "I didn't mean what you could maybe think I meant."

"No, certainly not," Molly said, all cool and calm and together. "Men rarely do."

"What's that supposed to mean?"

"Nothing. I'm sorry. It's been a long day. It was a lot of years with Louey. We're coming, Emma."

Emma stood patiently in front of the door while Molly pulled out her key. She slipped it into the lock and turned it easily. "Things look so beautiful because I've had a person coming to garden for me. One of my neighbors waters the indoor flowers and plants. Still, it's bound to be a bit on the musty side and—"

Molly got no farther. The stench hit them

full in the face the moment they stepped into the small foyer.

"Mama, this isn't good," Emma said, backing up. "It smells like there's bad food everywhere. It smells like Ramsey's house did when we went there."

Ramsey caught Emma as she raced back out the front door. "Get behind me, Emma. That's right. Your mother and I will go see what's going on. You stay right here."

• **"Oh,** no." Molly's once-colorful very cozy living room with high ceilings open to the dining room through an arch, filled with fat silk pillows, framed watercolors and photographs, and restored furniture painted in bright colors, all of it was trashed. Even the ivy had been pulled from its pots and dashed to the wooden floor.

"Let's see if your clothes and Emma's are all right. Pack up and get your passports, if they're still here, then we're out of here. We'll call the police from the hotel."

"I want to call my neighbors, too, and a cleaning service. Who did this and why? Is it ever going to stop?"

"It will. It has. This was done days ago."

An hour and a half later, the police met them at the hotel, in their two-bedroom suite on the ninth floor of the Brown Palace. The suite was huge, but the rooms were too warm. Ramsey had opened all the windows and complained to the front desk that the air conditioner was on the fritz. It was finally beginning to cool down a bit. Emma was seated on one of the sofas, watching a cartoon on TV. Ramsey, Molly, and Detective Mecklin of the Denver PD were sitting at the circular table at the other end of the living room. A pot of coffee and a plate of cookies were on the table.

Detective Mecklin was chewing on an oatmeal cookie from the Brown Palace kitchen.

"As I told you," Molly said, "I had a neighbor coming in to water my plants. Everything was fine three days ago. One of your people is speaking to her, right?"

"Yeah, right. But I doubt she saw anything, or we'd have gotten a call by now. Whoever did it, had guts. We didn't clear out of there until about five days ago."

The hotel doorbell rang.

An officer who'd accompanied Detective Mecklin answered it. He walked into the living room, a stoic look on his young face. Behind him stood FBI Special Agent Anchor, decked out in his dark suit, white shirt, dark thin tie, and wing tips.

Molly wanted to groan. Mecklin was enough. Now the both of them?

"Hello, Mrs. Santera. I'm still considering whether or not to arrest you."

"That's nice, Agent Anchor," Molly said, feeling the tension in her replaced by anger. It felt good, that wave of rage. She sat back in her chair and smiled at him. She realized she'd seen her father do this. She'd wanted to fry this guy since he'd first walked into her house after Emma had been kidnapped. He was arrogant and overbearing. "Hey, have you decided on the charge? Was it saving my daughter from a kidnapper? Was it perhaps escaping to avoid getting murdered? Or maybe it was keeping my child out of your incompetent hands? No, I've got it. You're going to arrest me for doing your job."

She'd got him. His face was red and his hands were stiff at his sides. He looked ready to explode. She loved it. "Oh, how about this— you want to arrest me because I trashed my own house?"

Agent Anchor managed to control himself. He even managed a very stiff smile at Molly. Ramsey was surprised and hopeful that perhaps the man would stop being a jerk. Agent Anchor said finally, "Your attitude isn't helping your case, Mrs. Santera." He then looked at Ramsey, a dark eyebrow raised. The raised eyebrow was met with silence.

Agent Anchor said finally, "You look familiar."

"He should," Detective Mecklin said between chews on another oatmeal cookie. "He's Judge Ramsey Hunt, you know the guy we've been hearing about from San Francisco and Chicago."

Agent Anchor froze. He was used to being in charge and then Molly Santera and this guy Hunt had treated him like he was a Keystone Kop. "What are you doing here?"

Ramsey just smiled at him. "Well, you

know, my house in San Francisco was trashed just like Mrs. Santera's. We were thinking that there just might be some parallels. What do you think? Just maybe Mr. Shaker is a very thorough man?"

"I don't appreciate your humor," Agent Anchor said. "I know all this. But she shouldn't have taken off to look for her daughter. She shouldn't have refused to return to Denver after she'd found her. She shouldn't have hindered my investigation." He stared at Molly, his thin nostrils flared wide with dislike. "And she shouldn't have insulted me when I walked in just now. Maybe if she'd done what I told her to, she wouldn't have ended up with a dead husband. But then, you got a live judge, didn't you?"

Molly shot a quick look toward Emma, who looked to be glued to the TV cartoon. Then she stood up in one smooth motion and kicked Agent Anchor hard in the shin. He gasped, grabbed his leg, then very slowly, he straightened. "I'm arresting you for assaulting a federal officer," he said when he could speak again.

"I don't think so," Ramsey said. "Actually, she beat me to it. Stop being an ass, Agent Anchor." He gracefully slid his hand to the man's elbow. He said close to his ear, "I think you're laboring under a severe misapprehension here. Listen up: *She's not her father*. You'd best get that right away. Now, why don't you put on your human clothes, sit down, and we can try to work together. If

310

that isn't to your liking, then I'll call up your boss and Agents Savich and Sherlock, who worked the case with us in Chicago, and we'll all have a talk. Your call, Agent."

Agent Anchor wasn't happy. On top of everything, the case of the murdered farmer in Loveland wouldn't ever officially get solved now. They hadn't even found the man who'd abused the little girl, and it had all started when she'd up and left Denver and gone out to hot-dog on her own. Ramsey Hunt was wrong about her. She was just like her father, he'd known it the minute he'd set eyes on her. She'd made the case go sour. And now this damned judge had taken her side. And he knew Savich.

Detective Mecklin pushed back from the table and rose. There were cookie crumbs on his solid red tie and on the white shirt that gaped over his belly. "Listen, we're not getting anywhere with all this crap. Agent Anchor, sit down, if Judge Ramsey will let you."

Molly said, "There's also my daughter, Agent Anchor. Children hear most things adults say. I think we've said enough."

Agent Anchor looked over at Emma, who was chewing gum, too fast. He had two kids. He knew when a kid was hearing things she shouldn't. And now he had this judge in the mix.

"Yeah," Agent Anchor said, and sat down.

There was dead silence. Detective Mecklin picked up another oatmeal cookie and said as he took a big bite, "If all this is connected, it

311

took power, men, and money, all of which this Mr. Shaker has in abundance."

Molly said, "Why do you think they trashed my house? Just for the fun of it?"

"Say it happened two or three days ago, Mrs. Santera," Detective Mecklin said. "That was about the same time your ex-husband was getting blown up. Maybe it was all part of the same puzzle. The word is that you and your daughter were the intended victims, to bring Mr. Santera in line. Yeah, it's gotta all be part of the same effort."

"All that," Molly said. "All that for some money, or to get Louey for his daughter? It sounds crazy."

Agent Anchor poured himself a cup of coffee. He hadn't said a word. He drank a bit, then poured in some cream. Finally, he said, "People like Shaker can't allow anyone to stiff them for a million bucks. He relies too much on people being afraid of him. God knows the money was there to hire the best."

Detective Mecklin said, "Shaker did it, all right. Trust me on this. It's over."

"You're probably right," Ramsey said. "There is no other answer." He turned to Agent Anchor. "Unless you can come up with something?"

Agent Anchor shook his head. "No, it's just my gut. Did Savich discover anything on that damned laptop?"

"Nothing solid yet," Ramsey said.

Agent Anchor shook his head. He had a buzz haircut, which was just as well since he was mostly bald. "I remember once when I was in Washington, I got to be in a meeting with Savich, and the person recording the minutes asked him what sex the laptop was currently enjoying. Nobody laughed."

Ramsey didn't particularly like to have a person start to turn human on him when he'd made the decision that the person was a jerk. Still, maybe the guy would relapse again.

Ramsey saw that Emma had curled up on the sofa, her piano clutched to her, sound asleep. One leg of her jeans was rucked up and he could see the pink sock over her Nike sneaker. He wasn't really shocked at the strength of his feelings for her, not anymore. He swallowed. Then he saw that her other sock was white. Well, it had been a hard day for all of them. He rose, still looking at Emma. "I can't see that this is leading anywhere. Maybe we shouldn't even have bothered to call you. Waste of time for all of us."

"No," Detective Mecklin said, rising as well. "All of it is part of the investigation. Maybe we'll turn up something at the house. Sooner or later, we'll snag that guy who hurt Emma. The Feds want him real bad. Hey, Agent Anchor, maybe you can get him on tax evasion, huh?"

25

It was sixty-two degrees and breezy in San Francisco, with a big unclouded sky overhead. Ramsey breathed in the clean air deeply and

313

smiled. He looked through the half-open window of his study that gave onto a small lawn and the Golden Gate Bridge beyond, off in the distance. He loved Sea Cliff, which was considered by many, himself included, to be the most spectacular area in the city. His house was among the first tier of homes that sat atop the line of the cliffs at the northwestern tip of the city. The ocean rolled in from the left, the Golden Gate stood guardian at the entrance of the bay to the right, connecting the city to the bleak naked Marin Headlands directly across from him. The Headlands stood stark in the afternoon sunlight. There was still some green on the hills. But it wouldn't be long now, deep into summer, until the Headlands would be unrelieved brown, seemingly barren of life. If the fog rolled in during the late afternoon, it would settle over the Headlands, and look for all the world like the setting for a Gothic movie.

His house had been photographed, fingerprinted, thoroughly cleaned up, and repaired. He'd spoken to his secretary and both of his externs, the two law clerks assigned to him as a federal district judge. The three of them had volunteered to refurbish his house. He'd given them color schemes, the type of furniture he liked, and a budget. They'd gone over budget, but given the furniture and draperies that had been delivered and lovingly arranged throughout the house, he wasn't about to bitch. He wondered what else would be arriving. It was interesting to see himself through other people's eyes. His study was more domineering and masculine now, full of leather and rich earth colors. They'd spent a small fortune on the leather sofa and chairs and the immense mahogany desk, and he'd approved that as well. The walls were still empty. They couldn't have bought the art he would like.

Given that less than a month had passed, they'd accomplished miracles.

"Ramsey?"

"Yes, Emma?"

"I like your house. The water makes me feel good."

He grinned as he leaned down and picked her up in his arms. He carried her to his huge leather chair and sat down. He put his feet up on the sinfully rich leather hassock, something he'd never had before. "Let's look at the view together, okay? We can let our souls commune with nature. Hey, where's your piano?"

"Upstairs. But my piano's not important right now." She sighed, that adult sigh. "I'm worried about Mama. I don't think she feels good even though she told me she was fine."

"What's wrong?"

"She's sick. She sent me down here to keep you busy, to keep you away. She doesn't want you to know, but I'm worried. Can you fix it, Ramsey?"

"Oh, damn. Sorry, Emma. Will you stay here and commune with nature for me?"

"Yes, but just for a little while. Mama's face is kind of green."

"I'll take care of her. You stay put, all right, Emma?"

"I won't go outside by myself, Ramsey."

"Good girl," he said, kissed her forehead, and took off upstairs. He heard her retching from the top of the stairs. There were three bedrooms, his master suite, a study, and a guest room, where she and Emma were sleeping. She was in the bathroom attached to the guest room. The door was pulled to, but not closed all the way. He inched it open. Molly was on her knees, her head over the toilet, heaving.

He didn't say anything, just gently reached down to rub her shoulders, then hunched down on his knees beside her. He pulled back her hair. She sank back against him. "You okay now?"

She moaned. "I don't want to talk. I just want to die."

He flushed the toilet. "Hold still, let me get you some water to wash out your mouth."

She moaned again. "I wish you hadn't come up here. I should have known Emma would get you. This is humiliating."

He handed her a glass of water. She eyed it, then rose slowly. "Let me brush my teeth."

"I've got some antacid. You want some? Oh yes, Emma was really worried. I'm glad she had sense enough to fetch me. More sense than her mother."

"Go away," she said, pushing him out the door and closing it. He heard her rinse her mouth out with mouthwash. Five minutes later, he was walking beside her to the bed.

There wasn't a great view in the guest room, but the row of three windows that were there gave a glimpse of the Golden Gate.

"At least while I'm lying here dying, the last thing I see will be beautiful."

"Nah, the last thing you'll see is my ugly face. That's enough right there to get you well again."

"I must have eaten something bad on the airplane."

She'd had the linguine with clam sauce. Both he and Emma had had the chicken. "Could be. That or it's stress." He gently cupped her face with his palm. She was sweaty and damp. He frowned. "I'm going to call my doctor, see what he has to say."

"I'm not going to any doctor, Ramsey. Forget it. My stomach's empty now. I'll be fine."

"We'll see," he said, in the same adult tone she used naturally with a child when she wanted to clamp down on any further arguments.

He brought her a couple of pills and a glass of water. "Take these."

She didn't even ask what they were. When she'd swallowed them, she leaned back against the pillows.

"How's your arm?"

"It's fine. How's your back?"

He just smiled at her. "I'm okay. Can you still see the stitches in your arm?"

"Some of them, but they're on their way. How's your leg?"

"Long healed. I want to see your arm."

She suffered his rolling up the sleeve of her pale cream-colored blouse. He gently pulled back the bandage. The skin was a healthy pink, the stitches obscene in her white arm, but the wound was much better, the remaining stitches disintegrating. He grunted and pressed the bandage down again. "Well, your heaving isn't from this wound."

"Where's Emma?"

"She's in my big leather chair staring out the French doors toward the bridge. But let me go check." He brought her back up five minutes later.

"Look who I found with her cute little nose pressed to the window?"

"My beautiful little princess?"

"Nah, she's mine, but I'll be willing to share her for a couple of minutes. You can see for yourself, Emma. Your mom's okay."

"Can I stay with her, Ramsey? I'll try to make her laugh. She says laughing always makes anybody feel better."

"Okay, but if she gets sick again, you holler and I'll get somebody over here with some needles to stick in her."

"Yuck," said Emma.

Three hours later, Molly was chewing on some dry toast and drinking hot plain Earl Grey tea. She still looked pale. At least she hadn't vomited again. The nausea had been gone for an hour, but his hand still hovered over the phone. He wanted to call Jim Haversham, an internist with privileges at San Francisco General.

"I don't think we're going anywhere tomorrow," he said at nine o'clock that evening. Both Emma and Molly were lying in the guestroom bed, the brand-new TV on low, providing background noise.

The doorbell sounded. Ramsey turned to leave. "It's just a friend of mine from the San Francisco PD. I called her. She's going to brief me on anything they've turned up."

"About your house being trashed?" Molly asked, moving the wet washcloth a bit to the left on her forehead.

"That and other things. You guys just relax. Emma, if your mom needs anything, you come and tell me. Can I count on you to mind me and not her?"

Emma looked worried. "I don't know, Ramsey, she's my mom. She's been around since I was born."

"I know, but right now she's on the pathetic side. She doesn't know what's good for her. Call me, all right?"

Emma still looked uncertain. She pulled her piano onto her lap. Molly groaned. She groaned again, a big funny groan that made Emma smile.

Good for you, Molly, he thought, gave them a salute, and took off downstairs.

Virginia Trolley was at the door, wearing her signature black boots, black slacks, black turtleneck, and a red blazer. "I'm glad you're home, Ramsey. All hell's broken loose."

He invited her into his study. There was a fire in the fireplace and the new heavy pale gold

319

draperies were drawn, making the room darker, more intimate.

"I love your house. The new stuff looks great. Did they bankrupt you refurbishing it?"

"The insurance will cover most of it."

"Good. Now that everything's brand new, do you think we could get married, then we could get divorced and I'd get the house?"

"No way you'd get the house unless you bribed a judge," Ramsey said, and poured her a cup of coffee from the thermos on a side table.

She sighed. "My husband might not understand, either. Would you consider adopting me?"

"You're older than I am."

"Ah, so have you heard of age discrimination?"

"Not me. Thanks for coming by, Ginny. What's going on downtown?"

"You know everyone still calls you Judge Dredd. It really fits now, what with all your flirting with the underworld. The media has been going nuts about all of it. I'm surprised they haven't found out you're home. Be thankful for small favors. It won't last."

He brought her up-to-date, finishing with, "Molly, Emma, and I are all going to Ireland day after tomorrow. We were going to leave first thing tomorrow, but Molly was throwing up her toenails all afternoon. She seems better now, but it doesn't seem too bright to fly right now. I think it was the linguine she ate on the plane. I'm praying it's not gastritis or an ulcer, though an ulcer wouldn't surprise me what with all she's been through."

Virginia Trolley rose from her chair, walked to the wide French doors, and pulled back the drapes. The clouds were hanging black and low. There was no sign of a moon or any stars. She sighed deeply. "We've all been talking about what's happened. This Shaker guy is bad stuff, Ramsey. If he is behind all of it, the chances of getting enough for an indictment are about the same as the Raiders winning another Super Bowl anytime soon. The odds are astronomical." She grinned. "Actually, it's looking like the Forty-niners aren't going to come up smelling like roses either this fall. Who knows?"

Ramsey sat down in the big leather chair behind his desk. He leaned back, cradling his head on his arms. "I'm hoping it is Shaker because it means the three of us are probably out of danger. Anyway, it's what the Feds think, it's what the Denver cops think. They're all still looking for the creep who took Emma.

"I'm praying we're out of here before the media discover we're back. I think all of us being out of the country for a while would be a healthy thing. Have you got anything new?"

Virginia turned from the French doors, letting the drapes drop back into place. "You're probably right. No leads as to who trashed your house. The neighbors saw nothing. There weren't any prints." She paused, looking around the man's study—dark wainscotting, rich leather furniture, and highly polished oak floor. "The cleaning service took real pride in fixing Judge Ramsey Hunt's house all right and tight. The *Chronicle* even wanted a photo of this room after your people refurbished it. It do sparkle, don't it?"

"Yeah, it do."

"Any problems?"

"No, everything is fine, at least for the moment. But I'm thinking it might be smart to have some protection."

"Agreed. I'll schedule a patrol to come by every half hour or so. Oh yes, I need to show you this, though we don't think it's much of anything. Anonymous, of course. It was shoved under your office door." She pulled it out of her purse and handed it to him.

It was short and to the point.

YOU ARE A MURDERER. YOU WILL DIE.

It was printed carefully with a thick-tip black pen. Ramsey handed it back to her, "No verbosity—it can't be a lawyer. Any reason to think it's more than the usual crank stuff?"

"Not much different from what you got right after you destroyed the scum in your courtroom. You haven't gotten anything else recently, have you?"

"No, not that anyone has told me about."

"All right, it's probably nothing. But be careful, Judge Dredd. One of the undercover cops was telling his buddies he'd pulled a Hunt maneuver. In other words, he kicked some butt. He said he'd just wished he'd been wearing a black robe, that would have made him the ultimate cool. Sorry, Ramsey, you're in the cop lexicon now." Virginia Trolley looked up to see a little girl standing in the doorway, holding a large portable piano against her chest. The thing came down to her knees. She was clutching it really tightly. She had beautiful thick mahogany-colored hair that was straggling out of a fat French braid.

"Hi," Ginny said easily. "Are you Emma Santera?"

"Yes, ma'am. Ramsey, Mama's throwing up again. She told me not to tell you, but I'm worried. Would you make it stop again?"

"Yes, Emma, I'll take care of it right now." He turned to Ginny. "I'm going to call Jim Haversham. He owes me. I'll never forget Savich telling me that it's always a good thing to have a physician on your debt list."

"He's your FBI friend?"

"Yeah. Listen, Ginny, I'll keep in touch. If anything comes up, you can fax me in Ireland. We'll be staying at Dromoland Castle just north of Shannon Airport for a couple of days. I don't remember the county name. I'll let you know after that."

"Okay. You keep yourself safe, Ramsey. Good-bye, Emma. Take care of your mama and Ramsey, okay?"

"Yes, ma'am." Emma slipped into the room

and stood by Ramsey while Ginny went out. As soon as she'd left the study, Ramsey picked up the phone.

When he hung up, he swung Emma and her piano up in his arms. "Let's go tell your mom that she's lucky. No going to any hospital. Nope, she's going to have a real live doctor make a house call to see her."

• **Dr.** James Haversham was forty-two, divorced twice, a man who sailed every free minute. He straightened and rubbed his jaw, a habit of long standing. He said finally, still looking down at Molly, still rubbing his jaw, "I need to do some tests."

"No. Forget it. If I ever go to the hospital, I'll be dead and I won't know about it. No tests."

He sighed. "All right, then. My best guess is that you ate something spoiled. Ramsey told me you had linguine with clams on the plane. From what he told me, nearly all of it is out of your system. But you're still having bowel spasms and that's why you started vomiting again. I'm going to give you a shot and some pills. They will help calm your stomach, make you drowsy, and take away the nausea. It'll take time for your bowels to straighten out. You're getting dehydrated. I want you to drink plenty of fluids tonight and tomorrow. Okay, the shot's for your butt. Turn over, please."

"Ramsey, please take Emma outside."

But Emma wasn't about to budge. "No,

Mama, you need me. I'll hold your hand."

"You need me, too. I'll hold your other hand. It's your hour of need, Molly."

Emma looked up at him. "Was that a joke, Ramsey?"

"All right," Dr. Haversham said, "both of you turn around so my patient isn't embarrassed."

They turned to face the television that was showing a rerun of *M*A*S*H*, without sound.

They heard a yelp, then Dr. Haversham's voice. "Now, two of these pills, Mrs. Santera. You're going to stay in bed, sleep and eat through tomorrow. Drink enough water so that you're in the bathroom every fifteen minutes. Any more vomiting, though, and you're coming to the ER. I mean it. Unless you feel better soon, it means there's something going on here other than food poisoning." She was shaking her head even as he leaned down and said, "You have a beautiful little girl who needs you. Pick something else to be stubborn about."

She sighed. "You're right, of course. Thank you for coming."

"You're welcome." He turned to leave when Molly called out, "What did Ramsey do for you? He said you owed him and that's why you came to the house."

"He saved my life."

"What did he do?"

"When my first ex-wife got drunk and was going to beat up my other ex-wife, but not ex then, Ramsey stepped in. He distracted

Melanie and had her dancing the rest of the night."

Molly laughed. "That's quite a debt you've paid off."

Dr. Haversham wasn't about to tell her that he'd made that up. She was a lovely woman with an easy smile on her face. And he'd put the smile there, brought the laugh. It was probably as effective as his pills and shot. "It sure was. Take care, Mrs. Santera."

She was nearly asleep. He smiled and shook Ramsey's hand.

"I heard what you said," Ramsey said. "I didn't know you could think that fast on your feet. We're even now."

"Oh, no. I still owe you another two or three more favors. I remember that water sure was cold. If you hadn't gotten me out of there, I wouldn't be doing favors for anybody."

He leaned down and automatically put his palm against Emma's forehead. She gasped and leaped back. Ramsey just smiled and patted her shoulder. "It's all right, sweetheart. Dr. Haversham just wants to make sure you're not sick like your mama. He's always checking everybody around him. Foreheads are his specialty."

Then Dr. Haversham remembered. This was the little girl who'd been kidnapped and sexually abused. He smiled down at her. "You seem to be in great health to me. You've got a fine forehead. You stick close to your mom, okay?"

"Yes, sir, I will," Emma said, but she kept back, staying close to Ramsey. He felt her hand slide into his. She was holding the piano up with only one arm. He quickly reached down and picked her and her piano up. "Let's see Dr. Haversham out, Emma. Then we can bring some water to your mama."

"She won't like having to go to the bathroom all the time, Ramsey."

"I wouldn't either, but it's her fate for a while."

26

Molly slept through the night. The next morning, she felt weak, but her stomach was settled. Ramsey gave her three slices of toast, thick with strawberry jam. Both Ramsey and Emma sat on the end of her bed, watching her take every bite. Finally, Molly laughed and said, "Enough. Look, two slices. I'm stuffed to my tonsils."

"You don't have any tonsils, Mama."

"Close enough. Now, I need a shower to feel really human. Ramsey, can you get us out of here today?"

He shook his head. "Let's give it another day, Molly. You've got orders to stay close and rest. Take those pills and keep drinking your water. I got you the bottled stuff. If you're good, if you're feeling even better this afternoon, we can go over to my favorite Mexican restaurant on Lombard Street for dinner."

Molly groaned and clutched her stomach. "Okay then. Chicken soup it is."

She was exhausted by the time she'd blow-dried her hair and dressed. She looked at the bed, freshly made, the comforter turned back, at Ramsey, who was just smiling at her, and flopped down. "A woman picked out this bed set. It's so bright and whimsical. Am I right?"

"Yep. Probably my secretary. I like it. Here, drink this entire glass, all twelve ounces. Then, take a nap. I'm going to take Emma over to Cliff House. The beach there is wonderful, right below what we call The Great Highway. She'll see some seals. We'll build a sand castle and throw a Frisbee for one of the many dogs that hang out with their owners over there. I'll bring her back dirty and happy. I want that bottle to be empty."

They'd been on the beach only twenty minutes when a huge panting black Lab came trotting over to Ramsey and butted his head against Ramsey's leg. A woman called out, "Just tell him to eat dirt if you don't want to throw that Frisbee for him."

But Ramsey patted the Lab's big head. "You up for this, fella?" He pulled his ancient chewed-up yellow Frisbee out of the old duffel bag that also held his and Emma's sandwiches, potato chips, and soft drinks, and flung it a good thirty yards. The Lab raced after it.

"Now Bop's never going to leave you," a young woman said, striding up to where Ramsey and Emma stood. Emma's eyes were on

Bop as he hurled himself into the air, but couldn't extend far enough to catch the Frisbee.

"He'll get it next time. He has to learn your style. Just tell me when you're tired of throwing for him. This your little girl?"

Emma quietly slipped her hand into Ramsey's. She pressed against his side.

"Yes," Ramsey said. "This is my little girl, Emma."

"I'm Betty Conlin," the young woman said and thrust out her hand. Ramsey shook it. The woman knelt down in front of Emma. "Hi. How old are you?"

Emma gave her a long assessing look. She said finally, "Bop's coming back. My mama's home in bed. We're here so I can play and try to forget about things. We're here so Mama can rest and get well."

"I see," Betty said and rose, and, naturally, she did indeed see. She smiled. "Here, Bop!"

Ramsey snapped his wrist and sent the Frisbee flying again. Bop had already begun running. He caught it on a three-foot leap. Ramsey yelled out, "Nice goin', boy, well done!"

He was laughing. There was dog slobber on his hands. Emma was playing in the sand one foot away from him. The sun was bright, making the ocean surface gleam like light blue diamonds. The sound of the waves sweeping onto shore was a constant rumble behind all the human voices. All they needed was Molly with them, lying on a blanket, drinking lots and lots of water and probably needing a bathroom, of which there were none anywhere close. He looked down at Emma and saw that she was staring at Betty Conlin. He didn't need to worry about any woman coming on to him. Emma would protect him. Well, for the moment they couldn't have Bop without Betty. Bop came dashing back, played tug-on-the-Frisbee with Ramsey, dropped it, and took off running. Ramsey let loose with a really long throw, skimming low toward the water. He shaded his eyes, watching Bop. The Frisbee caught a sliver of upward air and went flying even farther. Maybe fifty yards?

He turned when he heard Betty say something. He nodded and watched Bop finally catch the Frisbee well into the surf. He bounded back through a spray of water that looked like diamond droplets beneath that crystal sunlight.

"Did you see that, Emma?" He was grinning as he turned.

Emma was gone.

He felt instant overwhelming panic.

"What's wrong?" Betty was saying even as she was patting Bop.

"Emma," he said. "Emma." He whirled about searching. He heard a cry, jerked about toward the Cliff House, but saw a little boy fighting with his sister.

He yelled again at the top of his lungs, "Emma!"

Oh God no. This couldn't be happening. No, she had to be close. They couldn't have taken her far, not in just the couple of minutes Ramsey hadn't been looking at her. The sun was in his eyes.

Then he saw a man walking quickly down the beach, heading south. He was wearing a long dark brown overcoat. There was a huge bulge in that overcoat. He had Emma under that overcoat. How had he done it so fast?

Ramsey took off after him. He didn't say a word, didn't scream at the man, just sprinted. The man stumbled suddenly, lurching toward the water. Emma's head poked out of the side of the overcoat.

She yelled at the top of her lungs. "Ramsey! Ramsey!"

Now he did call back. "It's over!" He was nearly on him. The man jerked back his head, saw that it was over, dropped Emma, and took off back up the beach to the high concrete retaining wall. Ramsey started after him, then heard someone yell. He whipped back and saw Emma.

She was lying motionless on the beach. Two little girls were standing over her, one of them holding a blue bucket in her hand. A woman was running toward them. He ran back, gently pulled the little girls back, and knelt down beside Emma. She was drawn up in the fetal position, her eyes closed, her hair slashed across her forehead, strands stuck to her cheeks.

"Emma." He lightly touched his hand to her shoulder. "Emma, love. It's me, Ramsey. Are you all right?"

She moaned low in her throat. Slowly, she turned to face him, staring up at him.

"Are you hurt?"

She shook her head. "Well, just a little. He covered my face and hit me on my head."

The bastard had struck her, put her under his coat, and simply walked away. He looked toward the retaining wall. There were a lot of people milling around up there, but no man wearing an overcoat. Of course he could have just taken it off, and probably had.

He gathered Emma up against him, hugged her tightly, and kissed her. He'd nearly lost her. No more than three, maybe four minutes, and he'd nearly lost her. A woman said, "Did that man try to steal her?"

"Yes, he did. Did you happen to see what happened to him once he made the retaining wall?"

The woman shook her head. "No, I was looking right here."

"It happened so fast," Betty said, running up. Bop was pushing his head against Ramsey's legs, the Frisbee in his mouth. "From one instant to the next. She was just gone. I'm so sorry."

The woman didn't say anything more, just gathered her two little girls close. "We're leaving," she said. The children whined and argued, but the woman had a firm hold on their arms and dragged them away.

"Do you want me to call the cops?"

"No," Ramsey said, slowly rising. He still held Emma tightly against him. He was kissing the top of her head. "I'm so sorry, Emma, so sorry." He turned to Betty Conlin. "Bop can have the Frisbee and the sandwiches."

The police would question the people on the beach, all the people on the sidewalk at the top of the retaining wall, but Emma was burrowed against him, she was shuddering, he had to get her home. He kept her pressed against him even in the front seat of his old Porsche. It was a tight squeeze but he didn't care.

He was still holding her when he stood at his desk, calling Virginia Trolley. When she came on the line, he said, "Ramsey here. A man just tried to steal Emma on the beach near Cliff House. He dropped her when he saw I was about to catch him. I couldn't go after him because Emma was down. He was wearing a long brown overcoat, scuffed black-and-white running shoes, a brown knit cap on his head, dark sunglasses. He moved like he was over forty. No, not all that tall, maybe five-ten. Yeah, he was white. If you could send some people over there to find someone who saw the bastard. Yeah, thanks. See you in a few minutes."

He was still holding Emma when he hung up the phone. "Now, sweetheart, let me take a look at your head."

"Mama," Emma said against his jacket. "Mama."

"You're right. Let's go see that she's all right."

But Molly wasn't there.

Ramsey stared dumbly down at the empty bed. The water bottle beside the bed was empty. He yelled her name. He even looked in the bathroom shower.

"Molly!"

"Where's Mama, Ramsey?"

"I don't know, Emma, I don't know."

He ran back downstairs, Emma clinging to him like a limpet. He called her name again and again.

What the hell had happened?

He ran outside. There were two older people walking on the sidewalk. They knew him and waved. He waved back, even as he was turning to look the other way. No one else was around.

Emma was shuddering in his arms, crying, deep and low, harsh ugly sobs. "It's all right, Emma. She must have gone for a walk, that's all." He continued speaking nonsense to her, and that's what it was—nonsense. Where was Molly? He'd never been so afraid in his life.

Virginia Trolley pulled up with a young cop in her white Plymouth.

"Molly's gone," he said. "She's just gone."

Virginia Trolley saw the shock on his face, saw the little girl nearly hysterical in his arms. She said quietly, "Let's go inside and make some calls. It will be all right, Ramsey. Come along."

Virginia got on the phone. Ramsey started rocking Emma in his big desk chair. They heard a woman yell.

"Mama!"

Emma jerked out of Ramsey's arms and ran to the front door. It opened and Molly nearly fell inside, the young cop right behind her, his arm outstretched to grab her.

"Mama!"

Molly was on her knees in the foyer, Emma crying against her neck. The young cop said to Virginia, "I'm sorry, she wouldn't say who she was."

"It's okay. Now that Molly's here, you can go on over to Cliff House, Joe, and join the questioning."

Ramsey stood slowly. He waited until Emma had quieted a bit, waited until Molly finally raised her head.

"What happened to you?"

He sounded furious, at the end of his rope. Molly saw the policewoman standing by his desk. For a moment, she was so relieved she simply couldn't speak. She held Emma close.

"I got a phone call," she said, her voice strained and thin. "It came about ten minutes ago. I was sound asleep. It was a man. His voice was muffled, as though he was talking through a handkerchief. At first I was too asleep to realize what he was saying. But then he said everything again. He said something about the beach and he'd gotten her and I'd never see her again."

"Mama," Emma whispered. For a moment, Molly just held her daughter close. She rose finally, lifting Emma in her arms. She staggered. Ramsey walked to her and gathered them both close. He said against Molly's hair, "Thank God you're all right."

"Yes," Molly said. "What happened?"

Ramsey walked both of them to the sofa and sat down, holding each of them very close. He kissed Emma's forehead, then Molly's. "It's all right. We're all together. What happened is that a man did grab Emma, but I saw him running away with her and got her back. He ran away. Virginia's got police at the beach questioning people." He paused a moment, not releasing his hold on either of them. "But why did he call you? Just ten minutes ago? That means he called you after I got Emma back. Why'd he do that?"

Virginia said, "He did it to terrorize Molly. Now, who would like a glass of water?"

Ramsey started to say that Molly would, but he didn't. He realized that he was feeling very strange, as though his brain had slowed to a stumbling walk.

"I've been stupid," he said. "Even though I asked you about protection and you volunteered a patrol car, I still thought it was all over. I didn't really think there was any more danger. I never thought that man would come back."

"We've all been stupid," Molly said. "I didn't think there was any more danger either. The man's insane."

"That's probably very true," Virginia said. "Now, let's get down to it." Virginia asked him questions. She was infinitely patient, her voice pitched low. Ramsey realized, of course, that she'd played through scenes like this before, only most of them hadn't ended as well as this one had.

They sat close together, Emma on his lap, her face against her mother's shoulder, his arms around both of them.

Virginia said, "Mrs. Santera, please think back. Oh, I'm sorry. I'm Virginia Trolley, of the SFPD. I've known Ramsey for a while."

Molly nodded at the woman who was dressed all in black with a bright red blazer. "Call me Molly."

"All right. Good. Now, the man called at about—" She looked at her watch, did some calculations. "He called about ten after three. He said what exactly?"

"He said he had Emma. He said that stupid judge had just left her on the beach, didn't care about her at all, that he was flirting with this girl and throwing a Frisbee for her dog. He said it was a piece of cake. He said he'd never let her escape him again. He said I'd never see her again. Then he laughed. He said he was going to drive close to the house so maybe I could see him and Emma. He said he'd let Emma wave good-bye to me. Then he hung up. I was staring at the phone. I couldn't think of anything to say. Then I thought if I went outside maybe I could catch him. I ran outside. I've been running all through Sea Cliff. I'm surprised neighbors haven't called the cops to report a crazy woman."

"He called her after I got Emma back," Ramsey said slowly. "Just to frighten her?"

"Like I said," Virginia repeated, "he wanted to terrorize Molly. He wanted to make himself feel powerful. He'd failed to get Emma, but by calling Molly, he could win, at least for a while, until the both of you got back here."

His brain was beginning to function again, thank God. He could tell that Molly, too, was getting herself back together. As for Emma, he didn't know what they'd be facing with her. "Emma says he hit her on the head."

Molly patted her daughter's shoulder. "Em, does your head hurt?"

Emma sat up on Ramsey's lap. Slowly, she lifted her hand to touch above her left ear. "It's just a little lump."

"I saw you poke your head out of his overcoat."

Emma nodded. "I bit him through his shirt, too. Real hard. You told me never to give up and I didn't."

Virginia said, "In his side, Emma?"

"Yes."

"Which side?"

"His right side. I think it hurt him."

"Good for you." Ramsey cupped her face between his hands and kissed her nose. "Good for you, Em." He looked into that small face that had become so inexpressibly dear to him. It broke him. "Oh, Emma, I'm so sorry." He touched his forehead to hers. He felt the panic well up again, and that awful foreboding of sheer helplessness.

Slowly, Emma raised her small hand and lightly ran her fingers over his cheek. "I'm okay, Ramsey. You didn't do anything wrong. He was so fast. I was patting down one of my sand castle walls, and then he hit me."

Virginia Trolley turned away, cleared her throat, and said over her shoulder, "Emma, does your head hurt?"

"No, ma'am. It's just sore."

"Perhaps we should call Dr. Haversham again, Ramsey."

"All right. I'd sure feel better."

"I'm like my mama. I hate hospitals."

Ramsey and Molly exchanged glances.

"He wasn't wearing a mask this time, but he still had bad teeth."

Her voice sounded almost normal. She was sitting up straight now on Ramsey's legs. She was looking at Virginia.

"Did you notice anything else about him, Emma?"

"He smelled funny, just the way he did before."

"Funny how?" Virginia asked, taking a small pad of paper out of her purse and writing on it.

Emma shrugged. "Strong. Not nice."

"Whiskey," Ramsey said. "Was it whiskey?"

Emma wasn't certain. Ramsey lifted her in his arms and carried her over to the sideboard. He pulled the cork out of a bottle and lifted it to her nose. "Is this the smell?"

She scrunched up her face and jerked back. "Yes, Ramsey, like that. It's not a nice smell."

"No, it's not."

"And he had bad teeth?"

"Yes, ma'am, all black and yucky. I remember one was missing." She pulled open her lip and pointed to one of the incisors on the left.

"Good," Virginia said as she wrote. "Did he say anything to you, Emma?"

She shook her head. Ramsey returned to the sofa with her and sat back down beside Molly. "Think, Em. What were you doing just before he hit you on the head?"

"I was packing down sand."

"Then what?"

"I heard something. I looked up but something hit me and I don't remember."

"That's fine, Emma," Molly said. "All done in an instant of time." Emma slipped her hand into her mother's.

Virginia Trolley quietly closed her small notebook. She nodded to Ramsey. "He's made a mistake. He's close. Now maybe we can get this monster. Emma, you're the greatest. Ramsey told me you got away from this jerk before. You did it again. Now, you need to take care of Ramsey and your mom, okay? They aren't doing so well right now."

"Yes, Officer, I will."

Ramsey said, "Emma, can you give a police artist a description of the man? This time he wasn't wearing a mask."

"I can try, Ramsey."

Virginia Trolley said, "I'll send someone right over. You're a good girl, Emma. I'll see you later."

"I don't think you should ever go to the bathroom again, Mama, unless I go with you. Ramsey either."

Virginia Trolley heard Mrs. Santera laugh

as she walked out the front door. It was a shaky thin sound, but still a laugh.

27

Both Emma and Molly were openmouthed when they stepped into the reception area of Dromoland Castle, with its circular, gray stone inside the same as outside, and its giant windows, ancient tapestries, and smiling Irish. Dromoland had once been the stronghold of the O'Briens and was now a huge, turreted Gothic-style stone building that had been turned into a hotel in the early part of the century. It was a sprawling grand mass of stone, set amid the most beautiful park they'd ever seen. They were in the Speath Suite, a vast square room with tall windows that gave onto the beautifully mowed sloping lawns, formal gardens, and a lake. There were two queen beds. They'd ordered a rollaway cot for Emma, but when it arrived with the smiling bellman Tommy, and Ramsey had turned to ask Emma where she wanted the bed, the lost panicked look on her face had made him quickly turn back to Tommy and order the cot taken away. Emma slept with her mother. She'd had no more nightmares since they'd arrived.

On their third full day in Ireland, the first day it wasn't raining heavily, the sun was so bright it hurt to look directly into it. It was late morning. Emma was wearing blue jeans, a white shirt, her favorite Nike sneakers, and a pair of plaid socks Ramsey had bought for her in the charming thatch-roofed village of Adare, where most of the picturesque cottages housed tourist shops.

Emma was feeding the ducks. Molly was crouched six feet from her, down on one knee, waiting for the late-morning sun to get to just the right angle for the perfect series of shots. She had a roll of thirty-six in her Minolta, her film four hundred ASA. She didn't have her light meter with her, and wished fervently that she'd bought a new camera with the light meter built into it. But she'd shot Emma so often, with so many different backgrounds, different lights, and angles, she wasn't taking too much of a chance. It's just that she wanted one of these photos to be absolutely perfect. She wanted it for Ramsey, the man who'd saved her daughter's life, the man she was coming to know as well as she knew herself. There was more light than dark in Emma today, and in her surroundings as well. White ducks glossier than the shine on a brand-new Corvette were surrounding Emma, and Emma was laughing, and throwing single pieces of bread, hoarding each piece, choosing which was to be the lucky duck. One of the ducks was fast and cunning. He'd jumped and flapped wildly several times now in front of one of his cousins and ruthlessly snatched the bread from her fingertips. Molly quickly closed the aperture one f-stop and increased the shutter speed to 1/125 since

342

she was hand-holding her camera and she didn't want to take the chance of blurring. Since the natural lighting was spectacular, she knew the background—the lake and the ducks—would be as clear and sharp as Emma's face. The sun was behind her so she could backlight Emma. She continued to meter off her face so she could get natural skin tones that would give her somewhat of a halo. The lake and the ducks would also be in focus, would show full stark color, full drama. She wanted fluidity, not a vaguely blurred motion shot with little detail, but the essence of constant motion captured at exactly the perfect moment. She wanted every crease in that shirt to be exactly as it looked, with no shadows or dimming, no unnecessary highlighting or overexposing. She wanted that incredible smile on Emma's face to be there just as it was at this moment, in one hundred years, sharp and warm and so real you could practically hear the laughter, feel its warmth. She snapped once, twice, three times, then shifted back on her heels for another series. Then she sat down on the slope, leaning back, looking up at Emma. The aggressive duck hopped high to grab a small piece of bread Emma had destined for the duck beside him. Emma jumped up and clapped, so pleased she thrust out a hunk of bread to the invader duck. The duck jumped up toward her, almost in counterpoint, his neck stretched out full length to get that bread. Molly snapped another series, ending up flat on her back, looking nearly straight up. She righted herself, and lay her Minolta SLR on her knee. She was out of film. The camera felt warm and comforting in her hand, just right resting against her leg. She and the Minolta were old friends. She was used to the weight of it, the feel of it. The new cameras were something, doing everything she still did manually; some of them were so fine-tuned, they could probably even make coffee for the photographer. Nah, she didn't need coffee. Her Minolta had a lot of miles left in it.

She was pleased with the photos she'd taken. One of them would be perfect, she'd bet the farm on it. Maybe even two. For a moment, she wished she'd had a tripod. Then she shook her head, remembering what a pain in the butt it was to cart around all the extra stuff.

She saw a sudden movement out of the corner of her eye, off to the left in a stand of pine trees. She froze when she saw it, panic spiking in her. It was a man, leaning slightly around a tree, wearing a long brown coat, a brown knit cap on his head. He seemed to be staring at them. Molly was on her feet in an instant, her heart pounding, just about to grab Emma when a man emerged from the trees, carrying a bag of golf clubs. The breath whooshed out of her mouth. The Irish and their incessant golf, surely a national addiction. There were courses everywhere, including here on the grounds of Dromoland Castle. She'd swear that the Scots, with their St. Andrews, couldn't be more golf-happy than the Irish.

He saw her staring at him, and took off his golf hat, calling out a good morning.

She waved back, feeling herself flush to her toes both with relief and chagrin that she'd panicked so easily.

But she knew she'd act the same way the next time a strange man suddenly appeared. She would until the man who'd taken Emma was caught. For now, he was still out there. He was still after Emma.

At the moment, Ramsey was making some phone calls, one of them to Virginia Trolley of the SFPD to see if she had anything to tell him. Emma's meeting with the police artist had shown a man in his forties, with thinning hair, a sharp chin, and whiskers heavy on his face. His eyes were a soft gray, and set wide apart. He'd had strange ears, large for the size of his head, sticking out a bit. Emma said that's why he wore a knit hat. He didn't like his ears. His bad teeth were the giveaway. Molly hoped the guy didn't make a trip to the dentist.

Molly had no idea—no one did—how accurate Emma's description was. But it was the best they had to go on. The drawing was in the hands of the SFPD and the FBI.

Having the picture out there would protect them somewhat, Molly thought, but he was still out there. She felt it deep in her innards. When they went back home, he would be there, waiting. Somewhere. She decided that when they returned to the U.S. she and Emma wouldn't go back to Denver. No, she'd take her to an entirely new city. She would change her name and Emma's. They would disappear. The man wouldn't be able to find them then. She had enough money from the divorce settlement. She was a good photographer. She would get better. She'd have to start over with her professional contacts, but that wasn't a big deal. Her biggest assignment had been photographing Louey for *Rolling Stone* magazine some six years before. They knew who she was, but that was about all.

She saw Emma molding her last pieces of bread in the shape of an apple. After she'd thrown the small glob to the ruthless duck, Molly called out, "Hey, Em. Maybe you can grow up to be a caterer."

The ducks stopped squawking. They knew the bread was gone. They were going back to the large pond, waddling gracelessly, flapping their wings, grooming themselves.

"What's that, Mama?"

"That's a person who's paid to cook for people on special occasions. You'd get to taste lots of different kinds of goodies. You'd get to be creative, make food look like different things, just the way you've made the bread look like an apple. You'd be a food artist."

"Would I have to feed all those people, too?"

"Emma, was that a joke?"

Emma thought about that, then gave her mother a small smile. "I don't think so."

"No, they wouldn't eat out of your hand. Well, they might, but not literally." Molly looked out over the beautiful grounds. She put her arms around Emma and drew her back against her. She desperately wanted to ask her what she was thinking, what she was feeling, but she was afraid that she wouldn't say the right thing if Emma were to tell her something awful. Instead, she said, her voice bright and warm with the overwhelming love she felt for her daughter, "We've got sun today, kiddo. What do you say we go to Bunratty Castle? Maybe have a picnic on the grounds? Since it was raining the other day when we went, you just got to spend ten minutes there. Ramsey says it's a great place to visit, when the sun's out."

Emma grinned every time someone mentioned Bunratty Castle, just west of Limerick, where William Penn had been born in 1644, and where his father, Admiral Penn, had surrendered in the civil war and sailed off to America. Ah, and that had led to stories of the Quakers in Pennsylvania, a good half dozen that Ramsey had been told growing up near Harrisburg.

Emma wiped her hands on her jeans as she said to Molly, "I'd like to climb all those steps. Maybe I'll get all the way to the top this time without Ramsey having to carry me. Yes, let's go, Mama. Tommy said that the tourist buses will start coming soon. But it's still early, he said."

Molly blinked. It was the end of May. Life had changed so irrevocably that Molly had forgotten the day of the week, much less the month. "Yes, it is very early in the tourist season. Isn't that something?" A month before she'd been taking pictures, trying to polish her craft, her life busy and fun. Not really full, but that was okay. Emma would be starting first grade in the fall. They'd both looked forward to that. Then Emma had been kidnapped and their lives had flown out of control.

Suddenly, Emma held out her left hand. "Tommy gave me this." It was a small elaborately worked dark silver ring with a purple stone in it. "Tommy said it was Celtic."

Molly held her daughter's small white hand and looked at the lovely child's ring on Emma's middle finger. "It's beautiful. He gave it to you this morning?"

"He said if I ate my oatmeal, he had a small present for me. It was yesterday."

Molly felt a sudden jolt of fear. She'd seen Tommy speaking to Emma, but when had he given her the ring? Was Tommy one of those monsters? Was he trying to seduce Emma into trusting him? For a moment she was so afraid she couldn't breathe. No, she was being ridiculous. He was a nice boy, no older than seventeen, hair as red as a swatch of crimson silk, face very fair and freckled. No, Tommy was simply a nice boy. Still, she found herself taking Emma's hand for no good reason at all.

"Mama, you're hurting me."

"What? Oh goodness, Em, I'm sorry. Look, there's Ramsey. Let's see if he wants to go to Bunratty."

They left Dromoland grounds an hour later,

a picnic basket packed in the backseat beside Emma, with ham-and-cheese sandwiches, nothing else, because the Irish, Molly said, evidently didn't believe in mayonnaise or mustard or tomatoes or lettuce. They did, however, have potato chips. And lots of local cider.

The lanes were so narrow that if another car came along, they had to back up into one of the bulges, Emma called them, and park until the other car passed. "I'm nearly used to driving on the wrong side," Ramsey said as they passed a car on a turnout. "In the east of Ireland there are lots more people and better roads. By the time you get over Dublin way, you're pretty much used to all these strange things."

There was only one tour bus parked at Bunratty. They had nearly the entire shaded park to themselves. Emma climbed the castle's main stairs all on her own.

• **"We** think we've found him, or at least we know who he is."

Ramsey gripped the phone tight. It was midnight in Ireland, seven o'clock in Washington, D.C. Savich said again, "Ramsey, you there? Damned telephones. We got a poor connection?"

"No, it's fine. You really found him, Savich?"

"Yep. Well, we don't have him in the slammer yet, but we know who he is. His name's John Dickerson, aka Sonny Dickerson, aka Father Sonny. He's forty-eight years old, an ex-priest, finally booted out by the Church because he'd been so flagrant that the good

349

bishops and the cardinal had to oust him. You remember how they used to just ship the pedophile priests from one unsuspecting parish to another after having sent the offending priest off for spiritual and psychological rehabilitation?"

"Yeah. Thank God the Church now hands them over to be prosecuted."

"Yes, once they realized there were no cures. This guy was so over the edge that at the last parish they sent him to the people found out about him within a week of his arrival. Unfortunately, he had time to molest a little girl while her mother was in the church bathroom. There was a wedding rehearsal going on at the same time. Everyone came running out when they heard the mother yelling her head off. The bride and groom got an eyeful. He was in prison until about a year ago. He was supposed to register when he got out, but he didn't. He's been a fugitive, but no one ever really tried to find him, not enough cops, larger cases, until now."

"Does he look like Emma's description?"

"Have I got a surprise for you. I inputted the police sketch, just as if it were a photograph, into what we call the Facial Recognition Algorithm program. The general public doesn't know about this program yet; I got it from a friend who helped develop it for Scotland Yard. I've made modifications and have been working on it for the FBI. We've already uploaded photographs of every convicted child molester in the United States, and several other groups of violent felons too.

"With MAXINE's help, we treated the police sketch like a photograph and ran the program. What this program does is compare the photo, or the sketch in this case, to the photos in the database. It compares, for example, the distance between the eyes, the length of the nose, the exact size of the upper lip, the distance between various facial bones, you get the idea. Since MAXINE and I are pretty flexible, we managed to make the comparisons and came up with a list of a couple of hundred who resembled the sketch. We found Father Sonny in the group in under an hour. He fits all the other characteristics: he's a heavy smoker, has rotten teeth, drinks too much, and he's been out of Folsom for about eight months. His prison records indicate he refused any dental care. He said, and I quote: 'I won't have any of those drill-wielding assholes in my mouth.' He's a real hard case, Ramsey, real hard. They only let him out because they didn't have a choice."

"Did he molest both little boys and little girls?"

Savich said, "Evidently he didn't have a particular preference, at least then. Obviously if Shaker hired him to kidnap Emma, in order to bring Louey into line, he's no longer on Shaker's payroll since Louey's dead, and since Emma managed to get away from him."

Ramsey said, "I can't imagine that Shaker

would ever want to see this guy again, unless it was to have a little talk with him. No way Shaker knew he was a child molester when he hired him to kidnap Emma."

"So what Father Sonny did in San Francisco was all on his own." Savich paused a moment, then added, "He took a hell of a risk taking Emma right from under your nose. That's really out of control."

"Yeah, that's close to obsession. I'd say, bottom line, he's left common sense way behind."

Savich cursed, something rare for him. "Fixation, obsession, whatever the shrinks want to call it, Father Sonny's there. Our shrinks who deal with child molesters say it's common. A guy can come to believe that a certain child will save him. In this case, since the guy's an ex-priest, he might even believe that Emma can save his soul and cleanse him, heal him, maybe even make him acceptable to God again. Usually, though, after they're done with the child, they'll carefully select another child and believe the same thing all over again. Why does he want Emma back? Was it because she managed to escape him and so he wasn't the one who got to decide? He wants the control, the power? His can be the only voice?"

"Or maybe," Ramsey said, "he still believes that only Emma can save him, that she wasn't through cleansing him, so he's got to have her back. She said that he needed her more than God needed him, something to that effect. You know what? I want to kill the fucker."

"Yeah, you and about a zillion other people. We've got everyone countrywide clued into Father Sonny. That's what most of the other prisoners called him. He'll surface sooner or later. Someone will see him, recognize him. We'll get him. Your cop friend in the SFPD, Virginia Trolley, she's heading things up out there. How is Emma doing? She love Ireland?"

"Oh yeah. She's big into feeding the ducks here at Dromoland Lake and into visiting castles. She hasn't had any nightmares since we've been here. You know, I was getting worried since she was always so quiet, so well behaved. Today she was a real kid, Savich. She finally whined this afternoon, didn't want to do something her mother told her to do. It warmed me to hear that fretful, obnoxious little voice. Molly says it's tough not to spoil her because of all that's happened to her. But we're trying." He paused, then said, "I saw Molly shooting photos of her this morning. Emma was feeding ducks, laughing, the sun bright, the ducks carrying on madly."

"And?"

"I don't know," Ramsey said. "I really don't know why I was telling you that." He saw Emma's beautiful face in his mind's eye, then, suddenly, saw her lying on her face in the forest, saw the marks on her small body, the blood on her legs. Vicious deep rage nearly overwhelmed him. It drummed all the way into his bones. He was clutching the receiver so tightly his knuckles showed white.

"It's not right, Savich. This shouldn't have happened. Not to Emma, not to any little kid."

"You know how common it is, Ramsey. God knows you saw enough of it in your time in the U.S. Attorney's office, and probably some when you were a trial lawyer. And now as a judge."

"Some people in the San Francisco area think I've been too tough on crimes like this, but I don't agree. There isn't a cure or rehabilitation for child molesters, as the Church finally discovered, so it behooves us to keep them well away from children for the rest of their lives."

They spoke of Paris, of Sherlock's continuing reaction to the word *pregnant*. Savich was laughing as he said, "I accidentally said the accursed word in a three-star restaurant on the Isle St. Louis. She nearly puked in her fancy French mushrooms stuffed with something I can't begin to pronounce. I'll bet it means something like "greasy tourist innards" but I could be wrong. In any case, our waiter was wild-eyed, flapping his white waiter's towel around, but he got her to the women's room just in the nick of time."

"The bathroom was very nice. It was too bad that I didn't make it to the toilet."

It was Sherlock and she was laughing. Ramsey said, "It shouldn't last much longer, should it?"

"The doc says another month. I'm thinking of taping Dillon's mouth shut to keep that word stuck in his throat, but then he couldn't kiss me properly. It's a tough call, downsides everywhere. How's Molly?"

"She's hanging in, taking lots of pictures, even of me. I look up and there she is, turning all these dials on her camera, assuming strange contorted positions, muttering about backlighting and the like. She's spending a fortune on film. You want to speak to her?"

Molly slipped out and came around to Ramsey's bed. Thank God Emma was sound asleep. She listened, then spoke to Sherlock. She laughed, a warm infectious sound that made Ramsey smile. She was humming to herself when she slipped back into her bed beside Emma.

28

Ramsey brushed his teeth, put the cap back on the toothpaste, and rinsed out his toothbrush, standing it bristles-up in a glass on the sink. He was leaning into the small shower stall to turn on the water. He heard something, straightened, and turned back toward the bathroom door.

Molly was standing there in her cotton nightgown, her hair tousled from sleeping, and her eyes were remarkably bright and focused. She was staring right at his cock.

"Molly?"

"Uh? Oh, Ramsey, I'm sorry. I wanted to

go to the bathroom, I wasn't listening, I didn't realize you were in here and I—" Her voice fell like a rock off a cliff.

She continued to stare at him. Even when she'd spoken, she hadn't looked at his face. She hadn't even gotten as high as his chest.

She said now, still not looking at his face, "I guess I'd better leave now."

"I'll be out in just a few minutes."

"I can hold it." She was out the door in a flash. He looked down at himself. He was getting erect, fast. Well, damn, he was a man and a man didn't have any say over that. It was the only completely independent organ of his entire body. Actually, given all the time they'd spent together, it was surprising this hadn't happened before. Actually, he rather wished, as he lathered soap on his chest and belly, that he'd been the one to walk in on Molly. He wondered how she'd have reacted if he'd just stood there staring at her body, his eyes not getting above her neck. He also found himself wondering what she'd thought of his body. She'd seen him with a hard-on before, particularly in the mornings when they'd slept in the same room. But he hadn't been naked.

He hadn't worked out in a month except for that session with Savich in Mason Lord's state-of-the art gym. Sure he'd walked a lot, kept his cardiovascular system going at a fast clip through sheer stress, but it wasn't the same thing. He needed to work out. His body missed it. He flexed and stretched. He wondered if there were any gyms in Ireland. He'd just have to hike more, maybe carry Emma on his shoulders as a free weight.

He was whistling as he thought: So what'd you think, Molly? Did you like what you saw? He was whistling when he came out of the bathroom, completely dressed. "All yours," he said, and smiled at her.

She forced herself to look him straight in the eye and said, "Thank you."

• **Late** that afternoon, sitting on the Cliffs of Moher, waiting for that huge brilliant sun to sink down into the Atlantic, Ramsey took Molly's hand, lifted it to his mouth, and kissed her fingers, one at a time. She became instantly as still as a deer in the glare of headlights. He said quietly, still holding her hand, "Emma's not looking right now. I think she wants us to buy her another Celtic ring from that vendor over there. She's looking at every piece of jewelry he has. I've got my left eye on her. Don't worry. So, Molly, I think we should get married. What do you say?"

Molly jumped to her feet and took three quick steps back. Ramsey didn't move, just twisted around and looked up at her. Then he looked at Emma, who was now strolling not ten feet away from them, hovering near a man and a woman and their two young girl children.

Molly wrapped her arms around herself. She was shaking her head, her red hair a wild halo, corking out in all directions, simply beautiful. The sun, stark against her, turned her hair molten. She didn't look at him as she said, her voice low and strained, "Just because I saw you naked this morning and just stood there and stared at you, my little heart filled with lust, you think you've got to marry me? That doesn't make any sense, Ramsey. I know what men look like. I'll admit that you look the best of all the men I've ever seen—"

"And how many does that make exactly?"

"Two."

"You've made my day."

"Two, counting you."

"I take it back."

"Don't be ridiculous. I've seen lots of pictures, movies with men very nearly nude. You're as good-looking as the best of them, and you surely know it, you're not blind." She stopped suddenly, as if aware in that instant of what was coming unbidden out of her mouth. She pursed her lips, like a pissed-off grade-school teacher. "Just because I can still see you clearly in my head, it won't do to speak about you at any more length. No, I didn't mean to use that exact word. It was just a slip of the tongue. Yes, enough about your body."

That was probably a good thing since he was getting hard and they were in public, and he wanted to laugh. "Okay, that's fine, at least for now. Incidentally, I didn't ask you to marry me just because you happened to walk in on me. I was thinking it's kind of surprising that it hadn't happened before. Do you think if the shoe had been on the other foot, so to speak, you would have felt compelled to propose to me?"

"Oh, goodness. I would have sunk into the floor. I'm not beautiful like you, Ramsey. I'm so skinny."

He looked at her face, at her glorious hair, and said, "Don't you ever speak ill of yourself again. It really pisses me off."

She swallowed, looked down at her feet. "It's just the truth."

"Bullshit." He looked back at the sun, getting lower now. He said, not looking at her, "Sit down. I don't want you to miss this."

"Then you shouldn't have said what you said at such a precious moment. It beat out the setting sun for sheer drama."

"I thought putting the two precious moments together was a bang-up idea."

Molly looked at Emma, who was playing now with the two children, the parents looking on. Molly waved to them. The woman waved back.

She sat back down, slowly, carefully, as if she were wearing a dress that he could look up if she wasn't careful. She sat Indian style, her palms flattened on her thighs. Her fingernails were short, blunt, like his. She was wearing black jeans and black half-boots. Her vivid yellow windbreaker was billowing out behind her as the stiff offshore early-evening winds swept in.

She didn't look at him, just stared at that bright red sun that was close enough to the water now to turn it a gleaming golden red. "Have you ever been married before, Ramsey?"

Getting down to it now, he thought. "Yes, when I was twenty-two and just starting law school."

Her voice cynical, she said, "You knocked her up?"

"Nope. She was a marine, had just finished her basic training and was going to be shipped out to some god-awful place in Africa. We wanted to be married just before she left."

"What happened?"

"We did well together. She was the one always on the road, off to someplace I'd never heard of, but it worked out okay. She wanted to wait on kids and I was agreeable. Then it was all over." He found his body tensing, becoming clammy, just as it had that day he'd walked out of the courtroom, elated because he'd just won an important case, only to have one man and one woman, both in uniform, waiting for him. He'd known, oh yes, he'd known in that instant that Susan was dead.

"She was killed when her helicopter crashed in the Kuwaiti desert at the end of the Gulf War in ninety-one. She would have shipped home the very next week."

"I'm sorry," Molly said, "I'm so very sorry."

"Shit happens."

She laid her hand on his arm. "No, don't act like a man about it."

There was clean anger in his voice as he turned to her. "Why not? At least now I can sound all flippant and macho, but for a very long time I couldn't even say her name without stuttering or bawling. And you, of all people, Molly, know that shit does happen."

She didn't understand how he'd felt, given her own experience with marriage. She said, "You must have loved her very much."

"Yes, but Susan died a long time ago, Molly. Fact of the matter was that we didn't really know each other all that well. She was gone too much of the time. When she was home, it was nonstop sex until it was time for her to leave again. We talked, sure, but for the life of me, I can't remember many conversations. And, as I said, I know more about you than I did her. For example, I don't remember how she squeezed a tube of toothpaste, whereas I know that you flatten the tube in the middle. I don't know what kind of nightwear Susan really preferred. You love floaty silk nightgowns. I saw you rubbing the one you couldn't help but pack, you loved it so much. But with me around you wear only those cotton jobs that start at your throat and end at your toes. I never knew what her favorite breakfast was. You like to eat Grape-Nuts unless you're on the run—and I do mean that literally. She liked my body, she told me that whenever we were together, but I can't remember that she ever looked at me the way you did this morning. You licked your chops, Molly. I don't think you once got up to my face. I felt like a sex god. It was great.

"Isn't that strange? To be married for nearly

four years and not really know your mate very well?"

He stared at the sun again, then over at Emma. He saw her laugh at something one of the kids said. After the man had taken her off the beach nearly right under his nose, he automatically checked on her every fifteen seconds, or less. Usually it was less, especially after San Francisco.

"Maybe, but I never knew Louey all that well either. Like Susan, he was gone most of the time. Unlike Susan, when he was home, he was usually a jerk." She sighed. "Louey's dead. It's just over a week. It seems much longer. Goodness, it feels as if I've known you forever."

"That's because we got thrown together in the same pot with the lid plunked down and lots of heat. No time-outs."

"I guess so." She studied his face in that special way she had, as if she were going to photograph him. "You're really meticulous with the toothpaste. You roll it up carefully from the bottom. When you're alone, do you sleep nude?"

"Most of the time."

"Listen, Ramsey, my father's a big-time crook and you're a federal judge."

"I deal all right with your father. I prefer dealing with your stepmama, but hey, I can make do."

She grinned at him. "Eve's something else, isn't she?"

"Yeah. Most of the time when I was around her, I would have sworn that she married your dad for his big bucks and power. Then, at other times, I'd be willing to swear that it was something else entirely." He shrugged. "Maybe we'll find out someday just what she's all about."

"My father treats her like dirt."

"He does have that problem with women. But again, I have this gut feeling things are going to change." He looked over at Emma. She had started rigging up a kite with the other kids, the father showing them what to do. He smiled. Emma knew exactly what to do. Molly had taught her and done a really good job of it. He saw her then, flying her dragon kite in the meadow by the cabin. And then those men had come with their guns. It seemed an eon ago, another Ramsey Hunt. He shook himself. "Let's get back to us, Molly. There's nothing either of us can do about our families. We'll cope."

"Tell me about yours."

"My father's a dentist. First thing he'll do when he meets you is check your mouth, just the way they do with horses. Because you've got great teeth, he'll probably fall in love with you on the spot. My old man's easy that way. Give him a beautiful tooth and he's in ecstasy.

"As for my mom, she's a retired school-teacher, high-school history. I remember she cried when I announced I was going to law school. She believes all lawyers are pond scum. She only forgave me when I told her I wanted to be one of the good guys. She approved of the U. S. Attorney's office. She still tells me all the lawyer jokes though."

"What about when you went back out to be a trial lawyer."

He ducked his head. "It was only for a year and a half. I hated it."

"So?"

"I didn't tell her. Since I'm a judge now, she treats me like I'm on the Supreme Court and asks me all sorts of questions about Sandra Day O'Connor and Ruth Bader Ginsburg, both of whom I've met only once, but that's about all. A neat woman, my mom. Uh, she doesn't look a thing like Eve. I also have two older brothers. One's career Army, a two-star general, three kids. The other brother, Tony, is a political speechwriter. Tony's an okay guy, lives in Washington, D.C., nice wife, two kids, neither of whom takes drugs or is in jail."

He looked over at Emma at exactly the same time Molly did. Their eyes met. They smiled at each other.

"It will probably be a habit of a lifetime," Molly said, "checking on Emma. I'll probably have my antennae up when she's a little old lady."

"Do you want more kids, Molly?"

"Maybe. Two would be nice, maybe three. I like kids."

He realized he'd been holding his breath. He let it out and laughed. "Just the number I had in mind. I'm thirty-four. That's really young to be appointed to a judgeship, but as for my biological clock, it's running out fast. I heard it isn't good for a guy to father kids after he's forty. The risks are too great."

She poked his leg. "You mean you'll be too paunchy and too run-down to keep up with them?"

He leaned over, took her chin in his hand, and kissed her mouth. He pulled back, studying her face. "You've also got beautiful eyes. They're a bit on the vague side right now and I do like that."

They heard applause. They both jerked around to see Emma running away from the cliffs, her leprechaun kite high in the air. She was letting out the string perfectly, just as Molly had taught her. She was laughing, the wind whipping her hair, just as the crimson shadow of the sun floated above the water before disappearing.

He looked at Molly then back at Emma. The look on his face was tender, filled with quiet joy. He said, not looking back at her, "We're both smart. We can work out any problems. Let's do it."

"Could you kiss me again, Ramsey?"

"My pleasure." He kissed her a bit longer this time, but he didn't let it get out of hand. He tasted her, nibbled on her bottom lip, wished she'd open her mouth, just a little bit. On the other hand, it probably wouldn't be smart to have his tongue in her mouth here on the Cliffs of Moher with Emma flying a leprechaun kite not thirty feet away. He pulled back. He wanted her a whole lot, more than he'd ever wanted any woman before. The fact was, he really couldn't remember now what he'd felt like when he'd been with Susan. She was in the past, a past that held dear memories, a past that was becoming more blurred each day that passed with Molly and Emma. He'd found a new focus, new feelings that were sometimes overwhelming they were so rich and powerful. He kissed her again, lightly, just a recognition kiss, and it was there, this knowing of each other. He smiled at her and said nothing, wondering what she was thinking.

Molly knew why he wanted to marry her, knew it, and accepted it. He wanted Emma. To get her, he had to make Mom part of the deal. She licked her bottom lip where he'd nipped her, saying, "You just want to keep feeling like a sex god."

He loved the humor in her, coming so seldom because life was so excessively grim. It made it all the more precious. He could look forward to her laughter for the rest of his life, he hoped, if she married him. "How'd you know?"

She looked at him a long time, studying his face, again as if she were setting her camera shot. She cocked her head to one side. "Sex is part of things. I know you like my hair, you even like my eyes. But I'm skinny, you know that. Will you mind having sex with me?"

He said, never looking away from those very nice eyes of hers, "I know it's expected, so I'll try."

She wanted to run her hand up his thigh but instead, she just laughed, then almost immediately sobered. "What about Emma?"

"I guess at first we'll have to sneak around, that, or abstain for the time being. I spoke to Dr. Loo about Emma needing to sleep in the same room with either or both of us, that or in the same bed, and she said not to worry. She said of course it wasn't a good idea to have kids sleeping with their parents as a regular thing, but this was different. She said Emma would probably be the one to break away when she was ready. So, Molly, will you marry me?"

Molly got to her feet, dusting off her bottom with her hands. "It looks like the family is about ready to leave. Let's go get Emma and tell her she's going to have a new daddy." She started walking away, then said over her shoulder, a big grin on her face, "Yeah, I'll put you out of your misery, Judge Hunt."

"Say it," he called after her, raising his deep voice loud enough for several people to hear him and turn to look at Molly. "I want to hear you say the words."

She knew people were staring and listening and she laughed, shaking her head. She called out, "I'll marry you. It would be my pleasure to marry you."

There was some applause and a couple of groans from some men, who got punched by their wives.

"That sounds wonderful," he said, walking to stand beside her. "It sounds more than wonderful. We'll be a family for real now.

Yes, I quite like that." He looked over at Emma and her new friends. "I think that man is going to give Emma the leprechaun kite. Let's go thank them for watching her." He stopped then, turned, and brought her against him. "Did I ever tell you that you're the most beautiful woman I've ever known? That you've even gotten more beautiful each added day I know you?"

"No. You just told me I had beautiful hair."

"That, too. That's your crowning glory, I'll admit it." He raised his hand and curled a thick strand around his finger. He smiled at her. "Feels like springy silk. Yeah, you're beautiful. I think every skinny little bone in your body is beautiful."

He looked over at Emma, who was panting from her run, dragging the kite behind her, looking tired and pleased. "You're sure you like me enough, Molly?"

"I like you enough." She looked down, scuffing the toe of her black boot in the dirt. She said then, making his eyes nearly cross, as she looked back up at him through her lashes, "I particularly like your body."

She thought for a moment that he was going to grab her, and she wouldn't have minded, but he didn't. He just smiled and said, "Excellent. That's a really good start. Let's get married, Molly, as soon as we get back home. We can stop off in Nevada. Let's have the honeymoon before the wedding. What do you think?"

What was love anyway? she thought, as she slowly nodded.

They didn't have the opportunity either to honeymoon in Ireland or to tell Emma that she was getting a new daddy. Waiting for them at the reception desk at Dromoland Castle were two phone messages and a fax from Savich.

• **They** flew from Shannon to Chicago O'Hare in Business Class, in the middle section that holds three seats, putting Emma between them. She slept most of the way, propped up on three pillows on Ramsey's armrest, covered with a blanket, holding her piano close, the top keys sticking out from beneath the blanket. The piano had sat in the corner of their suite, seemingly forgotten by Emma, until the phone call had come, her mother had paled, Ramsey had cursed quietly, and they'd started packing quickly.

Molly saw that the shoelace from one of her Nike sneakers was dangling. She stared at it, then finally reached down and simply pulled the sneaker off. She had one plaid sock on her small foot. Molly had washed out the pair the night before.

They'd said very little. Life had spun out of control again. Molly felt numb, nothing else, just a numb blankness that had taken over both her brain and her body. She supposed she should be grateful for it.

Finally, Molly said quietly, so as not to awaken Emma, "I'm having a hard time accepting it. I keep thinking it's a mistake, that someone really screwed up, that Eve was utterly wrong."

"I know."

"Will they get Rule Shaker now?"

"I don't know. We'll find out exactly what happened when we get to Chicago. Listen, your father's not dead yet. God knows how he's managed to survive so far, but he has. That's a good sign."

"Maybe he's already been able to tell the cops who shot him." She stopped, staring at the blank movie screen directly in front of them. "Or maybe by now it's over and he's dead."

Ramsey started to pick up the phone on the armrest. "No," she said, placing her hand over his. "No. I don't want to know, not just yet. For the moment, I want to think you're right. He's told the cops who shot him. It will all be over by the time we arrive at O'Hare."

But Ramsey knew this wasn't likely. In fact it was well nigh impossible. He said quietly, "Remember I told you it was a distance shot, from a good seventy-five yards away, given the trajectory. The assassin probably fired from the roof of the four-story building just across the street. Mason never saw his attacker. Savich said the preliminary ballistics report was that the bullet, a heavy 7.62 mm, was from a sniping rifle, like a SIG-Sauer SSG2000. That's a popular military rifle." He didn't tell her that the bullet had ripped through Mason Lord's chest, hurling him into a car parked at the curb. The impact had smashed the driver's-side window of a new blue Buick Riviera.

"Gunther was just a single step in front of your father. He wasn't touched."

Emma groaned in her sleep. Ramsey reached over and gently began to rub her shoulders and back. She pushed against his hand, then quieted.

"We had to tell her. She's not stupid."

"Yes, I know. This is her escape," Ramsey said, his voice pitched even lower than before. "First chance we have, let's call Dr. Loo again."

"He's not dead, Ramsey."

Ramsey didn't say anything. He kept lightly rubbing Emma's back. He leaned his head back against the headrest and closed his eyes. They'd just gotten over the jet lag of flying to Ireland when they'd gotten word. Now they'd get to do it all over again.

He wanted to get married.

He wanted Emma to know he'd always be with her, as in forever, as in she was his now. The woman who would be his wife as soon as it could be managed was two feet away from him. He didn't know what to say to her either. He wondered what the hell was going to happen now.

"Ramsey?"

"Yes, Molly?"

"We're going to have to wait until things are sorted out."

He looked over at her and said, "Well, hell."

29

Detective O'Connor was waiting for them at the Lord mansion. Miles was there, but no one else. Gunther and Mrs. Lord, Miles told them at the front door, were at the hospital. "Do come in. Mr. Lord is holding his own. He's not out of the woods yet, but he's holding steady. I'm sorry, Molly."

"Thanks, Miles. This is hard on everyone. Thanks for being here to hold down the fort."

"Hello, Judge Hunt, Mrs. Santera," Detective O'Connor said, stepping out of the living room and walking toward them. "I'm sorry you had to come back to this. It's unexpected. No one quite knows what to make of things. I hope you don't mind, Mrs. Santera, that I waited for you here?"

"No, Detective, not at all." Molly went down on her haunches in front of Emma. "You want to go with Miles to the kitchen and have a goodie to eat?"

"I made some chocolate-chip cookies just for you, Emma," Miles said. "They're still warm, right out of the oven."

Emma gave her mother a long, patient look. There was such weariness in her eyes that Molly wanted to fold her up against her and cry. "Your grandfather is in the hospital, Emma. He was hurt. We told you that. Now Detective O'Connor needs to speak to Ramsey and me. He wants to know what we think about things."

"All right, Mama, I'll go with Mr. Miles."

"Thanks, Em. I'll be in to see you soon. I want one of those cookies myself."

She got another long-suffering look. She didn't get back to her feet until Miles had taken Emma's hand in his and they were walking toward the kitchen, Emma holding her piano close against her chest. She rose and sighed. "Do come into the living room, Detective."

"It was verified," Detective O'Connor said. "The bullet was a 7.62 mm sniping round." He turned toward Ramsey. "You probably know that this bullet is heavier, to give it more energy and a flatter trajectory. That's particularly important over a long distance."

"Any sign of the shooter?"

"We went to the Ames Building, to the roof, which is the top of the fourth floor. We found a couple of cigarette butts, a to-go coffee container, and, wonder of wonders, there was this small wet spot."

Molly blinked at the detective. "Wet spot? Why is that a wonder?"

"He spit, Mrs. Santera. The shooter spit. That means DNA, if we're lucky. That means if and when we catch the guy, we'll have indisputable proof that he's guilty. The forensics folks think he's a smoker with a bad hacking cough. His vices might end up bringing him down.

"Since Mason Lord is a very powerful man, despite his more questionable associations and business practices, this case is very high profile. The press is starting to understand there isn't much to see around here. But they'll start showing up again at dawn, you can count on it. I'm glad you made it back so early. They'll find out soon enough that you're back, Judge Hunt."

"What do the doctors say about Mason's condition?"

Detective O'Connor checked his watch. "It's nearly midnight. I told his surgeon that you'd be arriving about now. He said you could call and he'd give you the latest word."

Detective O'Connor pulled out his cell phone and dialed. After five minutes of being sent from one person to the next, he handed the phone to Molly.

Ramsey watched her face as she took in what was being said to her. Her expression didn't change. That was odd. He watched her press the *Off* button, then hand the phone back to Detective O'Connor.

"He's alive. The surgeon, Dr. Bigliotti, says he's got a fifty-fifty chance—if, that is, he manages to survive the night. He already woke up." She looked at Detective O'Connor. "He whispered to the officer sitting next to his bed that Louey Santera shot him."

"You're kidding," Detective O'Connor said. "He must have been out of his head, what with the drugs."

"Yes, that's what Dr. Bigliotti said. My father hasn't said anything more. Dr. Bigliotti also said the media was all over him personally and the hospital in general. One of the night nurses nabbed a reporter who was carrying

around a mop—as a disguise, I suppose—
trying to find Mason Lord's room. Do you guys
have any ideas? Any guesses that might help?"

Molly and Ramsey just looked at him. He
knew defeat when he saw it.

• **The** hiss of the regulator was obscenely
loud in the momentary quiet of the ICU at
Chicago Memorial on Jefferson, the closest
trauma center available when her father had
been shot down in the street. Molly looked
down at her father's white face, the tubes in
his mouth and nose, the lines running into both
arms, the bag emptying his bladder hanging
from the side of the hospital bed. One officer
sat not six inches away from him, a recorder
on his lap, holding a police procedural mys-
tery novel in his right hand. He nodded to them,
then did a double take when he saw Ramsey.
He nodded again, this time, his head going
lower, a sign of excessive respect, Molly
thought, to Ramsey.

The ICU was huge, impersonal, filled with
high-tech equipment. There were six other
patients, with just curtains around their beds,
and they weren't quiet. Moans of pain mixed
with that damnable hissing sound, low voices
of relatives speaking to patients, curses from
the bed in the far corner, a nurse's hurrying
footsteps.

Her father was as still as death. If it weren't
for the machine, he would be dead. She lightly
touched her palm to his cheek. His skin felt
slack and clammy.

She realized in that moment that she wanted him to live. No matter what was true, he was her father. She wanted him to live. The nurse motioned them to leave after five minutes.

In the corridor, Molly said to Detective O'Connor, "Has anyone called my mother? She lives in Italy."

He looked at her blankly, scratched his ear, and shook his head. "Can't say anyone has, Mrs. Santera."

"I'll do it then when we get back home." It was nearly two o'clock in the morning. Molly had wanted to come, to see his face, just to see for herself that he was alive. Life was there, huddling deep inside her father, barely.

There was no traffic on the drive back to Oak Park. Ramsey kept a hard focus on the road in front of him. He was nearly cross-eyed with fatigue.

Even if they'd managed to get married, he was so tired right now, he doubted he could even stay awake long enough to kiss Molly's ear, even if she offered her ear to him to kiss. She was in pretty bad shape herself.

When they finally drove to the gates of the Lord mansion, they saw a man jump from a dark car just up the road. A reporter.

"Just what we needed," Ramsey said, and quickly called out to the guard in the security box at the gate. "It's Judge Ramsey, open the gates, quickly. A reporter is coming."

"Putrid little maggots," the guard snarled, and got the gate open just before the reporter got to the rear end of the car.

"Wait!" the reporter yelled, but Ramsey just roared through the open gate. The reporter started through, then saw the wild maniacal grin on the security guard's face in the lighted booth as the huge gates began to swing shut.

He stepped back, cursing. "Hey, haven't you heard of the First Amendment? You jerk!"

The security guard, still grinning like a mad scientist, said over the loudspeaker, "Sure, you little shit, and Prince Charles is a Tampax."

Ramsey heard that. It made no sense at all. It all of a sudden seemed hilarious. He began to laugh. Molly joined him. They walked into the house, holding hands, laughing their heads off.

"Oh, dear," Miles said.

• **Both** Miles and Gunther had alibis. Warren O'Dell also had an alibi. So did Eve Lord. Of all things, her mother had come over for a visit. They'd been drinking iced tea by the swimming pool at the time of Mason Lord's shooting.

The media had exploded. Since Eve was young, beautiful, extravagantly rich, she garnered immense sympathy and support, bolstered by the media, who always wallowed in beauty and money, particularly if it was possibly tragic beauty.

Molly's mother had expressed sympathy, but wasn't about to fly back to the U.S. "Why ever should I, my dear? I have no desire to hold his limp hand or let the paparazzi leap out of bushes at me. Just keep me informed, Molly."

Not unexpected, Molly thought, given that the new Mrs. Lord was young enough to be her daughter, and that her ex-husband hadn't been in her life for a good number of years.

Mason Lord, who lay unconscious, his life in the balance, was nearly forgotten. The attention was on the beautiful young wife, who just might at any moment become a widow. But then again, to be fair, what reporter wanted to risk his own neck questioning the background of Mason Lord?

He survived that night. They'd nearly lost him once, but they'd been able to control his blood pressure with a medication dripping into his IV, and he seemed stable. Molly and Ramsey hadn't gone back that morning, staying with Emma and watching as Eve Lord negotiated her way through the press when she visited her husband, all in glorious color on a special news bulletin on all three major local stations.

"I wish I had a clue as to what she was thinking," Molly said.

"So does Detective O'Connor," Ramsey said. He turned to see Emma walking slowly into the living room. "Hi, Em," Molly said. "Come on in and tell us what Miles is making for lunch."

Emma just stood there, holding her piano against her, looking bewildered. "Mama, when can we go home?"

Home, Molly thought. Which home?

"Where would you like to go?" Ramsey

asked. He patted his knee. Emma went to him instantly. She carefully set her piano down on the floor beside the sofa and let him lift her onto his legs.

"Where?" he asked again.

"Home," Emma said. "To San Francisco."

"Ah," Ramsey said. "You got it right. What would you say, Em, if your mom and I were to get married?"

She turned to look up at him. She slowly raised her hand to lightly stroke his cheek. She said with all a child's appalling candor, "My daddy just died, Ramsey. He wasn't with us much, but he was my daddy."

"Yes, he was. He'll always be your daddy."

"I don't think so," Emma said then. She leaned against his chest, her cheek against his shoulder. "I can't take the chance, Ramsey, I just can't."

"What chance, sweetheart?"

"If you married Mama, someone might blow you up too."

"Oh, Emma," he said, and hugged her tightly against him. "No one's going to hurt me, no one."

"They already did. You got shot in the leg at the cabin and when my daddy blew up your back got hurt, too."

"Just minor stuff. A big guy like me can take lots of minor stuff. Don't worry, Em. Please."

She leaned down to pick up her piano.

Her security blanket, he thought, wondering what the hell to do. "You know something, Emma?"

She lightly stroked her finger on middle C, not looking at him. Afraid to look at him, he thought.

"I think when we're all a family and everything's okay again, we're going back to Ireland. Shall we all spend our honeymoon at Bunratty Castle?"

She gave him a small smile. She turned away from her piano and pressed herself against his chest. "I don't know, Ramsey. Will Mama be happy?"

"I can make her delirious, just ask her."

Emma raised her head and stared at her mother. "Mama, do you think we can keep Ramsey safe?"

This was a wallop in the gut, Molly thought, smiling at her daughter, whose piano was slipping off Ramsey's lap. She nodded. "Yes, I think we can keep him safe. You see, Em, he's right. He's big and strong. We're not as strong as he is, so we'll be thinking more. We'll be the brains of the operation. Yes, we'll keep him safe."

Emma nodded slowly. "Who shot Grandfather?"

"We don't know yet," Molly said. "But he's alive, Em, and they're taking care of him at the hospital."

"Look at the time," Ramsey said. "We've got to get going or we'll miss your appointment with Dr. Loo."

"I hope we can avoid the media," Molly said, worry lacing her voice as she looked down at Emma.

They did manage to lose the press, and in Dr. Eleanor Loo's office thirty minutes later, Emma said, "Dr. Loo, Ramsey and my mom are going to get married. What do you think?"

"I think," Eleanor Loo said, fascinated, "that I need to have my secretary go buy us a bottle of champagne. You, Emma, can have a Sprite, is that all right?"

"I'd rather have a Dr. Pepper, Dr. Loo."

"That's great." Dr. Loo got on her phone for a moment, then turned back. "In half an hour, we'll have a toast. Congratulations to both of you. Now, Emma, tell me why you're worried."

"Because Ramsey could get killed like my daddy."

"That's true," Dr. Loo said slowly. "But you see, Emma, anything can happen to anybody in the world at any time. Remember when Princess Diana died so tragically? I'll never forget the shock of it, the realization that none of us has any guarantees on anything. Life is one day at a time and trying to enjoy each day we're given. You've got to discover the knack for doing that. Do you understand?"

"That was different," Emma said. "Bad people are after us. It isn't just bad luck."

"You understand all too well," Dr. Loo said. "Okay, let's look at it this way. Ramsey and your mom want to give you a home. They want the three of you to be a family. They love you and want you to know that they'll always be there for you."

Emma sighed. She looked for a very long time

at Ramsey, saying nothing, just studying him. Then she looked at her mother. Then, she turned back to Dr. Loo, and smiled. "I think Ramsey will make me a good papa. He already loves me bunches."

"He does, does he?"

"Yes. He went crazy in San Francisco when that bad man grabbed me again."

Molly had told Dr. Loo on the phone what had happened on the beach.

"Were you scared?"

"Yes, but it was over so fast. Ramsey said I saved myself again."

"What did you do?"

"The man hit me real hard, but I stayed awake. I bit him through his side. He's kind of fat around his stomach. I bit him real deep. He jerked and I got unburied by his coat. Ramsey saw me and the man had to drop me." She turned to Ramsey. "I wish you could have caught him."

"Me too, kiddo."

Dr. Loo spoke alone to Emma for a while and then they drank champagne, Emma drank her Dr. Pepper, and they all accepted congratulations from the staff there and two waiting patients.

One of the patients, an old man with a severe eye twitch, said, "I saw a blurred photo of you, Judge, in one of the rags. You were hugging a little girl."

"No," Emma said loudly, holding her piano really hard to her chest, "he was hugging *me*. He was upset."

• **"No,** I didn't see anyone," Mason Lord said to Detective O'Connor. He paused, sucking in his breath with a sudden twinge of pain. He shot a hit of morphine into his vein by pressing the medication button.

Detective O'Connor waited until he saw the pain clear from Lord's eyes. "No shadows, no warning, nothing?"

"No. Gunther and I were just coming from a friend's office. We'd had a little chat with him. A good fellow, a politician."

"His name, sir?"

"State Senator Quentin Kordie. Don't worry about him, Detective, he wouldn't try to shoot me. We're simply friends, that's all."

"Very well. Now, sir, who knew where you would be?"

It was obvious to Molly that her father had thought about that. She hated the calculation in his eyes, the drawing of pain as he sorted again through the few people he believed had known where he would be at that particular time.

Finally, Mason said, "A number of people knew, but, of course, only people in my organization." He paused, pumped another hit of morphine into his vein, and said, "If I've got a traitor in my midst, I'll deal with it, Detective."

"No, Mr. Lord, this is a police matter. It's called attempted murder."

"Then you know who's behind it, Detective. Rule Shaker." He shook his head in bewilderment. "He's never been frankly stupid before. The moron."

Detective O'Connor rose from his chair. "It seems to me, Mr. Lord, that if indeed Mr. Shaker was a moron and did try to kill you, then you've got a big problem. You seem to be well protected for the moment. Naturally, I assume that Rule Shaker has heard that you're still alive. If you're right, I can imagine what he's saying right now."

• **Rule** Shaker wasn't saying anything. He was standing close to the huge glass window in his office that looked out over an endless stretch of desert. He hadn't ever wanted a view of Las Vegas. He lived in a city of kitsch. He wasn't about to look at it unless he had to.

The desert was clean, the air pure, so hot that all life sheltered during the hottest part of the day. Including people. He couldn't see a single soul in that vast expanse. He turned slowly as Murdock said, "Rudy's still hanging out at that motel in Oak Park," waiting for orders."

"Let him continue to wait. I hear that Lord is getting stronger every day in that hospital. He's going to live."

"That's the word," Murdock said, uncrossing his legs. He'd gained weight since he'd gotten back from Germany. He hadn't liked following Louey Santera around, but that's what Mr. Shaker had ordered him to do and that's what he'd done. Now he was home and could eat all the KFC he'd missed in Germany. He'd put on six pounds since he'd returned.

"Is there anything you'd like me to do, sir?"

"I'm thinking about it, Murdock. For the moment, we'll just let him lie in his bed, feel lots of pain, and think about his transgressions."

"Mason Lord doesn't believe in transgressions," Murdock said. He studied his boss, the man who'd taken him out of the street six years before and trained him to be one of his forward men. Yes, he was one of the FM now, a group everyone important had heard of. He was respected and admired. He should get the six pounds off.

Mr. Shaker wasn't tall and aristocratic-looking like Mason Lord. Nature had shortchanged him, topping him off at a mere five foot seven inches. But he was a fit little man, hard and lean. He dressed beautifully, mostly in handmade English suits from Savile Row. But he was cursed with a swarthy complexion, flat black glass for eyes, scary eyes that made him look like a Middle Eastern terrorist or a religious fundamentalist, and a five-o'-clock shadow that started at nine o'clock in the morning. Actually, he looked like the Hollywood stereotype of exactly what he was: a crime boss. For all that, the man had more women than he could reasonably keep up with. Murdock suspected it was danger that brought the women. For all his smallness, Shaker looked like danger. He'd heard that Shaker had serviced two women the night before, and he was fifty-eight years old. Amazing.

Service. Murdock liked that word. He wished he could service women the way Mr. Shaker did. Maybe if he lost the six pounds, they'd come around him a little more here the way they had in Germany. Of course they'd wanted to use him to get close to Louey Santera, the little slime.

"He believes in transgressions, all right," Rule Shaker said. "Just not in his own. Let's just wait and see. Tell Rudy to keep alert. I'm going to have my helicopter fly out over the desert now. It's time to scatter Melissa's ashes."

"That's what she wanted, sir?"

Rule Shaker said, "Melissa was twenty-three. She didn't even know there was such a thing as death."

30

There were six bodyguards on duty around the clock, three shifts, one man always in the hospital room with Mason Lord and another outside his door. Mason Lord didn't trust the cops to do the job.

He said to Detective O'Connor, "If I'm not paying someone, then I can't be sure he's working for me."

"Fine by me," Detective O'Connor said. "It'll save the taxpayers some money. In Chicago, the good Lord knows they need a break."

The mainstream media finally got bored and left, but some paparazzi, hoping for another strike on Mason Lord, stayed on speculation of blood and gore. They were like a plague of locusts only not as benign, said one of the hospital administrators. They camped out at the Lord mansion, too. One of them got a shot of Emma sitting in the shade of a big rhododendron bush in the garden of the estate, playing her piano. It was taken from a goodly distance, a bit on the blurred side, from magnification, but it was still clearly Emma. She'd been labeled as the *Granddaughter of Crime Lord*.

When Mason Lord saw the photo, he said quietly to Gunther, "How clever the play on words is. Isn't it odd? It's this photo that has broken my patience, my indifference. Get the name of the paparazzo who took the picture."

• **Just** after lunch that day, Eve Lord came out of the living room into the grand foyer to hear Ramsey say to Molly, "There's no reason to stay longer. Your father is over the worst. We all know who likely shot him and there's not a thing we can do about it. As to the actual person who pulled the trigger, the cops are on it. Chances are slim we'll ever know. This could mean that the violence will escalate. I don't want us here if it does, particularly Emma. Let's get married. Let's go home."

And Molly, frumpy plain Molly with her wild red hair and too-skinny body, gazed up at the big man whom Eve would take to bed in a minute, stared up at him like she wanted to eat him, and she probably did. Then she laughed and jumped into his arms. She clearly caught him off guard, but he was fast, managing to catch her and bring her tightly against his

387

chest, his arms locked around her. She wrapped her legs around his waist. Then he laughed and swung her around. "Home," she said, kissing him once, twice, a half dozen more times. "I like the sound of that."

Slowly, he slid her down the front of his body. When she was standing, staring up at him, laughing, he leaned down and kissed her mouth. Molly's hands were on his shirt. She looked ready to pull it off him.

Eve cleared her throat. "I see there's more going on here than a little friendship."

"Yes," Ramsey said, lifting his head, releasing Molly slowly. The taste of her was still fresh, still drawing on him, the memory of her body was still warm against him. "You can congratulate us, Eve. Molly and I are going to be married." They hadn't told her before. It felt a bit on the indecent side to tell that to a woman who'd nearly been made a widow.

"Congratulations," Eve said. She looked down at Molly's waistline. "You pregnant already?"

"No, I'm not," Molly said. "Getting in that condition would be kind of hard, what with Emma sleeping in the same room, don't you think?"

"I would say that in my experience, men always find a way. My former fiancé nailed me once in the coat closet with his family not six feet away."

Ramsey laughed. "Then he deserves to be a former." He hugged Molly to his side. "Is Emma eating chocolate-chip cookies in Miles's kitchen?"

Eve pulled on soft pale cream leather gloves that matched her silk dress. "Not chocolate chip, but her new favorite—peanut butter. Mrs. Lopez was chattering about it. I'm going to see your father, Molly. Does he know about this?"

"Yes, we told him last night."

"I see. So I'm the last to know. Will you two be here when I get back?"

"Depends," Ramsey said. "You want to bring back something to celebrate?"

"Sure," Eve Lord said, then called out, "Gunther, I'm ready!"

• **In** the *Chicago Sun-Times*, on the bottom of page ten of Section A, there was brief mention of a man who had been found just off Highway 88 between Mooseheart and Aurora by a passing motorist. The man had been beaten severely, but was expected, in time, to make a full recovery. His cameras had been crushed and left beside him. The newspaper called him a free lance photographer, but bottom line, what he was, was a paparazzo.

• **"I** think we should pack our meager belongings, grab Emma, and hop a plane to Reno. I was thinking Las Vegas, but Rule Shaker's there, and I can't quite handle getting married anywhere near to where he is. I don't want any more magazines or tabloids with pictures of Emma. She saw the one in the *National Informer*. She'd made out some of the words before I managed to get it away from her. I just pray she hadn't gotten to the part about her playing the piano as well as her murdered father, Louey Santera. Can you begin to imagine the field day the media will have if we get married either here or in Harrisburg at my folks' place? They always find out, no matter how careful you are."

"Oh, God!" Miles came running out of the kitchen, a dishcloth in his hands. "Thank God you're both here. I just don't believe this. Somebody just tried to kill your daddy again, Molly. Oh God. Where's Gunther? Where's Mrs. Lord?"

"Is he all right, Miles?"

"Yes, he is. That was one of the guards we hired to protect him in the hospital. The guy fired from the building across the way— a good hundred and fifty yards—right through the window. He wounded a nurse who was taking your father's blood pressure."

"That's an enormous distance," Ramsey said.

"Is the nurse all right?"

"Took off a lot of her right ear; she bled all over everything, which made everyone believe that your father had been shot, but yeah, she's fine."

Ramsey squeezed Molly's hand. "I guess we'd better get to the hospital. Miles, will you make certain Emma is never out of your sight?"

"No problem, Ramsey." He'd been wringing his hands, but now at the mention of Emma, her need to be protected, he instantly calmed down. By the time Ramsey and Molly were out the front door, Miles had pulled himself together. Emma stood beside him. He was holding her hand.

Detective O'Connor from Oak Park and two detectives from the CPD were in Mason Lord's room when they arrived.

"Show them in," Detective O'Connor said. Introductions were made quickly. Miles was right. There was blood everywhere.

"Ears bleed like stink," one of the CPD detectives said. He pulled on his own ear and Molly realized the bottom part was gone. He'd never be able to wear pierced earrings. She nearly laughed. She was losing it.

She slipped her hand around Ramsey's. He looked at her briefly, saw her too-bright eyes, and slowly, very slowly, pulled her closer. "It's all right," he said quietly, his mouth nearly touching the top of her head. "It will be just fine. Breathe slowly, that's it."

The hospital window was shattered. Two technicians were busy very carefully extracting the bullet from the wall just about ten inches off the floor. The woman was using tweezers.

Detective O'Connor looked tired and harassed, but that wasn't anything new. She felt tension between him and the other cops. He told them in his concise way, "Nurse Thomas was standing right next to your father, taking his blood pressure. Suddenly he seemed to weaken and fall back against the pillow. Nurse Thomas immediately leaned over him, holding on to him, when the shooter fired. If your father hadn't gotten suddenly weak, if the nurse hadn't pressed him down even more, shielded him, all those things, then the chances are good that your father would have gone down this time, Mrs. Santera. At the very least he would have been wounded. The bullet went through Nurse Thomas's earlobe, downward. The bullet slammed into the wall less than a foot above the floor."

Molly leaned over her father. "Dad, Ramsey and I are here. You're all right, thank God."

"Yes," Mason said. "I'm fine, Molly. Actually, I've got to be the luckiest bastard in Chicago. As for Nurse Thomas, I'm going to cut her a nice check for her bravery."

They turned to see the technician holding up the bullet. "It's fairly intact," she called out. "Enough for identification."

"Excellent," one of the Chicago detectives said. "We'll do a comparison between this one and the one they found on the scene over on Jefferson after Mr. Lord was shot. Are you Judge Ramsey Hunt?"

"Yes," Ramsey said. "It seems likely the bullets will match, but unfortunately it won't tell us anything else."

"At least we'll verify that we've got just one perp here," Detective O'Connor said.

Molly, who was staring at that smashed window, said, "He blew out the window. I remember all of us mentioned the possibility, but the closest building is so far away. At least one hundred and fifty yards, probably more."

"I'm not blaming Gunther," Mason said, the first words he'd spoken in a good ten minutes. There were seven people in the room, most of them talking. The instant he spoke, everyone shut up and turned toward him. He continued in that calm cool voice of his, "I remember when you were looking out that window, Molly. I remember you were one of the people who brought up the possibility, but none of us considered it a threat. We underestimated him. Technology just keeps racing forward, and this time, our brains stayed behind. We're getting old and careless, Gunther. The guy had a clear shot at me through that damned window." He leaned back against the pillow, closing his eyes.

Gunther said, "That's why we've moved the bed away from the window." He was pale and tense, as close to distraught as Molly had ever seen him. He added, "One thing we do know is this guy has to be a world-class sniper. I've known of maybe half a dozen guys who could have made that shot through a closed window."

Detective O'Connor said, "We'd like you to provide us with the names of all the men you know who would be capable of such a shot." He paused a moment, running his palm over his bald head. "You know, if Mr. Lord hadn't fallen back on the pillow at that particular instant..."

Gunther nodded, then said to Mason,

"We're getting another room ready, sir. It's being seen to right now. No one will know the new room number. There won't be any window that has a building within a mile of it."

Mason laughed, then coughed. He was silent a moment, controlling the pain. "Gunther, you know a secret is impossible when more than one person knows about it. It'll get out, but it won't matter, because I'm going home."

• **"Tell** me how you're feeling, Emma."

"About what exactly, Dr. Loo?"

"Well, your grandfather came home from the hospital this morning. How is he?"

"I heard Miles say he's really tired and weak. Eve didn't want me to get near him because I'm a kid and I make noise, only I don't, not much. I think she kept me away because she doesn't like me much. Then I saw his face when they were carrying him in on a stretcher. He looked all gray and old. I never thought he was old before. I always thought he looked like one of those movie stars in the old movies Mama likes. Yes, he's all black and white." Emma paused, easing her piano down across her legs. She added, "This morning he looked old. I didn't say anything. There were people everywhere. I think three of them were doctors and they were all around him."

"How is your mother dealing with all this?"

Emma thought about that. She lightly touched the piano keys but didn't make any sound. Her dark hair, normally in a French braid, was loose this morning. Emma had some of her mother's naturally curly hair. It swung over, hiding most of her face as she said, "Mama's really quiet. I think she's scared. She's been scared for a long time now. She's scared about me. She doesn't want to leave me alone. Neither does Ramsey." Emma sighed. "Sometimes I'd like to be alone, but I know they worry if I'm ever out of their sight. But that's not often." She raised her head, pushed her hair back, then looked toward the closed door. Molly and Ramsey were in the waiting room. "I'm really glad that we're getting married, though."

Dr. Loo smiled, unable not to. Despite everything, this child was one of the lucky ones. She figured that Molly and Ramsey would love Emma so much she'd have no choice but to heal. "When are you all going to get married?"

"I heard Mama say that we couldn't leave for another day or so." She lowered her voice. "I think we're going to elope." Dr. Loo nearly laughed aloud this time, restraining herself when Emma sighed again, that too-adult sigh that made Dr. Loo wish for a tantrum, or at least the threat of one. She remembered Ramsey saying the same thing. What was going on here?

"Do you want to elope, Emma?"

"Oh yes, Dr. Loo. I'd get to be Ramsey's best man and Mama's maid of honor. I'd get to be the flower girl, too."

"Then what bothers you?"

"My grandfather wants us to be married in

his house. Miles said that he wants to give my mama away. But Eve wants us to leave. I think Eve will win."

"Why do you think that?"

"Because Grandfather is sick. He has to be standing to win." She lowered her head. "I heard Mama say that to Ramsey. They were talking really quiet so I snuck close so I could hear them."

"Well, you tell me tomorrow how everything is going, all right? Have you had any more nightmares, Emma?"

Emma shook her head. She scooted off the chair, her piano clutched close. "I think about him though, Dr. Loo."

"And what do you think, Emma?"

"That he's going to come back. I know when we go back to San Francisco there will be police officers close to make sure he doesn't get near us. I heard Ramsey talking to Officer Virginia on the phone yesterday. Ramsey told me his name is Sonny Dickerson. He showed me a photo of him. He's the man. I described him really well."

Dr. Loo had also seen the photograph. "Yes, you certainly did. Now, Emma, do you believe, deep down in your heart, and up higher, in your brain, that your mama and Ramsey will keep you safe?"

Emma thought about that. She looked hard at her Nike sneakers. She was wearing her favorite plaid socks that Ramsey had bought her in Ireland.

Dr. Loo patted her lightly on her arm. The

child was still too thin, but that was all right, for now. She imagined that it worried her parents, though. Emma finally said, "My heart's sure, but my brain isn't."

Dr. Loo nodded. "That's smart. Until this Sonny Dickerson is caught, Emma, it's really important for you to pay attention as well as your mama and Ramsey. Since there will be police nearby if he does come back, that should make you feel safer."

"I asked Ramsey to teach me to read more. Maybe I'll read about that man in a book."

"Yes, an excellent idea."

"Mama said I was so smart that I'd be reading about crime and punishment before I went to school this fall."

• **Molly** looked at her father, who was slightly elevated in his hospital bed, a newspaper on his lap, his reading glasses on. He wasn't happy, but she wasn't about to back down. She wanted Emma out of here, as quickly as possible. He said in that particular mildly contemptuous way he always spoke to her, "You will marry here."

She just shook her head. She wasn't going to argue with him. She said mildly, "You've already seen me get married once. You don't need to do it a second time."

Ramsey said, "We'd like to get Emma out of here and safe."

"She's so safe in San Francisco?" Mason said, his sarcasm biting. "That bastard took her from right under your goddamned nose, Ramsey."

397

Eve said, "Mason, there are Ramsey's parents. It isn't fair to them."

He didn't even look over at her. "Keep out of it, Eve. This doesn't concern you."

She merely smiled down at him, seemingly untroubled. She said, "I think I'll go get some tea. Oh yes, Ramsey, the car's coming for you at three o'clock, if that's what you decide." She looked down at her Cartier watch, smiling a small but quite amused smile.

They left at five minutes after three, Molly's good-byes to her father curt. The media knew their plans, naturally, likely from a leak from the limo company. Ramsey and Molly watched the media take off after the town car with its thankfully tinted windows. He smiled. "Let's go, Gunther. Good idea. Well done."

• **I'm** married, Molly thought, staring at her pale face in the mirror. Married again. Only this time I'm an adult, not a stupid immature kid. This time I married a good man and he's so sexy I don't think I can stand it. And he loves Emma to death.

She grinned at herself, touched on some lipstick, and slowly slipped the gorgeous peach silk nightgown over her head. Ramsey had presented it to her just ten minutes before, right in front of Emma, since there was no choice. "No more cotton tents," he'd whispered in her ear. "This is for both of us. Actually, tonight, I guess it's for Emma too." He looked as if he wanted to break into tears.

She walked out of the bathroom, leaving the

light on for a moment, knowing it backlighted her very nicely.

Emma called out, sounding awed, which really pleased Molly, "Mama, you look like a fairy princess. Ramsey and I have been waiting for you. And waiting. I want to get married so I can wear that, too."

Emma sounded as bright as a new penny, enthusiastic, about as far from being asleep as a new puppy. So what? In the long run, it wasn't important when she had a wedding night, when she was finally alone with her new husband. Things would happen when it was time. She gave Emma a big hug, making her squeak she squeezed her so tightly. "We're married and we're all together," she said, smoothing her fingers through Emma's hair. "We're lucky, Em. I really like our man."

Ramsey was still wearing a beautiful dark suit and pristine white shirt. His tie wasn't as conservative. In fact, it was a psychedelic mishmash of purple, pink, and yellow squiggles. He looked big and tough, and his smile would have charmed the gold out of a miser's teeth.

"He promised me he wouldn't ever get fat, Mama," Emma said.

"That's right," Ramsey said. "I don't believe in it. However, to help me keep that promise, you've got to get me to a gym before too much more time passes. Well, Emma, we're married. Do you approve?"

There was a thread of fine tension in his voice. Molly cocked her head to one side, staring at him. Surely he knew that Emma was nuts about him. She understood. He had to hear it. He was waiting, all quiet.

Emma pulled away from her mom and walked to him. She held up her arms. He picked her up and held her close. She drew back and said not five inches from his face, "You're the best man in the whole world, Ramsey."

"Thanks, Emma. I think you're about the greatest little kid. And just look at your mama. She's not bad herself. I got myself a fairy princess." He hugged her again, then said to Molly, "Emma and I are going to wake you up every hour and tell you how beautiful you are."

"In theory I like the sound of that," Molly said, walking toward the king-size bed. "Now, you cutthroats, how about we play some Old Maid?"

"No, Mama, you know I like gin rummy better."

"Emma, you always win at gin rummy. I just got married. Can't you give me a break?"

"All right," Emma said. "We'll play five-card draw."

Ramsey hooted with laughter.

Emma looked quite pleased with herself. After she'd won the first hand with three jacks, she said, "This marriage thing isn't any different. We did this in Ireland. Nothing's changed. That's good."

"That's painfully true," Ramsey said, and shuffled the deck.

31

Just after midnight, Molly awoke slowly when Ramsey curled her hair around her ear, licked her earlobe, bit it gently, and said quietly, "If you want to join the game, it's best if you're in on the kickoff."

"I've always loved football, from the very first kickoff. Where's Emma?"

He moved on his elbow, above her. "Our little darling was sleeping so deeply I thought she'd start snoring at any moment. I tucked her in in the other bedroom. I left the door open a crack so we could hear her if she woke up, so no yelling from either of us. Okay?"

She raised her hand and touched her fingertips to his face. Her eyes were adjusted to the night. She touched his nose, ran her fingertips over his black eyebrows, touched his lips. "You're a beautiful man, Ramsey. When I walked in on you in the bathroom at Dromoland, I wanted to jump you."

He grabbed her and pulled her tightly against him. He groaned against her hair. "I wish you had. As you saw clearly, I wanted to be jumped. I was shaking I wanted to be jumped so badly."

She touched his shoulders, ran her hand down his back to his flank, realizing in that moment that he'd shucked off his boxer shorts. "Oh dear," she said, leaning up to bite his shoulder, "I'm overdressed."

He had that gorgeous silk nightgown off her

in under ten seconds. She kissed his chin. "Do you want me to hang it up so it won't get wrinkled?" At the horrified look on his face, she lightly smacked his chest, and laughed. He rolled over on top of her, feeling the length of her against him. He breathed in her scent, feeling the textures of her flesh pressed up against him, the firmness, the softness of her belly. "I've thought about this so many times I nearly scrambled my brains. I surprised myself. I'd never thought I was such a horny bastard before, but with you, I am. I'm in a pretty bad way here, Molly."

"Will you try to nail me in the closet?"

He shook his head as he began kissing her, saying between kisses, "No, that's got no class. Well, maybe a closet would be all right if Emma's close by."

She arched up against him, found his mouth with her hands, and attacked him. "You don't know what a bad way is," she said into his mouth. "I want to eat you up." She was biting his neck, nibbling on his mouth.

"Nah, let me do that," he said against her breast. "That's my specialty. There's a whole lot of other stuff you can do. But later, Molly, a lot later." Then she opened her legs and he groaned in answer. He kissed her neck, her ear, her mouth, returning again and again. He balanced himself briefly on his elbow while his other hand went to her breast, then stroked down her ribs. "Well, hell," he said, his hand coming back up to her face, "I'm this big-time federal judge and we still can't do everything with Emma close. And the good Lord knows I want to very badly."

She was rubbing her foot along his leg. "Just keep trying. It's wonderful."

He lifted himself up onto his knees, shuddering with the effort to separate himself from her, and pushed her hands away when she would have brought him back down to her. He looked down at her, lightly touching her with his fingers, opening her legs wider. He brought his head down and began kissing her stomach. "This is a very good place to start," he said against her warm skin, moving downward until his mouth and his fingers stroked and pushed her, deepened inside her, until, in about the same time it had taken Ramsey to get her nightgown off, she was lurching up, choking out, "Ramsey, oh, goodness, this is too much. I think a yell is coming."

He clapped one hand over her mouth and she yelled against his palm, wondering if she were going to die, knowing she wouldn't, and never wanting the incredible, shattering feelings to stop. When she slumped back, quivering as the aftershocks of that wild pleasure continued to careen through her, he came inside her, deeper inside, until he was sealed to her. He froze over her, and in that instant, the knowledge that he was finally where he belonged, that she was his wife and his lover until they both left the earth, plucked him up, making him dizzy and hot, then shattered through him. He'd never realized there could be such a binding force in the world as what he was feeling now. He'd wanted Emma, wanted her safe, and he still did. Always it had been Emma and then, only after Emma, Molly had been in his mind. Now he didn't know. One thing he did know was that he hadn't expected being this consumed until there was nothing inside him but Molly and what she was making him feel. He shuddered like a palsied man as he climaxed deep inside this woman he'd known for less than two months, this woman who'd been married to a rock star and was the daughter of a gangster. Who knew about life?

Molly slowly opened her eyes only when she was certain she'd continue breathing if she tried such a violent movement. Nothing happened. She blinked. Nothing continued to happen. She concentrated on returning to life as she knew it. She couldn't believe the utter dizzying pleasure she'd just experienced. She said, "I'm going to try to talk now, not move, just talk. Yes, that was a complete sentence. Yes, I'm getting there, thank you. That was nice, Ramsey."

He was still deep inside her. It felt incredible. She closed her eyes again, just thinking about how amazing it was that they'd found each other. She lifted her hips. He groaned into her hair.

"What the hell do you mean 'nice'? Nice is a wussy word. It's close to an insult."

"Well, better than nice then. Really good. Maybe even getting close to superb."

He was quiet a moment, harder in her than

he had been just the instant before. "What you need is a comparison. Now, you might think I would be ready right this minute, but I'm not. My spirit needs to revive. Give me at least five more minutes."

He was lying flat on top of her, his head on the pillow beside hers.

Molly stroked her hands up and down his long back. "I forgot to check your back. Is the burn healed?"

"Yes, it's all right."

"It feels pretty smooth. How about your leg?"

"My leg is as good as new. How about your arm? Are the stitches all gone?"

"All gone. Just a little scar ridge. Ramsey, would you mind if I admitted that I sort of more than just like you a whole lot?"

He was silent. She began to fidget. "No," he said, still unable to move. "Truth be told, I more than sort of just like you as well."

He finally managed to lift himself above her again. He leaned his head down and kissed her mouth. "For so long now I would look at your mouth and wonder how you tasted, what you'd feel like. I wanted to make love to your mouth. Then I'd think how I'd feel with your mouth on me."

Not twenty minutes later, Ramsey's spirit completely revived, they made love again, and this time, he thought he'd die. It was close. It was wonderfully close. She could nail him anytime, anywhere.

At about four o'clock in the morning, Ramsey felt small hands patting his shoulder.

He'd had the brains to put his boxer shorts back on, thank God, which he'd believed was a miracle. He'd even gotten Molly to put her nightgown back on, and she'd been only semi-conscious.

He pulled Emma over his shoulder and scooted her down on the other side of her mother. Molly, still asleep, reached out her hand to touch him again. "Emma's here," he whispered. She quieted immediately. She smiled to herself in the darkness. She felt Emma's small arm come over around her waist. Emma said in her ear, "I know you're beautiful, Mama. It doesn't matter that I can't see you."

"Thank you, Em. You don't have to wake me every hour to tell me."

She settled again. Just before she went back to sleep, she saw the Justice of the Peace pronounce them husband and wife, saw Emma grinning from ear to ear and announcing to the judge's wife who'd sold Molly a bouquet for ten dollars that they were all together now and wasn't that just perfect. The woman, bless her heart, had agreed, distracting Emma while Ramsey kissed her.

She fell deeply asleep, her spirit so very content that she forgot ex-priest Sonny Dickerson, who had gone so far around the bend, he would probably die before he gave Emma up.

• **The** next morning, Molly said over the breakfast table in their suite, "You know what I think?"

She spoke softly, for Emma was close by, sitting on the floor, practicing printing her name in a notebook Molly had bought her in the hotel gift shop.

Ramsey looked up from his hash browns. "I know this isn't serious. You're about ready to burst into laughter."

"No, you're wrong. I'm dead serious."

"All right, but I don't know what you're talking about. What do you think?"

"I think being with you was beyond superb. It was so wonderful, maybe it should be taxed."

He nearly lost it right there. He gulped. He took a quick drink of his coffee and scalded his mouth. Then he clearly remembered how she felt and nearly shuddered his way off his chair.

Emma looked up from her printing and said, "What's my last name now, Mama?"

Ramsey looked at Molly, sex forgotten, sudden fierce possessiveness in his voice as he said, "I'd like you to be Emma Hunt now. What do you think?"

"Could you print it out for me, Ramsey?"

He took her pencil and wrote out Emma Hunt. Emma went to work. She said finally, looking back up, "It looks pretty good all written out. It's okay with me." She held up the paper for them to see.

Both Ramsey and Molly examined her effort. Ramsey said, "Well done, even good enough so I can read it. *Emma Hunt.* It has a ring to it." Emma grinned and went back to her printing. Ramsey lowered his voice. "I'm sorry, Molly. We never discussed it, but I want this very badly. I want Emma to be mine, legally and every other way as well."

"I'm torn," she said, cutting another slice of her grapefruit. "Louey wasn't ever around, but he was her father. It's like he'll cease to exist now."

"Let me ask you a question. If Louey were still alive and you'd divorced him and then married me, what would you decide?"

She forked down the grapefruit, then picked up a piece of wheat toast. She said quietly, so Emma couldn't hear, "I'd say he was a bum and never even wanted to see Emma anyway. Maybe I'd say he didn't deserve for her to carry a name that meant so little." She shook her head. "But because he's dead, I feel she needs to hold on to something. How about Emma Santera Hunt? We could ask Dr. Loo, but that sounds like a good idea."

"Emma will always know that he was her father."

"Yes," Molly said. "Are you going to eat your bacon, Ramsey?"

"No, you take it. You need to keep up your strength. I'm brimming with strength. The more times a man gets jumped, the stronger he gets. He gets pumped up. All his muscles start to flex. His fortitude increases exponentially. I can't wait to prove it to you."

"How do you think it looks, Mama?"

Molly looked away from her new husband, wishing she could fling herself on top of him and screw his brains out. "Ah, Em, let's see. Ah, you've printed it another six times. Each is better. Very good, love. Oh yes, that looks just grand. When you start the first grade this fall, you'll be Emma Santera Hunt."

"Miss Emma Santera Hunt," Emma said. "I won't be a Ms. until I'm eighteen."

Molly looked over at Ramsey, who knew what she'd been thinking. "And I'll be Mrs. Molly Hunt."

"That makes all of us Hunts," Emma said happily, then frowned. "I never even thought about a Hunt before Ramsey found me."

Ramsey called his parents. His mother and father spoke to both Molly and Emma. It went well, though Molly heard the disappointment after they'd gotten over their shock. They agreed to go back for a reception in their honor sometime toward the end of the summer.

"By that time, everything should be resolved," Ramsey said as he put the receiver back into its cradle. "You'll see how my mom treats all her daughters-in-law like they're perfect and gives grief to her three sons."

"Makes sense to me," Molly said. "I guess I should call my mom."

• **They** returned to San Francisco the following afternoon. It was close enough to midsummer to be chilly, with the fog from the Pacific rolling in through the Golden Gate.

Emma was wearing a sweater, walking around her new backyard, examining the flowers that grew well in the protection of a sturdy redwood fence. Her piano was on a chair in the kitchen. An unmarked police car was parked across the street.

"I'll get her a swing set," Ramsey said, coming up behind Molly, closing his arms around her. He leaned down and kissed her ear. "Maybe I can hang a tire from that branch on the pine tree over there."

She turned in his arms. "I want to have my way with you," she said, and so she did, right there in his study, their clothes on, ever watchful because Emma was close by. They were standing together, still breathing hard, when they heard Emma call out from the kitchen, "Mama, Ramsey's got a room that's filled with all sorts of cans."

Molly rolled her eyes. "Cans? All different sizes, I'll bet. You pervert."

"Mama? I can hear you laughing. Did you make a joke?"

"Oh yes," Molly said quietly. "Oh, yes."

• **After** a spicy dinner of Ramsey's favorite Chinese Szechwan Beef, and garlic noodles with eggplant, Molly said, as she watched Emma set down her fork, "It's time the three of us talked about this, Em. We've put it off long enough. You're ready to jump out of your skin." Emma's head came up. "Let me be real up-front with you. Ramsey's worried about you. He's worried because that awful man is still out there. We hoped he would have

410

been caught by now, but he hasn't. This means, Em, that you're going to have to be super-careful. That means whenever we leave the house, you've got to stay really close to either me or Ramsey. If one of us ever walks ahead of you, you grab Ramsey's hand or mine. Do you understand? Does that make sense to you?"

Ramsey would never have brought it right out in the open like this. He felt as if they were standing over an active volcano. He barely managed to make his throat swallow the strong black coffee he'd just brewed.

Emma said, "Yes, I think it makes sense too, Mama. Dr. Loo told me that this man thought I could save him from going to Hell. She said that wasn't true, but it was stuck in his brain like that, and so it was true to him."

She was talking. He supposed he was astounded that everything out of that small mouth made such sense.

"She's probably right," Molly said.

"If he thought I could save him from going to Hell, then why did he hurt me so much?"

Molly said, "Mr. Savich told Ramsey that the doctors at the FBI think that just maybe he hurt you because he believed you should take his punishment for him, that by hurting you, his savior, he was cleansing himself of his sins, readying to give himself into God's hands."

"I don't understand that, Mama."

"No one does, not really," Ramsey said. "He's

very sick and therefore he's very dangerous because he's out of control. That's why we've really got to be careful."

"I know he's still out there," Emma said. "He's just waiting."

"I know," Molly said. "I wish I could get him right this minute, but I can't. Until we do catch him, though, things are going to be tough for us. I'm sorry, but I can't change that. You're going to have to be on the lookout all the time and stick close. Now I want you to go to the front window and look at that light blue car parked across the street. Those are police officers and they're going to keep all their eyes open for that man."

"I see them, Mama."

Ramsey cleared his throat. But the reasonable sorts of words that had just come out of Molly's mouth were stuck in his throat. He tried to say something intelligent, something comforting, but what came out of his mouth was, "Emma, do you think you could come here a minute? I need to have you close to me. I'm not feeling so good."

Emma came running back to the table. Ramsey barely had time to push back his chair and lift her onto his legs. He drew her close. Emma was patting his arms. "It's going to be all right, Ramsey. We'll get through this. I promise."

He buried his face in her French braid. "I love you, Emma Hunt."

"I love you too, Ramsey. A whole lot." She

kept stroking his arm and his shoulder, giving him all the comfort she could.

• **That** weekend they went to Monterey to be tourists. They went first to the Monterey Bay Aquarium. Emma loved the jellyfish. The three of them sat on the bench facing the huge tank and watched the jellyfish for a good thirty minutes.

They walked through Carmel, played on the beautiful beach at the cove at the bottom of Ocean Avenue, drove down to Big Sur and picnicked off the road on the Seventeen Mile Drive.

They kept Sonny Dickerson at bay in their minds for a good three days, at least for most of the time. Ramsey called Virginia Trolley once they'd reached their hotel, gave her their number, and told her that everyone was settled in. Molly called her father. He was improving by the day. Miles missed them, particularly Emma. Her father was sleeping, Eve said, but maybe they could call him next week and he'd want to speak to them.

"Bitch," Molly said quietly as she hung up the phone.

Ramsey looked up from the Blackjack game he and Emma were playing. He'd just taught her the game two days before. She was beating him, which both surprised him and made him so proud he couldn't stand it. He said over his shoulder to Molly with a grin, "It's easier for Eve to deal with your father when no one else is around, particularly if it happens to be a stepdaughter who's older than she is and a step-granddaughter who's smarter at gambling than she is, and a guy who's really handsome and witty who isn't at all interested in her. Darn it all, Emma, I can't believe you took a hit on sixteen. You should have held."

Emma looked so withdrawn, so apparently locked into herself, that it scared Molly until she realized that Emma was just concentrating. Now Emma looked up and said in all seriousness, "I've been counting the cards real hard, Ramsey, just the way you told me to. I knew there were two more threes and two more aces in the deck. I don't remember how many twos there are."

He snarled, leaned over, and picked Emma up, falling onto his back and lifting her up over him, shaking her. She was screaming with laughter. "Molly," he called out over Emma's laughter, "can I go throw her in the jellyfish tank? Then you and I can sit there on that bench and watch her make friends."

"I remember now. There's one more two in the deck. It would be stupid to hold on sixteen."

"No, there aren't any more twos." He let her down. "Let's look. I'll prove it." There were twelve cards left. The very last card was the two of hearts.

• **The** next afternoon they were walking on the Monterey Wharf. Ramsey loved the smell of a wharf, a combination of salt and wood and creosote, a sealant used on the wood. Seagulls were thick and loud, begging handouts like the most aggressive panhandlers who flocked to Union Square in San Francisco. There were lots of fish stalls, and getting close to the stalls, particularly late in the afternoon, was nearly overwhelming—a putrid, briny odor that could bring tears to your eyes.

The smell of decaying seaweed was strong as well today. Flies swarmed over the seaweed. It wasn't an appetizing sight. Sea lions hooted near the wooden pilings, fat and bold, usually a dozen or so mesmerized children hanging around them, begging food from their parents to give to them.

And there were endless souvenir shops. Emma was wearing a Carmel T-shirt, her Nike sneakers, and her plaid socks. Molly had told Ramsey she'd wished he'd bought Emma a good dozen pair since they were her favorites. She washed them out each night.

Because it was summer, there were tons of tourists. The sun was bright overhead, but it wasn't hot. It was rarely hot by the ocean. It was usually just perfect. Normally, Ramsey preferred to carry Emma. He knew she was safe when he was carrying her. But she was independent, and after a while, she'd given him a long look and said, "Ramsey, I'll be all right. I'm not going to go run off."

She was walking beside him, holding his hand, either trying to speed him up or slow him down. She had her eye on a particular sea lion who honked loudly at every person who appeared to look easy. He was immense, and

Ramsey could see how he'd gotten that way. He asked one of the fishermen how long the sea lion had been in residence. "Two years," the man said. "Bloody beggar never stops eating. His name's Old Chester, the Gay Blade. Hey, what do you expect with San Francisco just up the road? No one's supposed to feed any of them, but they do. You can buy cheap sardines right over there. The beggars, they got no shame."

Was he referring to the tourists or to the sea lions?

"All right," Ramsey finally said. "But you're going to have to toss the sardines to him, Emma. I draw the line at that. And don't get too close."

She gave him one of her tolerant nods and bought three sardines, thankfully dead, and was given a paper towel. Ramsey stood right behind her as she eased up until it was her turn to feed the behemoth. She yelled with laughter when he honked very loudly.

At the same moment, Molly yelled his name.

32

Ramsey nearly tripped, he swung around so quickly. A boy was trying to wrestle Molly's purse out of her hands. He ran full tilt toward the tussle, yelling, "Let her go, you little punk!"

Emma.

Ramsey jerked back around to see Emma standing there, her hand close to that sea lion, not realizing what had happened. There were people all around her. She was all right. Then, just at the instant when he would have turned back to Molly, Ramsey saw him slithering through a knot of kids and parents near the sea lions. He would recognize the man anywhere, both in his nightmares and in real life. Just a few more feet and he'd be close enough to grab her. He was nearly on her, not more than three feet away, moving quickly now since he knew the distraction he'd set into motion couldn't last much longer. He had his hand out when Ramsey grabbed him by his collar, jerked him around, and sent his fist into his jaw.

"Hey, buddy! Why'd you hit that guy? He wasn't doing nothing!"

"Yeah, you can't go around hitting people. What is it with you?"

There were half a dozen people swarming close now, pressing in toward him, but no one had grabbed him yet. He yelled, "Emma! Get over to your mother!"

Dickerson was stumbling to his feet, rubbing his jaw, spitting blood, yelling, "Why'd you hit me? I'm a priest! Why'd you hit a holy man?"

"Hey, buddy, you shouldn't oughta done that!"

Ramsey was shoved back. Another man punched him in the shoulder.

"No, stop! He's my papa and he was saving me!"

But they didn't hear the little girl. Just kept telling him what a bum he was.

Ramsey was desperate. He didn't want to, but he saw Dickerson going for Emma again. "Leave her alone!" he yelled, but Dickerson ignored him, so intent on Emma that Ramsey wondered if he'd even heard him.

"Sorry about this." Ramsey levered himself up and kicked one man high on the thigh, sent his fist into another man's shoulder, and one final kick into a man's belly. He was free. Dickerson was close to Emma again. This time Ramsey didn't yell. He wanted to get his bare hands on Dickerson and beat the living shit out of him. He felt rage pour through him, violent, pure vengeance. Dickerson was two feet away from her. The look on his face was calm, even serene, as if he were looking at a beautiful scene, and perhaps he was, somewhere in his demented brain. A man turned sharply and bumped into Ramsey. Ramsey couldn't stop himself, he shoved the guy hard out of the way. Then Dickerson looked up. Ramsey heard him curse, saw him weighing his chances of getting caught. He must have seen the death in Ramsey's eyes. He stumbled away down the wharf, weaving in and out of people. Ramsey yelled after him to stop. He stumbled faster, then straightened when the wharf was clear, and began running, Ramsey behind him, Emma running behind them both. People cleared from their path. Dickerson looked back, saw that Ramsey was closing, then turned sharply and jumped into the water. Ramsey grabbed up Emma, turned to a large woman who was surrounded by little kids and looked tough as nails, and said, "He's a child molester. He was after my daughter. Please hold her and keep her safe." He nearly threw Emma into the woman's arms. He jumped into the icy water of Monterey Bay after Sonny Dickerson.

He thought his flesh would freeze off his body. He felt as if his lungs had seized up. He got to the surface, looking for Dickerson. He couldn't see him. He couldn't be far. He felt as though he'd jumped right on top of him.

He heard Molly yell, "He's heading for the pilings, Ramsey. Hurry! Be careful! Damn you, be careful!"

He was a strong swimmer, but the surge was vicious, yanking one way, then the other. There were rocks around them, sharp and dangerous. The water was so cold his chest was tight and his arms and legs felt rubbery. Then, finally, he saw Dickerson, slipping in between the slimy pilings.

This time he wasn't about to let that monster escape him. Not again. He believed in the laws and in the courts, to his very fiber he believed in the order of law, but he knew that no lawyer was ever going to get the chance to represent this man, not if he could help it. He surged through the wildly slapping waves, nearly on him, when Dickerson, his hair plastered to his skull, suddenly waved a gun.

"Stay away from me!" he yelled, then got a mouthful of water. He choked and spat it out. "I mean it, Hunt. I'll shoot you if I have to."

Ramsey treaded water, yelling back, his

voice strong and calm, even persuasive in his rage, "Listen to me, Dickerson, you'll never get Emma. All the cops have your photo and so does the FBI. Given what you've done, all of them want to shoot you down like the pathetic bastard you are. You're not going to get Emma or any other little kid ever again. It's all over for you. Give it up." Ramsey grabbed one of the pilings, his palm slipping because it was so slimy. "Come on, Dickerson, don't be stupid. It's over."

"That's a lie. No one knows who I am. I'm an expert at makeup and disguises. All she saw was Clinton. It was good!"

"Not on the beach you didn't wear any makeup. Emma described you very well. It's not as if you'd just emerged newly hatched from under a rock. You have a record, fingerprints, photos, the whole shooting match. It's over. You're never going to get near her again. Did Rule Shaker know you were a child molester when he hired you to kidnap Emma?"

"I never met him, it was one of his men who hired me. He told me over and over that I wasn't to hurt the little girl, that she had to go back to her mother after her father cooperated with Shaker. Sure I agreed. I needed the money. But when I saw Emma, I knew that she'd been sent to me.

"I knew she belonged to me. A week was only a beginning for us. But then she fooled me and ran away. It's just a matter of time and she'll be mine again."

Ramsey nearly lost it, but he wasn't stupid.

"You called up after she was gone and got those men up there to kill me, right?"

"Yes. I had to have her back, but you managed to escape."

"Yeah, and I got you too, didn't I?"

Dickerson yelled at that. He pushed forward, away from Ramsey, then veered toward a wobbly wooden ladder that looked as if it should have crumbled into the water years ago. He got himself halfway up before Ramsey was beneath him, grabbing his foot.

"Let me go! She's mine, do you hear me? I have to have her, she's all I've got. I can't survive without her. What I am is far more important than what she could ever be. I need her!"

Ramsey yanked as hard as he could on Dickerson's foot as Dickerson fired. Ramsey felt the heat of the bullet as it whizzed past his left ear.

An instant later there was another shot. It felt like a heavy blow striking his shoulder. He lurched backward, nearly losing his hold on Dickerson's foot. He didn't feel any pain, just more numbing cold. This numbness was different, colder than the water. It froze through his chest and down his arm, making it useless. He couldn't move his damned arm. He heard Molly's voice, Emma's voice. He heard someone scream out, "He's bleeding! That man's been shot."

Dickerson got his foot free. He kicked Ramsey hard in his wounded shoulder. Pain ripped through him and he fell back into the water.

He saw, as if from a great distance, Molly's

white face, saw her raise her sneakered foot, saw her smash her sneakered foot into Dickerson's face just when he reached the top of the ladder. The force of her kick knocked Dickerson back. He scrambled wildly, trying to keep hold of the ladder, but the ancient rotting wood collapsed, each step crumbling when his weight hit it. Dickerson went flailing into the water, crashing beside him, struggling frantically, choking up water, trying to find the ladder whose rungs now hung down drunkenly. This time Ramsey had him around the neck and he never intended to let go. Dickerson was waving the gun around, yelling, water filling his mouth, still yelling, only it was gurgling now, and Ramsey felt him weakening. It was just a matter of which of them lasted longer now.

Ramsey felt the god-awful pain in his shoulder, the uselessness of his arm. He shuddered with the force of it, felt the pain pulling at him, felt light-headed and dizzy. But he didn't let Dickerson go. He only squeezed harder. Dickerson was twisting wildly, trying to turn the gun toward him. He tried to bring up his useless arm, but it just hung at his side, blood streaking down it, plastering his shirt to his flesh, hurting so badly his teeth were clenched. He was squeezing now as hard as he could. Why didn't Dickerson go down? Of course it was the force of the waves that prevented it. He couldn't get enough leverage. The gun waved in the air around them.

It didn't seem at all strange to him when he

saw Molly scoot off the edge of the wharf to land in the water next to him. A moment later he thought he'd die of fear. He saw her grab Dickerson's arm, grab his wrist, and pull with all her might.

Dickerson screamed and yelled, but it didn't matter. Molly had the gun now. He saw her face was white, deadening fury in her eyes, saw her raise the gun to Dickerson's face, not a foot away from him. She was going to kill him. He realized in that moment that the last thing he ever wanted in his life was to have Molly kill another human being.

He said, "Don't shoot him, Molly, you might hit me. I've got him around the neck. See? I've got him. He's not going anywhere. It's all over for him. Please don't shoot."

She blinked, the blank rage receding. Dickerson heaved, shoving his elbow into Ramsey's stomach. The vicious surging water suddenly backlashed, shoving against them, giving Dickerson more power rather than slowing the force of his arm. Ramsey's hold loosened and Dickerson jerked free. He grabbed for the gun in Molly's hand.

There was a shot, wild, nearly straight up. Molly was heaving and struggling, but he was still on her. Ramsey kicked forward with his remaining strength to help her. God, he'd been a bloody fool to save the man's life. He was a fool and he was also losing. He heard Emma screaming his name.

Then there were two men in the water, and all of them were grabbing for that gun. When the gun went off another time, no one knew who had it, who had fired it.

All any of them knew was that there was an unconscious man on his face in the water, red streaked water flowing from beneath his body.

Ramsey said to the two men, "It's about time you two showed up. I'd just about given up on you."

• **Lieutenant** McPherson, of the MPD, a man whose face had come into focus just a couple of minutes before, said quietly, "Don't worry about anything, Judge Hunt. You're in Monterey. You're in a hospital room. The doctor and nurse just left before you woke up. You're going to make it, no problem. The only reason I'm here right now is I thought you'd want to know about Dickerson. He's still in surgery. The docs don't know if he'll make it. The bullet got him right in the chest. It's just too soon to know."

"I just wish they'd let the bastard die," Ramsey said. He couldn't move his right shoulder or his right arm. He looked down at a white sling. He remembered now how they'd wheeled him up to the operating room, side by side with Dickerson, Molly and Emma beside him, both of them white-faced and silent. He remembered Emma's small fingers lightly stroking his forearm. As for Molly, she'd held on to his hand for dear life. He vaguely remembered waking up in the recovery room. They'd just wheeled him into a private room, and he was alone with the lieutenant.

424

"Yes," Lieutenant McPherson was saying, "I hope he expires. "It'd sure save the taxpayers a lot of money. Well, at least you're going to be all right, Judge Hunt."

"Do you know what they did to me?"

"The surgeon spoke to you in the recovery room. You don't remember?"

"No, just this voice that wouldn't shut up. Do you know anything?"

"Yes. They worked on you for a good two hours. When the surgeon came out, he said you were lucky. The bullet went through your pec, and all you've got there is skin, muscle, and fat. He said you'd hurt like hell because the bullet also broke your collarbone and grazed a rib, but there wasn't any bad damage, it would just take a while to heal. You should be ready to take out more crooks in your courtroom in three or four months. Oh yeah, the doc also said he was real pleased that the bullet hadn't hit anything important, said he didn't want any complications with a big-time federal judge. He gave a big belly laugh then."

Ramsey couldn't think of anything to say. His brain seemed to be going in and out on him. At least he felt blessedly numb, all of him. He just wished Dickerson was dead. Surely it wasn't asking too much after what the bastard had done. If he lived, if they brought him up on kidnapping and attempted murder, he could still get out. Emma still wouldn't be safe.

He was losing it. Yes, she would be safe. By the time Dickerson ever got out of prison, Emma would be an adult. She'd be safe from predators like Dickerson just because she'd keep accumulating birthdays.

"Judge Hunt? Can you hear me? Do you want me to get a doctor for you?"

Ramsey hadn't realized that his head had fallen back against the very comfortable pillows. He opened his eyes to see Lieutenant McPherson looking very worried. He knew he'd been speaking, he'd felt the cadence of his voice, the underlying kindness, the concern, but he hadn't understood most of what he'd said. Ramsey managed to say, "I'm okay. I didn't think hospitals had comfortable pillows."

"These aren't the hospital's pillows," McPherson said. "These are from Mrs. Hunt, who's right now changing clothes along with your daughter. Actually they're from Mrs. Rallis, who went out and bought you pillows and your wife and daughter new clothes. She didn't like seeing them in hospital scrubs. Evidently she saw the whole thing on the wharf. She's a big name here in Monterey. If she says that you should have soft pillows, no one's going to argue with her."

Ramsey wanted to ask about Molly and Emma, find out if they were okay, but somehow, he just couldn't get the words out. It was a weird feeling, this knowing words, feeling what those words meant to him, yet being unable to get them out of his mouth. He felt the man lightly pat his arm. "The doc gave you a shot of something really strong. He said you didn't seem like the sort to kick back and relax, so he said he'd lay you out, it would be the best thing. Did you hear me tell you about your daughter and Mrs. Hunt? They should be here soon. The last I heard, Mrs. Rallis insisted that your wife and Emma have coffee and hot chocolate. I tried to stop the doc from giving you that shot, but I couldn't. Can you talk, Judge Hunt?"

"No. I'm laid out," Ramsey said, but McPherson never said anything more, so he guessed he'd spoken to him only in his mind.

• **He** smiled at Molly and Emma coming into his hospital room. Emma was wearing a new outfit he'd never seen on her before. As for Molly, she looked like a fashion plate in a pale yellow silky-looking pants outfit and high-heeled shoes, of all things, on her feet. Her beautiful hair was combed back, fastened with a fat gold clip at her neck. They both looked incredible to him, just incredible. He wanted to shout to them that this time they'd won. He wanted to yell at Molly for jumping in the water like that. He also wanted to thank her for saving his bacon. He wanted to tell them that he loved them more than he'd loved any two people in his entire life. But his mouth wouldn't say anything. He wondered again where the words were that would say what he wanted to say.

He heard McPherson say, "No, he's all right, ma'am, I promise. He's been in and out. The doc wants him to rest and so he's resting.

You and Emma sure look like a million dollars. How do you feel, Mrs. Hunt? Would you like to give me a statement now?"

Then he heard Virginia Trolley's voice, telling McPherson to leave Molly alone, that she'd speak to him once she was convinced that Ramsey would be all right. Boy, she'd gotten down here fast. He knew she'd take care of everything. He also knew she'd take a strip off her two cops who were supposedly protecting them. He thought he remembered one of the young cops telling him that he'd had to take a leak and that's why they'd just been a couple of minutes late helping him. What about his partner? Ramsey had wanted to ask, but hadn't been able to.

He smiled now vaguely at Emma, who'd slipped away from her mama to come to him. "I'm okay, Em," he thought he said, but her face didn't change expression. He felt her soft mouth on his cheek. He heard her whisper against his ear, "We got him, Ramsey. Mrs. Rallis promised me he wasn't going to escape from her hospital." He wanted to laugh, but he didn't. He just slid away. The last thing he felt was the touch of Emma's fingers on the back of his left hand.

• **"He's** going to live," Molly said. "They spent hours on him in the operating room, and now he's going to live."

Virginia Trolley said from his other side, with a deep sigh, "They knew who and what he was. I wish they'd just let him go. Now we'll have to try him, there'll be more garbage for you guys to go through."

"It's all right, Virginia," Ramsey said, his voice deep and gravelly this morning. He wanted a cup of coffee badly, but they wouldn't give it to him. The nurse had said he'd puke up his toenails if he drank coffee now. He wanted desperately to prove her either right or wrong. "Where's Emma?"

"I'm right here, Ramsey. Mama wanted me to pay attention to something else, but I told her I know what's going on. Does your shoulder hurt?"

"Nah, I'm a big guy, just like I told you. This isn't anything. I seem to be getting better at having my body parts shot all the time."

"I was afraid he would kill you, Ramsey," Emma said. "The water was all red. I would have gotten to you to help you, but that big lady wouldn't let go of me."

The thought of Emma jumping into the water like her mother had, maybe landing on Dickerson's head, had nearly made his heart stop. He said, however, "Your mom saved my hide for you. Thanks. Now, Virginia, what's going to happen to Dickerson?"

"Your friend Dillon Savich is on his way out here. The kidnapping is federal so it's the FBI's call. He wants to speak to Dickerson himself. Also a profiler is coming. You know they're always interviewing sickos like Dickerson. He should be a gold mine of information for them. Are you up to giving the local boys a statement?"

He spoke to Lieutenant McPherson and his captain, Daniel Mapes. It took quite a while. He was white around the gills when Captain Mapes said, "That's enough, Judge Hunt. If we have more questions, we'll see you tomorrow."

"I didn't think they were ever going to leave," Molly said, coming to the bed. "You don't look so hot."

"I want a cup of coffee."

"I know. Here you are." It was a miracle. He avidly watched her pull the lid off a Styrofoam cup. He took three long drinks, then promptly wanted to die. It was close, but he wasn't about to let himself throw up. The nausea subsided, finally. Then he panicked. "Where's Emma?"

"She's all right. She's with Virginia, telling her exactly what happened. From a child's perspective, it should be very interesting. Now, you're to rest for a while longer. It sounds stupid to tell you how lucky you were when you're lying flat on your back feeling awful, but you are. You'll mend. The surgeon said you'd be ready to take me dancing by tomorrow night. Well, maybe Wednesday night."

Molly smiled at him, closed the door, and climbed up with him on the narrow hospital bed. She kissed his ear, his nose, his mouth. "You taste like hospital," she said, nuzzling his neck. "But since I'm dressed in silk, maybe it's that opposites-attract thing." She gave a deep sigh. "I wish we could play doctor."

"Molly, please don't make me hard. I can't

33

By the time everyone had all the answers he or she wanted, Ramsey was feeling human enough to walk down to see Emma. She and Virginia Trolley were sitting in a corner of the cafeteria, their heads close together.

Emma looked up and saw him. She let out a yelp and dashed to him, wrapping herself around his leg. "It's all right, Emma," he said, patting her head. "See? I'm walking. It's for real. Nobody's holding me up. It was just another little bullet to a big macho guy like me. Now, let me pick you up so you can give me a proper hug."

"No, let me do it," Savich said and hoisted Emma up to eye level with Ramsey. She reached out and hugged him. He kissed her ear. "You smell good, Em. What is that? Oscar de la Renta?"

"No, that's the soap from the hotel." Then Emma drew back and said, "Was that a joke, Ramsey?"

Molly said to Sherlock, who was looking fit and quite beautiful and watching her husband with new eyes, "Ramsey loves her so much. Maybe someday he'll even love me."

"The man's found Nirvana and he knows it, Molly," Sherlock said in a matter-of-fact voice, still looking at her husband holding Emma, a besotted look on his face. "I've always liked Ramsey. Now that he's got you,

begin to imagine what Nurse Hayman would do if she walked in and saw me pointing to the ceiling."

"She adores you. She'd probably pull me off you and take my place."

"Okay, enough of this newlywed stuff," said a man from the doorway.

"Not nearly as bad as Nurse Hayman," Molly said, and scooted off the bed.

It was Dillon Savich, grinning from ear to ear. Behind him was another man who looked as if he'd never smiled in his life. He looked like a medieval monk, all stiff and long and narrow, with a thin rim of gray hair circling his head.

"Hi, Ramsey, glad you're well enough to kiss Molly. Guys, this is Thomas Galviani, otherwise known as Tommy the Eye, a gentleman whose specialty is child molesters. He's one of the world's leading experts."

The man didn't change expression, just calmly nodded and shook Ramsey's hand. He said, "Savich thinks I'm too serious, but I'm not. I'm glad to meet you, Judge Hunt. I read about what a hell of a good job you did on those drug dealers in your courtroom. Everyone in the Bureau is still talking about it. I'm more than glad that this time our perp was caught before he killed. Congratulations on bringing him down."

"Thank you, Mr. Galviani."

"Tommy the Eye," he said without skipping a beat, his expression all bland, and Savich laughed.

"Where's Sherlock?"

Savich said to Molly, "She's in the women's room, cursing me. I said the *P* word to a doctor who was worried because she looked a bit on the pale side. I told him it had been a long trip and she was tired because she was pregnant. That was all it took."

"I hope," Tommy the Eye said, "that Sherlock doesn't shoot you before she stops having morning sickness."

They were still grinning when Sherlock came into the room. She walked up to her husband and punched him in the arm. Then she greeted Molly and Ramsey, all smiles. She said, "I stopped by the ICU. Dickerson is still out of it. They'll let us know if and when he wakes up."

"I would like to speak to him," said Tommy the Eye. "I've read everything we've got, all the reports from his first trial, the transcripts of what he said when and to whom. He was a preferential child molester, that is to say, he's a pedophile who sexually molests children. The preferential abuses up to as many as a thousand children in his life, not like a situational molester, who may just abuse a dozen or so children. This guy is a classic, with one exception. He brutalized Emma as well as sexually abused her. We call that a sadistic molester. Add to that the fact that with Emma he became obsessional. You don't see this all that often in child molesters, but it does happen. One particular child, the pedophile must have that child, no other. He lost all sense of sur-

vival. Most molesters would have just shrugged and moved on to another child, but Dickerson didn't. He just couldn't stop.

"He's not a stupid man, but he had to have known on some level that this obsession he had with Emma would bring him down. But he just couldn't help himself, couldn't stop himself, couldn't leave and forget her. I understand he's also excellent at disguise and makeup."

"That's what he told me when we were in the water," Ramsey said. "That's one of the reasons Rule Shaker's men hired him. Since Emma was going to be returned when Louey came around, the kidnapper couldn't be recognized, thus the disguise."

Tommy the Eye just shook his head. "He must have thought he'd died and gone to heaven when he got the job."

Ramsey said, "How does all this get confused with his religious needs? He told Emma that he needed her, actually needed her."

"I would really like to talk to him about that. He seems like a boiling cauldron with all sorts of things tossed in indiscriminately, from beliefs of how Emma would save him to hurting her so that she would be taking his punishments for him. I can't wait to dig into his brain. But we're mostly just thankful that he's out of commission now."

Molly said, "If and when you reach any understanding about him, Tommy, please tell us."

"I will, Mrs. Hunt."

He was rubbing his palms together.

everything will be just fine. What do you think, Molly? Does Dillon look like a natural holding Emma or what?"

• **The** orderly had brought two cots into Ramsey's room the night before. The whole family was together. They were sound asleep when the door suddenly burst open and Lieutenant McPherson ran in.

Ramsey was out of bed in an instant, ready to fight, and he nearly passed out cold. He fell back against the bed, breathing hard. "What the hell's wrong?"

"No, it's all right, Judge Hunt," McPherson said, panting. "I was just worried that something could have happened to you as well. Here, let me help you back into bed."

"What are you talking about?" Molly said, helping Ramsey herself. Emma was halfway to Ramsey's bed, intent, he knew, on protecting him.

"It's Dickerson," McPherson said. "They think somebody put something, maybe potassium, into one of his IVs. He's dead."

• **"But** there are staff all over the place in the ICU," Virginia Trolley said, shaking her head, still looking utterly incredulous even though McPherson had been talking about it for a good ten minutes. She'd thrown on clothes and rushed to his hospital room when Ramsey had called her. Ramsey had never seen her without makeup before and her hair uncombed and her red blazer wrinkled. She looked cute. He'd never tell her that, of course, because she'd knock him out.

"How could anybody get in there," she continued, "stick a needle into the IV tube, and get out again, all without being seen by anybody? There weren't any guards on him, why would there be? He wasn't going anywhere on his own and no one ever thought he'd need protection. We've spoken to security and they've sealed off the hospital, but good luck on that. They're checking videotape right now to see if there's anything suspicious."

"Lieutenant McPherson said a nurse saw someone dressed in hospital whites," Molly said. "But that's no big deal. It's a little like wearing a uniform at the Pentagon. Nobody gives you much of a second glance if you appear to be someone who's supposed to belong."

"She's right," Ramsey said. "It's the only reasonable answer. Actually I don't think it's all that reasonable, but hey, this is a hospital, not a top-security area. The hospital staff weren't alerted to keep an eye out." He closed his eyes a minute. He was exhausted, his rib hurt, his shoulder ached like the devil, and he was ready to call in the cavalry for a pain pill.

He suddenly felt Emma's hand slip into his. He turned his head to see her studying him, knowing that he hurt, not knowing what to do about it. It was a lie, but he said cleanly,

"I'm just fine, Emma. But I like you right here holding my hand."

He also felt incredible relief. Dickerson was dead, long gone, no more threat to anyone. Emma was safe.

Lieutenant McPherson cleared his throat. "I also ran in here, Judge Hunt, because, to tell you the truth, you're the best suspect."

"I'm not moving too quickly right now," Ramsey said. "I nearly hung it up when you burst through that door. I think stealing a white coat, finding some potassium, since I don't carry any around with me, and walking nonchalantly into the ICU just might have been beyond even my abilities, astounding though they be."

"That was a joke," Emma said to Lieutenant McPherson.

"I know. I'm glad all of you were here. It makes things easier."

Not an hour later, when the three of them were finally alone again, though they could see news vans below them in the street, they discovered they were all still too hyped to go back to sleep. The phone rang. Molly answered it, then, with a strange look on her face, she handed it to Ramsey. "I don't understand. It's my father. He wants to speak to you."

Ramsey thought briefly about pressing the speaker button. No, Emma was here. He picked up the phone and identified himself. It was indeed Mason Lord. He said, "I'm much better and I understand that you'll survive as well, Ramsey. Oh yes, I'm also given to understand that there will be no more problems with that animal who was after Emma, and shot you."

Ramsey said very quietly, though he could feel the blood pounding through him, "How did you know, sir? Surely there hasn't been enough time for it to be on the news yet."

Mason laughed softly, then said, amusement lacing his voice, "I have friends everywhere, Ramsey. Of course I find things out very quickly. Actually, one could almost say that I find some things out almost before they happen."

Had it been Gunther who killed Dickerson? Or had Mason hired local talent for just this one assignment? Now that he'd had a second or two to think about it, he wasn't at all surprised. He didn't say anything. Why bother? What was there to say anyway?

"Now Emma doesn't have to be afraid, nor do you or Molly. I will expect the three of you here for Thanksgiving. That's my favorite holiday. No one expects extravagant gifts, just a great meal, which Miles always delivers."

"Yes," Ramsey said. "We'll be there." Slowly, he placed the phone back in the receiver. He looked at Molly and shook his head. She frowned a moment, then he knew she understood. She made a big deal out of yawning. "I'm ready to fold my tent. How about you, Em?"

"I'm sleepy too, Mama. What did Grandpa want, Ramsey?"

"He wanted to make sure we were all right. Nothing more."

"He was nice to call," Emma said, kissed Ramsey, and let her mother tuck her in.

Ramsey leaned back and closed his eyes. His shoulder was hurting like the devil. His fingertips tingled. His head ached. Now this. Molly leaned down to kiss him. He whispered, "He had Dickerson killed. What am I supposed to do?"

"Tell McPherson the truth. It won't matter, you know it won't. No one will ever take down my father. In fact I'll bet my father wants you to tell the cops. He's probably laughing right now, imagining it."

He suspected she was right. He called out, "Good night, Emma. Sleep well. You too, Molly."

• **It** was all over, Ramsey thought, as he walked up the stairs of their San Francisco home, Emma at his side. All over. He was thinking about Dickerson's mother in Duluth. She had paid for his cremation. Ramsey had actually gone, Savich with him, just to be sure, just to see the man before he was reduced to gray silt.

"Mama's asleep," Emma said. "She was really tired. I don't think she slept well last night."

That was true enough. He hadn't either.

Emma had said she'd wanted to sleep in her own room, which was the reason neither of them had slept much. It was odd, but he'd missed her cuddling against them, at least in the morning he had.

"I hope she's not still asleep," Ramsey said. "I want to see her smile. She's done a lot of that since we got back home yesterday."

He stood in the doorway of their bedroom. Emma had left him, running down to her bedroom to fetch one of her toys. Molly was lying on her side, her back to him. She was wearing only a pair of white panties that were high cut on the sides. Her bottom leg was straight, the top leg was slightly bent. There wasn't a more seductive pose for a woman. He swallowed. Her hair was a glorious mess, tangled over a beautiful expanse of white flesh that made him want to walk right over there and begin kissing her back, starting at the base of her neck downward, until he could pull her panties away. They'd made love three times the previous night. He suspected there would have been a fourth time this morning, but Emma had had other plans.

"Mama kicked off the blanket," Emma said matter-of-factly beside him. She walked to the bed and gently raised the blanket to cover her mother. Molly stirred. She fell over onto her back and opened her eyes.

"Emma," she said, and raised her hand to cup her daughter's face. "Have you been taking care of Ramsey?"

"Yes, Mama. He's a lot better. He promised his shoulder only hurt a little bit. The best thing is he's not worried about me anymore."

"Emma, I'll worry about you until you're ninety years old. Now if we could just get rid of the press then everything would be fine and dandy," Ramsey said. "I'd really like to take you guys down to meet all the people in my office. We've also got a dynamite view." He sighed. "But you can bet the press is hanging out there." He walked to the bed, leaned down, and kissed Molly's nose. "You have a good sleep?"

She gave him a long lazy look that made him start to get hard again. "Yeah, no bad dreams, just oblivion. It's nice for a change. I'd best call my mom before it gets too late in Italy. She was concerned about Emma, and I promised."

Later in the kitchen, Molly put through the call, while Ramsey stood at the counter chopping some carrots and broccoli. Emma was setting the table.

Molly smiled into the phone, balancing it between her neck and shoulder as she stole a carrot. "Yes, Mom. How are you?"

"Fine, dear. Is everything all right?"

Molly told her, in a highly edited version, how the man had been captured. She finally told her that he'd been murdered in the hospital.

Her mother was silent for just a heartbeat, then she said, with affection, "Your father was always very efficient. Did he call you shortly after the man was dead to tell you that you were safe?"

Molly stared at the phone. "Yes, that's exactly what he did. The police still haven't located the person who shot potassium into Dickerson's IV."

"They won't either. Not a chance. Your father always hires reliable help."

"Yes, I suppose so. But I'm still very worried for him. He's been nearly killed, twice. That Rule Shaker doesn't seem like the type to give up."

"No, he never was. I doubt he's changed."

Molly jumped up from her chair, nearly pulling the phone off the wall. "What do you mean, Mom? Do you know Rule Shaker?"

"Certainly, dear. I knew him a very long time ago, when both he and your father were just getting started in their businesses. They were excellent friends, way back when. Our two families did everything together. I very much enjoyed his wife, Lorna, poor woman. She died in an automobile accident some fifteen years ago. I always believed Rule Shaker was responsible for that."

"But, Mom, they're bitter enemies now. It was Rule Shaker who blew up Louey, when Ramsey, Emma, and I were the actual targets. It was Rule Shaker who murdered a farmer in Colorado. He's tried twice to kill Father."

"These things happen, Molly. Just a moment." Molly heard her mother switch to her musical Italian. "What, Maria? Oh yes, just put my tea on the table. That's fine. Do go to bed." Her mother returned, switching back to English. "Yes, dear? What were we speaking about?"

The good Lord give me patience, Molly thought, looking upward. "We were talking about the fact that my father and Rule Shaker are trying to kill each other. Why didn't I ever know about this? Why don't the police know about this? What happened between them?"

"I don't know about the police, dear. Surely they know. The split was no secret. As for you, why would you have ever known? The split happened when you were a little girl. Just before I left your father, actually. It was only a year later that Rule's wife left him."

"Do you know what happened?"

"Yes, dear. I don't suppose it matters now. You're all grown up with a daughter of your own. Rule Shaker wanted me to sleep with him, but you see, I was in love with your father. Too, I didn't really care for him. Rule looked like a gangster, if you know what I mean, the kind of gangster Hollywood put on the screen if they wanted no sympathy for the character, the kind who smokes. Your father never did look like anything but an aristocrat. He still does, in the photos I've seen of him over the years."

"But what happened?"

"Your father walked in on us. Rule Shaker was trying to force me, actually, and in a very crude way. Being a man, your father blamed me as well as his friend. It was the end of our marriage and the end of their friendship and business dealings. It was a very difficult time."

"I remember we went to Italy," Molly said slowly. "That was just after this had happened?"

"That's right. But it's a long time in the past, twenty years. Now, Molly, let me speak to Emma. I would like all of you to come to Italy for Thanksgiving. No worry about giving anyone a gift they won't like, just a very good meal. Our cook here, Magdalana, is just excellent. She'd never cooked a turkey in her life until she came to me. Will you come?"

"I'll have to get back to you on that, Mom."

"Oh, yes, I did see a photo of your father in *Time* magazine, with his wife. It appears he's going to live, yet again. Well, I suppose that's good. After all, he did remove the threat from Emma."

"He had Dickerson murdered, Mother," Molly said, then realized she was a damned hypocrite and said quickly, "Although I wanted to kill him myself. You're right. No matter what else Father is, he did save Emma from a horrible experience in the courtroom, at the very least."

"Well, he still should be careful, don't you think?"

"Naturally," Molly said. "I don't think Rule Shaker is the kind of man to give up. I'm sure Father knows him well enough to realize that as well."

"Oh yes, he'll think he's being careful, but

444

it isn't Rule I'm talking about. I just hope your father knows what he's doing."

"Doing about what?"

"Well, dear, it's his wife. I hadn't realized whom he'd married. In fact, it seems incredible to me that he would marry her, but evidently he didn't see any harm. Men are strange, don't you think? They think with their penises. That's what my mother always told me."

Molly shook her head. "I don't understand, Mom. What's strange about Eve? Admittedly she's younger than I am, but many older men have trophy wives, and yeah, I'd probably agree that most men do think with their dicks."

"Molly, dear, that's such a crude word. Now, that isn't what I meant. There was so much bad blood between your father and Rule Shaker and it just kept getting worse. They went after the same deals. Sometimes one would win, sometimes the other, but the rivalry has just gotten stronger over the years. That's why this is such a surprise."

"What's such a surprise?" Molly rolled her eyes toward Ramsey, who raised a black eyebrow.

"Your father's wife, dear. Eve. There was an excellent photo of her in *Time* magazine, just after your father was shot that first time. Didn't you know, dear? She's Rule Shaker's eldest daughter."

34

Molly walked into her father's magnificent study and quietly closed the huge double doors behind her.

Her father rose slowly from his desk, raised an eyebrow, and said, "What is it, Molly? I wasn't expecting you. Is everything all right?"

He was dressed immaculately. Very few people who knew him would realize that he was thinner, that the flesh on his face was drawn more tautly, that his color wasn't exactly right, that, actually, he should still be in bed recovering from a gunshot wound to his chest. She smiled at him. "Oh, yes, we're all just fine. You're looking well. Miles said you've been up three hours today. He's worried, you know. He thinks you're overdoing it too quickly. He also said you ate a big piece of chocolate cake last night."

"Yes. There was some of Miles's home-made vanilla ice cream on top. I was growing mold in that bed. I'm fine. Where is Ramsey?"

"Both Ramsey and Emma are with Miles. I do believe Gunther is hovering, eating some of Miles's chocolate-chip cookies himself." She paused a moment, smiled at him, and said, "Actually, I wanted to see you by myself."

"What's this all about? Why are you here?"

The slant of his eyebrows, she thought, was identical to her own. She wondered that she'd never noticed that before. She'd have to ask Ramsey if he saw the similarity. "As a matter of fact," she said, "I'm here to do you a very big favor." He frowned at that, just as she'd expected, since it was something he couldn't imagine. He waved her to a huge leather chair. "It's my favorite chair," he said, "but right now I can't sit in it. It's too difficult to get back out of it."

"Sort of like a pregnant woman."

"I doubt it. Now, what is this favor, Molly?" When she didn't answer immediately, he glanced at a paper he'd been reading, ignoring her. She'd seen him do this before. It really rattled a person wanting his attention. Odd how she saw and understood it, and was only tempted to tell him that he was a fine actor.

She let him scan a full page, then said finally, "Mother told me all about you and Rule Shaker, that you were best friends for so many years, your two families close. She told me how you blamed her as well as Rule Shaker when you came in on them."

His head came up with a snap. "I'll just bet she told you how innocent she was, that Rule was trying to rape her."

"Yes, that's what she said. She said she didn't really like him, that he was crude, that she loved you, but of course, you blamed her as well as him. You threw her out. You kept my brother and I went with her to Italy."

He shrugged and winced a bit with pain. "It was a very long time ago. I can't imagine why she chose to tell you now. As for Rule Shaker, I've dealt with him over the years without much problem. Perhaps not as well as I'd like recently," he added, frowning down at a letter opener that looked as sharp as a stiletto. He looked up at her. "Actually, he's taken more business than I'd have liked over the past couple of years, but it's a temporary thing. He's become a thug, nothing more. He's always been jealous of me and what's mine. He had bad teeth when we were young. I'll bet he's got false teeth by now." He paused a moment, a frown settling on his forehead, looking beyond her, into the past, perhaps.

"I accepted him, made him my friend," he continued after a moment. "I can't believe I didn't see him clearly until I happened to walk in on him and your mother.

"He's tried to kill me, twice. I'm going to have to deal with him once and for all. I don't like having to constantly look over my shoulder. Gunther worries. He isn't happy about any of this either."

"Rule Shaker didn't try to kill you."

Her father looked at her with amazed contempt. "What did you say?"

"No," she said, very slowly, as if she were speaking to a dim child. "He didn't ever try to kill you. Actually, it was your wife."

Her father bounded to his feet, his face paling, then weaved where he stood. She saw waves of pain washing over him, started to go to him, then stopped, realizing that he hated anyone, particularly her, to see any weakness in him. He chopped his hand in the air, waving her back. "Eve? You're saying that Eve tried to kill me? You're trying to blame Eve?

have no memory of her at all. When Rule Shaker and his wife divorced, Janice went with her mother to Boston and Rule Shaker kept Melissa, who was just two years old at the time. They split their kids just the way you did with me and Teddy.

"Janice married a Swedish engineer when she was only eighteen, her freshman year in college. Her husband was killed on a dam project a year later. She obviously got all her Swedish antecedents from her husband's family, including her husband's engineering degree that's hanging on your wall. In any case, somewhere along the line, Janice or her father came up with the idea to take you in. And they did take you in. Fooled you completely.

"She admitted to me that she murdered Louey. She hated him, didn't want her sister to be with him. She smuggled in the bomb that blew him up. Emma and I weren't the targets. And then when you killed Melissa, her sister, she tried to murder you. Maybe Eve would have tried to murder you eventually regardless of what happened. She didn't volunteer her plans. I don't know and neither will you. It doesn't matter. All of it's going to stop right now."

She watched him straighten, knew that the effect must be hurting his chest. Then he was utterly still, even his hands silent at his sides. He said, his voice as gentle as a soft spring rain, "If what you say is true, if she did betray me, then how could it possibly be over?"

She would have preferred rage, not this

calm dead coldness. She didn't know where she found it, but she reached down deep inside her and brought up a very big smile. "Because, Dad, I've saved your life and now I'm going to end it all. No one is going to kill anyone. You try to harm Eve or Rule Shaker and I'm going to turn you in. It's true that I don't have much hard proof, but I know enough to make things excessively uncomfortable for you. If you refuse to end it, I also promise you will never see Emma or me again. I will not take the chance of Emma getting between you and Shaker.

"There will be no more attempts on your life or anyone connected with you, including me and Emma. Eve and her father have agreed to it. You took one of his daughters and you're giving the other one back. Louey is dead and you were nearly killed twice. They both know I could bring them down, because, you see, I taped my conversation with Eve and played it for them. One copy is with Dillon Savich of the FBI and the other is with the San Francisco District Attorney's office. I've got it all and I'll keep it safe. It's over. Believe me on this."

He slowly raised his hand. In an instant, Molly thought he was going to strike her. She stood her ground, waiting.

Slowly, Mason Lord lowered his arm. His voice was nearly a whisper as he said, "You're my daughter and you're threatening me with this?"

452

"Yes, I am. It's my only way to protect both Emma and you. I don't ever want to have to worry that Emma could be the next victim in your war with Rule Shaker. What's more, I don't want him or his daughter to kill you. Now, I want your word that you'll leave the Shakers alone."

Mason stared at the daughter who looked so much like her grandmother, who hadn't wanted Alicia to marry him, who'd looked at him like he was some sort of back alley scum. She'd looked at him and known what he was to his very soul. He'd seen the knowledge in those gray-green eyes of hers—Molly's eyes—and he'd hated her with everything in him. Now here was Molly, more her blood than she was his, telling him what to do. What was wrong with him? She was just a woman, nothing more.

He wanted to straighten her out but good, but instead, what came out of his mouth was, "I eliminated the scum who hurt Emma."

His voice was defensive, with maybe even a hint of a whine. It amazed her and heartened her. "Yes, I know. That's why I haven't already called the cops. Do you know something, Dad? I don't think you're all bad. You tried to protect family. That's something in your favor. A very big something. Do you agree, Dad? It stops here and now?"

Mason Lord looked down at his long white fingers. The flesh looked loose on the back of his hands. Slowly, he raised his head. Molly was standing quietly in front of him, her wild red hair pulled back and fastened with a gold clip against her nape.

Her ears, he thought, her ears were Alicia's. He'd always thought Alicia had beautiful ears. He heard her say again, her voice calm and low, "Do you agree, Dad?"

The phone rang sharp and loud beside his left hand.

"Answer it," Molly said, looking at her watch. "It's Rule Shaker, right on time. End it, Dad."

Maybe it was time to end it all. She had guts, his guts, to come in here and face him down.

Well, what the hell. He picked up the phone and said to a man he hadn't spoken to in twenty years, "Rule. It's Mason Lord."

Epilogue

It's a boy," Ramsey called out. Both Molly and Emma came running into his study from the kitchen. He pressed the speaker button and put the phone down.

"Congratulations!" Molly and Emma shouted in unison. Emma's Dalmatian, six-month-old Kenny, barked madly, and jumped against Ramsey's leg. "When? How long? What's his name?"

Sherlock laughed, raucous and full-bodied, loud on the speaker. "His name is Sean Franklin Savich and he wailed his lungs out as he slid into Dillon's hands. He's big and healthy and everything's just great. Dillon came through like a champ, kept me up and walking around until I finally told him I'd punch his lights out if he didn't let me lie down and yell at him."

Emma wanted to know when they'd bring Sean out so she could play with him. Soon, Sherlock told her, very soon.

When Ramsey hung up the phone, he sat down in his dark brown leather chair and pulled Molly onto his lap. Then he brought Emma down on Molly's lap, wrapping his arms around both of them. It was a routine all of them were used to. He looked at the wall across from his chair. There were three neoimpressionist paintings hanging there, selected by him and Molly together over the past several months.

"I got a request from my law clerks and my secretary today, all three of them, that they want to see Emma," he said, kissing Molly's ear. "It's been at least a month, they said. They said I was being selfish with her. So, guys, would you like to come down to my office? Emma, you've got a holiday Monday so you won't miss any school. What do you say?"

"Will Mrs. Burger have some of her lemon bars?" Emma asked.

Ramsey laughed. "Greed always wins out. I'll ask her."

"If the answer's yes, then count us in," Molly said, and kissed Emma's ear.

When Emma jumped down to go play with Kenny in the backyard, Ramsey said to Molly, "I got a call from Lieutenant O'Connor from the Oak Park police. They found the man they believe shot your father in a dump site, somewhere in southern Ohio. He'd been dead quite a while, about six months. Rule Shaker didn't want any loose ends."

"Exactly. Eve must have told her father about the saliva the cops found and could do a DNA match on if they came up with a suspect. His spitting cost him his life."

"Yeah. Probably no big loss. That's over. No doubt it's a relief for your dad." He nuzzled her neck, fiddled with the small gold hoop in her left ear, and said, "Have you decided yet, Molly? Are we going to Italy or to Chicago for Thanksgiving? You'd best make up your mind; it's only a few days away and I imagine that there aren't many airline tickets left."

"No problem," she said, giving him a big grin. "We're going to Italy for Thanksgiving and to Chicago for Christmas. I told my dad that Emma wanted lots of really neat presents and that's why he got Christmas.

"He huffed and puffed, but then he laughed, said Gunther was already talking about getting Emma a G.I. Jane doll for Christmas, replete with appropriate weaponry. Can you beat that?"

"No, I'm not even going to try."

Molly rolled her eyes. "Well, since I still have my Detonics all safe and snug in a box on the top shelf of a closet, I guess I can't say much. Oh yes, I returned Mrs. Garcia's call. She said that Dr. Loo sends her love, that she's planning on spring skiing."

"What did she say about Emma?"

"She's pleased. She thinks it would be good for Emma to travel again. She's still very encouraged with the progress Emma's making. For now, she says that Emma's talked about it enough, and, in her own way, is ready to move on."

"Thank God for that. Am I spoiling her too rotten, Molly?"

"Nah, she's got a good head on her shoulders. She's spoiling you, actually. Imagine her running down here to the kitchen to make you some toast this morning so you wouldn't have to get your feet cold on the tile."

He laughed. "There are still crumbs in the bed. Oh yes, I forgot to tell you. You know how the district judges get their cases through the random lottery system? I just got handed another big-time drug case. I hope this one has a different ending than the last one."

"I think I'll hang out in the courtroom, just to make sure nobody tries anything."

He kissed her ear, her chin, the tip of her nose. "Emma spoils me and you protect me." He leaned back in the chair and gave her a big grin. "What more could a guy ask for?"